THUNDER IN THE DEEP

THUNDER IN THE DEEP
A Novel of Undersea Nuclear War

JOE BUFF

BANTAM BOOKS

NEW YORK   TORONTO   LONDON   SYDNEY   AUCKLAND

THUNDER IN THE DEEP

A Bantam Book / August 2001

All rights reserved.
Copyright © 2001 by Joe Buff.

Map by Jeffrey L. Ward.

Book design by Glen Edelstein.

Library of Congress Cataloging-in-Publication Data
Buff, Joe.
Thunder in the deep : a novel of undersea nuclear war / Joe Buff.
p. cm.
ISBN 0-553-80136-8
1. Imaginary wars and battles—Fiction. 2. Twenty-first century—Fiction.
3. Submarine warfare—Fiction. 4. Nuclear warfare—Fiction. I. Title.
PS3552.U3738 T48 2001
813'.6—dc21   2001025045

Published simultaneously in the United States and Canada

Bantam Books are published by Bantam Books, a division of Random House, Inc. Its trademark, consisting of the words "Bantam Books" and the portrayal of a rooster, is Registered in
U.S. Patent and Trademark Office and in other countries. Marca Registrada. Bantam Books,
1540 Broadway, New York, New York 10036.

PRINTED IN THE UNITED STATES OF AMERICA

BVG   10   9   8   7   6   5   4   3   2   1

In honor of submariner spouses,
perhaps the toughest job in the Silent Service
because waiting is the hardest part.

NORWAY

SWEDEN

• Goteborg

Skagerrak

Kattegat

DENMARK

• Copenhagen

JUTLAND BANK

Area of detail

60°N

15°W

0°

15°E

North Sea

Norwegian Trough

UNITED KINGDOM

SCOTLAND

ENGLAND

WALES

IRELAND

DOGGER BANK

London

NETHERLANDS

• Amsterdam

BELGIUM

GERMANY

LUXEMBOURG

English Channel

• Paris

FRANCE

50°N

North

Atlantic

Ocean

YMPUS
NOLL
OUNTS

PORTUGAL

SPAIN

40°N

M e d i t e r r a n e a n   S e a

Azores

Arquipelago
da Madeira (Portugal)

Porto Santo

Madeira • Funchal

MOROCCO

ANARY
BASIN

Santa Cruz de Tenerife

Tenerife *Lanzarote*

Las Palmas

Hierro *Fuerteventura*

Islas Canarias
(Spain) *Gomera*

Gran Canaria

30°N

WESTERN SAHARA

Canary Current

CAPE VERDE
PLAIN

MAURITANIA

20°N

Sao Nicolau *CAPE*
VERDE
TERRACE

o Antao

Vicente

Fogo *Santiago*

KAYAR
SEAMOUNTS

SENEGAL

PE VERDE

SIERRA LEONE

SIERRA LEONE
RISE

10°N

SIERRA LEONE
BASIN

0°

South Equatorial Current

15°W

0°

15°E

© 2001 Jeffrey L. Ward

70% of the earth's surface is covered by submarines.
—ADMIRAL HENRY G. CHILES, JR.
U.S. NAVY (RETIRED)

formerly CINCSTRAT
(Commander in Chief, U.S. Strategic Command)
and formerly COMSUBLANT
(Commander, Submarines, Atlantic)

The Submarine Review, *January 2000, p.32*

PROLOGUE

In mid-2011, Boer-led reactionaries seized control in South Africa, and restored Apartheid. In response to a U.N. trade embargo, they began sinking U.S. and British merchant ships. NATO forces mobilized, with only Germany holding back. Troops and tanks drained from the rest of Europe and North America, and a joint task force set sail for Africa—into a giant trap.

There was another coup—in Berlin. Kaiser Wilhelm's closest heir was crowned, the Hohenzollern throne restored after almost a century; a secret conspiracy planned for years. Germany would have her "place in the sun" at last. Coercion won over citizens not swayed by patriotism or the onrush of events.

Covertly, this Berlin-Boer Axis had built tactical atomic bombs. They ambushed the Allied naval task force underway, then destroyed Warsaw and Tripoli. France capitulated at once, continental Europe was overrun, and Germany established a strong beachhead in northern Africa. Germany captured nuclear subs from the French, and advanced diesel submarines from other countries. A financially supine Russia, supposedly neutral, sold weapons to the Axis for hard cash. Most of the rest of the world stayed out of the fight, from fear or greed or both.

Now, American supply convoys to Great Britain are suffering in another terrible Battle of the Atlantic. If the U.K. should fall, the modern U-boat threat will prove that America's overseas trade routes are untenable. The U.S. will have to sue for an armistice: an Axis victory. America and Great Britain both own ceramic-hulled fast attack subs— such as the USS Challenger, capable of tremendous depths—but Germany and South Africa own such vessels, too. Now, as harsh winter approaches in Europe, the British Isles starve, the U.S. is on the defensive, and democracy has never been more threatened. . . .

TWENTY YEARS AFTER DESERT STORM, IN A DIFFERENT SORT OF WAR.

IN THE MID-ATLANTIC OCEAN, NEAR THE AZORES

Captain Taylor told himself it must have been that convoy battle raging in the distance. The shock wave and noise from yet another tactical nuclear detonation rocked his ship, the USS *Texas*—a steel-hulled *Virginia*-class fast-attack sub, Taylor's home, his mistress at sea, his relentless yoke of command responsibility. Taylor knew from the feel of the shock that it was an Axis underwater blast, meant to shatter the Allied freighters' bottoms, now that their Royal Navy escorts were mostly neutralized. This far off, Taylor's sonar people wouldn't hear the breaking-up sounds or the screams. But by sheer chance the echoes from those A-bombs had given *Texas* away, mocking the quieting of her machinery, making useless the stealth coatings on her hull.

Robert Taylor, a beefy guy, was normally upbeat and jocular, but now he bitterly cursed his luck. The latest undersea blast-front bouncing off *Texas* would betray his depth and course and speed to the pair of Axis nuclear subs, which had him in a pincers—they'd never have spotted *Texas* without that endless searing thunder off to starboard, from the east. Taylor and his crew, and his Special Warfare passengers, had far more important things to do than tangle with them now. His orders even forbade his helping the U.K.-bound food convoy.

Taylor's executive officer said he was ready to open fire. The small atomic warheads on the Advanced Capability (ADCAP) torpedoes were all enabled, the outer tube doors open. The silent stalking was over with. Inside Taylor's head, twenty long years of Navy experience and training—and of constant physical risk and separation from his loved ones—all became sharply focused on the next few seconds and minutes of mortal combat.

"Firing point procedures," Taylor ordered, "tubes one and two. Target Master One, match sonar bearings, and *shoot*."

"Tubes one and two fired electrically!" the XO called out.

A heartbeat later the sonar officer reported four enemy torpedoes in the water, two each incoming from the port and starboard beams.

The *Texas* had six tubes in all. Taylor quickly launched another pair of his nuclear ADCAPs, targeting the other ex-French *Rubis*-class boat, Master Two. He decided to save the last pair for anti-torpedo fire, to try to smash the inbound weapons using area bursts. Anticipating this, inevitably, the wire-guided Axis fish began to spread out. Each *Rubis* had four tubes. Taylor was outgunned.

Suddenly there were *eight* incoming torpedoes in the water, *four* on either beam.

Taylor badly wanted flank speed, but the Advanced SEAL Delivery System (ASDS) minisub that *Texas* carried on her back created hydrodynamic drag. The SEAL team leader volunteered to man the little vessel to release it from its host, and a lieutenant (j.g.) wearing gold dolphins offered to serve as copilot. Taylor reluctantly gave assent. Another distant rumbling rocked the ship, reminding them all what was in store for *Texas*. The sonar officer put his passive broadband on the speakers.

The nerve-ripping whine of a dozen torpedo propulsion systems filled the Command and Control Center air, in 3-D quadraphonic. Taylor could almost feel those eight eager Axis A-bombs drawing closer by the second, ready to unleash new underwater suns. Their top speed was twice that of *Texas*, and the range was short enough to make survival touch and go. Taylor fought down his fear: Emotions like that had to wait. Repression and denial were survival tools.

The ASDS was ready. It was set loose.

Taylor snapped more orders. His tense helmsman made a knuckle in the water, then dialed up flank speed. *Flank speed*, everything *Texas* had. The normally mild-mannered XO, now frowning and sweating, kept launching noisemakers and acoustic jammer pods.

Taylor's eyes roved constantly, between the crewmen crowded

round him and the color-coded data on his command workstation. Briefly he watched the plot of the newest contact, the battery-powered ASDS, as it tried to sneak away. It was by far the slowest thing out there, and without it their whole mission would fail, before it had even begun. Silently Taylor beseeched his God, not for himself nor even for his crew and their dependents, but for the entire Allied cause. Ever since the Double Putsch in Berlin and Johannesburg some six months back, this war had not gone well, not for the good guys.

It was almost time for Taylor to launch his two available nuclear countershots—tubes one through four were still busy being reloaded. For the humans involved, Taylor told himself sardonically, time may have seemed to slow down, but the torpedo room loading equipment ran its oblivious pace.

Grimly Taylor forced himself to *use* every moment and think. The longer he waited, the more those incoming fish would bunch up, and he stood a better chance of wrecking several with each precious ADCAP. But the longer he waited, too, the smaller grew that narrow margin of distance between *Texas* and the hostile warheads' kill zones. Underwater, a mere one kiloton would be immensely destructive.

Taylor studied the geometries on his screen, watching the dozen torpedoes, projecting their tracks, asking himself what the enemy captains' next move would be. His judgment had to be perfect. *Now.* He gave the order to fire.

"Tubes five and six fired electrically!" the XO's voice shouted back.

The cacophony outside the ship increased once more—*fourteen* torpedoes in the water going one way or another, above the constant nasty hiss of *Texas*'s own flow noise, plus the unending ungodly roar of antiship A-bombs from that separate convoy versus U-boat battle in the distance. "Both units running normally!" a sonarman called.

Then came a deafening hammer blow, bad enough to shake the control room consoles in their shock-absorbing mounts. Plastic mugs flew from cup holders, splashing coffee on the deck. Taylor held on hard to an overhead fitting. He would've grabbed for a periscope shaft had there been one, but in the *Virginia*-class all outside imaging was done electronically.

"Whose weapon was that?" he demanded, as the turbulent shaking began to subside and his console began to reboot.

"Master One's!" the XO said. "One Axis fish went for our noise-makers!"

"How many torpedoes still running?"

"We need to wait for the reverb to clear!"

"What about our own units?"

"All six still functioning, sir. Good contact through the wires."

Taylor glanced at a depth gauge, then ordered his submarine shallower. This had always been standard doctrine in tactical nuclear war at sea, to benefit from surface cutoff effect, the venting of fireball energy into the air. The Cold War might be long over, the enemy different now, but the underlying physics hadn't changed.

Taylor went back to his screen. It was time to trigger those last two ADCAPs. Commands were relayed; the water around *Texas* heaved. The resounding cracks, so close, were much sharper this time, punishing Taylor's ears. The vibrations were much sharper, too. An overhead light fixture shattered, and nearby crewmen protected their eyes.

A phone talker, young and already scared, pressed his hands to his bulky headset, listened intently, and raised his voice. "Flooding in the engine room, lower level port side!"

Too many things were going on at once. Taylor ordered the XO aft, to oversee repairs. The weapons officer deftly stepped in as Fire Control Coordinator. The tactical plot was refreshed. The nearest threat icons showed up with very high position confidence, the enemy torpedoes so noisy now as they ran at endgame speed. Two Axis fish were still closing in from starboard, one from port, clearly picked up on *Texas*'s side-mounted sonar wide-aperture arrays.

The ASDS tried to raise the *Texas* by underwater telephone, but the message was unintelligible, conditions out there were so bad. Then the minisub started to ping, on maximum power. Taylor realized it was trying to act as a decoy, to protect its more high-value parent. The two men aboard, two good men Taylor knew well and liked and cared about, must know that they'd die: The ASDS was unarmed. One Axis torpedo acquired it; the others pressed on toward *Texas*. Again Taylor had to squelch down his emotions: Around him, man and machine were melded into a conflict that wiped out any possible sense of personal future or past.

Tubes one through four on Taylor's weapons status window flashed green, ready to fire. There was a heavy roar from astern, and the ASDS icon on the main plot pulsed, then vanished.

There was a pair of distant roars; more shock waves pummeled the ship. Taylor heard several men shouting at once.

"Units from tubes one and three have detonated!"

"Close-in hits on Master One and Master Two, assess both targets destroyed!"

Then from the phone talker: "Flooding aft is worsening, Captain, two feet deep in the bilge!"

The chief of the boat worked his console with tight concentration, trying to preserve neutral buoyancy and maintain level trim. He'd put in his papers to retire at twenty just days before the war broke out—forget about that now.

There were still two incoming torpedoes, spaced wide apart off the port and starboard quarters. Taylor ordered tubes one through four fired, more defensive nuclear snap shots. But the inbound weapons were so close now it was a toss-up whether they could be knocked down in time. Even if their proximity fuses were set very tight, buying *Texas* a few extra seconds, the ADCAPs might not reach safe separation quickly enough for survivable preemptive blasts. Again Taylor studied his screens. A week-old image forced its way into his mind, his wife and their two teenage girls, making good-byes on the pier in New London.

"Detonate the weapons," Taylor ordered. He knew it was too damned close.

The explosions, reinforcing each other, knocked him off his feet. His shoulder struck an unyielding corner; an awful pain shot through his chest. Console tubes imploded. The deck shook so hard his vision was blurred, and the air began to fill with pungent smoke.

He saw men dazed, others moving and speaking, then realized he was deafened and he tried to read their lips. The phone talker, bleeding profusely from a flattened nose, mouthed each word carefully. "Flooding in Engineering is out of control." The bilge pumps couldn't keep up.

Taylor turned to the chief of the boat, and commanded an emergency blow. Surfacing into the tons of radioactive steam and fallout topside appalled Taylor, but it was their only chance. The bottom-mapping sonar was useless in such chaotic acoustic conditions, but the inertial nav plot told him enough. The seafloor here went way down past their crush depth.

Compressed air screamed and roared. The helmsman tried to

plane up, just like he'd trained. The deck tilted steeply, and the vessel strove for the surface as her ballast tanks were forced dry. Taylor noticed more blood. One crewman had compound fractures of both forearms, from bracing himself the wrong way. Another man lay on the deck, the stillness of death upon him, his neck badly twisted, broken. Other crewmen donned their emergency air breather masks, before the thickening smoke could kill them all. Fire-fighting teams went to work. Taylor felt a jumble of pride and anguish, at their skill and their courage, their wounds and their dreadful pain. His people—kids, really, most of them—were his surrogate family, and around him they were dying.

Taylor struggled to his console, tried to lift the red handset to Damage Control back aft, and realized his right collarbone was smashed. He grabbed for the phone with his left. Every breath came with agony. He vomited, then almost blacked out.

He made himself go on, of sheer necessity; one-handed, he pulled on his mask. There were a hundred thirty-five people aboard—including the SEALs—all his to lead, to protect; their wives and kiddies collectively totaled twice that. He'd seen them on the pier, too, making *their* good-byes.

Taylor knew the crew needed to stop the flooding very quickly once on the surface, then resubmerge, or they'd be picked off by a nuclear cruise missile. The Axis antishipping campaign was conducted with numbing ferocity. As if to emphasize the point, more explosions rumbled in the distance from the now one-sided convoy/U-boat fight.

The *Texas* broached nose first, consummating her sickening upward trajectory, then smashed back flat on the surface, forcing Taylor to his knees. The ship wallowed, rolling heavily, obviously settling fast. The engineer back aft tripped the panic switch, valving shut all sea pipes, which shut down propulsion too, but the water kept roaring in. Vital welds had cracked, in places difficult to find amid the blinding incoming spray. COB had already blown what he could, but the *Texas* was going down.

Taylor knew that if he ordered Abandon Ship, the few men who'd get out would perish horribly. He didn't activate a photonics mast—to see the multiple mushroom clouds would alarm the men to no purpose.

He stared very hard at a digital chart. A few nautical miles away lay the spur of a jagged seamount peak, an extension of the Azores volcanic chain. The spur's depth was almost seventeen hundred feet, challenging *Virginia*-class crush depth, especially after the beating *Texas* just took. The remainder of the seamount was sheer-sided basalt cliff; if they missed the spur they were doomed. But it was their only hope, to huddle down deep and await a harrowing rescue, and pray their SEAL raid against a crucial German weapons lab could somehow be pulled off before it was too late.

Taylor ordered the sea valves reopened, to get the propulsion shaft turning again. He ordered all nonessential personnel to evacuate the engineering spaces, which were all one giant compartment when it came to truly watertight doors. He knew the men were coming when his aching eardrums crackled and he felt the air get warm; the incoming water was squeezing the atmosphere.

The watertight hatch was closed again, and Taylor told COB to put more high-pressure air in the engine room, to help hold back the water. Its influx would only grow stronger as *Texas* drove for the seamount spur, her depth increasing by the minute, all reserve buoyancy lost. American SSN's simply weren't designed to float with one entire compartment flooded.

The XO conveyed by sound-powered phone that he'd stay aft with a handful of seasoned men. He knew that what *Texas* needed the most was speed, and people had to be there to override the safeties as the freezing seawater rose. Taylor authorized the reactor be pushed to one hundred eight percent.

Taylor eyed a depth gauge and watched the vessel's rate of descent, then glanced back at the nav chart. Maybe they'd make it to the spur, and maybe not, and even if they did they might crash-land too hard to live.

In simulator training his crew would have called this scenario grossly unfair. Taylor was fatalistic, staying detached. He tried not to think about the men working aft, who couldn't possibly survive.

The COB and the helmsman fought their controls, as the main hydraulics failed. The turbogenerators went next, and console systems switched to batteries.

"Rig for reduced electrical," Taylor said, and *Texas* labored her heart out, the propulsor refusing to quit.

The phone talker reported the seawater aft had risen well past the tightly dogged watertight hatch. It was time to scram the reactor. *Texas* kept going on built-up momentum, sinking like a stone on her glidepath into oblivion.

"*Collision alarm,*" Taylor ordered, as the crucial moment neared. He hoped his inertial nav fix was good and the local bottom charts accurate—with the ceaseless nuclear reverb and swirling bubbles all around, the bottom-mapping sonar only showed meaningless snow. He wished his boat had a gravimeter, which would have removed any doubt, but someone had decided some ten years back that gravimeters were too expensive.

Wincing with every gasping breath, suspecting now he'd also broken some ribs, Taylor ordered an emergency buoy prepared. He had it programmed for a tight-beam laser microburst, and hoped that the satellite due to pass overhead in an hour was still operational. The deeply encrypted message gave his ship's position, his plan for survival, and asked for help. It also reported his two *Rubis* kills, two fewer nuclear subs in the enemy arsenal now; at least if his ship and her people all died, they wouldn't have died for nothing. The buoy was launched. Taylor flashed once more on all those faces on the pier; some were widows and fatherless already.

The surviving men around Taylor braced for impact with the spur. If they missed it they'd keep going until the *Texas*'s hull caved in. They'd know soon enough.

CHAPTER 1

TWO HOURS LATER.

SÃO VICENTE ISLAND, REPUBLIC OF CAPE VERDE

Water lapped against the submarine pier. Gulls called, machinery growled, the air stank of dead fish and diesel fumes, and the equatorial sun shown brightly near the zenith in a silvery blue sky. There were no clouds he could watch, nor ships beyond the breakwater, and on this leeward side of the island only minor swell on the sea. Dominating the horizon loomed the next volcanic peak in the Cape Verde chain, seeming indifferent and invulnerable. Lieutenant Commander Jeffrey Fuller fidgeted.

At last, above the sound of cranes and trucks and urgent, shouting dockworkers and marines, Jeffrey sensed a clattering roar. The Navy courier helicopter swung into view, first above the stuccoed homes sprawling along the parched rocky slopes around Mindelo harbor, then over the drab concrete warehouses of the waterfront itself. The helo flared and hovered by the pier, bringing with it the heady perfume of burnt kerosene exhaust.

Out of the corner of his eye, as she stood next to him, Jeffrey watched the aircraft's prop wash tousle Ilse Reebeck's hair. The engine noise precluded conversation now, but their conversation had already been cut short, back at the hotel. Ilse looked relieved to be coming with Jeffrey, and he was glad, too—the whole thing was very last-minute—but it only complicated matters between them to have her on Jeffrey's ship again. Lord knew in the last two weeks, with their atomic demolition raid on the South African coast, they'd shared enough experiences, and nightmares, to last a lifetime. He told himself it was worth it, for what they'd achieved for the Allied cause, but the personal price was so high. Now, with no chance to catch their breaths or succor the inner emotional wounds, they were headed right back into the all-consuming maelstrom of tactical nuclear war at sea.

As a marine guard on the pier helped the helo pilot pick his spot to land, Jeffrey glanced at the water. The last of the liberty party was already crammed into USS *Challenger's* ASDS minisub, moored against the pier—hiding under a special awning that helped mask the goings-on from Berlin-Boer Axis spy birds. Jeffrey knew some crewmen were forced to stand in the mini's swimmer lock-in/lock-out chamber. But the embark was on hold, because of this courier.

"I wish he'd hurry up," Jeffrey said out loud. For most of his life, Jeffrey had wished people and things would hurry up.

As the helo settled on the pier, Jeffrey reviewed what little he knew so far: The *Texas* was down and needed help, and time was of the essence. In this whole big, hot, North Atlantic-wide theater of battle, *Challenger* was the closest thing—the *only* thing—available. Images flashed through Jeffrey's mind, training videos he'd had to watch—ones all U.S. Navy submariners had to watch—of tattered human remains in tortured postures: the men who died on the Russian submarine *Kursk*. Smashed to pulp, drowned slowly, or cremated alive, then soaked in high-pressure seawater—a living medium full of creatures who sought and ate their flesh.

Was that what awaited Jeffrey's eyes, when he got to the *Texas?* His ASDS was supposed to double as a deep-submergence rescue vehicle, to try to dock with the disabled sub once *Challenger* arrived.

Someone stepped from the helo. Like Jeffrey, the courier wore no rank or insignia, for security, but Jeffrey knew him vaguely. He was a lieutenant commander, in fact a rear admiral's aide, and by Navy regulations he spoke for his admiral with equal force. Jeffrey, *Challenger's* executive officer, was now the ship's acting captain. *Challenger* herself was submerged somewhere beyond the break-water. She was much too high-value a target to bring into port here during this war, and her real captain, Commander Wilson, Jeffrey's boss, was confined at the hotel with a bad concussion.

"Sign, please," the courier said, handing Jeffrey a thick envelope.

Jeffrey eyed the Top Secret markings, the code words RECURVE ARBOR—whatever *that* meant—along with the notation to open only when north of latitude 30 north. "What is this?"

"I don't know," the courier said. "I have other stops to make. This *Texas* thing has everybody stirred up."

Jeffrey scribbled his initials on the courier's clipboard, and did the arithmetic in his head. At *Challenger*'s top quiet speed, twenty-six knots—the fastest she dared go for long in the war zone—it would take more than a day to cross the thirtieth parallel, almost two full days to reach *Texas*.

"Do we know what shape they're in?"

"A lot are still breathing," the man said, "at least so far. They managed to launch another buoy once they crashed. That's why you're being sent."

"Can't you get us a doctor?" *Challenger* would act as a stealthy undersea field ambulance, if and when the survivors from *Texas* were taken aboard.

The courier shook his head. "They're all in surgery, overloaded. A hospital ship put in last night, from Central Africa. . . . Your corpsman will have to do."

"Great." Jeffrey started a mental tally of his ship's medical supplies. His people would be sleeping on the deck, to free their racks for the injured. . . .

"We're not sure yet if the Axis also knows about *Texas*. You may hit opposition en route."

"Terrific." Jeffrey'd transferred on as *Challenger*'s XO well after the start of the fighting six months ago—he'd been more than glad to give up a fast-track planning job at the Naval War College. He'd wanted to get to the front. Now, with no qualified skipper available at this forward base to step in for Commander Wilson, Jeffrey was utterly on his own.

"Good luck," the man called as he ran back to the helo.

Jeffrey turned to Ilse. He saw her read the concern on his face. They were both still so exhausted, her expression seemed to say, and now *this*. Jeffrey shrugged. Ilse was a civilian, a Boer freedom-fighter, but she'd be killed as dead as the rest of the crew if something went badly wrong.

"After you," he said, letting her go first, up the aluminum gangway and down the top hatch of the little submarine. The sixty-five-foot-long

ASDS was their undersea taxi today, hopefully too small on its own for someone to waste a nuke, and too stealthy for the enemy to track it to *Challenger*.

Ilse climbed down the top hatch, into the minisub's central hyperbaric sphere, which doubled as entry vestibule. The packed crewmen, all familiar faces, tried to make room for her. She in turn eased out of the way, so Jeffrey could follow.

Ilse smiled to herself, a bit grimly. Stomach sucked in, elbows close at your sides, watch what you bump into, and respect the other person's personal space—this was how submariners moved about their cramped and self-contained world. Ilse was pleased with how quickly she'd learned these habits during her first trip on the *Challenger*, and how quickly the mindset returned now on this unexpected, hurried second mission. That first time, she'd volunteered; her special skills were badly needed. This time, no one asked; a message from the chain of command had ordered her to go. They were supposed to head for the U.S. East Coast and a needed stint in dry dock—and maybe some leave for Christmas, too—and then this *Texas* rescue came up. Now, Ilse was being swept along in the rush.

Ilse watched Jeffrey reach to close the top hatch. Before he could dog it shut, the heavy door from the minisub's forward control compartment swung open. *Challenger*'s chief of the boat looked into the sphere and made quick eye contact with Ilse.

Ilse smiled back, and her inner tensions died down a bit; it was good to rejoin these people she knew and trusted. They'd helped her relieve some of her earlier anger, her barely repressed rage. They were a family of sorts, to replace everything and everyone she'd lost after the Johannesburg coup. Was it worth risking death to be with them again? What was her choice, to languish as a displaced person, utterly alone? Besides, in *this* war nowhere was "safe."

COB winked Ilse a hello, seeming surprised to see her. He was the oldest man in the crew, a salty, somewhat irreverent master chief. He had an amazing charisma, in a tough and blue-collar way, and Ilse had liked him from the moment they first met two weeks ago. Right now COB was acting as pilot of the minisub, with a lieutenant (j.g.) copilot. The last time she'd ridden the mini, it had taken her into combat in her tyranny-ravaged homeland of South Africa.

Then, a U.S. Navy SEAL chief had been copilot. He didn't come back.

COB called out to Jeffrey, "Sir, another delay. More passengers."

"More?" Jeffrey said. The men standing around him groaned. The youngest, still teenagers really, looked afraid they'd get left behind.

The pressure-proof door to the rear transport compartment was closed, and Ilse wondered how many people were squashed in there already—the official capacity was eight. One of them, she realized, would have to be newcomer Royal Navy Lieutenant Kathy Milgrom; there was nowhere else Kathy could be.

Ilse saw COB glance at his console, as if he were reading a decrypted radio or land-line message. "They're arriving any minute, Captain," COB said.

Jeffrey sighed, handed the courier envelope to COB, and climbed back up the ladder through the top hatch. Out of curiosity, and because she liked to be where Jeffrey was, Ilse followed. Past the foot of the pier, beyond the big concrete obstacles and heavy machine-gun emplacements, a local taxi pulled up. Like clowns from a circus car, six big men piled out one after another, all in civilian clothing, as if for disguise. Ilse immediately recognized SEAL Lieutenant Shajo Clayton, his two logistics and backup people, and the three surviving operators from Shajo's blooded boat team. Shajo grinned and waved; he'd been with her and Jeffrey on the South Africa raid.

The men untied several heavy equipment boxes from the cab's roof rack, and pulled more from the vehicle's trunk. Some boxes were black: SEAL combat gear. Some were white with big red crosses: first-aid supplies, presumably for the *Texas.* Jeffrey called for crewmen to help, and everyone started carrying the stuff to the minisub.

Jeffrey shook hands very warmly with Clayton—they'd been through hell together, all too recently, and the resulting bond was tight. "Would somebody please tell me what the heck is going on?" Jeffrey said, smiling with pleasure at this unexpected reunion.

"If they do," Clayton rejoined, "then maybe you can let me know, sir." Then he clapped Jeffrey on the shoulder, equally delighted to see his proven comrade-in-arms again.

"What did they say to you?"

"We're supposed to be, you know, some kind of armed guard. Apparently you're in need of extra muscle."

"I'm liking this less and less," Jeffrey said, shaking his head.

"I know," Ilse heard Clayton say as they reached the brow to the ASDS. "The base admiral didn't like it too much either."

Under the awning, Clayton gave Ilse a brotherly hug. She'd helped treat one of his mortally wounded men during the raid, and Clayton had brought her back alive; she felt better to know he was coming this time, too. Shajo was in his late twenties, from Atlanta, easy to talk to and even-tempered, with a very hard body. To Ilse his eyes betrayed hints of a persistent sadness that was all too common these days, from the recent loss of friends and teammates in the war, and the loss of innocence.

Jeffrey put down an equipment case and shouted through the mini's top hatch. "COB, how's your trim?" The little sub rode very low in the water, and didn't have a conning tower. With all the crewmen and now the SEALs' gear, keeping the mini stable would be tough.

Ilse heard COB's voice from inside. "Too heavy aft, Captain, and there's nothing left I can pump or counterflood. Any more weight on board and we're gonna have to jettison the anchors."

"Do it," Jeffrey yelled, "right now. And unclip the passenger seats in the back and pass them up to the pier." This was the Jeffrey whom Ilse had quickly gotten to know, and maybe, sort of, to like; firm but informal, always improvising on the spot, and ruthlessly practical. Jeffrey was driven, coming alive under pressure, though sometimes impetuous or even reckless when in battle. Yet he was oddly hesitant with her—at least when they weren't both being shot at by the enemy. Lonely, too. Ilse had sensed that in Jeffrey quickly. He'd never once mentioned any family.

Clayton's men formed a human chain to pile the seats under the camouflage awning. Ilse couldn't help thinking that all this hubbub, the courier helo and then the taxi with the SEALs, had to get noticed by German or Boer recon assets.

Finally everyone was aboard with their gear, the shore power and mooring lines were stowed, the top hatch secured. Jeffrey went forward to stand behind COB's seat, in the little control room. Ilse started to follow him—she'd stood behind the copilot as they snuck in toward Durban, on the South African coast, the last time.

But Jeffrey held up one hand. "No, I need to talk with Shajo and COB about the rescue plan."

Shajo squeezed past Ilse and into the control compartment. Then Jeffrey closed the door in her face.

A FEW MINUTES LATER.

TRANSITING THE BAY OF BISCAY

Korvettenkapitan Ernst Beck paused outside the captain's stateroom door. This would be their first private encounter since leaving port for patrol.

Beck felt the deck tilting to a fifteen-degree down bubble.

Germany's ceramic-hulled nuclear submarine *Deutschland* had reached the edge of the continental shelf off occupied France—the minefields, friendly and enemy, were mostly behind them now. She was descending to deeper water per the captain's orders.

Beck hesitated. Even after three years of working with the man, to intrude made him feel cold. Beck dearly loved his wife and two young sons. He knew by now his *Kommandant*—commanding officer—loved no one but himself, and never would.

Beck knocked.

"Come," that polished, precise, unreachable voice called from within. Beck slid open the door, entered, and closed it again for security.

Fregattenkapitan Kurt Eberhard sat alone at his fold-down desk. The air was filled with tobacco smoke, swirling in delicate tendrils. On the bulkhead hung the portrait in oils of the new Kaiser, Wilhelm IV, in an expensive gilded frame—Wilhelm II was Kaiser in World War One; Wilhelm III was his son, the Crown Prince, who never took the throne after 1918.

Eberhard looked up. He seemed annoyed, then softened his features; he was polite, at least superficially.

"Ja, Einzvo?"

Beck was *Deutschland*'s so-called "1WO," the *Erster Wachoffizier*— executive officer, pronounced phonetically "einzvo." His rank equaled lieutenant commander in the U.S. or Royal navies. Eberhard was a full commander, intent on making full captain soon.

"Sir," Beck said, "a high-priority radiogram came in."

"Did you read it?"

"Yes, Captain."

"Well?"

"It's an assessment from Kaiserliche Marine Intel, sir." Imperial

Naval Intelligence. "Reliable sources indicate USS *Challenger* is putting to sea from Cape Verde."

Hard blue eyes confronted Beck.

"So they've localized our ceramic-hulled friend?"

"Yes, Captain. She's heading north."

"Does the message say *why*?"

"She might be tasked to assist a crippled American sub near the Azores, but that could be a deception, sir, a feint for some more important mission. . . . The odd thing is, it says combat swimmers were taken aboard, but not *Challenger*'s captain. Her XO's in command."

Eberhard stubbed out his cigarette. "I know Jeffrey Fuller all too well. A peasant."

Beck was careful not to react. The Coronation had done more than restore the glitter of Court, of which Eberhard was so fond: It had strengthened class differences in German society. Beck was the youngest son of a farmer himself, from outside Munich; his family was Catholic in the traditional Bavarian way. He'd joined the peacetime German Navy as a cadet in '91, right after Reunification. He did it to get a broader education than he could at the local technical school, and to help make the nation whole again with respect in the eyes of the world.

Also—as he put it to his trusted friends—by his late teens, Beck was tired of smelling manure and wearing lederhosen.

"Fuller and I once worked together," Eberhard said. He seemed distant for a moment, even more than usual. "Combined duty at the Pentagon, before the war."

"Is he good, sir?" Given the possibility of a contest with Fuller and crew, Beck had to ask.

Eberhard waved dismissively.

"He displeased me with his rebellious ways and casual style. I outranked him, of course, then as now, but the Americans put up with his antics."

Beck wondered what he was supposed to say to that. His job as executive officer was to meld himself to Eberhard's will, regardless of what he thought of the man.

"We're ordered to be on alert, sir. In case *Challenger* enters our operational area."

"Good. Let me see."

Beck gave him the message slip.

Beck glanced at Eberhard's desk. He recognized a file copy of *Deutschland*'s last war patrol report—he'd drafted it himself for Eberhard's signature three weeks ago. It was open to the final page, showing the vessel's cumulative totals since the start of the fighting.

Eberhard noticed him reading.

"Nine hundred fifty thousand tons of Allied shipping sunk," Eberhard said. "Already twice the previous world record, set by one of our submarine captains in World War One. Four times as good as Hitler's top-scoring U-boat ace." He went back to the message slip.

This damage wrought by *Deutschland* had earned Eberhard the *Ritterkreuz*, the Knight's Cross, one of Germany's highest military honors. It was deserved; Beck had no question of Eberhard's tactical skill. Beck himself got the Iron Cross First Class, prestigious enough, though he cared nothing for medals.

But he did want his own command someday. Beck did want his own command.

Eberhard put the message in his safe.

"How are the crew?"

"Getting back their sea legs quickly, Captain." They'd all been on leave in Bordeaux. Submariner skills were perishable—the men grew rusty away from the ship—but Beck was taking care of that with drills and refresher training.

"And the new hands?"

"I think they'll be ready."

"You think or you *know*?"

"They'll be ready, Captain."

"Good. I look forward to dueling with Fuller again."

"Captain, some of the seasoned men have been holding up an index finger to one another, when they think I'm not looking."

"An index finger, Einzvo?"

"Yes. For one million tons."

"This patrol we'll do it. A record for the ages."

As usual, Beck was torn by Germany's culpability in this war. But they had a right to their God-given place in the world, didn't they? Versailles, post-Nazi occupation by the Allies, endless, dreary Soviet domination in the East—all were made up for now. This was *good*, wasn't it?

"Sink one million tons, and then sink *Challenger*," Eberhard said. "What a Christmas gift for our monarch *that* would make!"

Beck figured Eberhard would be made a baron for sure.

Eberhard would like that: the nobleman's title itself. The validation independent of Eberhard's father, a crass, nouveau-riche investment banker in Stettin, in the Protestant north. The grant of a private estate in occupied French wine country. The long train of beautiful Frenchwomen warming his bed.

Yes, Eberhard would like that a lot.

"Destroy *Challenger*," Eberhard said, "and the self-infatuated Americans will be one big step closer to having to sue for an armistice."

Deutschland leveled off. Beck and Eberhard read the depth gauge on the captain's instrument display: eleven hundred meters. With her alumina-casing hull and sea pipes, the ship was capable of three or four times that—about fifteen thousand feet.

Eberhard lit up again. He sat for a minute, savoring the cigarette and thinking.

Beck waited.

"They have no sense of history, the Americans," Eberhard said. "None of what's happening ought to have surprised them. But it did. They're like children, thinking the world should be a nice place, and everyone else should agree with them."

"Unipolarism, they called it, sir, after the end of the Cold War."

"We're giving the world a *new* unipolarism, aren't we? Once we starve out the U.K., and link up with the Boers in central Africa, we'll control two continents. . . . You have to admit the Boers come in handy." They'd helped spring the giant two-step trap at the start of the war, and they were giving the Allies a two-theater conflict now.

Again Beck tried not to react to Eberhard's haughty attitude. He went to his common ground with the captain, as a fellow naval officer: patriotism and duty. But did Eberhard—Germany's greatest U-boat commander—love the sea and his ship as Beck did, or was the ocean to him just water, and *Deutschland* just a machine? Was Eberhard a patriot, or was he simply using this war for predatory self-advancement, the same way he used everyone and everything else?

CHAPTER 2

Ilse sat elbow to elbow with Kathy Milgrom, at the forward end of the sonar consoles lining the crowded Command and Control Center's port bulkhead. Although they'd both been there a while, the watch had just changed, and fresh crewmen were settling in all around them. Ilse sensed the mood of heightened urgency—they were halfway to the *Texas* now. Everyone put on a bright face, and fought to stay optimistic, but the relentless tension was taking its toll. The enlisted mess was turned into a war room for the rescue: stacked emergency tools and oxygen canisters, nonstop first-aid drills, constant damage control rehearsals; the men ate standing up. Jeffrey briefed his officers—and Ilse—as soon as *Challenger* got underway. His words about what they might find when they reached *Texas* had been pithy, graphic, chilling. Ilse regretted there was nothing she could do to help those poor waiting men, except help get there as quickly as possible.

The CACC, *Challenger's* control room, was rigged for red, despite the broad daylight twelve hundred feet above the ship, over the storm-tossed waves and distant mushroom clouds. The subdued lighting had little to do with preserving night vision. In the midst of tactical nuclear war at sea there was no way a submarine would raise a periscope mast by choice, let alone surface and man the bridge cockpit on the sail—the conning tower—even at night. The red fluorescents were used instead to make the computer screens easy on watchstanders' eyes.

"I'm about done with this module of code," Ilse said—an enhanced model of water temperature versus salinity dynamics.

"I'll be ready for your data bridge in a minute," Kathy said; she was the acting sonar officer. Ilse was the ship's on-board combat oceanographer, formalized now. She'd been teaching and doing research at the University of Cape Town, and was caught in the U.S. at a marine biology conference when the Double Putsch cost her her country—and cost her family their lives for resisting the old-line Boer takeover.

Ilse sat with headphones on, the left ear cup over her left ear, the right one on her cheekbone. This way she could hear the raw signals from outside, and still talk with Kathy. Intermittent thunder on the headphones formed a counterpoint: atom bombs going off, more than fifty miles away, in the latest battle between a supply convoy and the U-boats.

"This American combat systems software is splendid," Kathy said; she was crisp, but expressive, and clearly loved her work. A full-fledged Royal Navy submariner, Kathy was supposed to have had a quiet trip into dry dock to qualify on *Challenger,* before further combat duty after that. Now, like Ilse, she had been pulled willy-nilly into this rescue mission to *Texas;* she needed to master her new job very quickly.

The two women had already compared their life stories, so Ilse knew Kathy had grown up in Liverpool, then done the Royal Navy Academy at Dartmouth, followed by Oxford and active service in the surface fleet. Kathy's Liverpool accent, its edges softened now, sounded to Ilse's ear like Irish; she often talked with her hands, to the degree there was room at the consoles.

Ilse glanced at Kathy in profile, backlit in red, lit from in front by the blues and greens on her monitors. Kathy was a few inches shorter than Ilse, a few kilos overweight, and wore special submariner eyeglasses. These had narrow frames and small lenses, to fit under an emergency air breather mask. The glasses made Kathy look particularly owlish.

"Agreed," Ilse said. "The fiber-optic network's amazing." Each console did sonar or weapons or target tracking, depending which menu you picked—all three functions were vital in undersea warfare. Ilse typed on her keyboard, massaged the trackmarble with her palm, and touched her screen. It was possible to access the programs for quick enhancements using software tool kits, as she was doing now. . . . Ilse was getting her sea legs back. She lived in a giant *machine,* with a soul of its own she felt bound to already; the snug control room was its heart. Sonar was its eyes and ears, very dependent on how the sea transmitted and distorted sound—a topic she knew a lot about.

Ilse had grown up in urban Johannesburg, the oldest child of a media executive father and a city politician mother, and spoke English with a South African accent; she was also fluent in Afrikaans, the Boer tongue, related to German and Dutch. She'd always loved nature and scuba diving and had wanderlust in her soul—traits that took her to Scripps in San Diego for a Ph.D. in ocean science. During those four years she picked up American slang. She also, in those happier days, dated more than one American male naval officer from the bases around Coronado.

Lieutenant Richard Sessions came over and leaned between Ilse and Kathy. He read their screens—each station had a pair, one above the other, in high-definition full color.

"Quick work," Sessions said. "I see you two won't need much help from me."

This pleased Ilse; 'til yesterday *he'd* been sonar officer, reporting to Weps, the weapons officer, Lieutenant Jackson Jefferson Bell. With Kathy added to the crew, as an exchange officer from the Royal Navy, Jeffrey had promoted Sessions to navigator, a department head in his own right. The old navigator, Lieutenant Monaghan, was on a hospital ship, in intensive care with a broken neck. Kathy had served on the U.K.'s ceramic sub, HMS *Dreadnought,* as part of the Royal Navy's initial—and highly controversial—tryout of women in fast-attack crews, something made more palatable to most naysayers by the exigencies of war, the endless demands for talented people. Sessions was in his mid-twenties, from somewhere in Nebraska. Always earnest and polite, he was the sort of person whose hair and clothes seemed a little sloppy no matter what he did.

Sessions reached past Ilse's shoulder and pushed a selector button. Her lower screen changed from computer code to a broadband waterfall display. Ilse saw the snowlike traces of biologics and breaking waves, and watched the merged engine noise of surface ships fleeing from that beleaguered convoy. There were also weird tight spirals on the screen that Ilse knew came from acoustic jammers and decoys, and bright swellings here and there from the nuclear blasts.

"Looks bad," Sessions said.

"Yes." Ilse wondered why Jeffrey wasn't doing something to help, but figured his focus was on *Texas*. He'd been reclusive since the overcrowded ASDS docked with *Challenger*; she'd hardly seen him, and felt abandoned. One minute he'd been trying to ask her out, on leave at the hotel in Cape Verde, and she hadn't exactly said no. The next, after his hurried mission briefing, he'd foisted her off on Kathy and disappeared; for this watch, Lieutenant Bell had the deck and the conn.

Sessions straightened and returned to the digital nav table, to confer with his senior chief, the assistant navigator. Kathy spoke with one of the sonar chiefs. Ilse knew that in a very real sense the chiefs made *Challenger* go—and they'd be the first ones to tell you that. Ilse drank the dregs of her latest coffee, retrieved the computer code to her display, and went back to work.

She and Kathy discussed some further technical points. Kathy was approachable enough, but Ilse found her a bit reserved. This was probably just her needed persona as a naval officer, dealing with superiors and subordinates in the hierarchy of the ship. It could be because Kathy was new here, still testing the waters as it were. Ilse doubted it had much to do with the sex-balance on *Challenger*, since she'd had no trouble feeling welcome herself from the get-go: This crew was an *elite*, and knew no one would be assigned unless they also were very good. There was a strong sense of camaraderie on the ship, built from their shared first taste of combat two weeks ago, strengthened by this compelling new assignment, the *Texas*.

Well, maybe I'll get to know Kathy better, once we have a chance to unwind together alone in our stateroom.

Ilse felt Kathy stiffen abruptly. *"Here we go,"* she muttered. The Brit put both ear cups firmly in place, and frowned. "Console five," she said into her headset mike, speaking to one of the enlisted sonar techs. "Play back the last ten seconds, starboard wide-aperture array, on bearing zero two five true. Show me the power spectrum."

"What's happening?" Ilse said.

Kathy's lower screen changed to show a jagged, squirming oscil-
loscope trace, a plot of sound intensity versus frequency, on bearing
zero two five over time.

"That." Kathy pointed to a quick blip at about 2000 hertz that
stuck out like a sore thumb. On the tape, enhanced, it sounded like
a *clunk*. Kathy froze the picture and studied it. "Console three, give
me the ray trace." Her upper screen now showed a tangle of over-
lapping arcs and sine curves; Ilse's detailed knowledge of ocean me-
chanics made this plot more precise.

"Conn, Sonar," Kathy called out. "Mechanical transient, bearing
zero two five. Closer than our first convergence zone. . . . It isn't
friendly."

Jeffrey finished wolfing down a stale ham sandwich alone in the
wardroom. He felt his vessel shimmy for a moment, as she passed
through a dying shock wave from another distant atomic explosion.
He knew the second section of a huge convoy to the U.K. was under
attack way up ahead, part two of a shipment of food and heating fuel
on dozens of escorted merchant ships. The first section had run into
trouble enough the day before, near the path of the *Texas*. The convoy had sailed in two sections—a day apart and on different routes
past the Azores in mid-Atlantic—partly because the number of cargo
ships that started out was so large, and partly as a one-two punch to try
to overwhelm and blow past the Axis wolf packs. Similar tactics had
been used in World War II, with mixed success—and now the U-boats
had A-bombs, and silent air-independent propulsion if not nuclear
power, and didn't send constant radio reports for the Allies to home
on and decode.

Jeffrey heard and felt another detonation. He wished there was
something he could do to help those merchant mariners. Half a year
into the war, Great Britain was already starving, the initial six-month
surge capacity of the Allies' submarine fleets was nearing exhaustion,
and the killing North Atlantic storms had barely begun. But the convoy action was too far off for *Challenger* to make much difference.
Besides, she had a pressing engagement elsewhere, Jeffrey's preoc-
cupation: *Texas, Texas, Texas*. Her hundred or so combat-experienced
American submariners—or as many as would actually live and recover from their injuries—were a priceless war-fighting asset, even

with their ship herself lost. They were also an invaluable prize, if the enemy got to them first.

Jeffrey rubbed sleep-deprived eyes. Spread before him on the wardroom table were hard copies of *Virginia*-class blueprints and subsystem diagrams. Just as he had for most of the past twenty-four hours—often in conference with his engineer, Lieutenant Willey, and with COB—Jeffrey was trying to understand what the men aboard *Texas* might do to survive, and what *Challenger* might best do to aid them once she reached the scene. It would take several hours to evacuate the survivors, shuttling them from *Texas* to *Challenger* in Jeffrey's ASDS. It would be tragic indeed if some succumbed to wounds or oxygen deprivation while waiting their turn, when salvation was so near.

One of the wardroom intercoms barked. To Jeffrey the signal, the growler, always sounded like a shih tzu puppy. More stressed-out than usual, Jeffrey winced at this mental connection: His family had had a shih tzu when he was growing up, in a middle-class suburb of St. Louis. In a sick way, he was here now because of that dog.

He'd found the shih tzu, his family, his playmates, the town, all excruciatingly *ordinary*, and he didn't try to hide it. His father was a local utility regulator—a career bureaucrat—his mother a nondescript housewife, his two older sisters—and their husbands—painfully bourgeois. He had always felt a burning need to escape from there and achieve something really *special*. Jeffrey sometimes wondered if this was a genetic quirk, or if he'd been mixed up with another baby at the hospital. In fifth grade, by accident, he discovered the naval history section at his local library, and quickly became addicted to the stuff— it soothed that savage, painful craving in his breast. As soon as he could, in a rather heavy-handed way, he left home for Purdue with a Navy scholarship, and after that joined the SEALs, till bad scar tissue in a leg required he be transferred; he picked submarines. Basically, Jeffrey'd run away to sea and hadn't looked back, and his family, not nearly as dull as Jeffrey had judged them to be, resented it.

Jeffrey sighed. They had little contact with him now, and vice versa, and much of that was his fault. In fact, Jeffrey's father— deeply involved in America's desperate energy-conservation program these days—seemed to blame Jeffrey somehow for the war. After all, Jeffrey was Navy. The Navy should have known, should have done something sooner, not been suckered into that nuclear ambush off western Africa that cost three carriers.

Jeffrey forced himself back to the present: the growler. Its ringer was hand-powered from the other end by turning a little crank, which everyone had their own way of doing, their "fist." Jeffrey could tell this call was from his acting XO, Lieutenant Bell, who this watch was officer of the deck.

Jeffrey gulped the last of his iced tea, wiped his lips with a white cloth napkin, then lifted the handset. "Captain."

"Sir," Bell said, "Sonar just picked up a mechanical transient. Submerged, left of the bearing to the convoy, and much closer to *Challenger*."

Closer? Jeffrey's heart quickened. "What's Milgrom's best guess of the range?"

"Maybe fifty thousand yards." Twenty-five nautical miles.

Hmmm . . . "What's her assessment?"

"She thinks it was an underwater probe and drogue connecting, trying to hide in the reverb from that latest detonation."

"Some kind of undersea replenishment," Jeffrey said. "Probably pulled back for a breather from the running fight northeast of us."

"Yes, sir. Milgrom says she heard something like it once before, on *Dreadnought*, but that time the targets evaded. It's definitely Axis."

Good. That's why Kathy was here, a bit of cross-pollination between American and Royal Navy ceramic-hulled submarine crews. Jeffrey stood up decisively, from the sacrosanct captain's place at the head of the wardroom table. *Captain Wilson's place.*

"I'll be right there, XO. Rig for ultraquiet and deep submergence. Sound silent general quarters, man battle stations antisubmarine."

Jeffrey quickly piled the *Texas* work papers onto the sideboard. He ducked into the pantry to bus his dirty dishes. Lying loose they might become dangerous projectiles—and the wardroom doubled as *Challenger's* operating theater. On the way, for the umpteenth time, he glanced at the wardroom data repeaters. The ship was approaching latitude 29° 28' north.

Jeffrey was glad he hadn't opened that "RECURVE ARBOR" courier envelope. Some kind of secret orders? Which base to head for in the U.S.? Updated recognition codes for when they reached home waters?

Well, taking the fine print literally, he hadn't crossed 30 north *yet*—and there might be something in the package to limit his tactical discretion. For him, all the lives on the convoy—and the vital cargoes they carried—had to outweigh a single stranded crew on an already sunken submarine . . . didn't they?

Besides, here was a chance for Jeffrey's first independent kill. He was half afraid he *wouldn't* see combat before the East Coast and dry dock. Once hard and demanding Captain Wilson recovered, Jeffrey would revert to XO, taking orders in battle, not giving them.

Jeffrey climbed the ladder up one deck. He strode to the command workstation in the center of the CACC.

It occurred to Jeffrey that it hadn't occurred to him to be nervous making his first deliberate attack as acting captain, a big step in any naval officer's career. But as he'd discovered as a much younger lieutenant (j.g.), badly wounded on a black op in Iraq in '96, he didn't mind dying half so much as he minded being bored. The intense comradeship of people being shot at dispelled his gnawing sense of inner emptiness. The difference this time, though, was Jeffrey was almost forty, with everything *that* implied. And the burden of command was not one ounce diminished since his first taste of enemy fire; the unforgiving trade-offs of life-versus-life, that soul-wrenching calculus of war, only got harder, more wearing with age. He had never felt so lonely as in the past day, with no one, *no one,* to relieve the ultimate pressures of his responsibility as captain, or to share the blame in case he failed.

"Sir," Bell said, talking fast, "the ship's closed up at battle stations antisubmarine. We are rigged for ultraquiet. Our depth is twelve hundred feet, and we are rigged for deep submergence. Our course is due north, speed is top quiet speed, twenty-six knots." Unlike other American submarines, *Challenger* had in-hull hangar space for her minisub; the ASDS didn't slow her down.

Jeffrey repeated Bell's info per standard procedure, then took the conn. Bell slid over to the right seat of the desk-high console. Bell was an inch taller than Jeffrey, four years younger, and fit but not as muscular. Bell was a Navy brat, like his father before him, and had grown up all over the world.

Jeffrey announced in a loud clear voice, "This is the captain. I have the conn." The watchstanders acknowledged.

"What do we know?" Jeffrey said impatiently.

Bell relayed him the large-scale tactical plot. "Submerged hostile contact designated Master One, bearing zero two five true." Off the starboard bow, given *Challenger*'s course.

"Sonar, any further data since that transient?"

"Negative, sir," Kathy said. "Recommend splitting contact designation as Master One and Master Two, since I'm certain there are two vessels involved."

"Do it. Contact identification?"

"Speculation, sir. One Class two-twelve attack sub and one modified Class two-fourteen long-endurance milch cow."

"Makes sense," Jeffrey said. The 212 must be replenishing its liquid oxygen and hydrogen supplies, for its air-independent fuel cells (AIP). "The German boats won't be making more than three knots, cruising in close proximity, linked by fueling hose. A juicy target, *if* we can get near enough for a decent shot." An easy target, too.

"Sir," Bell said, "if our priority is helping the *Texas*, shouldn't we decline an engagement here? The closer we get to these U-boats, the more likely they'll pick *us* up."

"They'll have twenty or thirty nuclear torpedoes between them. We put 'em on the bottom in little pieces, more of our ships get through."

"Er, yes, sir."

Jeffrey turned to the phone talker. "Give me your rig." Jeffrey put on the bulky headphones and pressed the switch for the sound-powered mike.

"This is the captain." It got easier each time he said it. He made eye contact around the control room as he spoke. "Men . . . and women of *Challenger*. You all know we have somewhere important to get to, to help our friends on *Texas*." He paused to let the phone talkers stationed around the ship catch up, relaying his words to the other crewmen in earshot in each compartment. "Now we have a chance to do some good on the way. We are going to destroy two hypermodern Axis diesel submarines and neutralize their atomic weapons. Our actions will allow more ships to reach the U.K., on this convoy and future convoys. We must act quickly while they're still linked up for refueling and they're slow and vulnerable. Those AIPs are fast enough to be a threat to us and god-awful quiet on their fuel-cell electric drives. There's some risk, but it's worth it and we're taking it." Jeffrey paused again. "That's all." He took off the rig.

There was tense silence in the compartment. Jeffrey imagined some of the men chafed at this delay in the rescue mission. He decided to pretend he didn't notice: *He* was in charge now.

Jeffrey glanced toward the ship control station, on the forward bulkhead. COB was in the left seat, as general-quarters chief of the watch. Lieutenant (j.g.) David Meltzer had the right seat, as the helmsman. Both sat with their backs to Jeffrey; he couldn't read their faces.

"Helm," Jeffrey ordered, "make your course zero two five. . . . XO, I want to aim for the enemy's baffles." The blind spot behind their stern. "How long would it take a two-twelve to refuel, if it was running on empty to start with?"

Bell cleared his throat. "Intel thinks about sixty minutes, Captain."

"Then let's assume *we* have one hour, starting with that transient. . . . At our present speed we'll close the range to fifteen thousand yards in forty minutes. We'll launch our fish from there. . . . That won't leave much margin for close-in tactics. Face it, time's on *their* side."

"But, sir, if we shoot any sooner, and give our torpedoes too long a run, the enemy will hear them coming for sure. Then things could get very dangerous for us."

"Yeah," Jeffrey said. At Diego Garcia, *Challenger* had lost three torpedomen, and had half her tubes damaged, and it was a dry-dock job to fix her autoloader gear. "That's probably why they picked *us* to rescue the *Texas*. We're not good for much else."

CHAPTER 3

Jeffrey stood, leaning against the side of the command workstation as *Challenger* moved in on Kathy's now stale transient contact. Standing always helped Jeffrey think, and he'd been awake for thirty-six hours straight, so far. Sonar held no new data on the targets yet.

Jeffrey and his key people were debating whether to deploy *Challenger*'s one remaining towed array, for a better chance of detecting the U-boats early, through the very-low-frequency tonals they'd be making. The conversation had already gone in circles once. Basically, Jeffrey wanted to save the array for self-defense once they reached *Texas*; they'd had to ditch their other one at Diego Garcia, because it took too long to retract once there was an enemy torpedo in the water. But Kathy and Bell wanted to use the spare array *now*, or they might not be able to find the 212 and 214 at all.

A search for broadband noise using the ship's hull arrays would also be problematic. *Challenger* was hiding in the deep scattering layer, a zone of dense biologics that caused false echoes for enemy sonar; at this time of day in this season and latitude, the layer was comparatively shallow, twelve hundred feet. The 212's and 214's crush depth was a bit deeper than that, so they might be cloaked in the layer, too—it tended to block sound over any substantial distance.

Ilse suggested hunting for the U-boats by trying to look up at them from a greater depth—in sonar hole-in-ocean mode—using surface wind and wave noise to acoustically backlight the targets. The problem with that was they'd need to get very close to Master One and Two first, by sheer guesswork, before they'd have much chance of a contact. And even then, the Class 212 and 214 were tiny compared to *Challenger*—they'd be very hard to see as just two quiet spots against a noisy background.

Kathy stressed that any sonar search plan, in these conditions, would be at best an awkward compromise. Ilse looked like she wasn't sure *what* to think. She did point out that the seafloor here, at eighteen thousand feet, went way past *Challenger*'s crush depth. Bell hinted, not so gently this time, that maybe they ought to just press on to *Texas*.

The clock kept ticking. In his mind, Jeffrey decided. They'd follow the original line of bearing to the targets, course zero two five, and then assume the U-boats were slowly heading north to keep after the convoy fight while the 212 refueled. *Challenger* would use hole-in-ocean sonar: Kathy and Ilse had found two frequency bands where the biologic layer was relatively transparent to ambient noise.

For a moment Jeffrey felt self-doubt, or guilt or something. Had he picked this particular route for *Challenger* on purpose, to take him near the track of the convoy fight, for another chance to mix it up with the Axis while he held an independent command? There were certainly quieter, safer ways to reach the Azores, and home from there. . . . Was he trying to leave a calling card for that ceramic-hulled asshole, Eberhard, using nuclear torpedoes to settle old scores from office politics?

"People, it's our job to be aggressive. We're going after the German subs."

The others nodded, seeming to Jeffrey relieved a decision was made, and glad they weren't the ones to have to make it. He told Ilse to use her knowledge of hydrodynamics, to try to model what the flow drag of the U-boats' fueling pipes might sound like.

Jeffrey gave orders to arm the atomic warheads in torpedo tubes one and three, then flood the tubes and open the outer doors. The guys on *Texas* would have to hold on a little bit longer.

Jeffrey thought back to the courier envelope, unopened in his safe. What the hell did RECURVE ARBOR mean? Well, it would just have to wait. He certainly couldn't allow himself second thoughts now.

HALF AN HOUR LATER.

"Anything yet?" Jeffrey asked.

"No, sir," Kathy said.

Jeffrey went to talk to the navigator.

"It's been quiet out there for a while," Ilse whispered to Kathy.

"The convoy battle has died down."

"Think it's over?"

"No." Kathy brought up a different display on her console. "Still plenty of surviving merchant ships, see? The Germans must be lying doggo. Still a few surviving escorts, too. I can barely hear them pinging."

"Doesn't that convoy have SSN escorts?" SSNs were nuclear-powered fast-attack subs.

"Apparently not," Kathy said, "or the frigates wouldn't use active sonar, for fear of showing the Axis subs where ours are lurking, by an accidental echo off their hull, you see. Most of our fast-attacks are needed to protect the surviving carriers anyway, or for independent operations like we're on now. There aren't enough SSNs to go around, Ilse. . . . Besides, if there were, they might be sunk by friendly fire. Surface and airborne antisubmarine forces tend to treat any submerged contact as hostile, and shoot before they ask questions. . . . So our fast-attacks stay clear."

"I'm glad I'm not riding that convoy."

"Those merchant mariners are the unsung heroes of this war, if you ask me. Just like in the last big brew-up, before our time."

Ilse returned to her keyboard, refining ocean-model parameters to make better sense of all the raw data pouring in from the hull arrays.

Jeffrey came over and tapped Kathy on the shoulder. She turned.

"Any contact?"

"All five sonarmen are working on it, sir."

•   •   •

"Anything, Sonar?"

"Not yet, Captain."

"Have you run a systems check?"

"Several times, Captain."

Jeffrey fidgeted at the Combat Systems consoles. The tactical nuclear Mark 88 deep-capable torpedoes in tubes one and three were armed and ready to fire. Lieutenant Bell had the conn.

"Helm," Bell said. "Time for the next search leg. Make your course zero four five." Northeast. "Slow to ahead one third, make turns for seven knots." Going slower improved sonar sensitivity.

Meltzer repeated the orders verbatim for confirmation, worked the engine order dial and his control wheel, then called out when *Challenger* reached the altered course and speed.

Jeffrey was pleased with the young man. Meltzer had ranked high in his class at the Naval Academy, and in the nuclear qualification training, and Basic Submarine Officers Course, but nothing beat the test of combat. Since leaving Diego Garcia, not so long ago, Meltzer had showed nerve and confidence. He was a tough kid from the Bronx, and Jeffrey liked him. He'd piloted the ASDS on the Durban raid, and done very well, and then done well handling *Challenger* herself in the running battle which followed. Jeffrey decided Meltzer would pilot the mini again, rescuing the men from *Texas*.

Jeffrey smiled to himself. On his own junior officer tour, on a *Los Angeles*-class boat, a beginner enlisted rating had worked the helm, another the separate stern-plane controls, under the ever-watchful eyes of a diving officer. Back in those days SEALs rode free-flooding undersea scooters to the target, freezing their asses all the way—and a disabled sub had to wait for a deep-submergence rescue vehicle staged from the U.S. or Britain.

Jeffrey was less pleased with Bell. Bell was third-generation Navy, true. His father and grandfather had been enlisted men: his father a chief in riverine warfare toward the end in Vietnam, his father's father a steward on a battleship in World War II. Bell had earned a place at Annapolis, and an officer's commission, and had a strong service record since then, but he kept second-guessing Jeffrey in front of the crew. He also seemed at times lately to lack confidence, or backbone, or something. Was he distracted, too distracted, because his wife was expecting? Would he really make the grade as acting XO? He ought to stick to *that* task, daunting enough for a mere lieutenant, and let Jeffrey make the big decisions as acting captain. It was a captain's job to make the tough decisions.

Jeffrey turned to Ilse and Kathy, not smiling at all now. "So what have we got?"

"Still nothing," Kathy said.

"The more time we spend doing this, the closer that two-twelve gets to being refueled." Jeffrey pressed Kathy on purpose. The ship was going into battle, and Jeffrey had to take this new woman's measure fast.

Kathy nodded reluctantly. "Recommend we go deeper, sir, for a wider look-up search cone, so as to cover a larger swath with each sweep we make."

"Oceanographer, where's the axis of the deep sound channel here?" Sounds made near the axis tended to stay at the depth of the axis, a gambit to conceal *Challenger* from Master One and Two.

"Right around six thousand feet," Ilse said.

"We'll continue our look-up from there." Jeffrey glanced at the clock yet again. "We better spot them soon. Once they split up they'll make a smaller target, and be a lot harder to find."

For a moment Jeffrey worried someone or something might be lurking for *him* in the deep sound channel, a kind of horizontal acoustic superconductor. . . . He thought of the men waiting and suffering on *Texas*, who were depending on him for rescue. How much air did they have left? How much blood plasma, and morphine? He thought of the crews on those convoy ships, also bleeding, drowning, burning alive.

Jeffrey realized that if his choice to shoot for score against these two Axis submarines backfired, there'd be no salvation for the *Texas*. No one else was close enough to effect a timely rescue if *Challenger* was lost. Not for the first time, Jeffrey wondered what he was doing.

The ship was at six thousand feet.

"Still nothing, Sonar?" Jeffrey snapped.

"No, sir. Nothing. We haven't picked up anything."

"Was that transient a *mistake*?"

"*No,*" Kathy said, looking insulted. "It was much too clear on the tape. The system is *optimized* to pick up mechanical transients."

"Sir," Bell said, "we're almost out of time. Maybe we should just go back."

"No. We keep looking."

"I have something!" Kathy shouted. A sheen of sweat glistened on her forehead.

"What's target depth?" Jeffrey demanded.

"Within the deep scattering layer, Captain."

"Is it one or both of them?"

"Width of the target suggests it's Master One and Master Two, cruising side by side."

"Good job." Jeffrey saw Kathy grab a piece of toilet paper, used to clean the console screens. She wiped her face instead.

"Sir," Bell said, "we need horizontal separation."

"Concur." *They're practically on top of us; we'd get blown up by our own A-bomb.* "Give me the conn."

Bell slid over. "Target course is zero zero five."

Almost due north, as Jeffrey guessed. He smirked: He'd out-psyched the German captains beautifully. "We'll steer the other way. Let's get more vertical separation, too." Jeffrey ordered two two five, southwest, and a depth of nine thousand feet. Meltzer acknowledged. The deck tilted. The tension mounted.

Jeffrey kept one eye on a depth gauge: Nine thousand feet was very close to *Challenger's* test depth. "We'll use one Mark eighty-eight, set to run at slow speed for stealth. If we're lucky, Master One and Master Two won't ever know what hit 'em."

"Sir," Meltzer said, "my depth is nine thousand feet." The control room deck creaked slightly, from the compression of the hull.

Sonar still tracked the U-boats, on *Challenger's* starboard wide aperture array. Jeffrey cleared his throat. "Firing point procedures, Mark eighty-eight in tube one, area burst on adjacent sonar contacts Master One and Two."

Bell acknowledged, then relayed commands: Jeffrey had the targets cold.

"Six thousand yards separation, sir." In combat Bell was Fire Control Coordinator.

Jeffrey was satisfied *Challenger* wouldn't be damaged; the shock from a blast in deep water fell off quickly with the distance. The 88 warhead's variable yield was set on maximum, one-tenth kiloton—equal to three hundred high-explosive torpedoes combined.

Jeffrey saw Bell react to something on his console screen. "Sir! The contacts have changed course! Now steering zero eight five." Almost due east.

"Sonar, have they separated?"

"Not sure yet, sir."

"I said have they separated?"

Kathy stared at her screens. "Negative."

"XO, update the data to our weapon. Any sign they've detected us?"

"Negative," Bell and Kathy said.

"Good. Here we go. Tube one, match sonar bearings and—"

"Do not shoot!" Kathy shouted. "Revised contact classification! *Biologics,* adult whale and calf!"

Jeffrey turned to Kathy. "Christ, if we'd fired we'd've given ourselves away for sure. You almost got us killed."

Before Kathy could say anything, Bell gave Jeffrey a quick reproachful look. "Captain, the one hour you allotted has been and gone. They've probably secured the fuel lines and cleared the area, assuming it wasn't a diversion ploy to begin with."

Jeffrey ran a tired hand over his face. He knew Bell's real point, turn back now, was correct. He wasn't sure whether to be angry at Bell or himself. He apologized to Kathy.

"Nav," Jeffrey said, "what's optimum course to the *Texas?*"

"Recommend three two zero," Sessions said immediately.

"Helm, make your course three two zero. Let's get out of here."

"Captain," Ilse said, "urgently request permission to visit the head."

Jeffrey laughed, sheepishly. "Fine. One at a time, ladies first. Lieutenant Milgrom, you go next. . . . And Messenger of the Watch, please put up fresh coffee."

CHAPTER 4

As Ilse washed her hands, she was startled by a blast heard right through the hull, distant but very loud. *The convoy battle's heated up again.*

Then she realized something was wrong. *Challenger* turned hard to starboard, then to port, throwing her against the outside of a toilet stall. *We've made a knuckle.*

A muffled boom sounded from aft, the reactor check valves slamming into their detents. The ship began to vibrate, and kept vibrating, roughly and urgently.

Jeffrey's ordered flank speed. This can't be good.

Ilse dried her hands on her blouse as she ran to the CACC. She struggled to her seat, almost knocked flat by the sudden steep up-bubble. Ilse donned her headset, one earcup in place. Immediately she heard the nerve-grinding scream of enemy torpedoes in the water, close on *Challenger's* tail.

"The U-boats found us first," Kathy said. "That convoy shot, its echo gave us away."

Just like that, the tables were turned. *Challenger* was the hunted now. She'd been running deep; they needed to get much shallower for their countermeasures to work. The ship topped forty knots, accelerating hard.

"Range to inbound weapons is ten thousand yards," Bell called out as Fire Control. "Net overtaking speed is thirty knots." The Axis weapons were chewing up the remaining distance fast. They were wire-guided, and nuclear-capable.

Jeffrey ordered a steeper up-bubble. He grabbed an intercom mike. "Maneuvering, Captain. Push the reactor to a hundred five percent." The flank speed shaking grew much rougher, turbulence and straining propulsion plant as *Challenger* tore a tunnel through the sea—forty-eight knots now. Jeffrey told Meltzer to make another knuckle.

"Still two incoming weapons," Kathy reported. They were spreading apart, making it harder to intercept. Kathy's voice was even and clear; she wasn't sweating now.

Jeffrey told Bell to fire the Mark 88's in tubes one and three, as snap shots down the inbound weapons' bearings—Ilse heard them on her headphones, a deeper tone than the Axis fish and louder, too. But they still had no good data on Master One and Two, the small and stealthy U-boats.

"Depth five thousand feet," Meltzer said, "coming up to four."

"Bring our unit from tube one up to eight hundred feet," Jeffrey ordered. "Run the other at two thousand." Above and below the deep scattering layer. "Have them both go active *now*." To probe for the enemy submarines.

"Sir," Bell said, "don't you want to use them to knock down the Axis fish?"

"Negative," Jeffrey said. "I want the boats."

"They've got ten tubes between them. . . ."

"We'll try to evade the torpedoes, XO. Stand by to reload two more eighty-eights, in case we can't."

Slow work, Ilse knew—the torpedomen were down to block and tackle, and the ship was making radical angles, too. But if they closed the outer doors to reload prematurely, they'd lose the wires to the units they'd already fired. *Jeffrey was taking an awful gamble.* Those U-boats, somewhere out there, each held two dozen men, intent on killing *Challenger* and everyone aboard.

Meltzer reached three thousand feet. He leveled off. The ride was just as rough. Bell fired a noisemaker and an acoustic jammer pod. Jeffrey ordered a course change: south. He launched the brilliant decoy in tube five, to loop behind the ship, running back north.

He fired the conventional ADCAP fish in tube seven directly ahead, to run out in front of *Challenger*. Ilse saw he was trying to distract the inbound weapons.

"Shut the outer doors, tubes five and seven."

"Lost the wires, tubes five and seven!"

"Reload five and seven, Mark eighty-eights."

Bell acknowledged; backbreaking labor began.

The units from tubes one and three continued their active search: *still* no contact on Master One and Two. They must both be in the deep scattering layer, virtually opaque to the pings of the 88's. The U-boat captains weren't just sitting there, either; they were thinking and *fighting*.

"Inbound weapons have ignored our countermeasures," Bell said. "Weapons are tracking *us*, not the units from five and seven. . . . Both turning into our baffles."

The enemy fire control technicians, Ilse thought, *steering them through the wires.* Jeffrey's counterploy had failed.

"Range now?" Jeffrey said.

"Seven thousand yards, closing by one thousand every minute." Bell said the enemy warhead yields would surely be set at their maximum—one kiloton each—with a kill zone against *Challenger* of four thousand yards or more. The Mark 88's from tubes one and three had run well past the Axis weapons, too late to bring them back to make the intercept.

Jeffrey ordered more noisemakers, then a dive to ten thousand feet, to confuse the inbound weapons by jinking out of their search cones. Ilse buckled her seat belt; she'd forgotten to before. *Challenger*'s speed was steady now, 50.7 knots. The constant shaking showed how hard the ship was working. Consoles jiggled, making squeaking sounds.

"We still do not hold contact on Master One or Two," Bell said. This was an unforgiving contest in which every second counted; Jeffrey told Kathy to ping on the bow sphere, a powerful but last-ditch measure since it would surely give *Challenger* away. Kathy used a rising sawtooth tone, optimized to cut through the layer. The signal processors ran, ready to sift the returns.

"Active sonar contacts," Kathy reported. "Bearing zero two four, range eleven thousand yards, Master One. . . . Bearing zero three seven, range twelve thousand yards, Master Two." Two small blips on Ilse's display—with a murderous reality.

"Bring both our Mark eighty-eights to twelve hundred feet now," Jeffrey said. "De-enable their active pinging and slow them to thirty knots for stealth. Send one each at Master One and Two, on random approach arcs." Jeffrey would use the deep scattering layer, too.

"Launch transients," Kathy called a moment later, "from Master One and Two." Each U-boat fired a spread of weapons, assessed as countershots at *Challenger*'s pair of Mark 88's. *Challenger* kept diving.

"Hull popping, self-noise transient." Then, "Two *more* torpedoes in the water. Assess as aimed at *Challenger*."

Jeffrey ordered another course change; Meltzer acknowledged; something made a scary tone in Ilse's ear.

"Acoustic intercept contact," Kathy stated. "Closest inbound weapons have gone to active search."

"Range six thousand yards," Bell said. "They're locked on us for sure."

At this depth our stealth hull coatings are useless, Ilse knew, *squashed rock hard.* She admired Kathy's detachment.

"Two minutes till those warheads blow," Jeffrey said. "Then we're a mission-kill for sure, if not feeding bottom crawlers outright. *How's the reload doing on tubes five and seven?*"

Shajo Clayton and his SEALs were helping in the torpedo room, but even so . . . At last the reloads were armed. The acoustic intercept receiver made another scary tone.

"Inbound torpedoes still locked on!" Bell said. "They're getting echoes off our stern—we can't actively suppress!"

Jeffrey ordered tubes five and seven fired as countershots. Now Axis nuclear weapons ran at *Challenger,* and hers ran at the U-boats, both offensive plays. More Axis weapons ran at *Challenger*'s fish, and more of hers ran at theirs—these were the defensive races, all going on at once.

"Time to intercept the inbound weapons?" Jeffrey said.

"One hundred seconds," Bell said.

"Time till inbound weapons are in lethal range of *Challenger*?"

"Sixty seconds."

Too close. Jeffrey ordered *Challenger* back to three thousand feet.

Ilse heard sharp thunder, a staccato roar, and shock waves pummeled the ship. Master One and Two had begun to detonate their antitorpedo nuclear weapons. . . . They seemed to be shooting blind. *Challenger*'s units from tubes one and three still had live feed through the wires—but thanks to the deep scattering layer they also were running blind.

Jeffrey told Kathy to ping again; Bell updated his fire control solutions, then sent them to his weapons through the wires. "Forty seconds till our first two units are in lethal range of Master One and Two . . . and also till the closest inbound weapons are in lethal range of *Challenger*."

Jesus, Ilse thought, *it'll be a three-way kill*.

"Fire Control, fire two more noisemakers and jammers. . . . Maneuvering, push the reactor to one hundred eight percent. . . . Helm, *forty* degrees down bubble, left standard rudder, smartly."

Challenger seemed to twist sideways and aim straight down.

"No effect by the countermeasures! Inbound weapons still locked on!"

Ilse heard them pinging faster and faster. *Challenger*'s speed was fifty-two knots.

"Helm, forty degrees *up* bubble, *smartly*."

Ilse grabbed her armrests hard as the ship took off for the sky; the g-force pressed her neck onto one shoulder.

"Inbound weapons are rising to follow," Bell said.

"Chief of the watch, sound rig for depth charge."

"Rig for depth charge, aye."

"Fire Control, reset our units from one and three to detonate by timer. This way if we're dead, and the Germans try to evade, we still might take them with us." *Small comfort*, Ilse told herself, *for throwing away our lives*.

"Resets accepted!"

"Chief of the watch, do an emergency blow."

"*Sir?*" Bell shouted as compressed air made a deafening roar.

"I'm counting on some help from the surface cutoff effect!" A blast was less destructive very shallow.

Challenger kept driving upward hard. "Inbound weapons are *too close*. Our counterfire from five and seven will fail!"

"Reset units from five and seven, *maximum* yield, not minimum. Detonate them *now*!"

Challenger lifted violently, punched in the stern by a pair of atomic fists—her own antitorpedo shots, set off in final desperation. Ilse's headphones blanked out, the automatic amplitude filters, but she heard and felt the unforgiving concussions through the hull.

"Inbound torpedoes still running!" Kathy screamed.

"Any second," Bell said hopelessly.

The ship kept rising, almost straight uphill. Her depth wound madly down to zero, along with her life expectancy.

The shattering ocean erupted again with a hundred times the force, just as *Challenger* leaped out of the sea. The vibrations were so vicious Ilse's arms and legs flapped wildly; her bare knuckles rapped Kathy in the face. All the lights went out. A world-ending roar kept piercing Ilse's skull.

There are nuclear fireballs right outside, and tons of radioactive steam. Bile rose in Ilse's throat, as *Challenger* peaked in her trajectory. The ship dropped down so hard Ilse's headphones flew off.

"Fire, fire, fire in Engineering," the phone talker bellowed in the dark. "Upper level starboard side!"

Challenger pitched roughly, riding atomic tsunamis. Ilse caught a whiff of biting smoke. The CACC power switched to batteries. Everyone grabbed their emergency breather masks.

"Shut the main fore-and-aft air vents," Jeffrey ordered. "Do *not* ventilate. Keep the boat sealed up!" The ship rolled hard to starboard, then to port, her nose corkscrewing insanely on the tortured surface.

"Units from tubes one and three have detonated!" Bell said. "Assess Master One and Two destroyed! Assess surviving inbound weapons blinded by nuclear sonar whiteout!"

The crew finished donning their masks, then plugged the air lines into sockets in the overhead. Immediately the compartment filled with an eerie, repetitive hiss and whoosh, as twenty people each drew breaths through the regulator valves and exhaled. Ilse heard the crewmen speaking, badly muffled through their masks, half drowned out by the atomic cacophony beyond the hull. Inside her mask she felt terribly isolated; her heart pounded, and she fought to steady her respiration rate. *The ship's burning. . . . How bad is it?*

Having nothing to do only made the waiting worse. Jeffrey and Bell were talking, no, arguing, and Bell sounded angry. Jeffrey dashed aft. But wasn't Bell, the XO, supposed to go to the fire? Has Jeffrey's hero-playing gone completely over the top?

Ilse started to panic. *We can't get out, not here.* Suddenly the deck tilted steeply down, and *Challenger's* depth began to mount, though her forward speed was low. In terror Ilse turned toward COB and Meltzer. It looked like the ship wasn't sinking, yet—they were taking her deep on purpose.

Ilse glanced at Kathy Milgrom. Amid the lurid shadows cast by emergency battle lanterns, Kathy gave Ilse a determined, reassuring smile through her mask. But Kathy's eyes were worried, very worried. And Kathy was *experienced*; she'd been in action on *Dreadnought* since the very start of the war. Diego Garcia was *Challenger*'s first-ever taste of battle. How then must the young men around Ilse feel?

Bell's voice sounded again, tough, completely in control. He was ordering Kathy to find the U-boats. The battle wasn't over *yet*, but Ilse was amazed how reassured she felt just to hear—and *see*—Bell so confident, in charge. The bow sphere pinged, tuned to cut through the reverb and roiling ocean.

All right! Two separate clouds of metal fragments, falling through three thousand feet. The U-boats were dead. Their last torpedoes were running off to the south somewhere, no longer a threat.

Several men cheered, but Ilse just sat there numb. What about the fire back aft? What of other damage to the ship? And what about the men on *Texas? Challenger* might still die too.

Bell ordered flank speed. The ship sped up. Jagged vibrations began, all wrong, and they had to slow down right away.

The phone talker said something was wrong with the propulsion shaft or the pump jet. He relayed more status reports to Bell: The engine room fire had spread to oil that leaked in the bilge. . . . The number of wounded was mounting. . . .

They'd destroyed the U-boats, yes, but at what price? Wasn't the rescue mission enough for Jeffrey Fuller?

What could he have possibly been thinking?

CHAPTER 5

In the engineering spaces, Jeffrey surveyed the dripping turbogenerator. The charred casing was off now, the wiring melted and fused. The bulkhead behind it, and the overhead, were blackened and blistered from flame. The lubricant injector section smoldered. The deck nearby was covered with slippery fire-fighting foam, and waterlogged piles of torn heat insulation lay everywhere.

Lieutenant Willey, in his plug-in breather mask, stood next to Jeffrey on the narrow catwalk, leaning on a cane; Willey's left leg was still in a cast from the recent mission to Durban. Emergency lights cut harshly through the gradually clearing smoke. Jeffrey's air pack was heavy against his shoulders and hips—he'd need a new tank soon. He was very hot and sweaty under the firefighter's coat he'd borrowed from an injured man.

Just then Lieutenant Bell appeared; he'd gone from breather outlet to outlet, drawing air as he worked aft. "Lieutenant Sessions has the deck and conn." With his foot Bell nudged a foam concentrate can into line with a dozen others, making the pile of empties a little neater.

"Total loss for this piece of equipment," Willey said, looking at the auxiliary generator, one of two that gave power for everything but main propulsion.

"No way to just rewire it?" Jeffrey said. He liked the tall, straight-talking Willey—Jeffrey had been an engineer on his own department head tour, right before the Naval War College, right after the Pentagon.

Willey shook his head. "Too much damage, sir. . . . We also lost the main desalinators, Captain. We'll have to go to the backup system." The old-fashioned way: boiling.

"Water rationing, then," Bell said. "The crew won't like it."

"No," Willey said. "They never do. It'll be much worse, with an extra hundred people aboard from *Texas*."

"How badly will this wrecked turbogenerator affect our operations?" Jeffrey asked.

"Not by *that* much," Willey said. "The port-side unit is fine, and we can help meet a heavy domestic load from the main propulsion turbogenerators." *Challenger* had all-electric drive. "That should be okay, since we won't be doing flank speed anytime soon."

"How bad is it?" Bell said.

"The propulsion shaft is okay," Willey said. "I think the pump-jet rotors are okay, too. That leaves the fixed blades at the back end of the cowling. They're probably bent, from that nuclear near miss."

"It seems all right now," Jeffrey said.

"The vibrations start at thirty-two, thirty-three knots."

"What if we need to make flank speed again?" Bell said. "To outrun another torpedo, once we find the *Texas* or, God help us, before then?"

"Keep your fingers crossed," Willey said. "The propulsion power's there. The question is, what will the pump-jet do? It might just vibrate a lot, but that would cost some speed. It might break apart if we push it too hard. . . ."

Jeffrey looked down past the edge of the catwalk. He could see crewmen with tools and mops and machinery wipes, beginning to clean up the lower engine room level.

Jeffrey turned to Willey. "We'll make do. Good job fighting the fire. How long to get the air cleaned up?"

"Six to eight hours 'til we can stop using masks, twenty-four 'til it smells good, using air scrubbers alone. We can't exactly snorkel to refresh the atmosphere, can we now?"

Jeffrey chuckled. "No, probably not a good idea." Then he realized Willey was being sarcastic. "Keep me posted on the repairs."

Jeffrey and Bell went forward, out of the vast but crowded engine room spaces and through the maneuvering room. The reactor operator and throttleman looked up as they passed. Jeffrey eyed the instrument readings—nothing wrong there.

They squeezed around enlisted men, busy rolling up hoses. They walked into the reactor tunnel, then reached the watertight door. The crewman posted by the hatch lifted the canvas smoke curtain, so they could clamber through more easily.

They came out near the enlisted mess, stepping over gear and supplies mustered there for the *Texas* mission. Jeffrey waited while Bell drew fresh air from the overhead pipe. Some firefighters rested in an eating booth, recovering from heat stress, heads in their hands, their hair all shiny and curly, soaked with sweat. Assistant corpsmen tended the wounded, ranging from bad sprains or bruises to concussions and deep cuts and burns.

The cost of Jeffrey's victory had been very high indeed.

Jeffrey and Bell visited with the men briefly, offering encouragement, thanking them for their efforts. The men seemed listless, tight-lipped, distant, or dazed, several of them in very obvious pain.

The chief corpsman came out of the kitchen area, drying his clean hands with a wad of sterile gauze. He pulled on a fresh pair of surgical gloves. There was fresh blood on his rolled-up sleeves.

A cook-paramedic helped another wounded man stumble from the wardroom toward an open mess booth, where he lay down flat on the table, his eyes scrunched closed. His head was half concealed in bandages, already leaking more blood, and he breathed from a small oxygen bottle instead of a regular mask.

"Twenty-seven stitches," the corpsman said. "That's a new record for me."

He began to examine the next waiting crewman, reading the latest vital signs scribbled on a tag clipped to the patient's jumpsuit, and testing his reflexes.

"Will they recover?" Jeffrey said. He cast his eyes around the mess space.

"Yeah," the chief corpsman said through his air pack mask. "Eventually. Yeah. It'll be much worse on *Texas*."

Bell took another good breath from the overhead pipe, then he and Jeffrey walked forward.

When they were out of earshot of the mess, Bell said, "Skipper, we need to talk."

•   •   •

Jeffrey and Bell sat in Jeffrey's stateroom, both using plug-in masks now, their faces inches apart. Their air valves hissed and whooshed repetitively. The stateroom door was closed.

"Permission to speak frankly, sir," Bell said.

Jeffrey tried not to bristle. When he was XO himself, he'd always encouraged his department heads to speak their minds freely in private. Since the reshuffling from Captain Wilson's being injured, Bell, as acting executive officer, was Jeffrey's official interface to the entire crew. But there was something in Bell's tone that said this discussion would not be routine. "Permission to speak frankly," said the way Bell said it, by long naval tradition really meant "Permission to leave our difference in rank outside the room."

"Granted," Jeffrey said. He needed Bell's trust, now more than ever. To let a problem between them fester could lead to terrible consequences later, at a personal level or in combat.

"It is my respectful opinion, Captain, and I don't believe I'm alone in this, that you almost just got us all killed."

"We had to go after those German boats. We had to help that convoy."

"*Two* quiet enemy vessels? With *ten* torpedo tubes between them? With torpedoes that are smart and pack a bigger punch than ours? That constitutes a superior force, Captain. A clearly superior force. It's your job, with a command that is *not* expendable, to *not* risk the ship against a superior force."

"But we sank them. And there's no lasting harm done, as it turned out."

"We don't know that yet. *Sir.* We're a day away from the *Texas.* We do not know what we will find when we get there, or what Axis strength we'll meet. You compromised our strategic stealth."

"Granted," Jeffrey said. They'd just made one hell of a datum. . . . He remembered what he'd half warned himself about before: *a calling card for Eberhard.* "There's always risk. At least now you see why I didn't stream the towed array."

"*Negative,* Commander. We went in there half blind. The enemy got the jump on *us.*"

"It was a judgment call. And mine to make." Jeffrey sat back defensively.

"You should *not* have gone to the engine room fire. Sir, you're the *ex*-XO. You *must* not cherry-pick whatever parts you want to play."

Jeffrey realized he'd been irresponsible, carried away in the heat of action, carried too far. . . .

"The worst damage is morale, Captain, including the junior officers. After Durban and all that, the crew was very high on you. We were in a tight spot and you got us through. But this is different."

This *was* different. Back then, they were also against a superior force, but that time *not* by choice. Bell's help had been indispensable.

Jeffrey cleared his throat. "They think I'm a cowboy?"

"Something like that, Captain. Even General Custer's luck eventually ran out. In the Civil War he won the Medal of Honor. Medals reinforce bad habits, sir. Self-appointed heroes in command . . . well, they add to the friendly body count."

"You mean I'm reckless. Going for personal score, so it looks good in my service jacket."

"Something like that. Yes."

Jeffrey knew Bell knew he'd won the Silver Star in Iraq, for the same SEAL op when he'd gotten the wound in his leg. Jeffrey had recovered, but one of his men was still in a wheelchair from *his* wound.

Jeffrey had to clear his throat again. "We should have little trouble departing this area stealthily. An Axis air strike, or any long-range cruise missiles, ought to be stopped by Allied air cover from the Azores or the Canaries, not to mention the carriers protecting the convoy. That's the whole reason the second section came through here, not west of here."

"I know that."

"With this big storm topside, enemy airborne ASW will be badly degraded. By heading north we're steaming under a heavy-beam sea. Any Axis destroyers or frigates would have to steam right through it. They can't possibly keep up with us like that, nor can any diesel-AIP."

"I *know*. I knew that all along."

Jeffrey felt himself tensing, and told himself to calm down. With both men in their masks, needing to work for every breath and shout to be understood, this conversation was getting surreal.

"There's more, isn't there?" Jeffrey said.

"Your treatment of Miss Milgrom, in front of the entire CACC crew, violated every principle of good leadership."

"I apologized."

"You need to do a better job, in private."

"What's your real point here?"

Bell took a deep breath inside his mask. "You gave the crew the impression *you* think we got stuck with a sideshow rescue mission, at this critical stage in the war. Now everybody thinks that, too. . . . We're the *Challenger*, Captain, the state-of-the-future boat. We're supposed to be in the middle of the fight, doing things no other sub can do."

"I agree. I'm not happy about it, either."

"Instead we're being worn down bit by bit. More damage here, more crew casualties there, mental stress all around. I'm not a mind reader, sir, but as the new XO it's my job to try. I believe the crew now believe that one reason we're heading for the *Texas* and then home is that our present acting captain does not have the full confidence of the powers-that-be."

Jeffrey looked away, not saying anything, not daring to.

"Three responsible specialists advised you in almost so many words to keep on going to *Texas*. Sonar, Oceanography, and myself as XO and Weps. You plain ignored us all, in front of sixteen of the crew."

"But—"

"I helped build *Challenger*, Captain. I'm a plank owner, like most of the men. You got here two months ago. Me playing devil's advocate with you is *not* a knee-jerk game."

Jeffrey opened his mouth, but Bell cut him off.

"As an African-American myself, I am well aware of the problems of bias. I have never once sensed that with you, which is to your credit. But your blatant reaction to Miss Milgrom as a female submariner, a woman in uniform serving on this warship, simply has to change."

Jeffrey's face was burning. He realized Bell was right on every count, but still Bell didn't quit.

"You're responsible to the people, the chiefs, the junior officers, the department heads, and me. They're all courageous and tough. But at this point, if they could, as a matter of principle half the crew would put in for immediate transfer to another front-line boat. Think how *that* would look in your service jacket."

Jeffrey sat there, stunned. It would ruin his career.

"It is my considered opinion, sir, that the crew now believes that if you continue your current tactical and leadership style, it will be a miracle if we ever complete this rescue mission and reach the East Coast of the United States alive."

A half hour later, Jeffrey sat alone in his stateroom. This time the door wasn't just closed—unusual enough for him—it was locked.

Spread across his fold-down desk were the formal orders, and briefing papers and data disks, from the Cape Verde courier's envelope.

Jeffrey was feeling much better than when Bell left to take back the conn. He was also feeling much worse. RECURVE ARBOR.

The powers-that-be *did* trust Jeffrey, and the crew, after all. They *did* know what *Challenger* could really do, even when damaged.

This damaged, though? Jeffrey blushed, thinking about his attack on the U-boats, and about what Bell just said. Half of Jeffrey wished he'd opened the envelope sooner. On the pages in front of him, he was directly ordered to avoid all contact with the enemy whatsoever until reaching the USS *Texas*.

But *Texas* was a red herring. It wasn't a rescue mission at all. *Challenger* was ordered to stop at *Texas* only long enough to take off her specially trained surviving SEALs—with certain unique items of equipment, including two briefcase atom bombs.

Challenger was being tasked to complete the job originally given to *Texas*. They were going all the way. Up through the narrow, shallow waters between occupied Denmark, and occupied Norway and aggressively neutral Sweden, to penetrate the impenetrable German bastion, the Baltic Sea. When they got there, they were to pull off a nuclear demolition raid that made Durban, as frightening and important as it was, seem routine by comparison. A demolition raid so vital, apparently, that the rest of the men on *Texas* had to wait.

Jeffrey's tactical personality might indeed get everyone on *Challenger* killed. But now, he hoped, considering what they were up against, his on-the-edge way of war-fighting at least gave them a chance to succeed and survive.

Their involvement at Durban was, and had to remain, covert. Their role now was direct action. Jeffrey saw this new mission was also meant to aid the lasting effects of the Durban raid, as a double bluff: If *Challenger* set off A-bombs in Germany's face, so soon after the mysterious mushroom cloud in South Africa, then the U.S. wasn't behind the previous blast. Jeffrey hoped it worked.

Jeffrey thought some more about what Bell had said and implied. Jeffrey *had* been selfish, and too judgmental of people whom he needed and who needed him, and they'd seen it all over his face in the control room. It was just like with his family twenty, thirty years before. Second-guessing, and not listening. Condescending, burning bridges that might never be rebuilt. *Walking out on them.*

Jeffrey'd seen—too late—how it felt to be on the receiving end of *that*. After Iraq, during his year of painful rehab, when he'd struggled to learn to walk again and wondered if his Navy career was over forever, his fiancée dumped him.

Jeffrey held his head in his hands, mask and all. Dear *God*, he had soul-searching to do. His job was to *protect* his crew.

Finally, Jeffrey put his highly classified orders back in the envelope, and took a deep breath. He unplugged the mask's connector hose; the compressed air made its usual *pop*. Jeffrey took the envelope to the CACC. He decided to hold an impromptu mission briefing right there, within the limits of security.

First, though, he owed his XO a heartfelt thank-you, and his people a sincere public apology. If they ever got through this new mission, they'd get through it *together*.

CHAPTER 6

ON ANTICONVOY PATROL,
SOUTHWEST OF ENGLAND

"I hate this war," Ernst Beck said. He looked at the pile of papers on the fold-down desk in his cabin and then at the man sitting opposite him.

Oberbootsmann Jakob Coomans was a seasoned noncommissioned officer. He was *Deutschland*'s chief of the boat. At age forty-one the oldest man aboard, he hailed from Hamburg, that great port on the North Sea facing England. Coomans's build was slight, but he ruled the ship's enlisted ranks by the force of his personality and the sharpness of his tongue.

Beck sighed. "I never thought when I signed up that someday I'd sit in a German nuclear submarine, censoring crewmen's letters home, in the middle of tactical nuclear war at sea."

Coomans's eyes sparkled. "A war against our own NATO allies. A war *we* started."

"You always had a strong sense of the ridiculous, Chief."

"Or the grotesque, sir."

"Be careful," Beck said. But he smiled. "Someone might think you disapprove of the new regime."

"Crew morale is good," Coomans said. "The first batch of letters after leave, you expect some homesickness. That's when the men's fears and regrets show most, in their words to wives and lovers."

"Wives *and* lovers?"

"Very funny, sir."

"But no, I agree. Their spirits seem high. They *are* high. Good morale is hard to fake, living cheek-by-jowl as we do." Beck had pictured each of the men as he read their letters: a name, a face, a distinct personality, each with his hopes and concerns, his strengths and foibles. Most of the hundred-plus crewmen Beck knew well, from their secret fast-attack sub training in Russia, and *Deutschland*'s not-so-secret construction at Emden. Then came the quiet practicing under the ice cap, the ultraquiet snooping off U.S. and British naval bases . . .

"And why *wouldn't* their spirits be high?" Coomans said. "In the Great War our forefathers took fifty percent losses in the U-boats. In Hitler's war, it was *eighty* percent killed in action. Now our little Class two-twelves amount to suicide machines, but there's *still* no end of volunteers."

"And how will it all end this time?" Beck said. "How many dead? Widows? Orphans? Grieving parents and girlfriends?"

"You know what Bismarck said."

"Remind me, Chief."

"There are two things you never want to see get made: politics and sausage."

"So?"

"I'll paraphrase our soldier-statesman thusly: There's a third thing you don't want to see being made: empire."

"I never knew you were such a philosopher."

"Yes, you did, sir. That's why we're such great friends."

"I thought we were friends 'cause neither of us has anyone else we can talk to on this boat." In public, Beck and Coomans had to mirror their captain's detached interpersonal style.

"Don't be such a cynic, sir. You might hurt my feelings."

"That's bloody unlikely."

Coomans chuckled. "But you do see what I mean. Consider the Brits in their heyday. Killing wars over the centuries on almost every continent. The Boers haven't forgotten."

"But South Africa was on the British side in World War Two."

"Because they didn't like getting swallowed by Hitler's juggernaut. So this time we offer the Boers their own fair share of empire. At the right price *every* nation's soul is for sale. Empires come and go. Right now we have a Kaiser again, and a half-finished empire."

Yes, Beck reflected, *a nation's soul is always for sale. But what of man's soul? Why are we here? What about our responsibility to our own morality?* Beck stared at a battle map taped to the wall. *Yes, a sailor always has his duty, but what if that duty becomes a trap?* "I sometimes wonder if it'll end up finished, Jakob, or *finished.*"

While Beck spoke, a far-off nuclear detonation sounded through the hull, drawn out and growing to a crescendo before dying off. The tragedy of his words was heightened by the reality of their tactical situation.

"If we lose this time," Coomans said half to himself, "it will be very bad." Beck nodded somberly. There could be no quitting halfway now.

The two men, lost in their own interior journeys, were startled from their reverie by a knock on the door: a messenger.

"Sir, the captain's compliments. Enemy Convoy Section One is approaching. We're almost in attack position, and he requires your presence in the *Zentrale.*"

Beck forced a smile; it was his job to help put this convoy on the bottom of the sea today. . . . He thought of his twin sons, now ten. He thought of having grandchildren someday, of playing with them when he retired, long after this war. Germany's place in the sun. He was doing it for them.

He followed Coomans wordlessly, down the short corridor, past the Christmas decorations.

Deutschland's crowded Zentrale, her control room, was rigged for red. The men were *up,* excited, and Beck took an inner pride in their readiness. He'd taught them, drilled them, *made* them the eager tools they were for Kurt Eberhard. "Attack stations manned and ready, Captain." Convoy Section One was the target.

"Very well, First Watch Officer. I *don't* like surprises."

· Beck winced. Intel on the rendezvous of relief warships from England with the convoy had proven inaccurate. The enemy reinforcements were coming hours ahead of expected.

Beck saw Eberhard study the tactical plot and frown.

"Now we're caught between the convoy's frigates driving from the south, and fresh destroyers converging from the north. And the escorting carrier battle group has us boxed in from the west."

Beck nodded ruefully: The carrier was the nuclear-powered *Harry S. Truman,* one of America's latest and best, probably escorted herself by four Allied fast-attack subs.

Eberhard gave Beck a withering look. "If this first convoy section does get through, in spite of the beating it took off the Azores yesterday, and the second section suffers acceptable losses, Allied morale and logistics will get such a boost this war could drag on for years!"

Beck shuddered to think of the consequences if *Deutschland* failed today. Whole continents were waiting to choose sides, or to pick through the cooling ashes when the First World immolated itself: all of Asia, half of the Middle East, and most of South America were holding back from the fight. *Everything* hinged on starving out the U.K. quickly, exposing America's impotence, and scaring U.S. voters to sue for peace.

Beck told himself there was no choice but to press on. Luck and timing, good or bad, were always crucial factors in armed conflict. Merchant ship tonnage sunk was what mattered.

"I will *not* settle for sniping at the convoy from the flanks," Eberhard said. "To hit the priority targets with confidence, we need to get in very close, and *damn* the escorts."

Beck eyed the large-scale digital tactical plot on his console. *Deutschland* steamed due west, on an interception course with Section One. She made top quiet speed, thirty knots. Her depth was fifteen hundred meters, exploiting a temperature/salinity layer caused by conflicting currents deep in the ocean—excellent concealment from searching Allied planes and surface ships.

"Sir," Beck said, "recommend update target motion analysis on the carrier group. They may cease steaming semi-independently and close up with the convoy for the rendezvous."

Beck knew his ship had a clear playing field here today, which meant she'd get no interference from Axis forces, but no help: The German Class 212's, and captured French SSNs, were striking Convoy Section Two way off to the south. This made sense, to avoid friendly fire, but Beck suspected Eberhard had had a hand in it: no friendly forces present, no credit shared.

"Concur, Einzvo, update the data. A more concentrated target for us if they *do* close up, but better all-around protection for *them* . . . which only adds to the time pressure."

Beck turned to the sonar officer, who sat at the head of a line of consoles on the Zentrale's starboard side. He was a likable young man, Werner Haffner, an *Oberleutnant zur See*—lieutenant junior grade—from Kiel, a major base and port on the Baltic. Haffner was earnest and talented, though high-strung.

Beck asked Haffner the optimum depth and course for a good passive contact on the enemy carrier group. Haffner conferred with his sonarmen, then responded to Beck. Eberhard issued the piloting orders. Jakob Coomans, the battle-stations pilot, acknowledged; Coomans sat at the two-man ship control station, on the Zentrale's forward bulkhead. *Deutschland* went deeper.

"Einzvo, prepare for arming nuclear weapons."

Beck and Eberhard went through the sequence with their special keys. *Deutschland* had eight wide-body torpedo tubes, and sixteen vertical launch tubes for her cruise missiles. Soon, the Sea Lion deep-capable eels, German Navy slang for torpedo, and the Modified Shipwrecks, supersonic antishipping cruise missiles purchased from Russia, were ready to fire. Each carried an advanced U-235 warhead of Axis design.

Beck eyed Eberhard, standing there in his austere black jump-suit and beautifully polished sea boots, with the diamonds of the Ritterkreuz glittering at his throat, next to his bloodred arming key. Eberhard looked eager for what was to come.

That's the difference between us. I fight to make a better peace, and to protect my family. He fights because he likes it.

CHAPTER 7

ONE HOUR LATER,
ON USS CHALLENGER.

Ilse heard a beep on her headphones: Someone was breaking in on the circuit she and Jeffrey and Clayton and Bell were using during this SEAL mission briefing. The air in the front of the boat was still toxic from the engine room fire, and the foursome wore spare sonar headsets under their respirator masks; this way they could talk more easily, and privately. Bits of duct tape made airtight seals for the lip mikes. At this point people had gotten used to pausing rhythmically to draw breath; Ilse hardly noticed the constant hissing and whooshing all around.

"Captain, this is the Conn," Lieutenant Sessions's voice reported—he was the one who beeped.

Jeffrey turned from the digital navigation plotting table at the rear of *Challenger's* CACC.

"Your requested ten-minute update, sir," Sessions said from the command workstation. "The ship is at ordered depth, three thousand feet. We have fifteen thousand feet of water beneath the keel. Our course is three one five." Northwest. "Making for the Azores at top quiet speed, twenty-six knots."

"Very well, the Conn," Jeffrey said.

With water so deep, Ilse knew, long-range sonar conditions were perfect. Jeffrey wanted to stay above the deep sound channel now, to hide.

Another beep.

"Captain, Sonar," Kathy Milgrom said. "Your requested ten-minute update. One distant nuclear detonation, range and bearing match Convoy Section Two. No other new sonar contacts, sir."

Ilse, standing next to Jeffrey, saw him face Kathy and give her an appreciative nod, mask and all—*Some fences had been mended there.* "V'r'well, Sonar."

Kathy smiled behind her faceplate, clicked off the circuit, and turned back to her console.

Bell keyed the intercom switch clipped to his belt. "Sounds like Section One is having a quiet day, Captain." Bell leaned against the nav console, right next to Jeffrey, their elbows often touching. The tension between the two men had melted quickly—as had bad feeling in general—once Jeffrey had made public amends for losing his cool. His sincerity had been moving to see, and now, if anything, people felt more tightly knit than ever.

And it's a good thing, Ilse told herself. There was lingering tension enough from those A-bombs going off like strings of firecrackers during their close call with the 212 and 214. There was added tension from *Challenger's* new destination, their new target. The enormous responsibility placed on their shoulders was almost staggering.

"Play it again," SEAL team leader Shajo Clayton said. *He* wasn't smiling. The assistant navigator, a senior chief, pressed buttons on his keyboard. Ilse watched the horizontal large screen on the plotting table.

The satellite image looked down at Earth from hundreds of miles in space. Northern Europe was shrouded in rainy overcast. There were gaps where the cloud cover was thinner.

The computer overlaid the northern coast of Germany and occupied Poland on the picture, tracing the edge of the land-locked Baltic.

At first there was nothing to see. Then *it* started.

There were quick flashes in some of the cloud gaps, unevenly spaced. The flashes occurred from west to east, from Germany toward Russia. They were arrayed in a line that stretched about a hundred fifty nautical miles. A very *straight* line. The whole thing took under a minute.

"Initially," Jeffrey said, "the Joint Chiefs thought it was a cruise missile training exercise."

"Missiles ripple-fired from a line of frigates or submarines?" Bell said. "That would explain it." Ilse knew that Bell, as weapons officer, was in his element here.

"No," Jeffrey said. "The coordination of the flashes is too perfect. Computer analysis tracked one for a fraction of a second, and studied the engine's exhaust spectrum. There's no question we're seeing a *single* missile, liquid hydrogen powered, a ground hugger, doing Mach eight."

"Jesus," Clayton said as he stood next to Ilse.

Bell whistled. "Nothing we own can intercept Mach eight . . . except for a nuclear area burst. We have trouble enough with *ballistic* missiles, the type that follow a nice parabola up in the sky."

"Our side doesn't have something like this, too?" Clayton said.

Jeffrey shook his head. "NASA's work on hypersonic flight was all for high-altitude scramjets. Single-stage-to-orbit reusable low-cost spacecraft, or something to replace the Concorde."

Bell nodded ruefully. "And that technology's not much use for cruise missile hardware. *These* platforms skim the wavetops."

"There's a mole inside the missile lab," Jeffrey said. "Code name ARBOR. She was recruited by the Israeli Mossad long before the war. The Germans have been rolling up Mossad's network, but they haven't found ARBOR yet. . . . She worked her way to the top of human resources at the lab. She's our way in. The nuclear demolition itself is code-named RECURVE."

"And this satellite data proves ARBOR hasn't been turned," Bell said. "She's not feeding us false information under duress, as a trap."

"I almost wish she were," Clayton said.

"The location of the lab right on the Baltic makes sense," Jeffrey continued. "It was built, supposedly, as a hardened underground communications center, during the war scare in Asia five years back, when Germany started rearming in earnest. It's huge, subdivided, self-contained. Now it's been disguised as a depot-level repair facility for the German Navy."

Jeffrey gestured, and the nav chief brought another picture on the screen.

Ilse read the caption. "Greifswald." The old houses and shops had exposed beams, Tudor style. The colorful church steeples were picturesque. Evergreen forests covered undulating hills beyond the town.

"Greifswald is near the Polish border, in what used to be East Germany. It's not far from Peenemünde, where the Nazis perfected the V-2 rockets. Isolated, easy to protect, with the Baltic as secure test range right there."

"If we know where it is," Ilse said, "why not just hit the place with big high explosive bombs?"

Jeffrey sighed. "Won't work. NATO ground-penetrator munitions can't get through the forty-foot composite armor roof."

Bell thought for a moment. "A U-235 bomb would throw up massive fallout. The whole Baltic rim is heavily populated, and the winds are unpredictable."

"We have to go inside," Jeffrey said. "Two man-carried warheads, each yielding a kiloton. Detonators coordinated by atomic clock."

"Okay," Clayton said. "A self-contained tactical nuclear blast. Underground, no fallout . . . That works for me." As Ilse had seen, *very* up-close and personal at Durban, Clayton was an expert in atomic demolition.

Jeffrey went on. "This mole ARBOR says they're about to start mass production of the missiles, inside the lab. . . . But it gets worse."

Another picture came up. It showed a schematic of a submarine.

"The Germans are building a boomer?" Ilse said.

"Not an SSBN. An SSGN. A guided missile sub. They got the idea from us. The U.S. Navy reconditioned some *Ohio*-class ballistic missile subs a few years back."

"They put collars in the silos," Bell said. "Instead of one large ICBM, each silo can hold six or eight conventionally armed cruise missiles. Tactical Tomahawks or whatever, for power projection on land. Almost two hundred in all, based on the Trident boats' two dozen silos."

"Tomahawks are subsonic," Ilse said.

"Yeah," Jeffrey said. "Imagine instead a ceramic-hulled SSGN, able to dive to ten thousand feet or more and hide there. Armed with two hundred unstoppable Mach eight cruise missiles, each one tipped with a Hiroshima-size A-bomb."

Clayton stood there with arms crossed tightly on his chest, staring at the deck, his lips pursed in tense concentration, his eyes very hard.

"In one blow," Bell said, "they could smash the entire eastern United States, or wipe out Great Britain. Nuclear antiaircraft fire over the friendly homeland, to shoot down the missiles, would be self-defeating."

Ilse frowned. "But the Axis said they wouldn't be the first to hit cities with atom bombs. After the first two, I mean. Poland and Libya."

"The Axis *said* a lot of things," Jeffrey responded sourly. He looked at her and Bell and Clayton in turn. "There's concern that if this ceramic SSGN gets underway, armed with those warheads, our side may have to sue for an armistice. The threat is just too great. *Deutschland* or a squadron of Class two-twelves equipped with a clutch of the things would be devastating. Probably cost us the war at sea. A new iron curtain descends. The Axis wins."

There was stunned silence.

Ilse heard more nuclear explosions. Kathy broke in to say they came from the northeast.

Convoy Section Two is taking a beating.

Clayton cleared his throat. "So why don't we go after this fancy sub?"

"We're not sure where it is yet," Jeffrey said. "Maybe Kiel, maybe Gdansk, maybe even Trondheim. The most dangerous thing is the missile. We have a very tight window, from two factors. One, this year is a solar maximum. You all know that. The eleven-year sunspot cycle."

"Some people think that's why the Axis picked 2011 to start the war," Bell said.

The nav chief brought up another slide.

Stellar meteorologists had recently identified a new, massive twisting of magnetic field lines on the surface of the sun. In another two or three days they would split asunder and a record-breaking solar flare would erupt, releasing a billion tons of charged particles into space—reaching Earth in forty-eight hours.

"The effects of the flare should persist for a day or two, once it hits," Jeffrey said. "That's our target window: electromagnetic disturbances worldwide. Disruption of enemy comms, good masking of our signature from a lot of enemy sensors."

"That's an awfully compressed schedule, sir," Bell said. "Get to the *Texas,* do what we have to do there, then get way over to the Baltic and do what we have to do *there.* . . ."

"And then extract and egress," Jeffrey said. "I know. We're playing catch-up ball."

Ilse had a question. "You said there were *two* factors. The solar flare, okay. What's the other one?"

"Based on the timing of this flare, and using her position, ARBOR is supposed to plant a delayed-action virus in the lab's security system. She's a talented hacker, unknown to her bosses. Seems as a teenager she once pulled off a harmless but *very* clever intrusion. German police never found the culprit, but Mossad managed to track her down. That's why they recruited her."

"This virus'll help us get in?" Clayton said.

Jeffrey nodded. "ARBOR's role is critical. Once we're inside she'll meet us, show us around, then help us get out. . . . That last part is absolutely vital, because we're also tasked to receive from her copies of the missile design and control software, off their supercomputer."

"Right," Bell said, thinking aloud. "With that the Allies could design an interceptor, one that works with high explosive, not a mushroom cloud."

"Or at least build our *own* missiles, I suppose," Ilse said. "To stay even with theirs." *This war is a terrible arms race. What a perversion of the efforts of some of humanity's smartest people.*

"Do we have blueprints of the lab?" Clayton said.

"We're clueless on the layout," Jeffrey said. "The place is shielded against ground-penetrating radar. But ARBOR works there."

"If the Germans are busy shutting down the moles," Ilse said, "how safe is ARBOR *now*?"

"If they grab her before we get there, we're in a heap of trouble . . . and so is she."

Ilse nervously rearranged the intercom wire and air hose, leading from her neck to sockets in the overhead. Her own brother and his girlfriend had been hanged on TV in Johannesburg, for standing up to the old-line Boers. The executioners always made it take a while. Since the Durban raid, Ilse kept having dreams she was next. . . . After all, she'd help set off an *atom bomb*.

"What about a contingency plan?" Clayton said. "You know, in case ARBOR can't deliver?"

"There's nothing in the mission brief," Jeffrey said.

"Don't you think we need one, sir?"

"I'll have to think about that."

Two machinist's mates came through the CACC, lugging heavy canvas sacks full of repair tools. Their jumpsuits were soaked with sweat. The nav chief punched a button to blank the briefing screen while they passed by, for security. The men paused to plug their air hoses into unused sockets, drew deep breaths, then continued aft.

"Anyway," Jeffrey said, "assuming all goes well, this raid should set the Axis missile project back at least a year, and give us a chance to catch up."

Lieutenant Willey, the engineer, hobbled into the CACC, cane and broken leg and all. He and Jeffrey huddled, speaking through their masks. Ilse caught snatches about material condition and damage control. Satisfied, Willey went back aft.

"Have Allied submarines gone into the Baltic like this before?" she said.

"During hostilities with Germany? Last time was at the start of World War One. Three Royal Navy coastal subs snuck through."

"But that was a one-way mission," Bell cautioned. "When Russia fell to the Bolsheviks in 1917, they couldn't get out. They were scuttled near Finland."

"That's right," Jeffrey said, a bit too abruptly.

"Are you going on the mission this time?" Ilse said.

"Yeah. I need to be there in person. The same reason as last time, Ilse." Verification of the rules of engagement for using atomic munitions in populated areas, independent of the SEAL team leader—who might be a little too biased toward blowing up something once they got there. "The lab is barely five miles from Greifswald town itself."

Clayton nodded. He knew how important these burdensome ROEs were, both to human decency and to world opinion. Ilse knew they had to look to the future, too, when today's current events would become part of history, and would be judged.

"Sir," Bell said, "as acting XO I should go."

"It isn't our decision," Jeffrey said. "It's in my orders. You'll take the conn on *Challenger*, while we're off in the minisub."

"Er, yes, sir."

"Do I have to go this time?" Ilse said. "I don't know a thing about missile technology."

"No," Jeffrey said. "You're here to help us pick the best approach route, and choose stealth tactics to get in and out of the Baltic."

"But I don't know those waters at all. I'm South African, remember? Durban was near deep water, right on the Indian Ocean. Greisfwald is two hundred miles inside a shallow Axis choke point tighter than a hangman's noose!"

"And you were very helpful at Durban. You had the best data available. That area didn't matter much to NATO, when the big threat was the Sovs. But don't worry. Everything's provided." Jeffrey handed her a packet of laser disks.

"What is this?"

"Remember the MEDEA project?"

"Sure. A committee of civilian scientists got special clearances to look at all the classified oceanographic data the U.S. Navy collected during the Cold War. They recommended releasing it, for research purposes." Pure science, resource planning, environmental protection, oil and mineral exploration. "I'm not sure what actually happened."

"Some of it was declassified," Jeffrey said. "But none of the best stuff. Now you have *everything*. You should feel privileged."

"I'm supposed to digest this in *three days*? Do you know what you're *asking*?" Ilse made eye contact with Jeffrey through their respirator masks.

"Join the club."

Ilse felt angry at Jeffrey again. He'd barely made up for his temper in the control room before, and now he was Mister Imperious again.

"This is Cold War era data?" Ilse said.

"Yeah. Is that a problem?"

"It sure is! All the salinity and currents and temperatures in that whole area, they're *cyclical*. There are broad *directional* trends, too. That only became clear in the late nineties! Twenty-year-old data could be all wrong!"

"Miss Reebeck, I want to see a more positive attitude."

"I—" Ilse was interrupted by a beep.

"Conn and Captain, Sonar!" Kathy said. "New passive sonar contact on the starboard wide-aperture array! Submerged contact bearing zero three four! Designate the contact Sierra Seven!"

"What is it?" Jeffrey said.

"*Amethyste II* Axis SSN! Range twenty thousand yards and closing! Conjecture tasked to intercept this ship based on our recent surface datum!"

Ilse unplugged herself and dashed to her console and plugged in again. The steel-hulled *Amethyste II*'s were war prizes from France, state-of-the-art and very dangerous.

Jeffrey took the conn.

"Helm, slow to ahead one third. Chief of the Watch on the sound-powered phones, repeat rig for ultraquiet. . . . Sonar, Oceanographer, give me optimum depth to evade Sierra Seven!"

CHAPTER 8

Above *Deutschland* Allied aircraft and frigates searched, but she was lost deep amid the countless rugged transform faults of the Mid-Atlantic Ridge. Beck watched the forbidding undersea volcanic terrain go by on the gravimeter display. He saw the jagged talus slope, the pileup of huge unweathered boulders, at the base of the latest canyon *Deutschland* followed. Soon it would be time to open fire.

Now, over the sonar speakers, Beck could hear the sounds of Convoy Section One, bouncing off the canyon walls. The noise grew louder and louder, a heavy mechanical throbbing churning whine, the signature of a combined one-million-shaft horsepower striving for Great Britain—vital for the supplies they carried, and vital as a symbol of this clash of arms between cultures that could only have one winner.

Beck saw Eberhard listen to the noise, then glance at a chronometer again. The escort reinforcements from the north, too distant for human hearing, were also getting closer by the minute.

Beck snuck another glance at Eberhard, intent on his attack plan and his screens. Beck's captain—his boss, king, god, role model all in one—seemed more unreachable than ever. The man clearly savored the final moments of stalking his grandiose prey, but this was a pleasure he would share with no one. Off the ship, at banquets and balls, Eberhard was polished, suave, even charming. Now, here was a different Kurt Eberhard, the driven Germanic warrior incarnate, whose very essence Ernst Beck, a German naval officer himself, had always found enigmatic.

Eberhard and Beck finished deploying their initial salvo of weapons, like ticking time bombs. Sixteen Shipwreck cruise missiles bobbed deep in the water in special capsules, positioned away from *Deutschland*, their chronometers steadily running down to the preset moment of launch. Two groups of Sea Lion torpedoes, and two brilliant decoys, were also loitering out there at stealthy slow speed, their fiber-optic wires leading back to the ship. Unlike those of Allied submarines, *Deutschland*'s outer tube doors could be closed for a reload without losing the wires to units already launched; tubes one through seven held another salvo of nuclear eels.

Beck heard a string of distant rumbling roars. Each swelled and then died away. Several overlapped: more atomic detonations, near far-off Convoy Section Two.

"Load tube eight," Eberhard ordered, "quadruplet of Honeybee unmanned aerial vehicles." The low-observable Honeybees were miniature helicopters, and a built-in autopilot made them easy for Beck's technicians to fly. They were hardened against the electromagnetic pulse of a tactical nuclear blast, and linked to *Deutschland* by rugged fiber-optic tether. Their live imagery would be fed to the Zentrale's wide-screen displays.

"Arm the atomic warheads, tubes one through seven."

Beck followed Eberhard through their special weapons arming procedures. "All commands accepted," the weapons officer said; the warheads were armed. In battle, Weapons and Sonar reported to Beck.

Beck's mouth was suddenly dry, and he felt a peculiar lethargy coming over him. . . . In his younger days, he'd pictured the romance of rounding Cape Horn in a driving gale, or showing the flag for peace and prestige at naval reviews abroad, or maybe patrolling for gunrunners off Kosovo under U.N. auspices. But never *this*. . . .

There was a little time before the engagement would begin; Beck asked the messenger to get him some hot tea.

Eberhard glanced at Beck. For a split second there was a harshness in Eberhard's eyes. It gave a whiff of consummate arrogance, of moving in social circles where Beck knew he could never go. There was a whiff of something else though. *Not* the warrior ethos Beck expected and could respect—warriors had honor, and practiced teamwork, and loved their men. What he saw now in Captain Eberhard, what he sensed for the first time, was something very different, directed not at Beck but at the world: a sociopath, amoral coldness.

"Launch the Honeybees," Eberhard ordered, dragging Beck back to the matter at hand. Beck focused his mind on business, all his doubts and regrets buried deep.

Beck drew a breath, in awe.

The air was clear, and cloud cover minimal. The entire miles-across convoy was spread before him, in crisp view from different angles. Hardworking merchant vessels, of all different sizes and types, rolled and pitched through the North Atlantic's mountainous winter swell. Whether steam turbine-powered or diesel, many smokestacks gave off thick smoke, white or black—the white suggested fuel oil tainted by seawater leaking in. The strong wind merged the exhausts into a gray haze blown southwest, above the countless whitecaps of the gale.

The surviving escort warships did what they could to guard their charges, but many of the frigates—the ones still afloat—were visibly damaged from nuclear battle near the Azores the previous day, their superstructures or helo decks charred, their masts bent at an angle, their bilge pumps discharging heavily.

Beck's technicians busily tallied the targeting data: a fleet oiler, *Cimarron*-class, good for forty thousand tons. A group of large grain ships, and refrigerated meat transports. A giant liquid natural gas carrier. Two so-called troopships, improvised in desperation: the *Cape Fear* and *Sgt. William R. Button*, both actually U.S. Navy cargo-container vessels. The hundreds of big steel boxes were modified as habitation modules, each for an infantry squad; *Button* also carried a million gallons of transferable bulk fuel. Beck spotted the convoy commodore's flagship, a large mixed-cargo vessel in the center of the formation, with extra antennas and armor to harden her bridge.

Each of the fifty-plus cargo ships and dozen frigates looked small and insubstantial against the vast ocean, but Beck knew there were four or five thousand people in their crews, plus six to eight thousand soldiers on each of the troopships—an entire city underway, an armada of sustenance bound for the U.K., that thorn in the side of the Axis. Beck tried to dehumanize these people in his mind, to prepare for the killing to come, but it was difficult. Most of the frigates were U.S. Navy, *Oliver Hazard Perry*-class, and they and their helos were pinging aggressively. Beck knew from past experience that they'd fight and die very hard—today's confrontation might well be decisive to the outcome of the war.

Eberhard's voice broke in. "Show me that natural gas carrier again."

"We'll let the convoy run right over us," Eberhard said. "They're so close now we're golden even if they zigzag."

Beck kept monitoring the huge formation.

"How quaint," Eberhard said a minute later. "Flag signals from the flagship."

Beck saw them, too, through his Honeybee. Then searchlights blinked in code. Two escorts traded places. Some stray merchant ships got back where they belonged.

"Sir," Werner Haffner interrupted from his sonar console, "sudden high-speed blade rate from one escort on convoy's eastern flank."

"Contact classification?" Beck said.

"Appears to be a U.S. Navy auxiliary, an oceanographic research ship."

"Visually confirmed," Beck said. "The small-waterplane twin-hull *Kaimalino*."

Eberhard snorted. "They're at the end of their rope, pressing her into service in an atomic war zone."

Beck had to agree. He knew the Allies were badly short on escort craft, after six months of mostly losing battles on the high seas.

Beck went back to his tactical plot and the Honeybee screens. In a few more minutes, he frowned. The *Kaimalino* moved to the head of the convoy. It deployed a deep-towed side-scan sonar sled, and started searching the canyons in the armada's path.

Whoever's commanding the convoy defenses is *good*, Beck told himself. He'd realized *this* was the time and place of maximum danger, the last few hours and nautical miles before the escort rein-forcements arrived—and he was taking no chances.

Deutschland was trapped. If she stayed still she'd be spotted for sure, a very distinct hull shape against the rock-hard bottom. But if she moved, the side-scan sled would pick her up on Doppler even sooner.

The encapsulated Shipwreck missiles wouldn't launch for sev-eral minutes yet—they were autonomous, with no wires back to *Deutschland*. Eberhard's attack plan was coming unglued.

And he knew it. "*Achtung,* Einzvo, *open fire!* Direct all prelaunched Sea Lions to attack! Target one eel at the *Kaimalino* before they find us!"

Beck barked out the orders. Commands went through the wires. The escorts reacted at once. High-speed propellers and pump-jets sounded, much more shrill than the merchant ships, racing in differ-ent directions, the frigates and eels. Eberhard ordered Coomans to steer toward the convoy at thirty knots.

Deutschland began to move. Her bow pulled up. Coomans banked her hard into the turn. Eberhard ordered Beck to have both prelaunched brilliant decoys mimic Class 212's, as a distraction, to buy *Deutschland* time.

The Sea Lion reached the *Kaimalino*—*Deutschland* was barely outside the self-kill zone of her own one-kiloton warhead. Through the Honeybee, Beck watched as the sea around *Kaimalino* blasted toward the heavens, like three thousand conventional torpedo hits at once. The vessel, a huge steel catamaran, split from stem to stern. In the blink of an eye the two hull sections, each the length of a soccer field, flew into the air and tumbled and spun. An instant later the fireball broke the surface. The image whited out.

When the image cleared, the fireball broiled and fulminated. The airborne shock wave spread.

The waterborne *boom* that struck next badly hurt Beck's ears. *Deutschland* was lifted by the stern. Beck watched the gravimeter as the seafloor loomed too close. Coomans fought to bring the ship back on an even keel. Fireball pulsations, then more surface reflec-tions of the underwater blast, tried to pound *Deutschland* into the razor-sharp basalt bottom.

Beck forced his eyes back to the surviving Honeybee feeds. He saw the next thing Haffner heard. The frigates were launching updated ASROCs in retaliation, rockets that each dropped off an anti-submarine torpedo.

"*Flank speed ahead,*" Eberhard ordered. Coomans acknowledged. *Deutschland* sped up.

Beck watched the rockets leave the frigates, shrouding their foredecks in boiling flame. Soon the booster stages fell behind, plunging into the waves. Each booster left an American Mark 50 torpedo arcing through the air. Each 50 hit the ocean with a giant splash. They were a brand-new design, the 50's, and deadly.

"*Four torpedoes in the water,*" Haffner shouted.

Beck heard their propulsion systems scream. They were targeted at the points where *Deutschland's* loitering Sea Lions started their high-speed runs, on the assumption that German submarines were there. Soon there were four undersea atomic blasts. Four white fountains burst into the sky. They rose higher and higher without slowing down, and grew wider and wider. The ocean spawned a four-some of new suns. The combined undersea pressure waves, from off the port and starboard quarters, threatened to shatter *Deutschland's* hull. Damage reports poured in—the torpedo room autoloader gear was jammed.

"*Lost the wires,*" Beck shouted, "all units from tubes one through seven. Brilliant decoys destroyed!"

"Convoy aspect change," Haffner said.

Beck saw the convoy wakes hook sharply left. "Convoy's new course west." *Deutschland's* fourteen Sea Lions still ran south.

"Sea Lions now on preprogrammed active search," Haffner said.

Beck tracked his own torpedoes by their pings. "All Sea Lions converging on frigates guarding convoy eastern flank." The eels were out of control; *Deutschland's* element of surprise was hopelessly lost; and the smashing blow of her Shipwrecks, meant to open the battle, still hadn't come.

The eastern frigates detected the swarm of inbound eels. They fired their antitorpedo mortars, but the high-explosive bombs fell short. Beck could see the frigates' towed noisemaker sleds, designed to draw off Axis acoustic-homing weapons. The sleds were useless at the lethal range of a tactical nuclear blast.

Several Sea Lions went off at once. Mushroom clouds marked the warships' graves.

The spreading airborne shock waves reached the Honeybees; the pictures went blank. Eberhard ordered another brace of Honeybees launched immediately. There were plenty more frigates up there, and their seasoned captains were very angry indeed, and the sonar white-outs would only hide *Deutschland* so long.

"Sonar whiteouts clearing somewhat," Haffner shouted. *"Inbound torpedo, bearing zero seven five!"*

Amid the undersea chaos, an ASROC's Mark 50 had found *Deutschland*. Eberhard ordered a Sea Lion fired as antitorpedo snap shot. The inbound weapon's range was eight thousand meters, closing by one thousand every minute.

"Copilot," Eberhard snapped, "status of autoloader gear?"

"Both ship-sides out of action due to bearing pins sheared off from shock. Starboard autoloader will soon be repaired."

"Achtung, Einzvo, tubes two through seven, fire a spread at the convoy. Spiral our units to three hundred meters at stealth speed to mask our launch depth. Limit attack speed to fifty knots to mimic Class two-twelve-launched weapons. Match sonar bearings and *los!"*

Launch! *Deutschland* had to do as much damage as possible, before she was forced on the defensive by the outnumbering frigates.

"Inbound Mark fifty still closing," Beck said. "Unit from tube one converging on intercept course. Unit in range of inbound weapon *now."* He detonated the warhead through the wire.

Deutschland's stern slammed sideways, knocking the vessel off course. A monitor fell from its mounting bracket, tore out the power cable and coaxial feed, and imploded on the deck.

"Starboard autoloader badly damaged!" the copilot shouted. "Flooding through number two countermeasures launcher!"

"Chief of the Watch," Beck said, "give them a hand at the flooding." At this depth no leak was minor—Eberhard was playing it very close, hugging the nuclear blast zones for better shots at the enemy, hugging the sonar whiteouts in order to hide.

The relief pilot took over, and Coomans hurried aft. Haffner announced new rocket motors, igniting underwater—the encapsulated Shipwrecks' timers had wound down at last.

Beck called up the pictures from the new Honeybees; the next blasts would be air bursts.

Sixteen long, thin, matte-gray missiles leaped from out of the deep, riding trails of urgent flame and billowing smoke. Their winglets unfolded on leaving the water. They accelerated to near Mach 1 in the twinkling of an eye. The missiles settled on course, gaining speed steadily, skimming right above the surface, blowing spume back off the waves. They quickly reached full speed, Mach 2.5—faster than any carrier-borne fighter plane could go. Some aimed for the convoy; others targeted the distant *Truman* carrier group, far beyond the horizon.

Beck sensed a change in the pitch of the convoy noise. They'd seen the Shipwrecks. The escorts tried to shoot them down with Sea Sparrows, Mach 3.5 antimissiles of their own. But they were too late, perhaps because of battle damage and human stress.

Beck looked at his screens. Missile trails crossed every which way. The convoy flagship—the commodore's ship—was changing course, trying to veer away from the inbound Shipwrecks, trying to defend herself. Red tracers arced toward the missiles as men on deck used heavy machine guns. Countermeasure launchers on the flagship loosed off bursts of silvery chaff. Magnesium flares on parachutes began to burn as infrared lures. Aluminized decoy blimps inflated, stiffened, and drifted on the wind.

The Honeybee picture bloomed featureless white, making Beck's eyes ache. When it cleared, a violet-lavender fireball blossomed off the flagship's starboard side. Her paint burned off in an instant, and blew away in a puff of smoke. Her American flag simply vanished, her machine gunners shriveled to ash. The masts, the superstructure, the hull, all cast stark shadows away from the blinding, sizzling glare.

Beck could see the airborne shock wave of the A-bomb begin to spread, like a swelling sphere of ghostly condensation. The force of the blast hit the ocean. A tsunami grew. The air- and waterborne shock waves hit the flagship; the vessel broke in half. The aft end still drove forward as her insensate props kept turning, scooping up tons of seawater. The bow section flipped on its side, exposing red bottom paint and green sea-growth fouling. The sea growth began to smolder at once, from the heat of the blast. The swirling atomic fireball, now a beautiful orange-yellow, rose higher into the air. Beneath it a pillar of smoke and steam formed rapidly, drawn by the powerful updraft. A zone of fine mist spread from the pillar, dispersing as the mushroom cloud shot even higher. Lightning flashed on its crown, near an ethereal purple glow, the very air fluorescing from the radiation's intensity. Other Shipwrecks struck their targets.

"Convoy not dispersing," Beck shouted. "Frigates heading toward sites of the Shipwreck launches!" Eberhard's neat attack had become a disorganized melee. Coomans reported through the copilot that the countermeasures-room flooding was secured, but both launchers would be out of action for at least an hour—an eternity. Three men were dead from the force of seawater influx.

Beck shuddered: They'd been dashed to pieces by the jet spray at three hundred atmospheres pressure. But that was the least of his concerns. "Sea Lion from latest salvo about to reach troopship *Cape Fear*."

"Put *Cape Fear* on a main display screen," Eberhard said.

Beck hit the command. There was the container ship, with its stacks of habitation modules. The vessel tried to fight back; launchers fired off antitorpedo snares, voluminous nylon netting laced with explosive detcord. But the snares fell short.

Cape Fear was hit. She heaved and snapped in two. Cargo containers went flying, and seawater rushed for the heavens with ultimate force. The makeshift troopship was swallowed whole, as the ocean gave birth to another brand-new sun, a too-fast dawn from the wrong direction, west. *Cape Fear* simply evaporated amidships, steel and soldiers vaporized in a million-degree nuclear furnace. The stubs of her stem and stern were thrown bodily into the air in opposite directions, spinning end over end, spewing flattened containers. It was impossible in this chaos to make out bodies, but thousands of people had just died.

Other eruptions sounded all around through *Deutschland*'s hull, as technicians called more Sea Lion detonations. More antisubmarine rockets from surviving frigates' launchers went off, too, aimed at invisible tormentors that weren't there—the nonexistent Class 212 wolf pack, Eberhard's sleight of hand.

Beck knew the frigates wouldn't stay fooled much longer, and then *Deutschland* would pay. "Shock force from *Cape Fear* blast will reach the liquid natural gas carrier soon."

"Show me," Eberhard said.

The vessel loomed on the screen. The spreading shock fronts overtook her through the sea and through the air. She shuddered as the twinned forces pounded her hull. The airborne shock wave dented the big domes on her deck, the tops of the spherical tanks containing the super-chilled natural gas. They tore open, and insulation flew.

"That mist," Eberhard said. "The cold gas is condensing moisture in the air. . . . We should get a nice gas-versus-oxygen mix very soon."

The crew realized it—they were jumping over the side. Several of them staggered, then collapsed on deck.

"Asphyxiated," Eberhard said; he was transfixed. The freezing mist continued to spread, forming ice slurry on the sea. The men in the water grew still. "Now all we need is a good ignition source. A static spark from all the charged atomic particles up there, a bit of burning debris from the sky . . ."

Whatever did it, the LNG tanker suddenly vanished in a heaving white-hot plasma jet that shot higher than the clouds in a gigantic V. The resulting quasar flare-up was more powerful than the air-burst that had killed the commodore's flagship. The pressure wave expanded in all directions.

The blast front reached the Honeybee. The Honeybee disintegrated. The detonation's undersea force reached *Deutschland*. Its impact was unbearably loud.

The force knocked the submarine out of control. Light fixtures shattered in their mountings. Crewmen were pounded in their chairs, saved from broken limbs and concussions only by their seat belts. A sonar screen imploded, then caught fire. A hideous roaring reverb went on and on.

The gravimeter display went blank.

"Working to reboot," a nav tech shouted.

"Pilot, decrease depth," Eberhard ordered. "I don't want us hitting terrain. . . . Make your depth two thousand meters."

Coomans and the copilot fought their controls.

"Crewman trapped in port-side autoloader mechanism," the copilot said.

"Get him out of there," Eberhard said. "I don't care how! *Get that equipment repaired."*

"Convoy aspect change," Haffner said.

"Confirmed," Beck said. "They're fleeing toward the carrier group. New course is northwest."

Beck eyed the imagery screen, and gasped. Two dozen mushroom clouds were visible, twisted, distorted, savaged by each other's conflicting blast fronts. The tons of radioactive steam had started to condense, and some of the clouds shed rain like infernal thunderheads.

The surface of the ocean was an insane whirlpool of blowing spray and rogue waves, as each rising fireball sucked air toward its base, and each tsunami traced an ever-enlarging circle. Everywhere were giant splashes, as smoking wreckage plummeted from the sky.

The convoy formation was ruined. The ocean itself seemed to burn, as huge pools of oil and gasoline marked where fuel tankers had gone down. The pyre of the LNG carrier loomed over everything else.

Yet still, beneath it all, U.S. and Royal Navy frigates did their work. They were well poised now to wreak a terrible vengeance: *Deutschland* was almost helpless with her autoloaders damaged and with empty tubes.

"*New ASROC torpedoes in the water,*" Haffner screamed. "Random spread, six or eight weapons . . . One is closing on us fast!"

"New weapons are between us and the convoy," Beck announced. "They're trying to drive us back."

"Status of autoloader?" Eberhard snapped.

"Both sides out of action," the copilot said. "Crewman is badly pinned. . . . Manual loading will take several minutes."

"Pilot, steer due east." Coomans turned the ship hard.

"Incoming torpedo has active lock!" High-pitched *dings* came over the sonar speakers.

"Pilot, make a knuckle."

Beck was rocked to port and then to starboard. "No effect."

"Captain," the copilot said, "torpedo room man-in-charge requests avoid all radical maneuvers, to aid repairs."

If they couldn't make good knuckles, and they couldn't launch any countermeasures, and they had nothing to shoot back with . . .

The *dings* repeated, louder. *Deutschland* was making flank speed. "That Mark fifty is gaining on us," a fire control technician yelled.

"Sir," Beck said, "I should go down there."

"Einzvo, get a Sea Lion loaded, *any way you can.*" Eberhard eyed Beck meaningfully.

The weapons officer stood in for Beck. Coomans returned from aft, waterlogged and breathless, blood oozing from a scrape on the side of his head. He joined Beck; both men dashed below.

When they reached the torpedo room it was a scene of frantic efforts amid the weapons on the holding racks. Crewmembers tried to repair the damaged port and starboard autoloading machinery, while others rushed to rig the chain falls—block and tackle—needed to load by hand. Still others struggled to free the trapped crewman, whose face twisted in grim agony.

Beck was almost thrown off his feet when *Deutschland* made another knuckle. He felt the ship begin to fishtail, just as she did on trials when Eberhard pushed the reactor to one hundred ten percent. "Sir," the local phone talker shouted, "the captain indicates incoming torpedo will be in range in ninety seconds tops! You *must* reload a countershot or we'll be destroyed!"

Beck assessed the situation quickly. The culprits were two big Sea Lions themselves, sitting on the jammed reloading guides. They'd been right on the weakest parts of the guides when *Deutschland* suffered those blast shocks. The eels became harmful dead loads, twisting the guides out of alignment, snapping the bearing pins.

"The captain orders you fire when ready on local control. He has entered his warhead arming code."

The starboard gear was hopeless. The chain falls would never be ready soon enough. The port-side gear had just a chance. But the crewman's arm was trapped amid the robotic cams and actuators, and it would take forever to dismantle the equipment enough to pull him free. Beck looked at Coomans, then at the Sea Lion looming over the crewman. They had to get it into the tube, had to launch it at the inbound nuclear Mark 50. But there was no way.

How? In the name of God, in the name of an end to the war, *how?*

"Less than sixty seconds," the phone talker shrieked. Beck could tell the youth was panicking. He eyed the worried faces all around the cramped compartment, and he saw the panic spread.

Coomans grabbed a sledgehammer and began to drive the autoloader guide back into alignment. With each blow the trapped crewman grunted like a Neanderthal, as Coomans's pounding tortured his mangled arm. Pain didn't matter, ultraquiet didn't matter, nothing mattered but getting that long, thick, oh-so-heavy bastard eel into the gaping hole, the tube. But Coomans couldn't get past the crewman's body to replace the broken bearing pin, and they couldn't run the equipment this way, even assuming it still worked.

Beck spotted the big red fire ax. He knew he had no choice. *God forgive me.* He grabbed the ax. The injured crewman saw what was coming. Through clenched teeth he urged Beck to get on with it. But Beck hesitated, appalled at what he meant to do.

Again *Deutschland* fishtailed. Both errant two-metric-ton Sea Lions shifted more, and metal creaked. Hydraulic fluid oozed to mix with dripping blood. There was so little time.

Beck remembered what Eberhard said. *Any way you can.*

Beck swung the ax with all his strength. The crewman bellowed in animal rage. Beck tried to leave a stump—for a tourniquet—but he missed. The arm came off at the shoulder, the man fell away, and now the smell of blood was very thick.

Beck reached into the workings, right past the severed arm, and held a replacement bearing pin in position. Again Coomans worked with his hammer, driving the bearing pin home. More precious seconds ticked away; men shouted for Coomans to hurry.

At last Coomans grabbed for the power switch and then the portside activating lever. With a sickening crunch the equipment ran past the jamming sinew and bone. The Sea Lion entered the tube, but the equipment refused to retract—it was broken now beyond repair.

Coomans leaned in headfirst to connect the arming wires, then slammed the breach door shut. Beck hurled himself at the weapons panel. He pulled his arming key off his neck so hard the lanyard snapped. He shoved it into the slot and turned and typed his password as fast as he could. *But there was no time.* Beck felt everyone's terror mounting; he fought hard not to wet himself in front of the crew. He flooded and equalized and opened the outer door, shouting at each step to give himself courage. He lunged at the tube and worked the emergency firing lever. The eel roared from the tube and into the sea.

Beck grabbed the phone talker's mike. *"Tube six fired on local control."* Beck despaired he was too late; he dared not look at his watch. He and Coomans stared at the inner tube door, hearing the shrill hum as the fiber-optic wire played out. There was nothing more they could do. Beck wondered, if he somehow survived and was rescued by the Allies, whether he'd be shot for war crimes.

Beck saw the status indicator on the weapons panel change. The unit from tube four had detonated, but was it far enough away? Would it stop the much bigger warhead of the 50, or would the next eruption send *Deutschland* to her grave?

The concussion, when it came, was smashing . . . but they were alive. Men laughed and congratulated each other, but Beck knew their little victory was fleeting. *Deutschland* had been localized, pinned down by the enemy. More torpedoes would be coming at her very soon. "Sir," the phone talker said. "Captain requires you in the Zentrale at once."

Beck nodded wearily. Eberhard, this battle, this war—they were relentless.

Beck wiped the injured torpedoman's drying blood off his hands with a piece of cotton rag. The corpsman reported the man was dead, of shock and cardiac arrest.

In a real way, Beck had killed him. *How many others have I killed today, so far? How much blood is on my hands? What do I do, deny they were human beings?*

Beck forced himself to stay focused. Eberhard worked *Deutschland* deftly through the latest whiteouts at top quiet speed, to recover lost ground against the convoy. He offered no thank you to Beck for helping save the ship, and no condolences to Beck for his latest crewman who had died.

Fresh Honeybees showed barely twenty merchant ships still floating—from the original fifty—all steaming northwest, slowly gaining distance from the burgeoning forest of mushroom clouds. The half-dozen surviving frigates still hunted the Axis sub, pinging and launching ASROCs.

"Sir," the copilot reported several minutes later, "torpedo room reports tubes one through seven reloaded manually by chain falls."

"Finally," Eberhard said. He and Beck armed the weapons.

Beck reminded himself he'd *volunteered* for submarines—but never dreamed it would lead him to such tormenting madness as this.

"Copilot," Eberhard said, "deploy a short length of the starboard towed array. I want to hear up and behind us." Eberhard seemed unaffected by everything around him, the slaughter, and the crew's fatigue or grief or fear—after all, some of his men were close friends of the four aboard who'd died.

Coomans returned to the Zentrale, looking disheveled. He snuck Beck a halfhearted wink, and resumed as pilot.

"Achtung," Eberhard said. "Nuclear Sea Lion salvo, tubes one through six, maximum yield. Target as perimeter bursts against surviving convoy formation."

Beck, beyond exhaustion, relayed the orders.

"Tube one, *los!*" Eberhard ordered. "Tube two, *los!*" One by one all six weapons were fired. "We'll save the unit in tube seven as insurance."

"New sonar contact," Haffner said. "Enemy frigate, *constant bearing, signal strength increasing.*"

"It heard us," Eberhard said.

"Weapon transients. ASROC motors igniting!"

That frigate's captain is a brave man, Beck told himself. *If we had our normal rate of fire his ship would die for sure.*

"Torpedo in the water!" Haffner screamed. "*Second* torpedo in the water! Third! Fourth! Four ASROC-launched Mark fifties, inbound, overtaking."

"Flank speed ahead."

"All inbound torpedoes on constant bearings, signal strength increasing fast."

"We can't possibly hit them all with just one nuclear eel. Einzvo! Reload more Sea Lions, *now.*"

Beck, stung, issued commands. "Sea Lions aimed at the convoy have gone to full attack speed. . . . They're too far ahead to double them back to intercept the inbound fifties."

The frigate pinged on maximum power. One good echo would give *Deutschland*'s depth, too deep to be any German sub but *Deutschland.*

Eberhard cursed. "We're losing our stealth." Once the enemy had *Deutschland* identified, they'd stop at nothing to destroy her. *"Achtung,* snap shot, tube seven, at the incoming frigate. *Los!"*

The frigate launched an antitorpedo ASROC. Beck saw its aim was perfect. . . . "Unit from tube seven is destroyed." The blast shocked *Deutschland* hard. Her tubes were empty again, with four enemy nuclear torpedoes closing rapidly. Eberhard ordered Coomans back to the torpedo room, and Coomans reported from there—the reloads would never be ready in time for effective countershots against the inbound 50's.

The nearest frigate pinged again. Beck spotted yet more rocket plumes, from the frigate's stern this time, launched in a fan to port and starboard, over-the-shoulder shots. If he didn't know what they meant, they'd be beautiful. "Six *more* Mark fifties in the water aimed at *Deutschland!*" Other frigates joined the chase, closing in as well.

"They've got us in a vise," Eberhard said.

Beck thought fast and hard. "Sir, recommend we shelter under the convoy. Conjecture Americans preprogrammed their weapons to not harm friendly forces." ASROC-launched Mark 50's weren't wire-guided. Using the convoy for refuge was a gamble, but *Deutschland* had no choice.

The frigate pinged again.

"It's highly likely they know exactly who we are." Eberhard sounded disgusted.

"I doubt the United States would risk nuking their own ships, sir, even to sink *Deutschland.*" Or would they? Beck watched his screens as the 50's gained on *Deutschland,* and she gained on the convoy. It was touch and go who'd win. The 50's went to active search.

Eberhard grabbed an intercom mike. "Push the reactor to one hundred *twelve* percent." Beck waited for something in their Russian-based reactor plant to explode.

"Mark fifties continue to gain on us." Beck saw crewmen shaking their fists toward the stern at the enemy eels, heard them urging *Deutschland* to go faster. "Torpedoes in lethal radius any moment."

"Rig for nuclear depth charge."

Then Beck shouted, "Fifties are veering away." Several crewmen cheered.

Deutschland's Sea Lions didn't veer away.

Around the edges of the convoy, six phalluses of solid water thrust high into the air. Six breathtaking fireballs punched through the surface of the ocean all at once, like dawn on some alien other-world with multiple suns. The air- and waterborne shock waves bloomed and met and embraced, reinforcing each other strangely, the speed of sound varying in different places with the heat. The older mushroom clouds to the southeast, some topped now by exquisite smoke rings, were lashed by blast winds as new mushroom clouds asserted themselves. Surface and bottom reflections pounded *Deutschland* endlessly. The noise was utterly deafening.

"Severe injuries among reloading party," the copilot yelled.

"Pilot," Eberhard shouted cold-bloodedly. "Put us directly under the surviving troopship, the *Sergeant Button.*"

Deutschland had decimated Convoy Section One, and she gained a precarious sanctuary under the remnants of the convoy. Beck drew no comfort on either count. Where was the satisfaction in serving a captain who had no conscience?

Deutschland steamed on, much more sedately, almost two kilometers deep beneath the *Button*. The Honeybees that still functioned showed the troopship was shadowed closely by that pesky American frigate, now identified as the *Aubrey Fitch*. Other escorts and helos kept watch, too, from several sea miles away. Everyone headed northwest. Now and then *Button* tried to shake *Deutschland* by changing course, without success. Now and then the *Aubrey Fitch* pinged, getting echoes off *Deutschland*'s stern.

"There's just one little problem," Eberhard said. "We're in what the Americans would call a Mexican standoff. If we move away from the *Button*, they'll all be able to fire at us. We can't possibly sink every warship fast enough to get away."

"No, sir," Beck said reluctantly.

"And we certainly can't keep steaming like this in concert," Eberhard said. "What do we do, follow them right into Liverpool? . . . Einzvo, this was your idea. What do you suggest *now*?"

"New visual contact!" a technician shouted. The surviving Honeybees zoomed in. "Airborne visual contact!"

"Type of aircraft?" Eberhard demanded.

"A squadron of jump-jet Sea Harriers," Beck said. "And Super Stallion heavy transport helos."

"From the *Truman*," Eberhard said. Some of the Harriers dropped big pods where convoy ships had gone down. The pods inflated into giant orange life rafts. The Stallions began to lift men from the sea. "Their cavalry comes over the hill, too late to do much good."

"Sir," the copilot said, "Chief Coomans reports a Sea Lion manually loaded in tube seven."

"Load another in tube five."

But Beck had an awful idea. "Captain, recommend instead we load two Seehecht units."

Eberhard stared at Beck. "They're conventional eels, and slow, and if we launch below a thousand meters they'd implode."

"Understood, Captain." The escorts' torpedoes also had a crush depth of about three thousand feet. "We need to create a distraction." Beck hated himself for what he intended to do—he saw he was forced from minute to minute to imitate Eberhard's heartlessness, of sheer necessity in this fight. *Where will it end? War dehumanizes the living.*

"Explain yourself," Eberhard said.

"If we hit the *Button* with high explosive weapons on opposite sides, she'll go down slowly, on an even keel. Then the Allied forces will have something to worry about besides *us.* An undersea nuclear blast anywhere near here will create such an overpressure, all the men in the water will get fatal internal injuries. The escorts will be forced to come to the aid of the men on the *Button,* and they'll have to leave *Deutschland* alone."

"Hmph. It may not work, but we've no choice, time isn't on our side. Prepare to fire two Seehecht units." When they were ready, Eberhard ordered *Deutschland* just shallow enough. He had the Seehechts fired, to hide in the deep scattering layer as long as possible. *Deutschland* quickly returned to the seafloor under *Button,* much too deep to be hurt by an enemy high-explosive eel.

"Unit outbound legs complete," Beck reported. "Units turning to attack. . . . *Button* aspect change! She's trying to comb the torpedo tracks."

"*Keep us under her.* Course-correct each Seehecht through the wires."

"Impacts in ten seconds." Beck watched the image from the one surviving Honeybee. The *Sgt. Button* tried to launch her antitorpedo snares, but the now-damaged launchers exploded on deck. The *Aubrey Fitch* fired her antitorpedo mortars, but the mortar shells all missed.

The Seehechts hit the *Button* with a double metallic *whang.* The twin fountains of dirty water were anticlimactic, but that wasn't the point. Some cargo containers were blown into the sea, bobbed briefly, and sank—no one escaped. *Button's* million-plus gallons of fuel oil poured from the hull and caught fire, and bright red flames reared up. The burning oil spread across the water. The scene was half shrouded by heavy black smoke. The picture rippled from curtains of heat.

Button's passengers began to stream out of the habitation modules and up from the internal vehicle decks. The soldiers rushed to the sides like thousands of khaki ants. The Harriers and Super Stallions rushed in to do what they could. Coomans had to slow *Deutschland,* to keep station under the troopship.

The water was thick now with little black dots. The *Aubrey Fitch* had stopped, and was lowering climbing nets over her side.

"*Fitch* has ceased pinging," Haffner called out.

"Move closer with the Honeybee," Eberhard said. "It's our duty to record this imagery, and document our success. . . . Pan around to show all the mushroom clouds again." Their pillars were cooling, turning brownish from nitrous oxide smog. A meager handful of merchant ships remained. "Zoom in on those people down there. Be careful to avoid the smoke. I don't want the camera degraded by soot."

The little black dots resolved into human heads. Some were black from burns, others from a thick coat of oil. *This was my idea,* Beck told himself. Every man in the Zentrale could see the main wide-screen display. Beck was very glad the picture didn't have sound.

"Catch those soldiers floating among the flames," Eberhard said.

Now Beck saw human figures literally on fire, lipless mouths gaping in silent torment, arms flailing wildly with their fingers already burned off. *Does this foreshadow* me *in the afterlife?*

Beck glanced around the Zentrale. The crew had smashed their sought-for record of one million enemy shipping tons destroyed, but no one smiled. Whenever Beck made eye contact, the men looked away. *I'm their executive officer. They saw me as Eberhard's better half, but now I've become half-Eberhard.* Coomans was still below. Beck felt completely alone.

"I think we should make our egress." He was sick to his stomach.

"We've done this before," Eberhard snapped. "Was it somehow less terrible then because you didn't *see* it?"

Beck heard damaged steel creaking and moaning directly above, as the *Button* began to settle.

Eberhard sighed. "Very well, we've done our job. Now we see if the Einzvo's clever exit gambit works. . . . Pilot, maintain course. Full speed ahead, make revs for thirty knots."

"That takes us toward the *Truman,* sir," Beck said.

"They won't expect us to egress in that direction."

Beck went back to watching the Honeybee screen. Some Super

Stallions sprayed foam on the water near the *Button,* to try to hold back the flames.

"Interesting," Eberhard said. "I haven't seen that tactic used before."

Other helos were busy retrieving burn victims from the sea. One aircraft, full with wounded, flew back to the distant carrier. The *Fitch's* decks were swarming with huddled figures now, and many more still weakly climbed her nets, but there couldn't be more than a hundred or two survivors there, and the *Button* had carried eight thousand.

Beck saw other escorts approach the *Button* to help. He spotted a Viking orbiting overhead, a fixed-wing four-engine sub-hunting plane, acting as local air traffic controller for the rescue. More antisubmarine Seahawk helos, twenty knots slower than Stallions, arrived from *Truman,* to relieve surviving Seahawks low on fuel. But instead of deploying to threaten *Deutschland,* they formed a line and used their downwash to drive the burning oil away from the life rafts and the troopship's stern. The perverse armistice between *Deutschland* and the escorts was holding. Soldiers continued jumping from *Button's* side in droves. Her main deck was barely ten feet from the water now.

"New airborne visual contact," a technician said. "Two helicopters approaching from north, range thirty sea miles."

"Zoom in more," Eberhard said.

"Those are Royal Navy sub-hunting aircraft, long-range Merlins." Beck saw each had only one torpedo—their maximum load was four, but that reduced their combat radius.

"They must have launched from the escort reinforcements," Eberhard said.

Beck felt uneasy. "Sir, recalling the Brits' behavior in World War Two, against our U-boats giving aid to Allied seamen, they're quite likely to drop nuclear weapons in spite of the rescue efforts underway."

"I concur."

"Surface-tension impacts!" Haffner said. "Contacts on acoustic intercept, bearing north. Royal Navy active sonobuoys."

"Use Polyphems, Captain?" Beck said. Polyphems were antiaircraft missiles, launched from a torpedo tube.

"No, I want to send the Americans a message. . . . *Achtung,* Sea Lion in tube seven, preset maximum yield, maximum attack speed. Snap shot, due north. *Los!*"

The weapon was fired. Beck watched the visual imagery, and monitored the data from the Sea Lion through its wire. "Local escorts not reacting to our weapon."

"They don't want to break our little truce."

Beck waited while the unit ran, under the Merlins and past them. The helos heard it and tried to escape.

"Teach them a lesson, Einzvo."

Beck ordered the weapons officer to detonate. Another mountainous geyser blasted into the sky, well beyond the horizon. The fireball rose a moment later; the shock wave caught the Royal Navy helos from behind. They shattered, and flaming aviation gas rained to the sea.

Eberhard smiled. "Now *Fitch* knows we haven't exhausted *Deutschland*'s atomic arsenal."

The image from the Honeybee wobbled, then steadied.

"Last Honeybee's fuel is running low," Beck said.

"Give control to me."

Beck watched as Eberhard used his joystick to focus near the *Button,* on two rescue swimmers putting a soldier into a litter in the water, under a hovering Stallion. The litter started to rise on its winch cable, toward the door of the big helo. The rotor downdraft punished the surface of the sea. Eberhard followed the litter, moving the Honeybee closer.

Beck saw the soldier was badly burned from head to foot. Beck realized the soldier had breasts. He realized she was alive. *I did this,* he told himself. He knew he'd be haunted by the memory for the rest of his natural life.

The litter arrived at the door of the helo. The crew chief steadied the winch cable, and two other Marines shifted the litter into the aircraft.

The crew chief, in flight helmet and rubberized protective anti-radiation suit, suddenly noticed the Honeybee. The man's dark autopolarizing visor was up, so he could see what he was doing. He stared at Beck through the camera, as if to accuse him personally. Through the gas mask, Beck watched the marine sergeant's features harden with rage. He disappeared into the passenger compartment, and came back to the door with an M16. He knelt and aimed at Beck. The rifle's muzzle flashed. The picture went blank.

CHAPTER 9

The air was breathable now, though to Ilse it smelled like bus exhaust and burnt plastic. She rubbed again at the deep marks on her neck, from hours in a breather mask.

Ilse stood up as straight as she could and knocked on Jeffrey's stateroom door. She knew he was alone right now. She felt butterflies in her stomach.

"Enter," she heard him call.

She slid open the door and went in and closed it behind her.

Jeffrey nodded. "Miss Reebeck."

This isn't going well, she thought right away. *Even in private, we're back to a last-name basis.*

Jeffrey sat at his fold-down desk, littered with maps and briefing papers. His laptop was open and on. She tried to peer at the screen. He shook his head and closed the computer.

"How's your leg feeling?" Ilse tried to bring up something from their shared experience two weeks ago.

"What?" Jeffrey seemed puzzled. "Oh. Yeah. It's funny, it stopped hurting before we got to Cape Verde. It must've been stress, not decompression sickness after all."

Ilse sat down in the only guest chair. Jeffrey frowned.

"You mean, like psychosomatic or something?"

"I don't like big words like that," Jeffrey said, a bit sternly. "How can I help you?"

Ilse tried to recover. "I, um, I wanted to mention. I took a first look at the data you gave me."

"And . . . ?"

"It isn't quite as bad as I thought. There's this thing called the Navy Meteorological and Oceanographic Command."

"Yes. METOC."

"They, they have an assessment of basic tactics, for infiltration and stealth. You know, into the Baltic? It needs some work, and it does lack recent cyclical trends, but it seems pretty good for a start."

Jeffrey looked right at her. "Did you think you were the first oceanographer to ever think about undersea war-fighting?"

Ilse decided to get to the point, before Jeffrey threw her out of his office. It dawned on her, all at once, that he was a very busy, very important man. The shy, stammering guy who'd tried to ask her out at Cape Verde was gone from her reach, maybe gone forever.

"I wanted to ask you, Jeffrey. What exactly is my status now?"

"First of all, it's Captain, or Commander Fuller."

Ilse looked for something in Jeffrey's eyes, some hint of personal feeling behind the mask of authority. She didn't find it.

"I mean, sir, where do I fit in on the ship? Am I part of the crew? What am I supposed to be?"

This was the first time she'd called him sir in private, too.

"So far as I know, a formal status hasn't been specified. I suggest you concentrate on the immediate task."

Ilse took a deep breath, and exhaled, and felt like half her spirit left her body with the exhalation.

"Do you know what will happen to me, after this mission?"

This was her last attempt to hold open a bridge to Jeffrey Fuller. Maybe they'd have time later, after the mission, when he could unwind.

"Frankly, I hadn't thought that far ahead."

"I mean, do I—"

"Look. Miss Reebeck. Does Lieutenant Bell even know you're here?"

Oh, God, Ilse told herself. What the hell was going on?

"Er, no, Captain."

Jeffrey went back to his desk and picked up a map. Ilse could see it was a topographic chart for Greifswald. Without even looking at her, he cleared his throat.

Ilse stood. On different levels she felt humiliated, badly embarrassed, and angry. She left without saying another word.

Since Ilse wasn't a watchstander, her schedule was fluid. She decided to go to the enlisted mess for coffee—less chance of running into one of the officers. But then she heard Shajo Clayton's voice from in the mess, busy practicing with his SEAL team. She turned around.

There in the passageway she bumped into COB.

"You look so serious," COB teased her.

"Thanks for noticing," Ilse said. Maybe COB would be the right person to talk to. He was mature, and a great people manager, dealing with all kind of issues with the enlisted men and their families.

Ilse forced a smile. "I guess I'm trying to figure out, what do I want to be when I grow up?"

"Having one of *those* days, are we?" COB smiled back, a warm and reassuring smile. Ilse figured he'd taken a whole bunch of training courses on interpersonal leadership. For all she knew, he had two dozen kinds of smiles, for different occasions, and could turn them on or off at will.

But, not COB. He was just too genuine.

"Is there somewhere we can talk in private?"

COB laughed. "On a nuclear submarine? Are you kidding?" He seemed to step back from her, internally. His face hardened subtly, and he began to rock slightly on the balls of his feet. As if he were saying, Whatever it is, *don't* cling or whine.

Ilse blushed again, and felt very lonely. She knew COB could see it.

"Actually," COB said, "right here is good. People come and go in the corridor, but nobody'll linger. It's an unwritten rule on *Challenger,* my rule, that if you see people whispering here, you make a point not to listen."

Ilse frowned.

COB shrugged. "Best I can do." He looked at his wristwatch.

"You don't use the chiefs' quarters for one-on-one meetings?"

COB laughed again. "If we aren't at battle stations, Ilse, there'll be lots of guys working or sleeping in there. So, what's up?"

"I'm not sure I should say this."

"Say it," COB said. "I'm half the crew's father confessor and surrogate mommy as it is."

"I guess you could say I'm having an identity crisis."

Ilse saw a junior enlisted man coming down the passageway. The man nodded and quickly wriggled by.

When he was out of earshot, COB said, "Welcome to the U.S. Navy, Ilse. Last mission was an adventure, right? This time, the novelty's worn off, you realize it's hard work and dangerous, and you feel you've lost control of your life. Right?"

Ilse nodded reluctantly. "I keep trying to figure out how I fit in."

"You mean, the gender thing?"

"It's not that. Everyone's been perfectly nice. . . . No problems at all in that respect." Except for Jeffrey now, Ilse told herself, and whose fault is *that*?

"Good," COB said. "I put the word out, you and Lieutenant Milgrom are part of the family."

"Thanks," Ilse said.

"I told the guys to think of you as their sisters. . . . That makes hanky-panky incest."

"You don't pull punches, do you?"

"I leave it to officers to speak in tongues," COB said. "If that's their style. It isn't mine. It was never Captain Wilson's."

"Which is your clever way of getting right to the point, isn't it? About Captain Fuller."

"Look," COB said. "I know the two of you kind of, well, *noticed* each other, a while ago."

"Definitely make that past tense."

COB sighed. "That was then, this is now." He got formal. "Commander Fuller first and foremost *must* comport himself as the captain of this ship. He can't show favoritism, or allow any personal feelings whatsoever between him and someone in the crew. It's regulations, and tradition. And it's essential in combat. It has nothing to do with you."

"But that's just it. I'm *not* part of the crew. Refugee, partisan, mercenary. What *am* I, COB?"

"You're on this ship. We're going in harm's way together. That's good enough in my book for you to be part of this extended family."

"Thanks. . . ." Ilse felt tears coming. She blinked hard.

Good, no tears.

"Look," COB said, "I know it's tough. If it's any comfort, none of us here in uniform, of any rank or rate, turn off our feelings just because we're here. Everybody wants to be liked and wants to fit in. . . . I think you're doing just fine."

"You do?"

"You did a terrific job at Durban, and everybody knows that. People *know* you haven't had their kind of training in teamwork and self-assessment."

Ilse stiffened. *That last bit.*

She saw COB read her face again. He hesitated.

"What is it?" she said.

"You just need to beware of the celebrity syndrome."

"Excuse me?"

"Sometimes when we have riders, they get kind of overwhelmed. By the bigness of it all. You know, the United States Navy, an SSN at sea, and now with this war."

"What are you getting at, COB?"

"It can get a bit depersonalizing, I know. Sometimes, well, people, they react, sort of overcompensate, by acting like a prima donna."

"A *what*?"

"Look, Ilse. Everyone here has self-esteem, self-confidence, an ego. They're the best, or they wouldn't be here."

"COB?"

He made hard eye contact. "Look deep inside yourself, and ask if you haven't been thinking and acting like this whole show was being put on for *you*. That you were the most important and special person here. That the whole mission to South Africa was set up just so *you* could get even with some people."

"Where the hell did *that* come from?"

COB didn't say anything.

"I've been *discussed*, haven't I? There's some kind of personnel file on me, isn't there?"

"See, Ilse? There you go again. There's a file on *everybody*."

"So you and Jeffrey talked about me. You two think I'm a prima donna."

"You said it, not me."

"But you *did* say it, before. In *private*."

COB paused. "Yes."

"Now I feel really awful. . . . I'm such an idiot."

"Ilse, do a little soul-searching. You're still new. People know you're an outsider. They'll cut you slack, up to a point."

"Thanks a *lot*."

"Watch it." Now COB wasn't smiling. "*That* sort of attitude, there's no room for here at all."

Two hours later, Ilse was bent over the laptop they'd given her. She was grateful for the privacy of her cabin. She *really* didn't feel like seeing anyone right now.

Kathy Milgrom came in without knocking, and shut the door.

"Working hard?" Kathy said.

Ilse nodded. She felt herself perk up. "This stuff is neat. Saltwater transport processes, from the North Sea into the Baltic and back."

Kathy started getting undressed.

"All quite relevant," Kathy said. "Buoyancy, sound propagation, biologics."

Ilse yawned. As Kathy stripped to her underwear, Ilse turned away to be polite.

In a minute Kathy said, dramatically, "You can look now." She was wearing flannel pajamas, navy blue with little red and white submarines all over.

"Is that official issue?" Ilse said.

"No, no. I found these once in Harrods. They had them in different patterns, sailboats, dolphins, whales. . . . I wanted to be a submariner since I was a little girl."

"You come from a naval family?"

"Eighth generation, and proud of it."

Kathy put her eyeglasses and wristwatch in the little storage space beneath her mattress.

Ilse watched as Kathy reached up, and with both hands grabbed the heavy rod that supported the curtain in front of the top sleeping rack.

Kathy's face grimaced. She scrunched her stomach muscles, took as much weight as she could on her arms, and literally walked up the bulkhead. She rolled into the top rack in one smooth motion.

"I didn't know people could do that." Ilse used the middle rack—easy to get in or out. The bottom one held stationery supplies.

"I need all the exercise I can get," Kathy said, "which is why I didn't buy the pajamas with the whales."

Both of them giggled. Ilse yawned.

"You look completely exhausted," Kathy said.

"I am."

"When was the last time you got some sleep?"

"About twenty-four hours ago."

Ilse reached for her coffee, which was cold and stale.

"Don't," Kathy said. "Change and turn in. You *have* to rest."

"I have so much to do."

"That's an order," Kathy said, as a joke.

"Ouch," Ilse groaned.

If Kathy was surprised, she let it pass. "Look, you've got to grab sleep whenever you can. Put on your pajamas. Get in your rack. The messenger will wake you when he knocks for me. In about four hours."

Ilse remembered what COB had said. She realized how right he was. She wanted to resist Kathy, and she resented being told what to do—by anyone.

Instead, Ilse changed. She slept in heavy cotton p.j.'s, green-and-black plaid. She also wore thick mountain-climbing socks, and used an extra blanket. It got cold on USS *Challenger*.

"Mmmm," Kathy said. "Delicious beddie-bye."

"Yes," Ilse said. She got in her rack. She knew she sounded depressed.

"Jeffrey trouble?" Kathy said, from inside the top bunk.

"Crap, is it *that* obvious?"

"Basically, it is."

Ilse didn't say anything.

"Don't worry," Kathy said. "These little flirtations do occur. It's meaningless, mostly just displaced stress, homesickness, fear of getting killed in action. . . . I think guys do it aboard ship sometimes because they know it's safe."

"You mean, nothing really happens."

"Usually not. Maybe I should say, hopefully not."

But that didn't fit, Ilse told herself. Jeffrey wasn't a flirt. And I'm not sure anyone who used to be a SEAL, wounded on some secret op in Iraq back in the '90s, could possibly be considered "safe." But in a way, Jeffrey *was* safe.

"Still," Kathy said, "he *is* single, so that's all right. Love and family are natural. . . . Not my type at all, but I can see he might be yours."

"I'd rather not talk about it."

"Okay. My advice, which you didn't ask for, is just relax and be patient."

"I'm sure you're right," Ilse said. But she wondered what would happen if and when they did reach port.

"Do you have a steady boyfriend?" Ilse said.

"We talked about getting married. He got killed."

"At sea?"

"His destroyer was vaporized."

"I'm sorry."

Kathy sighed. "I miss him a lot, but life goes on."

"You're okay about the way Captain Fuller treated you before?"

"Certainly." Kathy put on a mock upper-class accent. "One cannot take it personally when a superior officer criticizes one, justified or no." She went back to her normal voice. "If someone's landing all over you, Ilse, you just act like a helo pad. It's for the good of the ship."

"I guess that's the whole point. The ship comes first."

"Starting to feel your individuality get submerged?"

Ilse didn't say anything.

"That was a *pun*," Kathy said. "*Submerged.*"

"Very funny."

"I know what you mean, though. It's part of being in the Navy. Everyone has a boss. Every captain has a commodore, or an admiral. The First Sea Lord has the First Lord of the Admiralty. *He* has the Minister of Defence, and *she* has the PM and the King. It's the same in the U.S. Navy, just different titles, and they spell defense with an *s* while we Brits use a *c.*"

"I'm beginning to see how war is so depersonalizing."

"To me that's the worst part of it," Kathy said. "I'm not afraid to die. I've led a clean life. I say my prayers. But war-fighting is so *relentless,* so *complicated,* so *huge,* it can make you feel very small. You get completely gobbled up."

"It's different for you," Ilse said. "You *chose* this, as a profession. The Royal Navy, I mean. You knew there could be war someday; you *trained* for it. I got dragged into something horrible I wish never happened. It ruined my whole life."

"You and a few hundred million other people, Ilse. So far."

"There it is again. We each become a cipher, a cog in a little wheel, in a world full of wheels within wheels."

"Just do your job. Concentrate on the small things, and do them as well as possible. Take the track you're given to run on, and run it *splendidly*."

"Is that what you do, Kathy?"

"Think of yourself as a vital organ in a special organism. An instrument of peace-restoration and statecraft. It helps maintain your sense of self."

"It just all seems so, I don't know, so *regimented*, so horribly rigid."

"Have you ever tried to run a warship, my dear?"

"Of course not."

"Then don't talk. Routine and hierarchy are what hold everybody together. The rules and procedures get us back alive."

"So you enjoy the work, day to day?"

"Immensely. Sure. Don't you?"

"Yes, I do. And I *am* good at it." *Take that, COB. Take that, Jeffrey Fuller. At least I don't have to go on the SEAL raid this time. . . . Best put Fuller out of my mind right now. He could easily get killed, like Kathy's boyfriend.*

"Anyway, Ilse," Kathy said, "sleep well."

"Good night, Kathy. Thanks for the advice."

Just as Ilse was about to drift off, Kathy looked down from her rack.

"You know," Kathy said, "the submarine is *not* a penis."

Ilse was wide awake now. *"What?"*

"Everyone thinks it is. The shape, how it launches torpedoes. How it's so nice and long and thick and hard. But they're wrong."

"You're not a Freudian?"

"I am, I am," Kathy said. "But listen to this." She smiled. "The submarine is a *womb*."

"You know, you're right. . . . I never saw it that way before. . . . It's snug and cozy. It protects you from the outside world."

"It goes into the sea, which represents Mother."

"I guess it takes a woman to realize that," Ilse said. "Or at least, to admit it."

"And on that note, Ilse, good night."

THAT SAME EVENING,
ON DEUTSCHLAND.

Off the starboard quarter, many sea miles away, another air-dropped nuclear depth bomb detonated. The roar and reverb engulfed *Deutschland*. The shock wave made her pitch and buck, but Ernst Beck got no new damage reports. There was pain and a feeling of pressure in his ears, from an endless day of such punishment. Beck wondered if it'd make him go deaf in old age, assuming he lived that long.

"They're dropping them at random," Eberhard scoffed.

The temporary stalemate at the sinking troopship *Button* was over now. Allied carrier aircraft, and fresh destroyers and helos, were hunting *Deutschland* with a vengeance—but she was too stealthy, especially in this rugged seafloor terrain.

Another A-bomb went off, further away. A heavy manual slipped from a console top, and the crewman caught it just before it hit the deck. Eberhard gave him a withering glance.

Deutschland's bow nosed up as she climbed a canyon wall deep in the Mid-Atlantic Ridge. Then she nosed steeply down, to take the next in the endless series of canyons at an angle. Beck watched the gravimeter. Soon the vessel climbed once more. She topped the volcanic escarpment.

"Sir!" Haffner said. "New passive sonar contact." It was a long-range secure acoustic communication; the message address was *Deutschland*. Beck knew the top-secret transmitter was in the Biscay Abyssal Plain off occupied France.

Beck's intercom light flashed—the junior officer in charge of the communications room. "Sir, incoming message is in captain's personal code."

Beck told Eberhard.

"Pass the message packet to me."

Beck saw Eberhard enter the password to access his private decryption routines. The algorithms ran. It took ten seconds for the plain-text to come onto Eberhard's screen.

"*Scheisse.*" Shit.

"Sir?"

"We're congratulated on sinking an official total one point four

THUNDER IN THE DEEP / 97

million tons, based on reconnaissance satellite imagery, but we're ordered to avoid all contact with the *Truman* carrier group."

Beck hesitated. "*Why,* Captain?" They were stalking *Truman* now; bagging her would be a perfect capstone to *Deutschland*'s victory against the Allies' Convoy Section One.

"I suppose it's not so bad. We're to proceed immediately to the verge of the Celtic Shelf." Just west of the U.K. "To establish a barrier patrol and ambush USS *Challenger.* She's expected to be making for the North Sea."

"Does the message say her objective, sir?"

"Intel suspects they're headed for Norway. A commando raid against the ceramic SSGN we're building in Trondheim."

"That *would* be a high-priority target for them, Captain."

"The only problem for *Challenger* is that Trondheim is a diversion. The activity there is fake. Even *I* don't know where they're really hiding the new boat. . . . With our superior sonars, we'll pick up *Challenger* easily, whatever longitude she follows north. We'll turn my old friend Jeffrey Fuller into radioactive fish food."

CHAPTER 10

The CACC was hushed. Jeffrey took a deep breath—and regretted it; the air still stung as it went up his nose.

The final search for the USS *Texas* was about to begin. However it ended, it wouldn't take long. For the umpteenth time Jeffrey wondered if the enemy had gotten here first, and was waiting for him. He hoped the long-term mine reconnaissance system (LMRS)—a remote-controlled probe vehicle—wouldn't give *Challenger* away.

"Captain," COB said, "LMRS approaching next-to-final way-point. Now on the southern flank of Seamount 458, hovering at depth twenty-seven hundred feet as ordered." The fiber-optic feed was working properly.

"Very well," Jeffrey said. Each seamount here was named by the depth at its peak in meters, based on British Admiralty nautical charts. Though *Challenger*'s charts were on-line, easily converted to feet or fathoms, the metric reference persisted.

"Sir," COB said, "advise that the tether is now strung out for twenty-four nautical miles, nearing the end of both the torpedo tube's and on-probe reels."

Jeffrey frowned. "If it breaks or isn't long enough, we'll have to go on with autonomous link."

"For that we'd need to shift *Challenger*, sir," Bell said. For a good acoustic line of sight to the probe. "We'd make a datum by moving, and another by signaling the LMRS."

Jeffrey thought hard for a moment. "No, I like our hiding place here. . . . COB, just be careful with the probe."

"Understood," COB said.

"Helm, any trouble maintaining ship's position?"

"Negative, sir," David Meltzer said, in the seat on COB's right. "*Challenger* holding well against the bottom cross-current." Their depth was ninety-one hundred feet, at the base of the southeast slope of a different seamount, labeled 960.

Jeffrey eyed the gravimeter again. The huge bulk of the seamount completely masked *Challenger*—that was the idea.

"A dozen seamounts all together in this cluster," Jeffrey said. "The Olympus Knoll."

The cluster formed a rough oval, with its long axis running north-south. The formation lay some three hundred nautical miles due north of Graciosa, a small island in the western Azores.

"Collectively," Ilse said, "they mark an ancient hot spot in Earth's mantle, like the Azores or Hawaii."

The Knoll's peaks loomed high above the local seafloor, an undulating plain ten thousand feet deep.

"And only one of them," Jeffrey said, "Mount 458, is tall enough near its summit, shallow enough, for a *Virginia*-class sub to survive. . . . The Axis has to know that, too."

"Sir," Ilse said, "why don't we search for *Texas* with our gravimeter?"

"At this range the resolution is much too coarse to see it," Bell said.

"Sonar," Jeffrey said, "any new contacts?"

"Nothing but biologics, sir," Kathy said. "But advise that surrounding terrain blocks our arrays on many bearings."

"I'm not comfortable with how thorough our area search really was," Bell said.

"Me, neither," Jeffrey said. "But we can't dawdle and play things safe. There are badly injured people on *Texas*. . . . We don't know what shape *any* of them are in by now, and we have another pressing engagement ourselves."

Bell nodded glumly. "It would be difficult to try to hit Greifswald with just Clayton and his men."

"I've been thinking that if we need to, we could try to rig the warhead from one of our own torpedoes, and somehow carry it into the lab."

"Wouldn't work, sir," Bell said. "Security. They're very specifically designed to not be removable from the unit in the field."

"In extremis? Clayton's good at that sort of thing."

Bell shook his head. "Once, on a bet, a special weapons surety guy from Johns Hopkins and I tried to figure out how."

"And?"

"We spent a solid week on it—we were bachelors then, on leave. No can do, sir. Period. Without the right tools and electronic pre-authorization, which they didn't give us at Cape Verde, you'd disable the arming suite permanently, and damage the physics package, too."

"Yeah," Jeffrey said. "I'm sure you're right."

There was an uncomfortable pause.

"My biggest worry right now would be *Deutschland*," Jeffrey said. "She could dig us out of this bottom terrain, with her hull and her sensors and weapons."

"The briefing papers said she's under the ice cap, far from here." The assessment supplied before *Challenger* left Cape Verde said that *Deutschland* was sneaking toward Canada, for a raid against Halifax or the St. Lawrence Seaway.

"There could still be German subs somewhere above us, XO, playing hide-and-seek around the mountaintops. Waiting for us to make just one mistake."

"Agree, sir," Bell said. "*Texas* is perfect bait, for them to use against *us*."

Jeffrey looked Bell in the eyes. "A disadvantage of our hugging the seafloor is, one Axis nuclear fish in seamount nine-sixty's chin, six thousand feet above our heads, and we're buried alive down here."

Jeffrey took a deep breath. He glanced around the CACC.

"All right, people, we don't have all day. . . . Chief of the Watch, bring the probe to the final way-point."

"Probe holding at way-point," COB said, "depth two thousand feet. Inertial nav agrees with dead reckoning plot for probe. Position checks complete."

"Very well," Jeffrey said.

Bell recommended testing the probe's sensor functions, and Jeffrey agreed. Jeffrey configured his console to show the data from the torpedo-shaped LMRS probe. He watched his screens. A computer image slowly sketched the near side of Mount 458. The slope was extremely steep, almost vertical. COB shifted the probe. More seamount features appeared, including a jagged protrusion.

"Don't snag the tether," Jeffrey said. The probe's sonars were functioning properly. Then COB turned on its passive imaging cameras. The picture was featureless, inky black.

"Changing to image intensification factor ten thousand."

Now Jeffrey saw a dull glow in the window on his screen, the barest trace of bright predawn moonlight, penetrating from high above, the photons picked up and multiplied by the cameras' CCDs. There was faint blue bioluminescence, too, as the LMRS stirred up microbes in the water.

COB brought the probe closer to the wall of the seamount. Deep-sea fish began to react to the movement. There were flashes in yellow and green, and flickers of sheet lightning, ghostly white.

"Image intensification fifty thousand," COB said.

The picture grew brighter, more detailed, though still fuzzy and murky. Jeffrey saw a swarm of small creatures dash by.

"Pelagic shrimp," Ilse said from her console. She was obviously watching, too.

"Confirmed," Kathy said. "Biologics. We're hearing the shrimp click and pop."

A huge jellyfish drifted past, translucent and gelatinous. Ilse said something in Latin.

Out of curiosity, Jeffrey selected *Challenger*'s own low-light-level TV camera mounted on the sail. He saw something black and ugly, with needle-sharp teeth, and a bright green lure dangling near its mouth.

"Demonfish," Ilse said.

Next COB tested the probe's active laser line-scan cameras. Now Jeffrey could see a small swatch of the seamount's slope, in crisp black and white. The texture of the bare rock was very rough.

"COB, it's time to break cover. Proceed to the peak of four-fifty-eight."

COB worked his joystick. "Bringing the LMRS up to fifteen hundred feet, sir."

Jeffrey saw Bell eye a chronometer. "LMRS battery level check," Bell said.

"Sixty-two percent," COB said.

"Very well," Bell said.

"Probe is at the summit."

"Sonar," Jeffrey said, "anything new?"

"Negative, sir. Not even any distant nuclear blasts in some while now."

"Quiet today," Bell said.

"Both sides are licking their wounds," Jeffrey said. "Very well, Sonar. . . . COB, begin the expanding snake search down the spur. Until we find *Texas*."

"Understood, sir."

"Use forward- and side-looking sonars in passive mode, to listen for transients and threats. Use passive-only imagery as a piloting aid. . . . I don't want the probe damaged, by an outcropping or uncharted wreck, or by *Texas* herself for that matter."

"Understood. LMRS has begun descent down the slope. Depth now fifteen hundred fifty feet."

Jeffrey saw a big boulder go by, lit by the living flashes and glows—or rather, the LMRS went by the boulder. The boulder's edges were softened by muck.

Jeffrey saw a starfish, waving an arm.

"There's silting on this spur," Ilse said.

"That would be organic waste, right?" Jeffrey kept his voice very even as he spoke with her. At least, he *hoped* he did. "Dead diatoms and plankton?"

"The bottom current transports nutrients," Ilse said. "The seamount makes it upwell, feeding an ecosystem over the summit. That's why the water turbidity's higher now."

Ilse was right. The image from the LMRS *was* murkier. For a while the only sense of motion came from floating specks and particles. They appeared out of the darkness, diverged to the edge of the picture, and were lost from view.

"If there's no erosion underwater," Jeffrey said, "how come the summit's so flat?" He hated to admit it, but talking shop with Ilse *really* turned him on. Since their little encounter yesterday, she'd been cool and professional. Good for her, but the widening gulf between them only made Ilse seem sexier to him.

"The top used to be a volcanic crater," she said. "The probe's in the bowl."

"Oh . . . But where's the rest of it? This spur is just a fragment." The downhill side of the spur ended abruptly in a sheer drop of almost two miles. There was no crater rim at the edge of the drop.

"Blew up, looks like," Ilse said. "Think of an undersea Mount St. Helens."

"Yikes," COB said. "That must have hit the Azores with one heck of a tsunami."

"Concur," Ilse said. "But that was millions of years ago."

Jeffrey chided himself on his one-track mind now of all times. He ordered his brain, the one in his head, to take back control of his thought processes.

COB continued to work the probe downhill, carefully searching.

"XO," Jeffrey said, "stand by with today's acoustic recognition signal and countersign."

"Recognition codes ready," Bell said.

"If anyone's still alive on *Texas*, this way they'll know we're here, and we're friendly."

"LMRS depth now sixteen hundred feet. Still no sign of *Texas*."

"How far past official crush depth do you think they could go?" Bell said.

"With the hull stressed by an atomic near miss?" Jeffrey said. "Lord, there's no way of knowing."

Jeffrey eyed the gravimeter. Past the end of the spur, at the bottom of the sheer drop, at a depth of over nine thousand feet, lay a huge field of boulders and lava extrusions.

"Probe depth now sixteen hundred fifty feet," COB said. "Still searching spur, now one thousand yards from the edge. No sign of *Texas*."

"What worries me," Jeffrey said, "is that after their second buoy got off, the ship may have slid down the slope. . . . *All* the way down the slope."

"I saw something!" Ilse shouted.

"Keep your voice down," Jeffrey said. "Give me a proper report."

"Um, sediment on slope appeared disturbed to the left. Striations, as if from a large moving object."

"Got it," COB said. "Good eyes, Miss Reebeck. Shifting LMRS to the left."

"Sonar, anything?" Jeffrey said.

"Nothing, sir," Kathy said. "No indications of enemy presence."

"Any signs of life at all?"

Kathy spoke to her people. "Negative, Captain. No *Virginia*-class tonals on sonar feed from LMRS, or other tonals for that matter. No broadband either, except for current flow noise."

"They must be conserving the battery," Bell said.

"Or they're dead," Jeffrey murmured.

Jeffrey watched the image-intensified picture from the probe. There was indeed a groove on the slope, gouged gradually deeper, running west. It went on and on.

"Debris now," COB said. "Stripped-off anechoic tiles . . . Something big, lying on its side. Yes, looks like the lower rudder."

"Careful," Jeffrey said. "Don't break the tether."

"This groove runs slightly downhill," COB said. "Present probe depth seventeen hundred twenty feet."

"That's too deep for *Texas*, sir," Bell said. "It's too deep."

"Keep praying," Jeffrey said. "At least it's in the right direction. Their last course would've been west."

"More debris," COB said. "Starboard towed array fairing, broken from the stern. . . . What's *that* mess?"

"Crumpled part of a wide aperture array?" Bell said. "Probably torn off by a boulder."

"They had *some* residual control," Jeffrey said. "She made a fairly gentle landing, from the looks of this groove. . . . The torn-off pieces are encouraging, actually. They'd've helped her slow down."

"Groove widening." COB. "Looks like she started slewing sideways. . . . More wreckage now."

"That's the starboard bowplane," Jeffrey said.

"Groove narrowing again. Depth seventeen hundred sixty feet."

Bell exhaled deeply. "We're almost at the edge now, Captain."

Jeffrey began to lose hope.

"There!" Ilse said.

Jeffrey saw it, too, upright, suspended several feet above the silt. Big slats, at the back of a cowling. The slats were twisted and bent, and the cowling was badly dented. To the cowling's right was the ragged stump of a stern plane. Just past the cowling, in the murk, loomed a huge cylindrical mass that took Jeffrey's breath away.

"We found her," he said quietly. "That cowling's a *Virginia*-class pump jet propulsor, for sure." Jeffrey eyed the probe's depth gauge once more. It was too far down for a *Virginia*-class hull to survive.

Jeffrey watched the latest grim picture coming from the probe. COB had already done a quick inspection of most of the disabled sub's exterior. For a moment, for a respite, Jeffrey glanced to the rear of the control room.

Lieutenant Willey and a junior officer from Engineering caucused there now, using a spare console behind the nav table. They carefully replayed earlier video from the probe. Willey and his j.o. were trying to tell exactly what sank *Texas,* and exactly what shape her forward compartment was in.

Jeffrey wasn't happy. From the outside, like this, there seemed no way to know if the front of the boat was filled with air, and the living, or with water and the dead.

COB kept working his joystick. The LMRS reached the bow.

"Look at that," Jeffrey said. "The streamlined cover for the bow sphere got knocked off. . . . Not surprising; it's mostly fiberglass."

"Where do you think it went?" Bell said.

"Pushed ahead of the ship, I guess. Kept going, tumbled off the cliff."

"We still can't tell what flooded her aft," Willey said. "From what we see, sir, and what their captain said in his two buoy messages, I suspect a main steam condensor shifted in its mount, from the A-bomb shock."

Jeffrey thought for a moment. "Yup." That could strain a cooling seawater intake or outlet pipe, and break a weld at the hull.

"We're still analyzing the forward section," Willey said. "No sign of cracks or implosion . . . or *explosion,* either."

"Very well," Jeffrey said. "COB, bring the LMRS to the *Texas*'s forward escape hatch again."

Soon the LMRS moved back behind *Texas*'s sail, to over the accommodation spaces.

"There's the hatch," COB said. "Her ASDS docking collar looks intact. No debris fouling the hatch."

"No sign an enemy minisub has been there?" Jeffrey asked.

"I'd need to go to active laser line-scan, sir."

"What do you think, XO?"

"We need to risk it, Captain. We'd radiate to send the recognition code anyway."

"COB, switch to active line-scan."

The picture got much clearer and sharper.

"Ilse," COB said, "from that little amount of silt and sea snow, can you tell if the collar's been disturbed?"

"I can't say," Ilse said. "If German commandos were here, or *are* here, wouldn't they cover their tracks?"

"Messenger of the Watch," Jeffrey said, "have Lieutenant Clayton come to the CACC. . . . Shajo ought be here for this. I should've thought of that before."

Clayton arrived a minute later.

"Oh, boy," he said when he looked at the screens. "You found her, didn't you?"

Jeffrey nodded. "It's humbling to see something so powerful lying there like that."

"Looks like her crash-landing ground to a halt just in time."

Clayton was right. From her bow to the edge of the cliff was less than the length of a football field.

"See the escape hatch and the collar?" Jeffrey asked. "Any way to know if the Germans were here?"

Clayton stared at the picture. "Sorry, no can say."

"Sonar," Jeffrey said, "anything now?"

"Still no sign of the enemy, sir, and no signs of life."

"Send it again," Jeffrey said.

"Recognition sign transmitted," Kathy said.

"Anything?"

Kathy paused. "Nothing, sir."

"Captain," Bell said, "we've been trying for twenty minutes now, with the highest signal power we dare. We aimed the LMRS transducer right at her port wide-aperture array, and what's left of the starboard wide array, and then her bow sphere. Nothing."

"They'd still have plenty of air reserve," Willey said, "assuming the compressed air banks in the forward ballast tanks survived the crash. . . ."

"It could be their hydrophones failed," Kathy said, "and they can't hear our signal. Or their transducers failed, and they can't answer back."

"Or their forward battery went flat," COB said. "Maybe it couldn't hold a charge after the crash. Or they drained it, running equipment to survive."

"Or they sprung a leak they couldn't stop," Jeffrey said. "Something small we can't see."

"Or German *Kampfschwimmer* are in control," Bell said, "waiting for us."

"You could always just bang on the hull," Clayton said.

"Not literally," Jeffrey said. "You heard the XO. We need stealth."

"What now, then, sir?" Bell said.

"COB, exactly what angle is *Texas* sitting at?"

"Down eleven degrees by the bow, listing twenty degrees to starboard."

"And the docking collar looks good?"

"Yes, sir."

"Can our ASDS mate properly, with those angles?"

"Tricky, Captain. Maybe."

"All right," Jeffrey said. "There's no choice. Shajo, get your men with their rifles. Messenger of the Watch, summon the medical corpsman. We're going to try to board her."

CHAPTER 11

Jeffrey stood, squeezed behind the pilot's seat in the minisub's cramped control compartment. David Meltzer was acting as pilot, and next to him sat COB as copilot. They all watched the imagery on one of the monitor screens, as the ASDS ultrahigh-frequency sonars built a picture of what lay outside.

There was *Texas,* listing to one side near the edge of the spur. There was the LMRS, hovering beyond the submarine's forward escape hatch.

Jeffrey reached past COB for the mike for the low-probability-of-intercept secure gertrude. "COB, lowest power, please, and keep the emitter aimed at the LMRS."

COB turned a knob, flipped a switch, worked his joystick, and flipped the switch again.

"*Challenger,* ASDS," Jeffrey called. "*Challenger,* ASDS. Communications check, over."

"ASDS, *Challenger,*" Bell's voice answered. "Read you five-by-five. How you me? Over."

"Same-same," Jeffrey said. "We're about to attempt the docking, over."

"Understood," Bell said. "Will monitor your approach through the probe's passive imagery, over."

"ASDS out," Jeffrey said. "COB, give me the transport compartment." Jeffrey keyed the mike again. "Shajo, come forward, please."

In a moment Shajo Clayton walked through the central hyperbaric sphere and dogged the hatch behind him quietly.

COB juggled the variable ballast, to adjust for the shift in weight. Shajo squeezed behind Meltzer, and looked at the screens.

"Almost show time," Shajo said. He wore a black bodysuit, a black ceramic flak vest, a black ceramic combat helmet, and had his dual-mode night vision visor flipped up. Jeffrey was dressed the same way, except for the helmet and visor.

"Pilot," Jeffrey said, "position us over the docking collar."

Meltzer took the main joystick now. He deftly turned the ASDS, using her side thrusters and her rudder and main screw propeller— all battery-powered, and silent. The minisub crept forward.

When they were over the collar, COB turned on the external light and the docking cameras.

Jeffrey could see the international-standard bright white lines and circle painted on the SSN's hull, like crosshairs around the escape hatch.

"I don't like these angles," Jeffrey said. "The collar's designed for a boat holding a zero bubble."

"The way the *Texas* is lying," COB said, "we could damage the collar. At this depth we can't equalize the lock-out chamber if it floods. No watertight seal to *Texas*, no opening the hatches."

"Can't you, like, tilt the minisub?" Clayton said.

"We're only eight feet in diameter," Jeffrey said. "We don't have the lever arm to put on a big list using the trim tanks. . . . Twenty degrees is too big."

"We *could* just flood negative," COB said, "come down heavy, and hope we settle on the collar just right."

"We'll have to try it," Jeffrey said.

Meltzer rotated the ASDS to line up fore-and-aft with *Texas*. He used his joystick and the side thrusters to fight the crosscurrent, almost two knots up here on the spur. COB worked his ballast control panel again.

Jeffrey watched the video screen. The round edge of the docking collar came at the camera. He could see the outer escape hatch now, down inside the collar.

The mini hit the collar hard. There was a scraping noise that sounded all wrong.

"Pull up!" Jeffrey said.

The minisub rose.

"This isn't working," COB said.

"Do you want me to try again?" Meltzer said.

Jeffrey looked at the screen. The part of the collar toward *Texas*'s stern was slightly dented. Paint particles floated in the water.

Jeffrey shook his head. "Too risky. We may have blown it already."

"We've come awfully far to give up now," Clayton said.

"We're definitely not giving up. . . . We have to think outside the box, folks. We're *not* a deep submergence rescue vehicle, we don't have a flexible ball-joint collar. We can't put on a twenty-degree starboard list. . . . So, what if we come in *sideways*? We'd only need an *eleven*-degree list in that case, right? If we could put on twenty degrees fore-and-aft somehow?"

"Um, yes, sir," Meltzer said.

"Easier said than done, Captain," COB said. "We're not designed for it. We dumped the back seats back at Cape Verde, so we're light at the stern. We can't make the *bow* any heavier, we've got max hot bodies crammed in here as it is."

That's true, Jeffrey thought. Shifting people around was the time-honored submariner's trick to alter bubble, but it only went so far.

"How about this?" Jeffrey said. "We bring the SEALs and their gear into the central chamber, and make us as nose-heavy as possible on variable ballast. Then we create a vertical twisting moment with our fore and aft rotatable side thrusters."

"It's worth a try," COB said.

"Think it'll work, Pilot?"

"Worth a try, sir," Meltzer said.

"Let's do it," Jeffrey said.

Clayton went aft and brought his people and some of their equipment into the lock-in/lock-out sphere. COB transferred all variable ballast forward as much as possible. Meltzer turned the ASDS ninety degrees, so it straddled *Texas* at a right angle, with the mini's bow hanging past the SSN's starboard side.

Clayton came back into the control compartment.

"Everybody lean to port as much as you can," Jeffrey said.

The SEALs gave each other doubtful looks, but complied.

"How are we doing?" Jeffrey said.

"So-so," COB said. "Six degrees port list, and we need eleven to mate with *Texas*. Ten degrees trim by the bow and we need twenty."

"Pilot, try using the thrusters."

Meltzer worked different knobs to position the retractable side-thrusters. "Thrusters going to maximum power."

The ASDS dipped more, and leaned more to the left.

"We're not there yet," COB said.

"Best we can do," Meltzer said, "and we're drifting away from the collar."

"Bring us back," Jeffrey said.

Meltzer did, using the main screw and the thrusters. "If I hold us over the collar, sir, I can't use the thrusters to angle us properly."

Jeffrey ran his hand over his face.

"So near and yet so far," Clayton said.

Jeffrey shot him a look, but Clayton was smiling.

"Think like a rifleman, sir," Clayton said. "We need to lead the target."

"You're right. . . . Pilot, can you put us upstream in the current just enough, and let us drift back over the collar as you lever the boat to line up?"

"Understood," Meltzer said. The ASDS moved forward. He and COB worked the controls. The mini tilted, and drifted crabwise, and descended toward the hatch.

"No good!" Jeffrey said.

Meltzer pulled up, and exhaled deeply. "I've almost got it, Captain. Let me try again."

"Begin when ready." Jeffrey noticed Meltzer was sweating.

Once more COB and Meltzer juggled their controls. The mini moved away, tilted, drifted, and came down.

With a satisfying *clunk*, the docking was perfect.

"Well done," Jeffrey said. He patted Meltzer on the shoulder. "Now for the next problem. COB, extend the docking pitot. Equalize the collar to one atmosphere and drain it. See if it's watertight."

Jeffrey waited tensely while COB went through the procedures.

"Collar is holding a good seal, Captain."

Jeffrey grabbed the gertrude mike, and kept Lieutenant Bell informed.

Then everybody listened. There were no signs of life from below, no loud banging, no gentle tapping, no voices calling, nothing.

"They *have* to have heard us docking," COB said.

Jeffrey nodded. "There's no point in us hammering now."

"It'd just make a datum, wouldn't it?" Clayton said.

"Now comes the scary part," Jeffrey said. "We don't know what's on the other side of the *Texas* escape hatch. Air at one atmosphere or so, or water at a thousand psi? . . . And there's no *way* to know, unless we crack the hatch."

"So what do we do?" Clayton said. "If the *Texas* is flooded, and we crack her escape hatch, we'll all die. The hyperbaric chamber can't withstand the pressure this deep."

"It's not *that* bad," Jeffrey said. "The dogs are designed to open the hatch gradually, for exactly this reason. If water squirts through, we turn it closed real quick."

"At least," COB said, "that's the theory."

"Yeah," Jeffrey said. "We don't know what a nuclear shock might have done to the mechanism. Even if the forward compartment itself is okay, the escape trunk might have flooded through a broken pipe or fitting. . . . Or I suppose the Germans could booby-trap the hatch, burn off the ends of the dogs as a nasty surprise with thermite lances, then flood the trunk on purpose."

"Oh, boy," Clayton said.

"We can't turn back," Jeffrey said. "The Greifswald mission is too important—we need those briefcase A-bombs bad. We say our prayers, and open the hatch."

Jeffrey knelt over the bottom hatch of the minisub. All ASDS lights, inside and out, were turned off. He wore his combined passive-infrared/image-intensification goggles. The image switched back and forth between modes every half second. He also wore his battle helmet now, and he had a K-Bar fighting knife strapped to one leg and his special .50-caliber pistol in a belt holster.

Around Jeffrey stood Clayton and his five SEALs, similarly garbed, gripping .50-caliber machine pistols—short-barreled assault rifles that fired subsonic bullets. The fully silenced, electric ignition weapons were turned on, with caseless rounds in the chamber. Black tape covered the digital round-count diodes and the tritium backup night sights; this way, they wouldn't give obvious targets to an enemy wearing night-vision goggles, too.

The men relied on the sighting reticle integral to their visor images, based on low-energy laser interferometers that always knew where their weapons were pointed.

Jeffrey turned the wheel of the ASDS lock-out hatch until it opened. He let it drop down on its hydraulically dampened hinges.

Below him was the hatch into *Texas*. On the other side of that hatch, Jeffrey knew, was the air lock of her forward escape trunk. There was another escape trunk—with another air lock—near *Texas*'s stern, for use from the engineering spaces. That part of the boat, Jeffrey knew for sure, was flooded.

The forward compartment might or might not be flooded. The men from *Texas* might or might not all be dead. There might or might not be Kampfschwimmer waiting on the other side of this hatch, or further into the ship.

Even as an ex-SEAL himself, Jeffrey was frightened by Kampfschwimmer. After all, the Draeger scuba combat rebreather was a *German* invention. Images came to his mind from old war movies, and captured Nazi documentaries, of relentless, merciless warriors in those ballistically-optimized coal-scuttle helmets. Picturing such men in wetsuits and swim flippers made it even worse.

Jeffrey climbed down into the space enclosed by the docking collar. It was damp and very cold—confirmed by the blue tinge of the image in infrared. *Challenger*'s medical corpsman—who, like the other men, appeared a multicolored aura when Jeffrey viewed him in IR—handed Jeffrey a stethoscope. The corpsman retreated to the transport compartment and dogged the door.

Jeffrey squatted by the hatch—it and *Texas*'s hull were much too thick, and too well insulated, to see through with wearable passive infrared. Jeffrey used his handkerchief to wipe away the slime. The steel hull was freezing, from immersion in seawater at 34° Fahrenheit. He put the stethoscope to the hull, next to the hatch, and he listened.

He heard a disembodied rushing sound: current flow noise transmitted by the hull. He heard occasional creaking, and metallic moaning: *Texas*'s hull as she complained about the outside pressure, or settled more on the uneven spur. Once he heard a sharp pop, as some item of equipment back aft—or maybe forward—could no longer hold out, and it imploded. He also heard steady clicking, which he guessed was the scrammed reactor as it continued to cool.

There were no voices, and no machinery running that he recognized.

Jeffrey looked up at Clayton and shook his head.

"Can't tell, or all flooded?" Clayton whispered.

"Can't tell," Jeffrey mouthed.

"How's the dogging mechanism?"

"Can't tell, without opening it."

Jeffrey saw COB watching through the door into the mini's control compartment—he and Meltzer now wore vision goggles, too. COB disappeared. He came back a minute later.

"*Challenger* says good luck, sir." In Jeffrey's crisp black-and-white LLTV image mode, COB looked worried, and suddenly seemed very old.

"It's now or never," Jeffrey said.

Clayton and his five SEALs looked at each other and shrugged, carefully expressionless.

"Ready?" Jeffrey whispered.

Clayton cleared his throat. "Will we feel anything?"

"Pressure, heat, wetness. Agony, then blackest death." Jeffrey was immensely satisfied to see that his hands weren't shaking.

With both hands, Jeffrey gripped the special wrench that would open the watertight hatch from outside. Through a fitting in the hatch, the wrench turned the inside locking wheel.

Clayton and his men aimed their weapons at the hatch, safeties off. Jeffrey dreaded a firefight—ricochets could kill them all and wreck the minisub.

Jeffrey turned the wheel. He waited for it to explode at him, propelled by a killing water cannon. He wondered if he *would* feel anything, if his brain would even have time to register before his skull was smashed. He turned the wheel more.

The hatch emitted a terrible *sssss*—he'd forgotten there might be air before the water, if there was a bubble of it trapped inside *Texas*'s hull. His brain formed the words "poison gas." He tried to crank the hatch shut, but it fought him and did burst open.

A blinding light pierced Jeffrey's eyes and bore into his soul—was this death?

"*Hande hoch!*" a deep voice shouted, German for "put up your hands." Five heavy-caliber muzzles stared through the hatch at Jeffrey and the SEALs.

"Drop *your* weapons!" Clayton bellowed.

There was a pause, then a tentative, "Shajo, is that *you*?"

"*Cripes on a pita with margarine,*" Clayton answered. "Chief Montgomery, you son of a goat! I could've killed you!"

As Jeffrey's eyes adjusted, the SEAL chief standing down inside the nine-man *Virginia*-class Special Warfare escape trunk looked up at Jeffrey and Clayton and smiled. His men put their weapons on safe.

"Commander Fuller, sir," Montgomery said. "I'm honored." Montgomery was just over six feet tall, and had a very powerful chest. "Welcome to the United States Submarine *Texas*."

"Permission to come aboard?" Jeffrey said.

Montgomery nodded. Then he winked at Clayton. "Nah, LT, I would've killed you first."

CHAPTER 12

"I'd already told the men not to expect to be home for Christmas," Captain Taylor said.

"I'm sorry there isn't more we can do," Jeffrey said.

Texas's captain, a full commander, looked exhausted but determined. He'd shaved recently, but clearly needed a shower—no dice, with the water rationing.

One arm was in a sling, and it obviously hurt when Taylor breathed. The air in the disabled sub was cold and damp and stale. There wasn't much smell of sewage or rotting garbage, at least not yet, but this deep *Texas* couldn't jettison waste *or* blow sanitary. The freezer was being kept running—they needed the food—so there wasn't a smell from there.

The lighting was very dim, to conserve the battery. The coffee was strong and hot. Near the sleeping spaces there *was* a smell: like a hospital, of disinfectant, wounds, pain, and of unbathed men, of sweat.

"The Greifswald thing has to come first," Taylor said. "We all know that. I'm just grateful it was you, and not some Germans."

"You didn't trust the recognition codes?"

"Frankly, no," Taylor said. "We've no idea what the Axis has been able to compromise. I decided to lie doggo, and find out. Chief Montgomery concurred."

Jeffrey nodded. "Captain Wilson said the same thing to me, before he was wounded. He said remember Ultra, when we read the German Enigma codes in World War Two. He said Lord knows what the Germans are reading now."

"It smarts, doesn't it, when the shoe is on the other foot?"

Taylor continued giving Jeffrey a quick tour of the unflooded part of *Texas*. The hardest thing was walking, with the ship tilted downhill and leaning sharply to the right as they faced forward. The whole place was strangely quiet, without the usual reassuring sound of air circulation fans, and with so little physical activity by the crew, to help save oxygen.

"Morale seems high, all things considered, sir," Jeffrey said. He was impressed that everything was *clean*. Broken glass had been swept up, blood and vomit mopped, smashed equipment tidied as much as practical, and there was no dust or litter *anywhere*.

"I'm lucky to have such a good crew," Taylor said. "The able-bodied men are helping care for the wounded. The ambulatory ones are doing what they can as well—I suppose I'm in that group myself. I'm grateful for the medical supplies you brought with you, and for the loan of your chief corpsman."

"It's the least I can do," Jeffrey said. "Our doc volunteered to stay until you're rescued. . . . I'm sorry about the men you lost."

Taylor grew sad. "My XO showed a lot of promise. If we make it back I want to put him in for the Medal of Honor. If he hadn't gone aft, led the others to keep the propulsion plant going . . . And my engineer, my engineer . . . My father's known his father for forty-five years; they were at the Naval Academy together." Taylor had to pause to wipe his eyes. "I'm not looking forward to breaking the news about his son."

"Maybe they'll be able to salvage her," Jeffrey said. "At least then the men aft can get decent burial."

"I keep hoping so," Taylor said. "*Texas* was, *is* such a fine vessel. . . . Compressed air bladders forced through the aft escape trunk, and through the machinery access hatches. Towed to friendly waters without changing her depth, for buoyancy control. . . . Won't be easy. But we need every ship we can get. I just wonder if this war will still be raging by the time she might be refurbished."

"I keep thinking, sir, that from where we are right now, a quick end won't be a happy end for the good guys. From the sound of things, that big convoy suffered horrible losses yesterday."

Jeffrey and Taylor reached *Texas*'s CACC, similar in size and layout to *Challenger*'s. The men on watch turned to greet Jeffrey, and Captain Taylor gave them encouraging words.

Just then COB came up a ladder, past the far end of the CACC. He was breathing a little hard and had clear, sticky grease on his hands and his pants.

"Well, sirs," COB said, "I think we can get tube four working, if we could bring some spare parts from *Challenger*."

"So you concur, Master Chief," Taylor said, "that torpedo tube two is operational?"

"Affirmative, Captain."

"At least we'll be able to defend ourselves," Taylor said. "No melee ranging without a working bow sphere, but the port wide-aperture array has a good field of view, the way we landed, from what you told me."

"And both port-side tubes are clear of debris," Jeffrey said. "We saw that with the LMRS." Jeffrey peered over the sonarmen's shoulders at their screens, out of curiosity and concern.

"Handy little gadgets," Taylor said, "those off-board probes. Ours were damaged, beyond repair."

There was a screeching sound, and everyone tensed.

"I forgot to warn you about that," Taylor said with a wry smile. "She doesn't like being so deep."

"It's a miracle the ship held up after such a beating," Jeffrey said.

"What really worried me were all the penetrations for pipes and cables leading aft through the main watertight bulkhead. If just one of those seals or flapper valves gives way, with ambient sea pressure on the other side . . . But General Dynamics and Newport News built *Texas* good."

Jeffrey glanced at the sonar screens again, but there were no hostile contacts.

COB cleared his throat. "I spoke to the Weps and made a list of things, sirs. I'd like to go back to *Challenger* to get them, in the ASDS with Meltzer."

"I'd appreciate that a lot," Taylor said. "What do you say, *Captain* Fuller?" Taylor smiled.

"I concur," Jeffrey said. "Just make it quick. We're way behind schedule already." He sensed Taylor was lonely for a peer with whom to unburden himself, and Jeffrey was it. Jeffrey had some idea of how the more senior man must feel. Jeffrey had never felt so lonely as since leaving Cape Verde.

"We better get most of your SEALs and their equipment over to my ship on this trip, too," Jeffrey said. "Otherwise the ASDS'll be overcrowded."

"Lieutenant Clayton and the men were assembling everything by the escape trunk," COB said.

"Let's go talk to them," Jeffrey said.

Ilse sat at a sonar console in *Challenger*'s CACC, busy working on the METOC oceanographic data. Kathy announced that Meltzer was calling from over by *Texas*. Ilse brought up the imagery from the LMRS probe. She saw the minisub sitting sideways on *Texas*'s back, with the little ASDS's nose pointed down at the muck along the much bigger SSN's starboard side.

The *Texas* seemed dumb, inanimate. Ilse tried to picture all the people in the hull, Jeffrey and Clayton and more than a hundred others. Then she remembered the corpses, near the stern.

"Put him on the speakers, please," Lieutenant Bell said. He picked up a mike. "ASDS, *Challenger*, g'head." Bell's voice went through the fiber-optic wire to the probe, then from the probe to the mini by low-power gertrude.

"Sir," Meltzer answered the same way, "am returning now with one load of SEALs and equipment boxes, including the two special items. COB has a list of things to bring back to *Texas* on our second trip."

Ilse guessed the "special items" were the pair of briefcase atom bombs.

"V'r'well, ASDS. Relay COB's list and I'll have people get them together immediately."

"Switching to digital datalink mode," Meltzer said.

"E-mail received," Kathy said.

Then Bell warned Meltzer that the LMRS battery level was low. They arranged for him to escort it back to *Challenger* for a recharge, controlling the probe by autonomous acoustic link from the ASDS— they would cut the miles-long fiber-optic and dump it in deep water.

Meltzer undocked from the *Texas*. Ilse watched on the probe's laser line-scan camera as the mini rose from the disabled submarine. The mini quickly righted itself—zero bubble, to use the proper term—and got underway. From the viewing angle now, Ilse could tell the probe was following off the minisub's port quarter, tucked in close.

"Acoustic control of LMRS tested and functional," Meltzer said. "Will follow predetermined dog-leg course to *Challenger*." For stealth. "No hostile contacts held on ASDS sonars. Am commanding LMRS to jettison fiber-optic cable."

Now, for a while, because of intervening terrain, *Challenger* would be out of touch with the minisub and *Texas*.

Jeffrey was chatting with some of *Texas*'s enlisted men in the mess. They seemed grateful for the company, and gladly stopped their millionth game of cards or checkers.

Shajo Clayton and Chief Montgomery came by for another cup of coffee. Overhead, they all heard a hard *clunk*.

"That wasn't hull popping," one of *Texas*'s senior chiefs said.

"No," Jeffrey said, "it wasn't." Adrenaline poured through his blood. "Somebody's trying to dock."

Clayton and Montgomery tensed.

Jeffrey reached for a growler phone to call the CACC, but it barked first—Captain Taylor. Taylor confirmed the ASDS was long gone, well on its way back to *Challenger*. Whoever was trying to land on *Texas*, it wasn't Meltzer.

Jeffrey spoke briskly.

"Concur," Taylor answered. "We didn't hear anything on sonar till that docking transient just now. They must have come in through our blind spot, over the stern. Smart bastards . . . I'm sounding silent battle stations. Prepare to repel boarders."

Jeffrey hung up the mike.

"Get everyone and everything out of here," Jeffrey said to the men in the mess. "Some of you, help keep the injured calm in the berthing spaces. The rest, hide as far forward as you can. Lie down, don't move, and don't say a word."

The crewmen disappeared. Clayton and Montgomery listened as Jeffrey thought and talked fast.

"I don't like the scenario we played out before, with rifles in each other's faces. If we'd been German instead of friends, there could've been a dozen dead, and a flooded mini blocking the escape trunk."

Clayton nodded. "We can't afford that."

"We have a mission to run at Greifswald," Montgomery said.

"We need to make this look *good*," Jeffrey said. He glanced at the overhead. "We better hurry up."

Montgomery summoned his men with their weapons, and they began laying out fields of fire. Jeffrey and Clayton ran the short distance from the mess, past the bottom of the escape trunk, round the bend, to the ship's freezer. Inside were three dead American submariners, in body bags.

Jeffrey and Clayton pulled the corpses out of the bags and dragged them along the deck to near the escape trunk.

"God forgive me for doing this," Clayton said.

"Put a breather mask on one, it'll look more realistic."

"I'll leave this other guy faceup, so the Germans know for sure he's dead."

"Must've had a broken neck," Jeffrey said, looking at the corpse.

"They don't smell bad enough," Clayton said. He used his strength to rearrange one dead man's arms and legs; the limbs were stiff.

"Get some garbage from the compactor room," Jeffrey said. "That and a soiled bedpan, with the lid up, should do the trick. Put them behind that mess booth in the corner."

"Right."

"And have the SEAL team use silvered blankets from the corpsman's cubicle. To suppress our infrared signatures."

Jeffrey put on his battle helmet and lowered the visor. The other SEALs did, too.

"Gas masks," Montgomery said.

Jeffrey lifted his helmet and pulled on his mask.

"Try to breathe real quiet when the time comes," Montgomery said. His voice was muffled.

Jeffrey nodded.

Clayton told the enlisted SEALs to get sacks of flour and oatmeal from the galley, to use as sandbags.

Montgomery handed Jeffrey an ammo clip for a spare electric machine pistol. "Hollow point only," the SEAL chief said. No armor-piercing rounds. "For use in an SSN's hull."

Jeffrey raised his eyebrows.

"We made these just in case."

Jeffrey charged his weapon, then used the growler phone. "Captain Taylor," he projected his voice through the gas mask, "cut all power to the mess deck."

The bug juice machine stopped gurgling, and the lights went out; the emergency battle lanterns came right on. Montgomery's men went around and smashed the bulbs with their weapon butts. Diodes still glowed to show the lanterns' batteries held charge—this gave the team's image-intensifier visors enough photons to see.

Clayton and Montgomery pointed to where each man should hide.

Jeffrey's heart was beating extraordinarily loud.

"Weapons off safe," Clayton whispered. "Selectors on semiauto."

"When you hear me shoot," Montgomery whispered, "everybody shoot."

"Make every shot count," Jeffrey whispered. "Make sure every bullet gets stopped by a German body." He pointed aft. "The watertight bulkhead's right there. Break the packing for a cable run, we flood the ship."

Jeffrey took his position, huddled on the deck, just inside the galley. He arranged the blanket, silver side in, to cover his body, except for where he needed to see. He hoped that to an enemy IR visor, he'd look like a corpse, still somewhat fresh, cooling.

Everyone waited. Soon there was another *clunk*.

Then Jeffrey heard more noises. The docking collar was being pumped dry. . . . The upper escape hatch was being opened. . . . Soon he heard the sound of many people coming down the ladder inside the trunk.

Jeffrey badly needed to take a leak. *Very* badly, all of a sudden. He decided he would, to add to the effect of a submarine full of dead men.

He felt better at once. The urine ran to the forward starboard corner of the galley, and puddled there. Jeffrey's gas mask kept out the smell. Someone undogged the lower escape trunk hatch from inside, and opened it just a crack. There was a long, pregnant silence, then Jeffrey barely made out confident, tough whispering in German.

Something small sailed out of the air lock and landed on the deck. There was a brilliant blue-white flash, then a hiss as some kind of gas filled the air. It spread, a fine aerosol, and Jeffrey thought it looked like military tear gas.

Then there was silence. Jeffrey tensed.

Another flash-and-gas grenade. Jeffrey's visor pixel antibloom control kept him from being blinded.

The first Kampfschwimmer dashed silently out of the lock-out trunk. Jeffrey saw him through his visors, on infrared, through the intervening aluminum bulkhead. The man was a giant, easily six foot six. His posture showed he held a short-barrel, two-handed weapon. It traversed as he peered in all directions fast.

Jeffrey had left a dental mirror, a standard Special Warfare item, in the galley doorway, camouflaged with a shriveled banana peel. As the German came closer, Jeffrey could see in low-light high-def TV mode that the man wore flat-screen night-vision goggles himself, outside an evil-looking respirator hood, with a full-body nuclear-biological-chemical protective suit. The thickness of his machine pistol's barrel showed it was silenced.

The German bent over and checked out the corpses, the real ones. Jeffrey worried he would think they were too cold.

The German turned and gestured to the lock-out trunk. Six more Kampfschwimmer appeared, just as tall and muscular as the first. One of them held something toward the stern, toward the reactor. A Geiger counter? Another held up something else—gas analyzer? Both men nodded to the others. One took out a long, thin wand—to check for trip wires in the dark? They advanced.

The SEALs were outnumbered. Besides Jeffrey and Clayton and Montgomery, only two had stayed behind when the rest went over to *Challenger*. The odds were seven to five against, and who really owned the element of surprise here?

Jeffrey wanted to move. The death-posture he'd adopted was dramatic, but his right leg had fallen asleep. The left leg, with his old war wound, started to ache horribly. He thought of what Ilse said, that it might be in his mind, from stress.

He pushed her out of his thoughts. He wanted to shift his weapon for a better line of fire. He dared not move a muscle.

The first Kampfschwimmer came down the corridor, toward the mess and the galley. The Germans covered each other skillfully. Two of them pulled out large canisters, more gas. As one Kampfschwimmer came to the door of the galley, Jeffrey saw through his goggles that the canister bore a skull-and-bones. *What was Montgomery waiting for?*

It also bore a large white cross. Jeffrey couldn't remember if that meant mustard gas or chlorine.

Jeffrey realized it wasn't to *kill* any surviving *Texas* crew—for that they'd use an odorless, nonpersistent nerve agent. The noxious poison gas was to force anyone still breathing to put on respirators, so they'd have to move, make noise as air valves hissed, be slowed down and partly immobilized.

Of course. The Germans would want to take prisoners, for thorough interrogation. But mustard gas caused terrible burns to bare skin. *What the hell was Montgomery waiting for?*

Jeffrey heard a silenced weapon cough—his heart raced out of control.

He brought his own weapon to bear on the Kampfschwimmer in the galley doorway. The man brought his weapon to bear on Jeffrey. The German fired first, hitting Jeffrey in the chest as Jeffrey tried to stand.

The force of impact against his flak jacket shoved Jeffrey backward. His weapon pointed wildly, and he saw the German's barrel aimed dead center at his face, but the German's neck exploded and blood spattered Jeffrey's visor.

Jeffrey tried to crouch but wobbled—his right leg was badly numb. He heard more weapons coughing, the thud and crunch of bullets hitting flesh and bone. He heard grunts and screams, then a whining ricochet forced him flat on the deck. Two bullets tore through the aluminum curtain wall, and zinged into the wardroom pantry where Clayton was firing steadily.

Two Kampfschwimmer charged the medical corpsman's cubicle and killed the SEAL who was shooting from there. The intervening bulkhead was structural, steel. They had the SEALs pinned down. The drinking fountain was hit and water sprayed.

Jeffrey belly-crawled to the corridor. His aim was blocked by bodies.

Jeffrey realized the SEAL who'd saved his life—by shooting that Kampfschwimmer in the back of the neck, between his flak vest and his helmet—had also been killed. His brains were smeared across the wide-screen TV at the front of the mess. The screen was spider-webbed with cracks.

The German minisub! Jeffrey was sure there'd be someone up there, who'd be calling their parent vessel for help.

While the surviving SEALs and Germans sniped at each other viciously, Jeffrey reached into the corridor and pulled dead bodies toward him. A hot bee snapped by his wrist, then another.

Jeffrey used the bodies as a bullet stop. More rounds hit home, making the corpses jump and twitch, as Jeffrey scrambled along the deck. Clayton saw what he was doing and threw a flash grenade of his own. Clayton and Montgomery pumped out rapid covering fire.

Jeffrey used the diversion to lunge into the air lock and slam the hatch. Bullets clanged against it a moment later, but it was pressure-proof high strength steel.

Jeffrey started to climb. Someone with a carbine looked down at him and he shot the man in the left eye, through his goggle lens and respirator mask. The mask and helmet held down the gore, but the German fell on top of Jeffrey and almost knocked him from the ladder. The German's helmet slipped off his shattered head, and Jeffrey was drenched in the blood and purple custard of his brain.

Jeffrey climbed as fast as he could, faster than he ever had in Hell Week. He used all his upper body strength to pull himself up—his damn right leg was still half asleep. Now he was inside the German minisub's central hyperbaric sphere.

Someone was forward, in the little control room. He was trying to dog the forward hatch. Jeffrey grabbed the wheel on his side, and tried to force it open. It became a test of will, and Jeffrey instantly realized how vulnerable he was.

If the man on the other side of the door could dog it fully shut, then jam the wheel with a wrench or a rifle, he'd be free to reach the mini's controls. He could flood the collar, and with it the trunk and the sphere, where Jeffrey stood. At this depth, free influx through a half-inch equalizing pipe would be like machine-gun fire. Jeffrey would be pulped before the pressure buildup threatened the German. If Jeffrey let go of the wheel, he might reach the mini's bottom hatch—but it was hydraulic, and if locked open Jeffrey could never get it closed.

Below him more bullets clanged. He remembered that the *Virginia*-class corpsman's cubicle also held two countermeasures launchers, miniature torpedo tubes. If the Kampfschwimmer rigged them with explosive, they could flood the whole front half of *Texas*. It was up to Montgomery and Shajo now.

For a moment Jeffrey thought of letting go of the door and retreating into the transport compartment aft. Instead he summoned desperate strength and forced the forward door undogged against the German's efforts.

The door flew open and Jeffrey stumbled through, and spun and landed on his back against the instrument panels. He aimed his machine pistol at the German. The man was a submariner, not a Kampfschwimmer, and unarmed. He put up his hands. Down below, more bullets clanged. Then there was silence.

Clayton called from the bottom of the escape trunk. The firefight was over.

"Check the countermeasure tubes!" Jeffrey shouted.

Jeffrey secured his prisoner hand and foot with duct tape, then threw him into the transport compartment. He clambered down into *Texas*.

The lights were on, the ones that hadn't been smashed by wild shots or ricochets. Jeffrey could see the air was heavy with gun smoke. The mess space was a scene of carnage. The fans were running, to clear the tear gas and the smoke.

Clayton came over, looking sheepish and very relieved. He held up two German detonators. "They had them rigged to the tubes, with lots of C-four. Set as dead-man switches, with ten more seconds to run." Clayton and Jeffrey looked into each other's eyes for a long moment, not saying anything, both knowing they'd all come *that* close to being killed. Then both men shrugged it off; they had plenty else to worry about.

Jeffrey glanced around. All eight Kampfschwimmer lay motionless in pools of blood, strewn from within the air lock to inside the corpsman's cubicle. Chief Montgomery's two enlisted SEALs were dead. Blood slowly soaked the scattered flour and oatmeal.

Montgomery looked okay, physically at least. He went up the ladder into the mini.

"How did you get the Germans in the doc's office?" Jeffrey asked.

Clayton smiled. "I switched to armor-piercing and shot them through the wall."

Jeffrey saw no spent shell casings; the Kampfschwimmer used caseless ammo, too. He picked up one of their weapons.

Crap. It was an exact copy of the one *he'd* used, down to the hookup for the special visor-aiming reticle. Except, the German model had a more effective flash suppressor, and a better grip.

The SEALs' electric machine pistols were supposed to be *top secret.*

Captain Taylor and the navigator—the acting XO—came aft. Their eyes began to water from everything in the air.

"Judas Priest," Taylor said, looking around and holding his nose. "We'll have to make sure nothing vital got hit." Taylor spotted the bullet holes through the sheet steel of the doc's office. He turned white. "There are sleeping compartments the other side of the medical space!"

"We checked," Clayton said. "A few close calls, but everybody's okay."

Taylor gave Clayton a hard look.

"I aimed as carefully as I could, sir."

Taylor shook his head. "You SEALs are absolutely crazy." Then he smiled, briefly. "Thanks for what you did."

Jeffrey noticed curious crewmen gathering in the passageway. Many wore bandages or neck braces, and had arms or even legs in air casts or improvised splints.

Other crewmen arrived and began to load the dead men into body bags. They started with their own three people, waiting to be reinterred, then did the SEALs, working silently, with respect. Someone offered Jeffrey a spare jumpsuit and towel, so he could get cleaned up.

Jeffrey just wiped his face. "We have to get out of here. The Germans may have been alerted. That minisub didn't get here on its own."

Jeffrey heard Montgomery up in the mini, speaking to the prisoner, in fluent German.

Montgomery came back down.

"He didn't get off a message."

"Are you sure?" Captain Taylor said.

"I held my K-Bar to his balls. He didn't get off a message. . . . They came in an *Amethyste II.* It's hiding north of here. That crewman doesn't know its zigzag plan."

"We need to get going," Jeffrey repeated. "They'll suspect something soon."

Taylor sent his navigator forward, to take the conn till Taylor returned, and have the weps prepare for battle. The crowd of crewmen dispersed to their stations or racks.

Taylor turned to Jeffrey. "How will you get back?"

"We'll use the German mini," Jeffrey said. "It'll be faster than waiting for Meltzer."

"I'm qualified as ASDS pilot," Montgomery said. "I checked, I can read the instruments up there. How hard can it be?"

"That's my man," Clayton said. He clapped Montgomery on the shoulder, but the humor was brittle. Jeffrey sensed they were both upset about the two men killed in action—*he* certainly was.

"Sorry about the damage, sir," Jeffrey said to Taylor. Jeffrey helped shift the bodies into the freezer. The flame-proof linoleum deck was slick with blood and other fluids; the effects of close-quarters battle were truly revolting.

In spite of himself, Jeffrey yawned—in the freezer, he could see his breath. The adrenaline was wearing off, and this made him very sleepy. His chest was sore, where the bullet had hit his flak vest. He was also incredibly thirsty.

Montgomery said a few words over the body bags holding his people. Jeffrey glanced at the ones with the Germans. Even in death, they frightened him.

Taylor hustled Jeffrey and the others to the escape trunk. Clayton and Montgomery grabbed samples of Kampfschwimmer gear.

"I wish *Challenger* could stay to help, Captain," Jeffrey said.

"I know your orders," Taylor said.

"It's the hardest thing I've ever had to do, sir, leaving you like this."

Taylor sighed. "We do have one good tube, with a nuclear fish loaded and armed, and plenty more on the holding racks."

"Atlantic Fleet can't just leave you here."

"Home in time for New Year's, then, maybe," Taylor said. He handed Jeffrey the rolled-up jumpsuit. "Change in the minisub, Captain. You stink."

Everyone wished each other best of luck. Taylor shook Jeffrey's hand, then began to close the door.

"We'll try to trick that *Amethyste* into the open for you," Jeffrey said. "Somehow."

"We'll be ready," Taylor said. "One way or another, no German's coming close without getting a bloody nose, and with the intel treasure *Texas* represents, nobody's taking us alive."

CHAPTER 13

Chief Montgomery sat in the left seat, Jeffrey in the right. Shajo Clayton stood behind Jeffrey. Their prisoner was nicely trussed up in the transport compartment. The bottom hatch was dogged.

"Collar is flooded and equalized," Montgomery said. "We're ready to separate."

"Do it," Jeffrey said. The German mini got underway.

A little later a red light started blinking. Clayton jumped. "What's this?" Neither he nor Jeffrey knew German.

"Uh-oh," Montgomery said. "Incoming message on voice."

"Don't answer it."

"What if we force our prisoner to feed them a story?" Clayton said.

"No. They've got world-class signal processors. Even if he *hates* the regime, and plays along, they'll see the microtremors in his voice. . . . Monty, can you get this thing to work on digital datalink?"

"If you help me, Captain. We better work fast."

With Montgomery as the on-board German language interpreter, and Jeffrey as a passable expert on undersea comms, they got the switches and computer commands lined up.

"Tell them our voice link is down, we took some damage during our melee with the SEAL armed guard."

Montgomery typed on the keyboard with one hand and steered

the mini with the other. He hit enter. His e-mail text in German on the screen meant nothing to Jeffrey, except for the acronym SEAL.

A message came back, at once. "They want the recognition code."

"Stall them."

"Leave this to me. Captain, please take the conn. Here's your depth, here's your gyrocompass. Just hold us steady." Jeffrey took the controls. Instruments and data screens responded.

Montgomery grabbed a box with a green cross: European-style markings for a first-aid kit. He rushed aft and closed the transport compartment door behind him.

"I'm glad I don't have to watch," Clayton said.

"Me, too," Jeffrey said. As he held the control joystick he realized his left wrist was sore. *Damn*, the crystal of his old Rolex was smashed, and the hour hand was gone. A German bullet must have done it. *That was close.*

Montgomery came back. "Got it." He sat, and typed on the keyboard.

"How do we know he didn't give you some kind of panic code?" Clayton said.

"I said if he did, I'd cut his dick and testicles off, then clamp the arteries with hemostats, and I'd hold his head between his legs and let him think about it till he died."

"Monty," Clayton said, "I'm *very* glad you're on our side."

Jeffrey just shook his head.

"Hey," Montgomery said, "I didn't actually *do* it." Another German message came back. "*Bingo.* They bought it. They want a status report. They say they heard a lot of bullet impacts on their sonar."

"Okay," Jeffrey said. "Okay . . . tell them the enemy submarine is secured, all the American SEALs are killed. Tell them the ship is identified as the USS *Texas*, SSN 775. Her captain is alive. The Kampfschwimmer are collecting the highest-value prisoners and crypto gear right now."

Montgomery typed.

"They want us to confirm Captain Taylor's laser buoy message, that the ASDS was jettisoned and lost in combat."

Jeffrey blanched. "They broke the code?"

"Yup." Montgomery sounded disgusted.

"Okay, tell them, Confirmed."

"They say their remote-control probe detected flow noise a few minutes ago, heading south. . . . *What* probe?"

Jeffrey blanched again. "They must have some kind of LMRS snooping around. . . . Uh, tell them it was probably a whale or a giant squid or something." Jeffrey wished Ilse was here. She was always good at this.

Montgomery smiled, and typed.

This is insane, Jeffrey told himself. We're busy holding a chat room with some enemy submarine captain, amid three warring SSNs all armed with nuclear torpedoes.

A response came on the screen. "They want us to investigate thoroughly. They're afraid an American sub may be in the area by now. Maybe what they heard was an LMRS or an ASDS."

"Tell them we'll investigate to the south. Ask them to rendezvous with us north of the spur for pickup in two hours. That should draw the *Amethyste II* into the open—we'll have to leave the rest to Captain Taylor. Let's get out of here. We need to catch up with Meltzer, and convince him it's us."

Montgomery resumed the conn. He followed the course he knew the ASDS would take.

Jeffrey looked around the German mini's cockpit more thoroughly. It was sophisticated, more futuristic than the ASDS. It was faster and had much longer cruising range, too, thanks to hydrogen peroxide power; Jeffrey saw a fuel gauge labeled "H_2O_2."

"What's this thing's crush depth, Chief?"

Montgomery called up a document labeled "Hilfe." Help. "Seven hundred meters."

Jeffrey whistled. "Twenty-three hundred feet . . . Good, we can use that. Dip down behind the spur and make flank speed. It'll take some juggling, but I want to jettison our ASDS and keep the German mini instead."

TWO HOURS LATER, ON CHALLENGER.

Ilse was glad that Jeffrey and the others had made it back okay. The ASDS was abandoned, lodged under a big outcropping of a different seamount. The German minisub was safely stowed in *Challenger's* conformal hangar now.

Ilse felt *Challenger* rock.

"Loud explosion bearing three two five!" Kathy shouted. "Range sixty thousand yards!"

"That matches Seamount 458," Jeffrey said. *"Whose weapon was it?"*

"A one-tenth-KT warhead, sir. Can't tell whose side."

"Torpedo screw-count?"

"None detectable at this range, Captain."

Ilse heard another blast on the sonar speakers, not as loud and different in character.

"Hull implosion!" Kathy shouted. "Same range and bearing! Full-size steel sub hull implosion!"

"What class vessel?"

"Impossible to tell in this acoustic sea state, sir."

"It was either the *Amethyste II*," Bell said, "or the *Texas*."

"Or both," Jeffrey said. He hesitated. "There's no more we can do."

Ilse felt the awkward, worried silence in the CACC.

Then she had a terrible thought.

"Captain, what if there were *two* German submarines near Seamount 458? That guy you captured might not even know."

Jeffrey turned. "Your point, Miss Reebeck?"

"What if the *other* German sub sent *its* mini to *Texas*, with more German commandos, and captured everyone and everything for real? What if *they* blew up the spur, to cover their tracks and keep the Allies from salvaging *Texas*? What if they tortured Captain Taylor till he talked? *What if the Germans know all about the Greifswald raid?*"

Jeffrey made a face and looked away. "Navigator, plot a course for the English Channel."

"Sir?" Lieutenant Sessions said. "Our orders are to transit *north* of Britain."

"They just say to do what *Texas* was supposed to do. We don't have time for that, and we've lost strategic stealth."

"But, Captain," Sessions said, "part of the Channel is barely a hundred feet deep. On a clear day you can see the Dover cliffs from the French beach at Calais!"

"Exactly," Jeffrey said. "Squeezing through there is the last thing the Axis would expect."

Ilse saw Jeffrey look around the CACC. He avoided eye contact with her, and she chided herself for feeling miffed. Besides, she thought he looked pretty silly, with the bulge of a chemical cold-pack under his shirt. What'd Jeffrey do, bruise himself on a stanchion?

"Think of it as a dress rehearsal, people," Jeffrey said. "For when we try to penetrate the Skagerrak and Kattegat."

Ilse heard crewmen inhale sharply. She saw one man grin, as if he'd won a bet, about where *Challenger* was headed. He didn't smile for long.

Sessions walked to the navigation table, and spoke with his senior chief. They studied the digital charts and ran some calculations.

"Captain," Sessions said. "Advise that from our present position, the distance to the mouth of the Skagerrak is two and a quarter times as great if we take the northern route through the Iceland-U.K. gap, compared to running the Channel."

"Exactly," Jeffrey said.

"But the southern route, through the Channel, sir, would require a much slower speed, because of the shallows and the intensity of antisubmarine measures. . . . We won't save any time, and may actually *lose* time."

"Ladies and gentlemen," Jeffrey said. "This ship has an appointment in the Baltic Sea. We need to get there before the upcoming magnetic storm winds down, and for another reason that some of you know, that I can only say is classified. From right now we've barely four days to get in position, and Lord knows if that's soon enough. We *are* going through the Channel, to regain strategic surprise, and we *are* going to make up lost time, because we have to."

Ilse thought of ARBOR, the mole. Was she already dangling from a gallows?

THIRTY MINUTES LATER.

Ilse knocked on Lieutenant Bell's door.

"Come in."

She entered.

"Shut it behind you."

Ilse felt her gut tighten. Bell looked at her as if she were a total stranger.

"The messenger said you wanted to see me." She reached for the guest chair.

"Don't," Bell said. "I'll keep this short and sweet."

"Sir?"

"You were completely out of line in the CACC."

Ilse bristled. "How so?"

"Your remark about a second German submarine."

"But it could be true, couldn't it?"

"*Yes,* it could be true. That long silence you felt so compelled to fill? Everyone in the compartment was thinking that already. Do you have some kind of a patent on undersea tactics? What could you *possibly* accomplish by giving voice to everyone's fears?"

"I, er . . ."

"Exactly. You didn't even *think* of that, *did you?* The submariner community's very tight. Half the people on *Challenger* have, or *had,* friends on *Texas.* You didn't even *think* of the effect you'd have on your shipmates' morale."

Whew. "Did Jeffrey put you up to this?"

"That's *Captain* Fuller to you," Bell snapped. "And *no,* he did not. Discipline is *my* job."

"I, look, I, I want to make a contribution here." Ilse knew she was stammering, and felt angry with herself.

"Don't you have any common sense on when to keep your mouth shut?"

"No, Lieutenant, I'm sorry, that's just too harsh. I'm here for a reason. Lieutenant Sessions talked back to the Captain, just before, in front of everyone."

"First of all, *Miss* Reebeck, you address me as Mister Bell, or *preferably* as XO."

"Well, I didn't know that."

"Second of all, *Lieutenant* Sessions has been in the Navy *ten* years. It's his *job* as navigator to devil's-advocate the Captain. *Your* job is to concentrate on your specific scientific tasks, under the direction of the sonar *officer.* Consider her your boss. Do *nothing* without her prior consent."

"No one told me that."

"Captain Fuller told you that. He said to work with Lieutenant Milgrom. Right?"

Ilse nodded.

"When the captain of a naval ship says something, it's not a request or a suggestion. It's an *order,* dammit."

"Yes, sir." Ilse moved to the door. "May I go now?"

"No. I'll tell you when you're dismissed. You realize, don't you, that you completely violated security back there?"

"Excuse me?"

"The crew is *not* supposed to know exactly where we're going. The same thing that happened to *Texas* could happen to us. RE-CURVE is highly classified. You just blurted it out. *Greifswald.* How careless can you be?"

Ilse hesitated. It all sank in at once. Celebrity syndrome; prima donna. She'd been warned by the chief of the boat, and just ignored it.

"Oh, God."

"Your wardroom privileges are revoked."

"Excuse me?"

"From now on you eat in the enlisted mess. That's all. Get out of here."

Ilse closed the door behind her, in shock. Two crewmen wriggled by. They read her face and looked away. She covered up as best she could and hurried to her stateroom.

THE NEXT DAY, ON DEUTSCHLAND.

"*Still* no contact on *Challenger,* Captain," Ernst Beck said. As ordered, *Deutschland* lurked at the Celtic Shelf, just west of the U.K.

"We can't afford to take the chance they snuck right past us," Eberhard said. "We'll have to try an end-around, to cut Fuller off. Einzvo, have the navigator plot a course for the English Channel."

CHAPTER 14

Ilse changed to pajamas, exhausted from work and her seesaw emotions. Visions of false-color 3-D bathythermograms danced in her head, colliding with probability isobars of early winter pack-ice drift.

She felt *Challenger* speed up.

"Fast, then slow, then fast again, over and over and over."

Kathy, reading a novel in her rack, grunted. "Sprint and drift tactics. It's the only way to get where we're going by the deadline, and have a prayer of not getting killed."

"But isn't it dangerous, going so fast for most of the time? Noisy?"

"Yes. That's why we stop to listen."

"But—"

"Don't say it," Kathy said. "Just don't."

Ilse climbed into her rack, then tried to adjust the covers without banging her elbows or her head. She awkwardly pulled the little curtain closed, then groped and turned off her reading light.

Oh, *God,* it felt good to just lie down and shut out the world.

"G'night, Kathy."

"I missed you at dinner," Kathy said from inside her bunk, with an interrogatory tone. Her light stayed on.

Ilse sighed. "It's a long story."

"I see; please go on."

Ilse realized she couldn't keep it from Kathy forever. *What if Kathy already knew?*

"The XO put me in hack. For shooting my mouth off in Control. He said I have to eat in the enlisted mess."

"I heard, and shame on you for being such a bad girl."

"Are you mocking me?" Ilse said.

Kathy changed her tone. "I was *trying* to cheer you up."

"Sorry."

"The food's the same as in the wardroom, Ilse, and the atmosphere in the enlisted mess is more relaxed."

"I know. It's a mob scene. Teenagers, family men, it's fun to sit with them all. Still, it stings to get yelled at, after everything I've been through with this ship. . . . It seems so *childish*. 'Go to your room.' 'No TV for you tonight.' "

"The XO is teaching you to do your job. Part of your problem is you spend too much of your time with the senior officers."

Ilse hesitated, then almost blushed when comprehension dawned. "This way I get to know the chiefs and other ranks."

"Stop feeling sorry for yourself. Adapt and learn. Fast as you can, is my advice. I said so once before."

"I'm trying. The more I try, the worse it seems to get. I mean, not fitting in. The honeymoon is definitely over."

"Poor baby."

"Ouch."

"What's the worst part of your punishment? Paper napkins instead of cloth when you eat? Give me a break!"

"I guess you're right." Kathy's tone had been sarcastic—was *she* pulling rank? "I feel just awful about that security goof."

"Good. You ought to. You could have gotten people killed. People who relied on you."

Ilse stayed silent.

"Well," Kathy said, "it's not *all* bad, as it turned out. At least not *yet*."

"How so?"

"The crew felt simply horrible about leaving the *Texas* behind."

"The XO said that."

"At least, now they understand *why*."

"The mission?"

"The captain and COB put the word out, after your gaffe. About the missile lab. Crew morale has skyrocketed. Didn't you notice? . . . No, I don't suppose you would. . . . People need to feel needed. They also need to know that fleet commanders do things for good reason."

"Um, so everybody isn't totally mad at me?"

"Now who's being childish? We need all the morale boost we can get, where we're going."

Ilse settled into her rack, mentally numb. She fought with herself, then decided to ask. Kathy was the closest thing to a friend she had on the ship.

"Were you ever disciplined, Kathy?"

"I got my share of bollockings when I was starting out. It's hard to avoid. I told you once already, remember how little training you have for this. Learn from the experience, and put the ship always first, and move on."

"I'll try."

"Try harder. The timeline of personal growth speeds up terribly during war. I sense we're covering the same ground as two days ago."

"That *did* sting."

"Success is not guaranteed," Kathy said. "You have to feel the calling. It's not for everyone."

Yeah, Ilse thought, it's not for everyone. Let's see how far *I* get, one of a hundred twenty ants in a naval anthill, where I'm censured for breaking rules no one even mentioned.

"First thing after breakfast," Kathy said officiously, "we go over halocline-induced horizontal signal loss in the surface wave-mixed isothermal zone. With the shallow bottom and so many wrecks coming up, and the chin-mounted sonar unserviceable, you and I have our work cut out for us."

"Yes, ma'am." Ilse felt the ship slow down again, then bank to port, so the on-watch sonar techs could listen for hostile contacts yet again.

It all just never ends. . . .

Kathy turned off her reading light, plunging Ilse into total darkness.

Ilse waited, hesitated, then said, "G'night, Kathy."

But the only response was snoring. Ilse felt utterly alone, and cold beneath her blankets.

PREDAWN, D DAY MINUS 3.

By 0415 local time Ilse was back in the CACC, as *Challenger* snuck into the English Channel. Ilse was busy integrating her updated version of the METOC data with the ship's latest readings of water temperature and salinity.

She glanced at the nav chart. Her modeling work was falling behind. While she slept, *Challenger* had climbed onto the European continental shelf. Already they were inside the western, widest part of the Channel proper.

Challenger favored the northern, English side, on Ilse's advice. In winter, the prevailing currents here ran east, helping gain precious minutes on the clock. Near the southern, French side of the Channel, because of the jutting Cotentin Peninsula, a gyre formed, and currents ran west.

Ilse saw Kathy watching as she studied once again an overlay of Commander, Submarines, Atlantic's latest data: friendly and enemy minefields in the Channel, Royal Navy safe corridors, and both sides' coastal antisubmarine obstructions. These were constraints that Ilse, as well as *Challenger,* would simply have to respect.

"Remember," Kathy said, "this is all several days old."

Ilse nodded. Submerged without trailing the floating wire antenna, they didn't have the baud rate to get a meaningful update through all the static and jamming, and they didn't have time to linger till they *did* get one. At least, Ilse told herself, the seawater blocking radio also shielded *Challenger* from most effects of solar storm disruption. The ship's magnetometers showed the storm was already starting: strength rating G2 on NASA's space-weather scale. "Moderate." G2 might or might not affect radar satellites and low-altitude magnetic anomaly detection sensor probes.

The surface wave-action showed the wind was from the west. This was good; warm air over cold water made fog. The fog would help hide *Challenger*'s surface hump and Kelvin wake—both giveaways at the surface of her passage through shallow water—especially during the mid portion of her Channel run, which had to take place in daylight.

Ilse ran more calculations. The sea was noisy, but not in the way she expected. The biologics were strangely quiet, even though this area should be good for mackerel, shrimp, and cod. The heavy peacetime shipping traffic had ceased. Instead, besides wind noise and rain and breaking whitecaps, the sonar sounds came mostly from the land, from coastal heavy industry, transmitted through the ground and into the water. England and occupied France, economies fully mobilized—of necessity or by force—were competing hard: to generate power, to dig in and harden surviving resources, and to make and transport matériel of war.

For now, the sounds of battle in the Channel were muted. For Ilse's conceivable future, *Challenger* had no friends. There was nowhere to run, nowhere to hide, if the sub began to draw fire; a trigger-happy Allied vessel or plane might be the first to shoot. Ilse reminded herself what Jeffrey had said, that he counted on luck and surprise. That was all the crew could count on, besides each other and their training and the ship. Ilse began to understand what teamwork really meant.

She glanced around. The CACC was busy. Fire control technicians worked hard to update the tactical plot. A new passive bow sphere contact was announced, Sierra sixteen: a Russian trawler, exercising freedom-of-navigation rights in these international waters, no doubt eagerly spying on both sides. The trawler was noisy on purpose, and would be well lit, to broadcast its neutrality. Ilse called up the data. The trawler's closest point of approach to *Challenger* would be inside five thousand yards.

"Sonar, Oceanographer," Lieutenant Bell said, "give me best course to evade Sierra sixteen." He had the conn.

"Recommend course one eight zero," Ilse said. Due south, away from charted mines. "That would bring us closer to the center of the current gyre. Eddies there make density cells, and chaotic Doppler."

"Concur," Kathy said.

Bell gave helm orders. Meltzer acknowledged and complied. *Challenger* turned.

Ilse listened to Bell confer with Sessions.

"We're losing ground," Bell said. "We have to go faster or we'll miss the tide. . . . Helm, make turns for twenty knots."

"Sir," Kathy said, "if we maintain that speed, as we get shallower we risk the propulsor cavitating."

Just then Jeffrey came into the CACC, looking tired. Ilse realized he'd sensed the change in course and speed—assuming he'd actually been asleep.

Bell gave him a quick update.

"Cavitating, surface wake, and thermal scarring," Jeffrey said, "we have to chance it. Sometimes you just play the percentages, and pray."

SIMULTANEOUSLY, ON DEUTSCHLAND.

Ernst Beck glanced at the navigation plot, as *Deutschland* snuck through the shallow waters ten sea miles due north of Île d'Ouessant, off the coast of occupied France. The ship was entering the English Channel.

It felt strange to be this close to home, and yet have home so far beyond Beck's reach. He pictured the base at Bordeaux, where his family now lived, and the industries of Munich, near his father's farm. Both would be high on the list of Allied targeting priorities, if the A-bombs or even H-bombs started to fly—the high-explosive cruise missiles and bomber raids were bad enough.

It was a very delicate gamble the Putsch leaders tried to play out now, confining atomic war to the high seas, or purely military targets on land in isolated areas, hoping to wear down the enemy's will to resist, hoping to force them to ask for an armistice. The Allies hadn't wrought direct revenge for nuking Warsaw and Tripoli, at least not yet—they'd been too shocked by such Axis blows that opened the war, and too squeamish since then to set off a nuclear warhead of their own in the middle of Europe. Perhaps the Allied leaders quietly agreed, as Kurt Eberhard once cynically put it to Beck, that Warsaw and Tripoli had been the two most expendable cities in the world.

But how long could this precarious balance last?

Beck heard Eberhard speaking with Werner Haffner at the sonar consoles. Beck wondered if *Deutschland*'s presence in the Channel, now that she was being hunted theater-wide, would itself be the wild card that led to the dreaded escalation, to mushroom clouds on London and Berlin, on New York and Johannesburg.

CHAPTER 15

Everyone on *Challenger* was at battle stations. Jeffrey had the conn. He finished his latest coffee, returning the plastic mug to his console's cup holder.

The CACC was rigged for black, the only light the glow of instruments and console screens. Conversation was kept to a bare minimum. *Challenger's* LMRS probe was two thousand yards in front of the ship, scouting for German mines and unreported wrecks, inside the narrow British submarine safe-corridor-of-the-day.

For the last few hours *Challenger* had steamed at a risky nine knots in mid-Channel, where the water was almost two hundred feet deep. Now, with Dover to port and Calais to starboard, barely eighteen nautical miles apart, the depth was half that; Jeffrey'd had to slow, but the fast tide and prevailing current gave them a push. Now, with deadest night above them, things were quiet. They were almost through, into the North Sea.

The magnetometers showed a solar storm strength of G3, what NASA called "strong." Jeffrey wondered if this could make mines go off on their own, including British mines. A manufacturing flaw, or sabotage by Axis agents, or combat damage could never be ruled out. A lot of the mines along here were CAPTORs, which unleashed a

Mark 46 torpedo to chase and destroy its quarry. Many mines lay inside the minimum arming run of *Challenger*'s antitorpedo rockets.

Jeffrey took a deep breath, and tried to ease the tension in his neck and shoulders. He lifted his coffee mug, then remembered it was empty. He opened his mouth to ask the messenger for a refill.

"New passive sonar contact!" Kathy interrupted. "On the starboard wide-aperture array . . . Surface contact, bearing zero nine five, range ten thousand yards." In such terribly shallow water, with the uneven bottom and shoals, detection ranges were unpredictable, and dangerously short.

"Range closing rapidly," Kathy said. "Tonals indicate *multiple Axis diesel engines.*"

"Classification?" Jeffrey snapped. He had no need of caffeine now—adrenaline surged.

"Class one-thirty corvettes! Three, no, *four* one-thirties! Advancing at flank speed in echelon formation, almost forty knots, directly at us!"

"Put it on the speakers," Jeffrey said. He heard the roar of all those diesels, four per ship, and the high-speed churning of many variable-pitch props.

"Those things are shallow draft, but I'm not taking chances. Oceanographer, what's the bottom?"

"Sand and gravel," Ilse said.

"Helm, all stop. Chief of the Watch, bottom the boat."

"Sir," Bell said, "if they spot us we'll be helpless."

"Not entirely. Bottom the boat."

"Captain, advise we use the wide-aperture arrays in active echo suppression and hole plug mode."

"Negative, XO. This close in that won't work well. I'd rather play dead. Let them think we're a wreck, if they spot us." Not that that would help much, Jeffrey knew. Both sides bombed wrecks all the time.

Ernst Beck watched the tactical plot as the squadron of Class 130's passed almost directly overhead. He could hear them through the hull, very easily. He felt as if he could almost reach and touch them.

Give them hell, he projected his thoughts to the corvette sailors, as *Deutschland* followed the German submarine safe corridor near the Out Ruytingen shoal off Belgium.

"New passive contact on the port wide-aperture array," Haffner said.

"What is it, Sonar?" Beck said.

"Multiple lift fans and airscrews . . . four Royal Navy Type two-thousand hovercraft!"

"Armed with Harpoon missiles and lightweight mines," Beck said.

"Hovercraft bearing two eight nine, range ten thousand meters. Signal strength increasing rapidly."

"Hostile contact's course is east-southeast. Type two-thousands making forty knots, on an interception course with our one-thirties."

"We're caught under a mining/countermining skirmish," Eberhard said. "Pilot, all stop. Let us drift with the current while they fight it out."

Jeffrey listened to the melee develop overhead. Fire control technicians tried to track the action.

Jeffrey heard the roaring *whoosh* as Harpoon antishipping missiles launched. The Germans retaliated, also with Harpoons. All contacts showed high bearing rates, and their engines strained deafeningly as they fought to evade.

Missiles struck home with dreadful *whumps*. Ammo and mine stocks blew up, crackling and erupting. Ships sank and men died.

Kathy announced more contacts. British light hydrofoils were moving in from the north to back up the surviving Type 2000 hovercraft. More volleys of missiles took to the air. Now Jeffrey could hear the steady pounding of Axis OTOBreda 76mm cannon. They were answered by Allied 30mm Oerlikons, faster but not as loud. Armor-piercing shells smashed home and burst, or missed and smacked the sea and burst.

Four Royal Navy frigates, *Cornwall*-class, rounded Goodwin Sands, making flank speed, thirty knots. Each one's twin gas turbines screamed louder still, at full military power. Another squadron of Class 130's was tearing west from Calais. Helos lifted from the ships. Their engines and rotors added to the din, as German Lynx fought British Sea Kings in an air war of their own.

More ship-to-ship missiles ripped by overhead, and engines whined and roared and roared and whined from all around, mixed with the clattering, beating roar of the helos. Still the Oerlikons and Bredas clashed.

A Class 130 was hit and blew up instantly, and *Challenger* rocked. The hulk struck the bottom almost at once, somewhere to starboard. A *Cornwall* was hit repeatedly by more Harpoons. It slowed. Another salvo peppered the ship as she beached on Goodwin Sands. Her magazine exploded, killing anyone still alive, and *Challenger* rocked.

Air-to-air missiles flashed between the helos again. More warheads detonated, avgas detonated, flesh and wreckage rained onto the sea.

A Class 130 streaked down *Challenger's* port side, less than a hundred feet away. Jeffrey heard a *slash-splash-splash-splash-splash*.

Mines.

Beck listened to the battle raging to port. *Deutschland* wasn't in the thick of it, but a stray Harpoon might hit the water above, and its warhead equaled a medium-weight torpedo's punch.

The navigator announced the tide was changing, falling, here on the French side of the Dover Strait. Beck knew the Calais tidal range was large, ten meters or more, forcing *Deutschland* toward mid-Channel, closer to the surface fight.

"COB," Jeffrey said, "put out a magnetic field like an *Akula Two*, smartly."

COB acknowledged.

Jeffrey hoped the mines, friendly and enemy alike, would all be programmed to ignore a Russian submarine. COB finished as the German mines landed on the bottom. None exploded, at least so far.

A quintuplet of Class 130's crossed *Challenger's* bow, and there were many more splashes. One of the 130's blew up just to port. Jeffrey heard the noises as its hull broke into pieces. Air boiled to the surface as the pieces tumbled down, and water roared, the ocean flooding in. The pieces thumped to the sand. Something set off a mine.

Jeffrey was torn whether to recover the precious LMRS. It was probably safer where it was. If they lost the fiber-optic wire, they could retrieve it by acoustic link. Two hydrofoils exploded a thousand yards ahead. Their pieces pelted the bottom. More mines exploded, and the fiber optic broke.

The surviving German corvettes began to withdraw, still lobbing Harpoons at the Royal Navy frigates. The frigates answered blow for blow. Their 114mm Vickers dual-purpose guns went into action.

One frigate roared by directly overhead. Jeffrey thought he heard the whine of turret-traversing gear, the clanking of its autoloading ammo train. The big gun fired. In the CACC, mike cords and lighting fixtures jiggled, and too late Jeffrey held his ears.

Another Class 130 was hit off *Challenger*'s port bow, but she barely slowed. She was hit again, and Jeffrey heard secondary explosions. The corvette started sinking, still moving at fifteen knots, right toward *Challenger*. Jeffrey had to move. He dared not go forward or to port because of German mines. He could back up in the safety corridor, completely blind, or take shelter to starboard amid the British mines and German wreckage. With the LMRS cut off, he ordered COB and Meltzer to raise the boat off the bottom and go back one third.

The bow sphere had a perfect view of the latest 130's death throes. Jeffrey heard the roar of flooding again, the sharper roars and cracks and bangs of the frigid sea on red-hot engine blocks. Added was the screech of tortured steel. *Things* inside the 130 still exploded as she hit the bottom hard, blocking *Challenger*'s pathway forward decisively. Another German ship crossed *Challenger*'s stern, disappearing for a moment in the sonar blind spot. Did she drop more mines? Jeffrey ordered all stop.

Kathy announced the *Cornwall*s were launching torpedoes. A dozen lightweight Sting Ray fish dashed at the Class 130's from the flank. Some scored hits, loud metallic *whang*s, followed by more sounds of disemboweled hulls dragged down by gravity. Other fish rushed for the Calais coast, looking for a target, any target.

"Torpedoes in the water!" Haffner shouted. "Bearing two seven zero, range eleven thousand meters. Sting Rays, attack speed forty-five knots!"

"If we fire antitorpedo rockets," Eberhard said, "we'll give ourselves away. *Achtung*, Einzvo, decoy in tube eight. Program it to sound like a Class two-twelve with a damaged screw and bilge pumps running."

"Understood."

"*Los!*"

Beck watched the decoy's track. The Sting Rays picked it up. Not wire guided, they mindlessly converged. One Sting Ray won the race, and set off all the others sympathetically. *Deutschland* vibrated sharply from the multiple concussions. She rolled to port as the shock wave echoed off the Calais shore.

"Captain," Kathy said, "loud explosion bearing zero nine zero, range twenty thousand yards."

"The Sting Rays?" Jeffrey said.

"Confirmed. . . . Sir, we have an ambient and hole-in-ocean submerged contact near the Calais coast, based on echoes from the Sting Ray warheads."

"Is it something on the chart?"

"Negative, sir."

"Size of contact?"

"Wait, please. . . . Appears to be beam on, length approximately three hundred feet."

"Must be a dead Axis corvette," Jeffrey said, "lost in some recent action like this one."

Beck listened as the hydrofoils and hovercraft wove in and out, and the corvettes and frigates thrust and counterthrust. One big ship, which side's Haffner couldn't tell, went down; her magazines exploded underwater.

"Ambient and hole-in-ocean submerged contact," Haffner said, "backlit against the Goodwin Sands."

"Size of contact?" Beck said.

"Appears to be beam on, length one hundred meters."

"A *Cornwall*," Eberhard said, "or a piece of one."

Beck watched the tactical plot, frigates chasing corvettes east. "They're coming in our direction, Captain."

"*First Watch Officer*," Haffner shouted, "new passive sonar contact to starboard! Many inbound aircraft, fast movers bearing one three five! They sound like our Tornado fighter-bombers!"

"Let's get out of here while we still can," Eberhard said. "Pilot, go to one-third speed ahead, RPM's for ten knots."

• • •

"Sir," Kathy said, "new passive sonar contact to port. More inbound aircraft, this time from the west. They sound like Royal Navy Sea Harriers."

"We have to get out of here," Bell said. "This skirmish is getting out of hand."

Jeffrey thought hard. "Sonar, is the acoustic sea state high enough you can spot wrecks and mines on the wide arrays in ambient passive mode?"

"Affirmative, sir! Engine noises providing good illumination."

"Chief of the Watch, recall the LMRS. Bring it back to one hundred yards off the bow."

"Recall the LMRS, aye," COB said.

"Helm, on auxiliary maneuvering units, stand by to slide to starboard into the British mine field." It was the least-bad choice; with the map they'd been given, and with luck, the mine field could be negotiated.

"Understood," Meltzer said.

"Captain," Bell said, "the seas up there will be chaotic for a while. No one will see our surface hump."

"Concur. Helm, as soon as we bypass the new German mines and fresh wrecks, bring us back to the safety corridor. Then go to ahead one third, turns for ten knots."

"Sir." Sessions. "Advise the tide has turned."

"Sir," Meltzer said, "we're drifting backward and our stern is being swung to starboard."

"*Captain,*" Bell urged as he pointed to his screen, "there's a British mine too close. *It's right near our pump-jet.*"

"Helm," Jeffrey snapped, "pivot us the other way using the forward auxiliary thruster *only.*"

Meltzer acknowledged, his voice an octave higher than before; they dared not use the aft thruster so close to the mine, and they dared not use the pump-jet. *Challenger's* heading changed, but she kept drifting crabwise toward the mine. Crewmen shifted nervously in their seats, and glanced at each other wide-eyed.

"There's nothing more we can do but ride it out," Jeffrey said. The forward thruster alone just wasn't strong enough to hold them against the shifting tide. Besides, any other course not blocked by wreckage would take them over a *German* mine.

Jeffrey watched his screens. *Challenger* kept drifting. Jeffrey felt everyone's blood pressure rising higher by the second. As the surface battle roared on in the distance—and downed aircraft and ejection seats and spent shell casings hit the sea—the British mine, sitting on the bottom, passed right under Jeffrey's feet. He stared down at the deck, not daring to breathe, wanting to scream. He waited for the mine to blow and snap the ship in two and kill his crew and ruin everything.

Nothing happened.

Soon *Challenger* was on the move again.

CHAPTER 16

IN THE NORTH SEA

Two hours later, that surface-and-air skirmish left behind and the LMRS probe recovered for a battery charge, Ilse was helping refine *Challenger's* plan for crossing the southern North Sea.

Bell came over and told her to go see the captain. Bell sounded grim.

Ilse went aft and knocked on Jeffrey's door. *What did I do now?*

"Come in!"

Not for the first time lately, Ilse thought Jeffrey looked tired.

"You look tired," Jeffrey said.

It's like we just read each other's minds. "I think everybody's tired, sir." Ilse made sure to use the "sir," but she noticed Jeffrey's attitude was softer now between the two of them in private, more personal, confiding. His shoulders were less stiff, his whole posture more relaxed—she liked his strong, broad shoulders and the well-toned muscles of his forearms and his neck.

"Take a seat. I have bad news."

"What is it?" Ilse said.

"Running so shallow, we picked up a VLF radio message. It took a lot of work to clean up the signal for decryption. ARBOR has been arrested."

Ilse exhaled. "We all saw this coming, didn't we?"

"Yeah," Jeffrey said.

"Do we turn back?"

"No. Her last dead-drop signal said the jigs and dies for mass-producing the missiles are ready at the lab. . . . The mission goes forward. We invoke the contingency plan."

"I thought you'd said there wasn't one."

"I lied. . . . No, I withheld information. For security."

"Oh, God." Everything fell into place. "Don't tell me—"

"Yes. You have to go."

"*Why?*"

"This isn't *my* idea. It's in the written orders. We need someone to break cover inside, and find their way around. You're it."

"What about the SEALs? Chief Montgomery."

"Look," Jeffrey said. "Navy SpecWar language skills emphasize just talking to the locals. Not blending in as one of them."

"But my German isn't perfect, either. I could never pass."

"You won't have to, Ilse. You go as who you are, a gen-u-ine South African Boer person."

"Like a visiting technician?"

Jeffrey nodded. "There's plenty of that going on. It's one more thing this German regime learned from World War Two mistakes: close cooperation with their allies from the get-go. With Japan, the cargo U-boats they sent over were too little too late. Crated jet fighters, V-two rocket parts, uranium oxide . . ."

"Um, I didn't know that." Ilse shifted in her seat, and crossed her legs. "But won't the Germans be expecting us, now ARBOR's caught?"

"Not necessarily, though for sure they'll be on heightened alert. We just have to take the chance she was able to plant that computer worm. Otherwise . . . They've arrested a number of Mossad moles the last few months. There's no reason they'd think ARBOR at Greifswald was special, not right away."

"What if they make her talk?"

"The moles were conditioned against that. The Israelis are state-of-the-art in counterinterrogation techniques."

Ilse shivered. "Short of suicide, you mean."

"You'll have to start hard workouts, and refresher training on the Draeger and the weaponry, at once. Sit in on Clayton's briefings from now on, rehearsals, all of that. You know the drill."

There was a knock on the door. Jeffrey looked annoyed.

"Come in!"

It was the messenger of the watch.

"Sir, the XO's compliments. He reports the shocks from our battle with the two-twelve and two-fourteen, and running repairs since then, appear to have freed the jammed foreplanes. He requests permission to deploy them, for enhanced maneuverability."

"Tell him negative. I'm afraid they may jam again while deployed. Keep them retracted."

The messenger, for confirmation, repeated the response. He left.

Jeffrey turned to Ilse. "The foreplanes deployed could make us unstable at very high speed."

"Oh." Ilse liked it when Jeffrey explained things to her.

"Sorry," Jeffrey said.

For the interruption, or for getting irritated by it?

"There's something else, Ilse. Your Government-in-Exile talked with the Pentagon . . . I know it's small compensation for having to risk your neck. You've been granted the assimilated rank of lieutenant in the Free South African Navy."

Ilse smiled. "What's that mean, exactly?"

"Pay and privileges equal to a naval officer of said rank."

"Have I been drafted?"

"No. Technically you're still a civilian."

"Can I eat in the wardroom again?"

"You need to ask the XO. I can't overrule him. I mean, I could but I won't."

"Um, okay."

Jeffrey laughed. "I'm sure it'll be just fine. Bell knew the contingency plan all along."

Aha. "That's why he was hard on me, wasn't it? To harden, condition me."

"Bell's in charge of training, and I sure know he likes to seize the initiative there."

Jeffrey grew distant for a moment, and Ilse sensed things between him and Bell she didn't understand—things in the recent past that were resolved now. But then, she realized, some of the things between her and Jeffrey were resolved now too, the censure for her bloopers, his standoffishness before.

"Look at it this way," Jeffrey said. "If we make it back from Greifswald, you can even have unlimited seconds on dessert."

The two of them made eye contact, and held it. Ilse fought down a grin. Jeffrey fought down a grin. Finally Jeffrey glanced at the bulkhead, then shuffled papers on his desk.

Ilse sensed the meeting was over. She stood up.

Jeffrey hesitated. He grew serious. "Please don't go, Ilse. . . . There's something else I want to talk to you about."

"What?" He seemed almost . . . needful?

"The message said *Deutschland*'s been spotted in the North Atlantic."

Ilse had to sit down again. "I thought she was headed for Canada. The briefing papers you got at Cape Verde, they said so." That courier package.

"That's what I was *told*. . . . And to think I felt *relieved* that *Deutschland* was so far away, after worrying about meeting her any moment when we stalked those U-boats." Jeffrey shook his head, annoyed with himself. "*Deutschland*'s supposed-attack on Canada was a ruse, which our side fell for. By now she could be almost anywhere. Including through the Greenland-Iceland-U.K. gap, into the Norwegian Sea. She may be damaged, heading home for repairs. *Maybe*."

"You seem worried," Ilse said. Jeffrey clearly wanted to share his concern with her; Ilse was worried enough herself. She came to better understand the awful pressure Jeffrey must be under constantly.

"I know *Deutschland*'s captain. Kurt Eberhard." Jeffrey said the name with disgust.

"He's good?" In spite of the tension, she could see another barrier between her and Jeffrey was being lowered; he was speaking to her now *as* Jeffrey, not as Captain Fuller. And soon they'd be off the ship together, on another SEAL raid. . . .

"Yeah, he's good. It seems he trained on Russian SSNs for several years before the war. Up under the ice cap, off of U.S. naval bases, trailing our boomers, you name it. . . . We worked together, three or four years back." Ilse listened, letting Jeffrey talk, unburden himself. "He was an up-and-comer in the *Bundesmarine,* the peacetime German Navy. A real charmer when he wants to be. This combined assignment in Washington, he had free rein in our group. . . . He hates my guts."

"Sounds like it's mutual."

"Well . . ." Jeffrey looked right at her. "Let's just say, we both had our egos, and in the case of him and me, opposites did not attract."

. . .

After lunch, Ilse sat at her console with sonar headphones on. Kathy and her techs were busy. The active wide arrays were working hard to cloak *Challenger,* suppressing ambient echoes and plugging holes in the ocean to whichever flank seemed most threatening. *Challenger* hid along the chaotic boundary between two major currents: the warm vestiges of the Gulf Stream, flowing east through the Dover Straits, and the frigid Nordic Current coming south from the Arctic Circle. In the confused sonar conditions where the currents met and fought, a sub-on-sub encounter could occur with lethal suddenness.

Ilse put down her SEAL raid briefing files for a moment, and strained to listen on the bow sphere. She was depressed by what she heard. There were no biologics. The mid-North Sea, once teeming with life, host to a thriving fishing industry, instead was now a barren desert. There were no shrimp or crab or lobster, no plaice or haddock or herring or cod, at least not alive.

Above the ship was a heavy oil slick. It went on and on, for countless miles. The thick sludge was good for stealth, Jeffrey said. It blocked airborne LIDAR. It smoothed the sea to hide *Challenger's* surface hump. It suppressed the surface capillary effects of her internal Bernoulli wave, which might otherwise be picked up by special radar. It also suffocated life.

There was no oxygen transport by air/water wave-mixing now. There was no plankton photosynthesis, the first step in the upper ocean's food chain. There was only darkness at high noon, persistent petrotoxins, and mass death.

Right now *Challenger* was passing one of the drilling platforms, several miles to port. This one tapped natural gas. Before the war the gas had been brought to the U.K. by seabed pipelines. Now, the pipelines and most of the gas and oil rigs everywhere were wrecked. Some of the emergency shutdown valves had been destroyed.

This particular natural gas platform still stood above the water, badly damaged. The gas burned uncontrollably. A huge flare rose hundreds of feet in the sky. Ilse could hear it hiss and roar on passive sonar; broken equipment clanked from the wind and waves and currents. The flame was virtually smokeless, Ilse knew—natural gas was clean. It burned day and night, as it had for months. She'd seen pictures of it on the news.

The platform fire is like an eternal flame, she told herself. A memorial to the dead, millions and billions of sea creatures, animals and plants, invertebrates, crustaceans, fish and mammals and birds.

Ilse, once more, thought about where she had to go in the Baltic, what she had to do there. Last time, Durban, it was for her brother and her family, and her rage had made her strong.

Again she felt the rage mount up. *Greifswald.* A searing instant of nuclear revenge. God *damn* the Axis for what they were doing to the world.

After dinner was cleared and his officers left, Jeffrey sat in his chair at the head of the wardroom table. Another afternoon of hard physical training and weapons drill was behind him. He'd've rather had an additional month to prepare. *Ain't gonna happen.* Now, Jeffrey rested.

Shajo Clayton's group filed in. Ilse returned from the head. Clayton opened the meeting.

Jeffrey watched as Clayton surveyed the room.

"I know some of you aren't happy about working with a civilian," Clayton said. "I know this violates our basic doctrine."

Some of the enlisted SEALs murmured. Chief Montgomery sat there stone-faced.

"Then let me disabuse you fast," Clayton said. "Miss Reebeck's been places, done things with me, that would've earned a man in uniform a Silver Star. She knows when to keep her head down, and when to shoot, and when she shoots she doesn't miss."

The three SEALs who survived Durban nodded.

"Besides," Clayton said, "there's no way we can pull this mission off without her help. *Do I make myself perfectly clear?*"

None of the SEALs from *Texas* said anything.

"You heard the lieutenant," Montgomery bellowed. "Did he make himself perfectly clear?"

Jeffrey had to smile inside. The SEALs left no doubt whatsoever they got the message now.

"Welcome to the team, Miss Reebeck," Montgomery said. The crisp, lively way he said it left no doubt *he* was sincere.

"Thank you," Ilse said to them all.

Jeffrey rose to get more coffee, on purpose, body language meant to get the others to relax. He sat down again.

Clayton turned to Ilse. "There are things you need to know *now*, Ilse, including the unknowables. It'll be important for your situational awareness."

She nodded.

"The rest of you pay close attention," Montgomery said in a threatening almost-whisper; Ilse thought he was even scarier when he whispered like that than when he raised his voice. Then Montgomery grinned, as if to say to his guys, No hard feelings.

Ilse cleared her throat. "I thought of some questions since Captain Fuller told me I have to go. The way my mind works and I learn, it'd be best if I could ask them first. Later, you can fill in anything else . . . if that's all right."

"Perfect," Clayton said.

"First of all, how do we really know ARBOR's been arrested? Maybe the message was a deception, sent by the Germans in our code to throw us off. You know, if they *can't* find the mole but they're afraid of us attacking."

"Let me field that," Jeffrey said. "There are authentication keys and backstop procedures for one-way comms to U.S. Navy SSNs and SSBNs. A lot's changed since the days of the Walker spy ring. . . . It's all top-secret, of course, like the name ARBOR itself. Let's just say certain items have to be inserted at the flag-officer level, an admiral personally I mean, for a message of this importance. At our end, everything checked out."

"Okay," Ilse said, "but there's something I don't get. If ARBOR had such high access at the lab, why didn't *she* just smuggle out the computer records to begin with? Why the rigmarole of handing them off to us?"

"May I, Captain?" Clayton said.

Jeffrey nodded.

"They have tight security, Ilse. People would be searched."

"What about those new holographic cubes? You could swallow one. You know, body pack."

"The searches are *very* thorough, imaging sensors that see under your clothes, others that look through your body. The critical hardware and software's heavily restricted within the installation, and completely isolated from the outside world. They use obsolescent magnetic hard-drive storage on purpose: it's bulky, hard to conceal, easy to erase by making you walk through an electromagnetic scrambler field."

"I suspect," Jeffrey added, "that if they even *find* you with unauthorized storage media or read/write units, they string you up."

"Then how did ARBOR manage to communicate at all?"

"Old-fashioned spy tradecraft," Clayton said, "from long before the microchip."

"Think of her as a datalink with an ultralow baud rate," Jeffrey said. "Only minimal information could pass either way, and very slowly."

"Okay," Ilse said. "That works for me. And I see why *we* need to sneak in covertly with the A-bombs. They wouldn't get through the front door. . . . Next question. I know the lab's supposed to be hardened against atomic attack. But it's tough for me to believe the U.S. doesn't have some conventional ground penetrator round that could pulverize the place."

Clayton sighed. "Beyond the fact that if we blew it up long distance, we'd lose the intel?"

"We lose the intel now! You can't expect *me* to hack their systems. I wouldn't know where to begin!"

"Calm down," Jeffrey said. "We didn't *know* ARBOR'd be arrested. *You* can still perform an invaluable visual recon."

"Visual recon, okay, right," Ilse said primly.

Again, Jeffrey had to smile inside. She's a cool one.

"Anyway, Ilse," Clayton said, "the roof is cleverly designed. Multiple layers of tungsten spikes, spaced composite armor, prestressed concrete and steel, explosion chambers vented to the atmosphere. Designed to break up gun-bomb fission warheads, deflect kinetic energy, set off H.E. munitions shallow so they just blow into the air, and incendiaries burn out harmlessly. The last few years, a lot of countries constructed places like that."

"Look," Jeffrey said. "In World War Two, the Nazis built bombproof U-boat bases all along the French Atlantic coast. They used a seven-layer roof system, including a predetonator superstructure, and reinforced concrete, and voids. The subs went in and out through three-foot-thick steel blast doors. . . . Despite what you may have seen in old war movies, the Allies never once really damaged a single pen. They're all still standing, being used again."

"Sixty-five years later?" Ilse said incredulously.

"*Yes,* sixty-five years later. And if you're wondering why they don't use hollowed-out caverns in the Alps or Harz Mountains for their weapons work, they *do*. Some of *that* dates back to Nazi times. There just isn't space enough for everything."

Ilse hesitated. "I have another issue, about the lab's hardening against nuclear attack. That's from the *outside,* correct?"

"Right so far," Clayton said.

"But this lab needs inlets and outlets for cooling water and air. When we detonate the bombs, won't the blast shoot through the openings?"

"Smart question," Jeffrey said. "The utility paths, air vents or whatever, are all protected by ultrafast-acting hardened shutters. They're triggered under local battery power by sensitive seismometers. When the A-bombs go off, a tremor will arrive first through the concrete and steel of the building, which have very high rates of sound transmission. That trips the seismometers. By the time the blast itself arrives, through the inside air, or through the fluid in the cooling pipes, or eating through the concrete, the shutters will've closed."

"It's just like our own modern hardened installations," Clayton said. "That much about the lab we know."

Jeffrey touched Clayton's shoulder. "We *suspect.* As the rules-of-engagement guy, that's one thing I have to check."

Ilse made eye contact with Jeffrey. "What if you decide the atomic demolition rules of engagement aren't satisfied?"

"We do as much damage as we can by conventional means, then fight our way out."

"What if we can't escape?"

"We surrender."

Ilse's eyes widened. She shook her head hard. "I'd be hanged."

"Everybody," Jeffrey said. "This installation *must* be destroyed. The orders say we have to go in. They don't say we have to come out."

"But, but, but why doesn't the U.S. Air Force or the RAF just paralyze the place, by knocking out its power supply?"

Clayton laughed. "Ilse, this isn't Iraq or Kosovo. For years, the Germans worked to protect their national power grid. A lot of trunk high-tension lines were buried underground, as part of the so-called Green movement, or at least that was the cover story. The open-air wires are heavily insulated against carbon-fiber weapons, and the power plants themselves are sealed. High-speed switches shunt power right past any point that's been disrupted, while crack emergency crews make quick repairs. Redundancy's built in."

"At this point," Jeffrey said, "Germany's practically turned electricity into a cottage industry. Every key installation has its own backup generators, just in case, a lot of them natural-gas powered. They get the natural gas from Russia, via pipeline through Eastern Europe. Like everything Russian, it's strictly off-limits to attack, by the Joint Chiefs' global ROEs. And speaking of Green, the Axis is *really* into alternate energy sources now, like solar and wind power, and the tides. And conservation, of course."

Ilse digested it all. "I have a different kind of question. What if ARBOR didn't get to plant the computer worm that's supposed to help us get in? What if the Germans found it and erased it? What if they're waiting for us?"

Jeffrey leaned forward. "Then the team is tasked to fight our way inside best we can, and if I say so, set off the A-bombs under fire."

CHAPTER 17

PREDAWN, D DAY MINUS 1.

The messenger woke Jeffrey as ordered at 0320 local. Jeffrey showered and dressed, and stepped into the CACC at 0328. The messenger was waiting with a mug of hot black coffee. He guided Jeffrey's hand to the mug in the dark.

After Jeffrey had taken a few sips, Lieutenant Willey said, "Good morning, Captain." Willey had the conn.

Jeffrey took a deep gulp while his eyes adapted to the rig-for-black. As he thought about his task this morning, his drowsiness vanished, replaced by a tightness in his chest.

"Morning, Engineer. How's the leg?" Willey sat sideways to the command console, since the cast kept him from bending his left knee.

"Not slowing me down much, sir."

"Good. Good."

"I'm real glad I never got off the ship at Cape Verde, Captain. They'd've never let me come."

Jeffrey chuckled. He took the right seat at the console. He studied the situation inside and outside the boat. On his backlit screen he read the digital log entries made since he'd turned in four hours ago. While he slept, it had begun to rain. This added some broadband noise, mostly across the 100-to-1000 hertz acoustic band, where detection ranges here were longest. This would help cloak *Challenger* on conventional passive sonar, but such cloaking cut both ways.

Satisfied, Jeffrey turned to Willey.

"I have the conn," Jeffrey said.

"You have the conn."

"This is the captain. I have the conn."

"Aye, aye," the watchstanders said. Jeffrey heard Ilse's voice, too. *Doesn't she ever sleep?* He listened to Willey hobbling aft, and called up the nav chart and the gravimeter.

Challenger lurked, almost touching the bottom, in one hundred ten feet of water, hidden from the nearby Denmark coast by Jutland Bank. The southern tip of Norway, at Kristiansand, lay sixty nautical miles due north. Halfway there, the seabed dropped off steeply, into an ancient geological feature, the Norwegian Trough, fifteen hundred feet deep or more. Jeffrey's night orders had been to make for the Bank, not the Trough, to stick to the unexpected.

The North Sea oil slick was left behind. As Ilse predicted, though, a recent gale had stirred the local bottom muck, and water turbidity was high, shielding the boat from enemy airborne LIDAR. Wave action mixing, and the slow current out of the Skaggerak mouth gaping just ahead, helped obscure *Challenger's* minimal thermal signature. Ilse had explained last night at dinner, in that sexy way she talked shop, that the half-knot current from the Skaggerak was the net effect of rain and snow on land: River runoff from ten countries on the land-locked Baltic had nowhere else to go.

Anyway, the current helped cool *Challenger's* reactor while the ship held position on autohover. As long as she didn't move, she made scant surface wake anomaly. The solar magnetic storm was stronger than forecast, already at G5, "extreme." No one would spot the ship's magnetic anomaly effects. Based on her success in shallow water so far, Jeffrey began to think *Challenger* could go anywhere, do anything.

It was a good thing, too, because their next task seemed impossible: Penetrate the German defenses at the entrance to the Skaggerak.

The deeper water to port was very thoroughly mined, with bottom-influence German CAPTORs. The mine field's extent was announced by the Germans, according to international law. The CAPTORs were known by U.S. Naval Intel to be switched on and off by encrypted acoustic signal and fiber-optic link, to constantly change the German submarine safety corridor. The corridor itself was patrolled by Class 212 diesel/AIPs, and *Rubis* SSNs. Not frontline boats against the best the U.S. and U.K. had, they were more of a submarine Home Guard, but dangerous.

The shallow water directly ahead of *Challenger* was blocked by a long line of sunken merchant-ship hulks, put there by the Germans, backed by high-tensile-strength antisubmarine nets. The nets were laced with shaped-charge contact mines that could do *Challenger* terrible harm. Jeffrey knew all about them, because he could *see* them, through the link from the LMRS. The picture was virtual, built up by low probability of intercept, frequency agile, super-high-frequency mine-hunting sonar. COB controlled the LMRS; he and Meltzer had the watch.

There was one narrow lane left open into the Baltic, along the forty-meter curve, for German and neutral ships to pass in and out, safe from underwater mines. This lane was thoroughly protected, by German patrol craft, and by naval guns on concrete caissons in the water, backed by antiship cruise missiles and antisubmarine aircraft based on land in hardened revetments.

Jeffrey knew there was no point in sinking the patrol craft, though it'd be easy. They were expendable to begin with, trip wires to give main forces warning of any intruder. The three-hundred-ton craft lacked sonar, but Jeffrey was sure the area was wired with sensitive hydrophones, ones that would test *Challenger*'s quieting to the hilt. There would be no way to know if Jeffrey's command had been detected and localized, till the ship came suddenly under attack; maybe they were being watched right now.

No, Jeffrey wasn't happy. *Challenger* was already three hours behind schedule. Jeffrey ordered battle stations. Almost instantly, Bell arrived. Kathy Milgrom arrived, too, to supervise the sonar supervisor, a senior chief. Kathy looked chipper, but thinner, maybe from overwork.

"Sir," Bell said, "all stations ready for action."

"Very well, Fire Control. Helm, make your course zero four five." Northeast. "Ahead one third, make turns for four knots."

"Make my course zero four five, aye, sir," Meltzer said. "Ahead one third, turns for four knots, aye."

Jeffrey worked best under pressure. Aiming right at the Germans, something would come to him.

"Captain," Kathy said, "new passive contact on the port wide-aperture array."

"Classification?"

"Appears to be a convoy of merchant ships. Estimate seven in number. Escorts too, sound like *Göteborg*-class Swedish guided-missile patrol craft. Two of them, sir."

"They're small," Bell said, "three hundred eighty tons, but well armed, including four deck-mounted ASW torpedo tubes."

"More military screw-counts," Kathy called out, "same bearing and range. . . . A pair of *Landsort*-class mine hunters, sweeping in front of the convoy."

"Not a direct threat," Bell said, "but they can plant mines as well as sweep them."

"Faint contacts on acoustic intercept," Kathy said. "Picking up scattered mine-hunting sonar now, five hundred twenty-five kilohertz, consistent with *Landsort*-class Thomson-CSF hull-mounted systems."

"Very well, Sonar and Fire Control," Jeffrey said. "The Swedish Navy must have met their merchies in the Norwegian Sea, in international waters. Now they're making sure they get through unmolested. The Skagerrak's the only access Sweden has in and out of the Baltic." The minesweeping escort was needed. A German mine might break loose, or the Brits may have secretly planted their own.

"Sir," Bell said, "recommend we try to follow the convoy through the Axis defenses."

"I was thinking that," Jeffrey said.

Over the CACC speakers, Jeffrey listened to the sonar broadband in quadraphonic: throbbing, churning, pinging, plus creaking and clanking from sunken hulks. There was also a clattering, beating roar: helicopters.

"Captain," COB said as he eyed the feeds from the LMRS. "Those helos are using dipping LIDAR to delouse the convoy."

"That's what I was afraid of," Jeffrey responded. The mercury-bromide lasers, dunked to avoid the problem of sea-surface interference, were looking for a reflection off something big underwater, or a *lack* of ambient backscatter due to something big and painted black.

"So much for the age-old trick," Bell said, "sneaking in under a merchant ship, sir."

Jeffrey was too disappointed to speak. He grunted.

"They must be on heightened alert," Bell said, "because of this magnetic storm."

Or worse, Jeffrey wondered—because of ARBOR and Greifswald?

"Sir," Bell said, "from the pattern on the tactical plot, I'm starting to think the Lynx aren't checking under the Swedish warships, just the merchies."

"Interesting," Jeffrey said. "We know the Swedes are aggressively neutral, even though they sell the Axis iron ore and arms. Could be they don't want the Germans getting too close, snooping on their naval assets. . . . So, let's put ourselves under the trailing *Göteborg*-class instead."

"We're twice as long as she is, Captain."

"Oceanographer, what's water turbidity now?"

Ilse typed on her keyboard. She cleared her throat. "On-hull sensors indicate a one-foot white Secchi reference disk will disappear at sixteen feet depth, Captain."

"The murky water will hide us from prying eyes, XO. At slow speed our wake effects should blend in nicely." Jeffrey spoke to Sessions, then gave the helm orders to close in behind the patrol craft.

"Blade-rate change," Kathy said, "on the *Göteborg*s and the *Landsort*s! Flank-speed blade rates! Rapid, repeated aspect changes!"

"Crap," Jeffrey said.

"They're one step ahead of us," Bell said. "They're much more nimble than we are, too."

Jeffrey nodded. "Dancing a high-speed jig, to prevent a sub from using them to infiltrate. They mean it, preserving neutrality."

Jeffrey helplessly watched the tactical plot and LMRS data. The sanitized merchant ships filed into the entrance lane, then the Swedish minesweepers and patrol craft all zipped through. The antisubmarine boom slid closed.

"All right," Jeffrey said, "we'll have to go in the hard way, through the Norwegian Trough and the deep-water mines."

"Captain," Bell said, "that'll take us fifty nautical miles out of our way, north and then back south again. It'll put us hours more be-hind."

"I know," Jeffrey said.

"New passive broadband contact on the bow sphere," Kathy reported. "Submerged contact! Designate Sierra thirty-four, bearing three five five, range eight thousand yards."

Jeffrey's heart raced. What he'd dreaded most was happening: a sudden, close encounter with an Axis sub, in Axis waters not as deep as *Challenger* was long.

"Mid-spectrum narrowband, harmonics of reduction gears and cooling pumps. Contact is nuclear powered!"

"What *class?*" Jeffrey said.

"Impossible to tell! It must be bows-on to us! Adverse range and aspect angle to pick up definitive tonals!"

"Helm," Jeffrey snapped, "make your course two six five, then all stop."

Meltzer acknowledged. The ship turned left, and her way came off.

"Anything on the starboard wide array *now?*"

"Affirmative, redesignate contact Master thirty-four. Contact is closing, a noisy one, sir, conjecture it's a *Rubis* class. Still no good tonals below one hundred hertz."

"We'll sit still to keep down our self-noise for you."

"Captain," Bell said, "Master thirty-four's course appears to be one three zero. She's practically on a collision course with us."

"Mechanical transient," Kathy said.

"What was it?"

"Possible weapon launch preparations."

"Fire Control," Jeffrey barked, "make tube five ready in all re-spects." Tube five held a conventional Mark 48 ADCAP. "Firing point procedures, tube five, on Master thirty-four. Open the outer—"

"Captain, do not fire," Kathy shouted. "Master thirty-four is a Russian Delta-four!"

"Are you *sure?*"

"Confirmed! Contact aspect change. Clear near-infrasonic tonals now."

Christ, Jeffrey told himself, *I almost started World War III.*

"What's a Russian boomer doing *here*?" Bell wondered.

"Increased flow noise and cavitation," Kathy said. "The Delta-four has gone to periscope depth."

"Whatever it is," Jeffrey said, "it can't be good."

"Sir," Kathy continued, "Master thirty-four is doing a main ballast blow. . . . Master thirty-four is surfacing. . . . Winch sounds. Master thirty-four retracting towed array."

"Curiouser and curiouser," Jeffrey said.

"She's going into the Baltic," Bell said. "It makes sense. Submarines are supposed to surface for the Skaggerak. She *needs* to, sir, she's *huge,* five hundred feet from stem to stern. On the surface she can safely make fifteen knots."

"XO," Jeffrey said, "I just had a wild idea."

"Uh, I think I know what you're going to say."

"Chief of the Watch, extend the foreplanes." COB acknowledged.

"People," Jeffrey said, "we've found our free ride in. With that Delta's heavy self-noise and her less-than-wonderful passive sonars, they'll never know we're there."

Jeffrey smiled, *Now* this *is using the element of surprise.*

FOURTEEN HOURS LATER.

Ilse grabbed a catnap in her rack, then had some pizza, and now was back at her console. She eyed the speed log—thirteen knots. The water depth was a harrowing 122 feet. *Challenger* still enjoyed her concealment right under the Delta, which Kathy's people hours ago identified as the *K-117,* commissioned in 1990. Fortunately, though much longer than *Challenger,* the Delta was slightly narrower— Jeffrey said it wore an ugly hunchback for its missiles, aft of the sail. This gave the Delta shallow draft for a boomer, providing *Challenger* a bit more headroom. Fortunately, the seas had calmed and came from astern; the Delta didn't roll and pitch much.

The available headroom was badly needed by *Challenger*'s ship-control station. The piggyback ride of the two submarines produced both suction and drift effects, some predictable, some not. COB and Meltzer, relieved for a head call and sleep and food, were back and had their hands full. *Challenger* shimmied and vibrated constantly. Even with the sonar speakers off, the machinery noise from the Delta with his two reactors, his thrusting through the seas and surface cavitation of twin screws, were noticeable through the hull.

It gave Ilse the creeps to be so close to another vessel, especially one whose main weapons had a single purpose: to unleash dozens of megatons on some foreign country, if deterrence failed. Ilse figured the yield of just one of those MIRVed ICBMs exceeded all the kilotons set off so far in the Berlin-Boer tactical nuclear war.

The first half of this chilling journey took both subs northeast, the entire length of the Skagerrak, some one hundred twenty nautical miles. The Axis safe-shipping route skirted the Norwegian Trough, and Jeffrey had ordered COB to send the LMRS into it, to get a partial map of the German mine fields. *K-117* bypassed the Swedish convoy in the wide part of the Skagerrak.

Now, *Challenger* and *K-117* headed south-southeast, beyond the bulk of German mines. The LMRS was retrieved, once more recharging its batteries. The ships were two thirds through the narrow Kattegat, itself a hundred twenty nautical miles from end to end, studded with islands and shoals. The two subs were six miles from the Swedish coast now, as the Delta exercised his right of peaceful passage in the navigable channel. Several times while in the Kattegat, *Challenger* had had to quickly sidestep, when the water got too shallow, and hide just to seaward of the Delta.

Kathy's voice brought Ilse to the present.

"I need another update of your projected salinity gradients."

"Working now."

Ilse knew just how important accurate data was, especially for predicting underwater sound speed and attenuation loss. Hiding under the Delta presented one big problem: The Russian sub's fathometer probed downward, and its mine-avoidance sonar—NATO code name Mouse Roar—searched constantly ahead.

Challenger blocked the Delta's look-down fathometer whenever it tried to take soundings.

The solution, easier said than done, was to detect its emissions using the acoustic-intercept hydrophones mounted on *Challenger*'s sail. Then, Kathy's staff reprogrammed their under-ice look-up sonar transducers to suppress the real return using active out-of-phase. Instead they sent a bogus echo, at the correct frequency and with a perfect time delay and decibel reduction, to give the men in *K-117* an accurate reading of depth, and the impression there was nothing between them and the bottom but water.

Jeffrey had joked that this made it okay to exploit the Delta. The global ROEs forbade *threatening* a Russian vessel. *Challenger* was actually *helping*. Bell was very uncomfortable, and wanted to enter his formal objection in the log to cover his ass. But he quickly thought better of it, and got into the spirit of things.

Ilse just hoped they knew what they were doing.

Besides, fair is fair. The look-forward Mouse Roar pings helped *Challenger*, too. Her mine-avoidance hydrophones on the front of the sail intercepted them, so the CACC crew could watch the bottom for obstructions without radiating.

Ilse checked the nav chart again. They'd just skirted several known wrecks to starboard, and the Stora Middlegrund shoal lay further off in that direction. Above her head, the Delta hissed and whirred and thrummed. Again she thought of all those hydrogen bombs.

"Captain," Sessions said from the nav table, "pings stolen from the Mouse Roar indicate several more wrecks to starboard and port, dead ahead and not on our charts." Bottom-mapping for navigation was his job.

"Confirmed," Kathy said. "Wreck seeping and settling noises."

"Very well, Nav and Sonar." Jeffrey called up the virtual imagery. "Detritus from a recent Royal Air Force raid, maybe." He saw a hummock, a bump, in the bottom terrain—overhead clearance would be tight.

Challenger topped the hummock.

"Captain," Sessions shouted, "more debris dead ahead inside the shipping lane!"

Jeffrey saw it, too. "Helm, can we maneuver past?"

"Negative," Meltzer said. "Insufficient lateral clearance due to wreckage."

"Master thirty-four blade-rate unchanged," Kathy said.

"He isn't slowing," Bell said. "*He* has plenty of room."

"Sir," Meltzer said, "*our momentum's too great*. Advise back two thirds smartly or we'll hit an obstruction!"

Jeffrey thought fast. A quick reverse would make the pump-jet cavitate. The Delta would hear. He studied the screens.

"Maintain course and speed. Take us through. We can make it."

"*Captain,*" Bell said. Jeffrey ignored him.

Meltzer and COB struggled at their controls. There was barely six feet between *Challenger*'s sail and the Delta now. There was less than that between *Challenger*'s keel and the mass of tangled steel.

Water squeezed between the two subs' rounded bows forced *Challenger* down. Meltzer pulled up to keep from shredding the sonar dome and making a terrible datum.

Challenger bucked hard.

Jeffrey saw COB reach for the collision alarm.

"Belay that!" Too much noise.

Challenger's sail, hardened for under-ice operation, kissed the Delta's belly with a thud.

Jeffrey's heart almost stopped. He waited for damage reports. He waited for the Russian captain to react: All he need do was dash to one side and signal for help. The Swedes and Germans would finish *Challenger* off.

"No blade-rate or aspect change on the Delta," Kathy said.

"We're past the obstructions," Sessions said.

Jeffrey shook his head, more wide awake than he *ever* wanted to be. "They must have thought they hit some bobbing debris, neutrally buoyant like waterlogged wood, missed by the Mouse Roar."

In unison, twenty people in the CACC breathed again.

Jeffrey told himself this was *Challenger*'s first collision at sea. "Assistant Navigator, record in the deck log that I take full responsibility for this mishap. Note that the helmsman and chief of the watch did their jobs well."

Jeffrey went back to watching his screens. He wondered how Devron TWELVE—*Challenger*'s squadron—and Group TWO—the commanding rear admiral—and the higher-ups would react to this part of his patrol report . . . assuming he lived to file one. Jeffrey blushed. *What would Captain Wilson think?*

Half an hour later, Kathy reported, "Master thirty-four aspect change. Master thirty-four is turning to starboard."

Jeffrey eyed the chart. "Don't follow. The water there's too shallow."

"Why's he heading *that* way?" Bell said. "The route through the Great Belt channel's twice as long as the run due south."

"Helm, make turns for four knots. Let the Delta pull away from us."

Meltzer acknowledged. Jeffrey heard the boomer's twirling screw slice overhead. His rudder would come very close to *Challenger's* sail.

"I *think*, XO," Jeffrey said when the Delta was past, "he's not going to St. Petersburg after all. He's heading for *Kiel*."

Bell sputtered. "What's a Russian boomer doing visiting one of the biggest German naval bases?"

"I doubt it's a transfer of ownership. The Russians wouldn't go *that* far. . . . No, I'll bet some of her missile silos are full of high-value cargo. Strategic metals, spare parts for the Russian weapons the Germans have already bought . . ."

"They expect to keep this a *secret*?"

"They know about the solar storm, too," Jeffrey said. "Any spy satellite that didn't shut down by now would've fried. . . . By the time this storm is past, he'll be underway again, either back into the North Sea or submerged in the Baltic proper."

"It's outrageous," Bell said. "How can they call themselves neutral, pulling an act like *this*?"

"Their H-bombs and ICBMs, that's how."

"Sirs," Kathy said, "think of Churchill and Roosevelt, with Lend-Lease before Pearl Harbor."

Touché, Jeffrey thought. While still officially neutral, FDR gave the Brits fifty old destroyers. "Meanwhile, folks, we just lost our umbrella, and we have thirty miles to go before we can drop off the mini-sub. . . . Plus, as a belligerent, we're violating Swedish neutrality ourselves."

Jeffrey ordered the helm to hold position on autohover. Now that the Delta was clear, he wanted time for the sonar and target tracking teams to update the tactical plot.

"New contact on the bow sphere and starboard wide array," Kathy said. "Range and bearing consistent with Master thirty-four."

"What is it?"

"A ship's whistle, sir." A foghorn.

"Good." Fog meant visibility would be poor. "We'll give the fog more time to thicken." Jeffrey was suspicious. Except for the Delta, and an unknown German warship distant and drawing away from *Challenger,* it was too quiet up there.

"*Sir,*" Kathy said. "New passive contact on the port wide-aperture array. . . . Surface contact, in our baffles, contact held by echoes off the shore."

"Where is it?" Jeffrey said.

"Wait, please. . . . Best estimate bearing three eight five, range four thousand yards. Signal strength increasing."

"She's awful close," Bell said.

"Can you classify the contact?"

"Wait, please," Kathy said, working frantically with her sonarmen. "MTU and MWM diesel engines now. Assess as a Class three fifty-one minesweeper control ship, sir, and a triplet of Troika HL three fifty-one remote-controlled minesweeping drones."

"The drones have magnetic minesweep solenoids," Bell said. "Retrofitted with mine-hunting sonar, too. Also able to trail two antimine paravanes."

"They're making sure the channel stays clear," Jeffrey said.

"They must have left the occupied Danish coast after the Delta passed through."

"Hmmm," Jeffrey said. "Are they following the Delta? Maybe they only trust the Russians so far."

"No, sir," Bell said. "Fire control indicates contacts not pursuing Delta's track. They're coming in our direction, speed nine knots."

They'll be on top of us in barely ten minutes. They can't possibly miss us. . . . Are they purposely trying to flush us?

There was nowhere for *Challenger* to dodge aside here. She had to move forward, at least as fast as the minesweeper, which was faster than Jeffrey—submerged in such shallow water—really dared go. He prayed, then ordered Meltzer to speed up.

The minesweeper didn't react.

CHAPTER 18

Two hours later, alone in her stateroom, Ilse stripped naked. She began to don her clothing for the raid: a fresh pair of panties and bra, South African manufacture. Thick wool socks and long underwear, top and bottom, U.S. Navy issue. Over that went her jet black dry suit, except for the SpecWar combat booties and flameproof gloves and thermal hood. She left the front of her dry suit partly unzipped.

Cold as Ilse felt, she held off bundling up or she'd work up a sweat. Later, wet underwear could cost her her life.

On second thought, Ilse pulled on the gloves—her hands were ice cubes. At least they weren't shaking, yet. She took one last long look at the photo of her family, taped to the bulkhead inside her rack. She wondered if there was an afterlife.

Jeffrey sat at the command console, all suited up. Meltzer, relieved by the relief pilot, was in the captured minisub. Jeffrey knew he'd be finishing the startup checklists there, with the help of *Challenger*'s chief Ger-ling—German language specialist. Clayton and Montgomery stood in the CACC aisle, hard to make out in their dry suits and face paint in the rig-for-black.

From sonar and LMRS data, Jeffrey understood now why it had been so quiet thirty miles back. To port, the west, lay Denmark's huge Sjaelland Island. To starboard, east, loomed the continental land mass of Sweden. Between them waited the Sound, the path into the Baltic. The entrance to the Sound was barely six thousand yards wide. This choke point was heavily defended by both the Germans and the Swedes—which hadn't been in any Intel brief.

Challenger sat in seventy-six feet of water, bottomed in the sand. She hid against a muddy shoal littered with wrecks both old and new, wooden-hulled and steel. The ship's propulsion was shut down, for both quiet and cooling, since there was nowhere she could run if found out anyway.

Jeffrey sighed to himself. *War-fighting is like a tournament with sudden-death elimination rules. One misstep and you're out— permanently. . . . Well, we're sure committed now.*

SIMULTANEOUSLY, AT TRONDHEIM IN NORWAY

Ernst Beck stood on *Deutschland*'s quarterdeck. It was really just the rounded top of the hull behind the sail, with a nonskid coating, by the torpedo loading hatch.

The naval brass band—hastily assembled when the ship announced, by undersea acoustic link, that she was coming in—paused for the moment. Captain Eberhard strode down the brow and onto the concrete pier, as the last strains of the martial tune echoed inside the giant underground space. He was off to make his demands of the yardmaster, for rushed repairs and a weapons reload. They had to get underway again very quickly: *Challenger* was coming.

This installation *Deutschland* visited was constructed by the Norwegian Navy, during the arms race after the war scare in Asia five years before. It was completed just in time to be grabbed by the *Kaiserliche Marine*—the Imperial German Navy—at the start of the real war in Europe. Built into the side of a granite mountain, thirty sea miles up a fjord, this was far more than a hardened dry dock. It was an entire subterranean submarine base. Norway had been an active part of NATO; some pens were large enough for the U.S. Navy's *Seawolf*-class. These accommodated *Deutschland* comfortably, too.

Ernst Beck watched as several of his wounded men were helped up the inclined ladder through the open loading hatch. He and Jakob Coomans gave them a hand. These, the ambulatory cases, made it down the brow on their own, to be met by nurses and orderlies. They were taken away in a battery-powered jitney, to the base hospital on the upper level. Next were the stretcher cases. An ambulance took them away.

The band struck up again, this time a funeral dirge.

Beck glanced at the Class 212 in the next pen. Her crew, two dozen officers and men, stood on the pier at attention now. They looked clean, well rested, excited—their first mission? Men from *Deutschland's* crew, some wearing beards, now began to bring up the body bags. Beck watched the proceedings silently. His jaw and throat ached from grief. It was hard to hold back tears. He saw dignitaries at the edge of the dock surreptitiously wipe their eyes.

"Look at them," Coomans said under his breath. He pointed with his gaze to the 212's crew. They were tall, and slim, and most of them blond. Handsome, Beck told himself, almost beautiful in dress uniform. Each time another body emerged from *Deutschland's* hull, they snapped a salute and held it till the corpse was off the brow.

"They look eager enough, and proud," Beck said.

"*Fools.* That captain is young enough to be my son. What does *he* know, what do *any* of them know, of mortality and death?"

"They see the bodies."

"They see glory and honor. They don't see cause and effect."

"They're ready to rack up some tons, after the fine example *we* set. It's their duty."

"Do they have any idea how many people we've killed, *murdered,* to score those tons? Have they any *idea* the odds *they'll* ever make it back in that suicide machine?"

The 212 did seem tiny next to *Deutschland.*

Beck watched as the fourth body bag came up the ladder. He knew it was the man he had cut free in the torpedo room. "Twenty percent," Beck said. "Last brew-up, their great-grandfathers' time, the survival odds were twenty percent."

"Look at them," Coomans said. "They're bloody *children.*"

Soon the grim ceremony on *Deutschland* was complete. The deck hands went back to work.

The band began to play again. This time it was a celebratory, triumphal march—a tune premiered at Wilhelm IV's coronation.

"They change gears just like that," Coomans said.

"It's all sheet music to them, I suppose."

"They huff and puff and work their fingers. They go home and sleep in a safe, warm bed, probably not alone. Look at them, the Kaiser's tootlers, how chubby they are, how soft their faces! They wouldn't last one day on patrol. *It's an insult for them to be here.*"

On a signal from her captain, the 212's crew rushed aboard her with military precision. Most of the men went below. Others took up the lines. Quickly the 212 started to move. The traction engines were towing her to the blast door interlocking. Once there she'd submerge, then transit through the deep fjord underwater. She'd come out in the Norwegian Trough, the same way *Deutschland* came in.

Beck made eye contact with her captain on the 212's bridge. He threw the man a salute. "Where are you headed?" he shouted.

"*Nach England!*" To England.

"Good luck!"

"And to you, Herr Korvettenkapitan! Again, congratulations on your new record!"

Beck turned away to get to work. As the 212 drew past *Deutschland*'s stern, he glanced at the back of the captain's head.

The man sounded confident enough, Beck told himself. But then, heading out, they always did.

And the band played on.

FIVE MINUTES LATER.

AT THE ENTRANCE TO THE SOUND, IN THE CAPTURED GERMAN MINISUB

Ilse stood behind Chief Montgomery as he piloted the mini. Outside the hull, small warships' screw-props swished, turbines sang, piston engines pounded, and active sonars whistled and chirped. Ilse's hair brushed the overhead; like *Challenger's* ASDS, the German minisub was barely eight feet high on the *out*side.

The control compartment was rigged for red. Lieutenant Meltzer, in the right seat, served as copilot: off watch, the last few days, he'd drilled to learn the German vessel's systems. Switches and knobs were labeled or tagged in English for him. Ilse glanced to her right. Jeffrey squeezed in next to her, half-standing behind Meltzer. Clayton and the enlisted SEALs and gear were in the transport compartment aft.

Ilse had a bad feeling. She wondered if she'd have to watch Jeffrey die, or one of the others. She wondered if the human soul is real, and whether it would have time to leave her body in that millionth of a second if she needed to set off an atom bomb in her lap. . . . She tried to shake her sense of foreboding.

Everyone studied the data on the mini's wide-screen displays. The mini sat on the bottom, in front of the choke point into the Sound. Threat icons littered the tactical plot and the nav chart.

"Mines, nets, wrecks, patrols," Jeffrey said. "German or Swedish, take your pick."

"We're a German mini," Meltzer said. "Maybe we should go through on the occupied Danish side." If Meltzer was nervous, it didn't show, except that his Bronx accent was thicker.

"Problem with that," Montgomery told him, "is we'll be challenged. We don't have the current recognition codes for here."

"What about down the middle?" Ilse said. "It's the deepest part, and the seam between the two countries' forces, right?" She liked the tight-knit feeling of this foursome, heading into danger together, improvising as they went. *Bonding.*

"We could draw fire from *both* sides," Jeffrey said.

"Which leaves Swedish waters," Ilse retorted. "You really think that's a better choice?"

"It's the least bad of the three. These minis were sold to the Axis by Sweden. Maybe they'll leave us alone."

"I dunno, Skipper," Montgomery said.

"Look," Jeffrey said. "In fourteen hours, tops, ARBOR's computer worm at the lab goes dormant again, assuming internal security doesn't find it first. After that, there's no way we'll ever get inside."

Montgomery picked up the mike to the transport compartment. He asked one of the enlisted SEALs to come forward. Montgomery turned to Jeffrey. "He speaks a little Swedish."

Meltzer stiffened. *"Hydrophone line dead ahead."*

"I see it," Montgomery whispered.

Jeffrey watched that screen, slaved to the mini's chin-mounted photonics sensor. The moored Swedish hydrophone heads showed all too clearly on the bottom, swaying gently in the image-intensified moonlight.

"Dense mine field to port," Meltzer said. "Big wreck right to starboard. We can't maneuver to avoid."

"Think they can hear us?" Montgomery said. He tapped the screen, one of the hydrophones.

"If we're close enough to see *them* through this turbidity," Ilse said, "they're close enough to pick something up from the mini. Main screw blade-rate, side thruster flow noise, machinery hum, something."

"Pull back?" Montgomery said. "Try again from more in-shore?"

"No," Jeffrey said. "Keep going or they'll be suspicious."

Montgomery worked his control joystick and the throttle.

Jeffrey watched the hydrophones disappear under the mini.

A light on Meltzer's console started blinking. "Incoming message. Undersea acoustic link." He brought it up on another screen. "Digital, but not encrypted. It's Swedish, sir, I think."

The enlisted SEAL, squashed between Jeffrey and Ilse, craned to read the message.

"It says, Identify yourselves."

"Ignore it," Jeffrey said. "Keep going. Pilot, increase speed to six knots."

"Aye, aye," Montgomery said. The light stopped blinking.

"I doubt the local troops have authority to shoot," Jeffrey said. "They'll need to follow ROEs, chains of command, just like us."

The mini kept moving south, toward the Baltic.

"So far so good," Ilse said a minute later. "The Sound gets much wider soon." She pointed to the updated tactical plot. "Our passive sonars say there are fewer ships patrolling ahead."

Suddenly Jeffrey heard a roaring, tearing noise, then a shattering explosion off the starboard bow. The minisub shivered and pitched—they'd been fired at by a shore-based naval gun.

The message light blinked again.

"It says, You are intruding in Swedish territorial waters. Surface and heave to for boarding or we will sink you."

"Now what?" Montgomery said. "We're boarded, we're finished."

Jeffrey ran his hand over his face. He worked his jaw back and forth. It was hard to think straight, amidst the reverb of the explosion and the vibrations from the shock.

The others looked at him expectantly.

"Answer in German," Jeffrey said. "Say we're on a training run. . . . Say we thought this was Rügen Island." Rügen was a German island that formed one side of Greifswald Bay.

Montgomery typed. The answer was in German. "They say we're not even close. . . . Surface and leave our waters at once."

Jeffrey heard another shell tear overhead and detonate in the water. He gripped the back of Montgomery's chair to steady himself. His ears hurt.

"They say that one went off due west of us. Head due west now or the next shell won't miss."

"You heard the man," Jeffrey said. "Raise the photonics mast and use image intensification. Don't surface."

Meltzer flicked a switch and the mast came up. He activated another screen to show the picture. The fog topside had cleared, but it was overcast. Jeffrey could see tall mountains on the Swedish coast, snowcapped.

Montgomery steered the mini due west. Meltzer adjusted the ballast and trim for the halocline—the variation in salt content which affected buoyancy.

"So much for stealth," Ilse said. "That shore battery woke up the whole neighborhood."

The message light blinked.

"Source this time is bearing two nine five," Meltzer said. From the direction of Denmark, not Sweden.

"Put the 'scope on two nine five," Jeffrey said.

Meltzer reached and turned a knob. "That's a German patrol craft, Captain, approaching fast." They were cornered.

The patrol craft was barely two thousand yards off, coming

straight at them on the screen. Jeffrey saw a big radar dome on a pylon over her bridge, and a big gun on her foredeck. He glanced at Ilse; she looked stoic, resigned. He saw her finger the pistol on her belt.

Montgomery said the acoustic message was in code. He couldn't decrypt it.

"Mechanical transient bearing two nine five!" Meltzer said.

Jeffrey saw it on the broadband waterfall. "Replay on speakers."

The control compartment filled with a clanking, a harsh electrical whine, then a thunk. There was awful finality to that thunk.

"That's a deck gun loading and training," Jeffrey said. On the screen the patrol craft's gun barrel seemed aimed right between his eyes.

"That thunk was the breach block closing, wasn't it?" Ilse said. "What do we *do*?"

Jeffrey could see she was panicking. He forced himself to stay levelheaded, which wasn't easy. He had an idea. "Chief, answer them on digital using plain text. Say it's our first day." The western Baltic was a German Navy training area.

Montgomery grinned, and typed.

The warship answered. "They want the recognition password."

Uh-oh. "Tell them, tell them you can't remember. In training they said to never write it down. That gun aimed down your throat is making you nervous. . . . Write with a lot of typos so they think you're flustered."

Montgomery took a deep breath. He typed.

There was a long, nerve-racking pause. Jeffrey waited for the gun to open fire. He'd see the flash, then hear it, then feel it, then feel nothing.

Montgomery frowned. "They say to stop where we are."

Ilse pulled the pistol from her belt. Jeffrey put out his hand to stay her. Jeffrey almost jumped when he saw flashes on the screen— but they were much too fast for a three-inch gun. A signal lamp, aimed at the minisub's periscope.

"Morse code, plain text," Montgomery said. "They're sending a minesweeper to escort us to the Baltic."

Jeffrey took the pistol from Ilse and safed it and put it back in her holster. "For the last time," he told her. "This is about the mission, not about *you*."

More lights flashed from the patrol craft, and another ship hove into view. That ship signaled.

"She's the *Konstanz,*" Montgomery said. "One of those Type three-fifty-one minesweeping-drone control ships. She says to fall in behind her, she'll send her drones out in front."

"Does this periscope have a signal light built in?"

"Yes."

"Then tell them thanks."

Montgomery keyed the message.

"They say they were going to make a routine sweep soon anyway. You never know when an Allied unmanned aerial vehicle might sneak through and drop a mine. . . . They also say, based on our performance the last few minutes, we might want to reconsider our career choice . . . like maybe the Army."

Ilse held on as the minisub pulled into the minesweeper's wake. The mini began to roll heavily. Ilse was glad she had taken a seasick pill before leaving *Challenger.*

"Try to keep the periscope aimed at their stern," Jeffrey said.

"Aye, aye," Montgomery said.

Ilse studied the picture. She could see boat davits on the *Konstanz's* afterdeck. Then came the superstructure, with a single mast. A yellow light blinked on the masthead.

"What's that for?" Jeffrey said.

Montgomery riffled through the mini's on-line database. "I am escorting a friendly submarine."

Two crewmen came to stand at the minesweeper's stern.

"An officer and a phone-talker, I think," Ilse said. They wore battle helmets and life vests over foul-weather gear. She saw the officer look at her through big binoculars. A third man came over with a handheld signal lamp. He flashed a message.

"They say it would be safer if we surfaced," Montgomery said.

"No," Jeffrey said. "Tell them we're low on fuel. We get better mileage submerged."

"They want to know how much fuel we have."

"How much *do* we have?"

"Eighty-two percent."

"Tell them forty."

"They want to speed up to ten knots. They have a lot of ground to cover. Can we make it to Bornholm Island at ten knots?"

"Why Bornholm?" Jeffrey said.

"That must be their training base for minis."

"Can we?"

"Yes, sir," Meltzer said, "running submerged. I memorized the speed/endurance curves."

"Can we make it to Greifswald and back to *Challenger* after that?"

"Greifswald, yes, sir, if we go slower. Back to the ship, no way, even at optimum cruising speed."

Jeffrey worked his jaw again. "Chief, tell them Bornholm is okay but we prefer to go slower."

"They say we can refuel when we get to barracks. They have work to do, and they're doing us a favor."

"Blade-rate increase," Meltzer said. "They're speeding up."

The signalman blinked. Montgomery translated.

"They said if we run out of gas they'll give us a tow. . . . The German inflection is hard to convey in English, Skipper, but it's sarcastic."

"Ten knots it is."

A few minutes later, on the periscope screen Ilse saw a sharp yellowish glare. There was a terrific detonation, ahead and to port of the *Konstanz*. She saw a mountain of water bursting skyward. It dropped back slowly, drenching one of the Troika drones.

The officer on the minesweeper's stern spoke to the signalman. They waved to the mini's periscope. Ilse thought they were laughing. *Cocky bastards.*

"Sir," Meltzer said. "I hate to bring it up again, but the mission. Getting back. How do we refuel?"

Jeffrey frowned. "We'll deal with that when we have to. . . . How long to get to the Baltic?"

"At this speed, Captain, six hours."

"Those of us who can ought to get some sleep."

"Concur, sir," Montgomery said. "The pilot and copilot reliefs will come forward soon enough." Some of the enlisted SEALs were trained in this duty. Montgomery reached for a thermos of coffee under his seat, and offered it to Meltzer.

"Ilse?" Jeffrey said. "Let's go aft. They saved the two front seats for us." Before he left the control compartment, he glanced at the fuel gauge and the chronometer.

We're falling more and more behind schedule with each new development, and lower and lower on fuel. This is starting to look like a suicide mission.

CHAPTER 19

Jeffrey jerked awake with a start: Something had scraped the top of the hull. He looked up frantically. *A tethered mine?*

"Just brash ice, sir," Chief Montgomery said from the aisle next to Jeffrey's seat. "Time to get up anyway, Captain."

Jeffrey looked at his borrowed dive watch: 1723 Berlin time— 5:23 P.M., after dusk already this far north, so close to the shortest day of the year, the official start of winter. Jeffrey had slept more than nine hours straight, for the first time in weeks. That explained why he felt so good.

The lighting was rigged for red. Montgomery handed him a steaming cup of coffee, then went forward. Jeffrey drank. He glanced across the narrow aisle. Ilse was wide awake.

"Where are we?" Jeffrey said. He ran his fingers through his hair.

"Entering Greifswald Bay," Shajo Clayton said from behind him. "Now comes the fun part."

Jeffrey looked aft. Beyond the fourth pair of sleeper seats, at the rear of the transport compartment, one of the SEALs used the chemical head. Jeffrey felt the call of nature. The others looked away and made small talk while Ilse took her turn.

Jeffrey and Ilse and Clayton went forward.

"How'd you get rid of the *Konstanz*?"

"Once we got to the Baltic proper," Meltzer said, "they gave us a course for Bornholm Island, then turned back north. We went east till we hit the German submarine training area, then headed south." He typed some keys. Their track, with time hacks, came on the nav chart.

"No problems along the way?"

"Negative, Skipper," Montgomery said. "We met a couple of two-twelves on exercise, some cargo ships serving as training targets, even heard a few practice torpedoes fired in the distance. Axis frigates screening the Swedish coast, against people like us. Some aircraft overflights. Everybody ignored us."

"What's our fuel level?"

"Peroxide's down to one eight percent."

"So we're still stuck for a way back up the Sound."

"Right now we're stuck for a way into Greifswald Bay, too."

"We had to avoid the dredged channel into the bay, sir," Meltzer said. "It's mined, and much too obvious."

Montgomery nodded. "We crawled over the Thiessower Bank instead." The bank was very shallow, Jeffrey knew, and salinity here was low, so the water would freeze more readily—that's why the mini scraped floating fragments of ice and slush.

"Then," the chief went on, "we found *this*." He typed, and a crisp image came on screen. Jeffrey could tell it was a laser line-scan picture from the mini's chin.

"This is live?"

"Affirmative."

"Give me the fine-scale nav chart."

The mini was at one of the less-shallow spots at the mouth of Greifswald Bay, all of twenty-two feet deep right here. Four thousand yards to starboard was Sudperd Point, on Rügen Island, heavily garrisoned by enemy troops. Six thousand yards to port was the military airfield at the tip of Peenemünde. The promontories—solid, inviolable land—seemed to devour the mini like giant incisors, with the bay as their gullet.

Jeffrey looked at the line-scan picture. Immediately ahead of the stationary minisub, underwater, lay a tangle of stainless steel concertina wire that stretched from the bottom to near the surface. The barrier was held in place and strengthened by vertical segments of railroad rail, driven into the mud and sand.

The mini's passive sonars tracked enemy helos patrolling overhead.

"We weren't briefed for this," Montgomery said, meaning the barrier.

"They must have done the construction work submerged," Jeffrey said, "hiding from our recon drones. Any sign of mines or booby traps, or hydrophones?"

"Not that we can see, but they might be buried."

Jeffrey nodded; they had no good way to check. The mini's magnetometers were useless in the solar storm now raging at G5+, and they dared not use their active bottom-penetrating sonar.

"Deploy the chin grapnels. Use the wire-cutter heads, and let's hope no one notices."

Montgomery repositioned the mini between two of the barrier rails. Meltzer worked his joystick in grapnel mode, and began to cut and cut. First upward, then once he got nine feet from the bottom he sliced sideways. The cutters made noise each time they scissored another strip of concertina, but constant surface wave action from the wind made the barrier rattle and clank anyway. Meltzer stopped when a helo hovered and dipped a passive sonar-head nearby, then continued when the helo left. There was no change in the pattern of the local airborne patrols.

"New contact on passive sonar," Montgomery said.

Ilse, quiet and thoughtful up to now, craned to read the screen. "Bearing- and blade-rate indicate some kind of speedboat. Constant bearing now. It's coming this way."

Meltzer stopped cutting, and turned off the laser line-scan.

"Photonics sensors picking up a searchlight," Montgomery said.

"Pass the word," Jeffrey whispered. "Rig for ultraquiet."

Clayton turned aft and made hand signals to his men.

"Speedboat's drawing away," Ilse whispered. "No change in blade-rate."

Meltzer went back to work. "Ready, Captain." His cutting was done.

"Push through."

"Retract the side thrusters," Montgomery said. Meltzer worked some switches. The mini began to slide sideways in the gentle current; Jeffrey knew there was almost no tide in Greifswald Bay. Montgomery worked the rudder and throttle, and the mini moved into the gap. When they were almost through, there was a scraping noise, then a strange *boing* from the stern. The mini stopped.

Montgomery increased the screw-prop turns, but the mini was trapped.

"We're tangled," Montgomery said. "Damn. Someone has to go out and cut us free."

"I'll do it," Jeffrey said. "Shaj, you be my swim buddy."

Jeffrey and Clayton donned their gear. First, their digital dive-computer chest packs, linked to heads-up displays in their masks, and the analog backups, strapped to their left forearms. Then came neutrally buoyant flak vests, just in case. Next, an adjustable buoyancy compensator, which doubled as flotation vest. Draeger closed-cycle rebreathers, worn over their chests. Weight belts, custom calibrated for each man. Titanium dive knives; the dive masks themselves with fiber-optic hookup wires; and big Special Warfare swim fins. They activated chem-glow cyalume hoops; each put one on his right arm.

They went into the lock-out sphere and dogged the hatches. They checked each other's rigs, then tested their two-stage regulators. On the intercom they told Meltzer to equalize the sphere. This took but a moment, the mini was so shallow. Clayton opened the bottom hatch and let it drop down.

In the hatchway Jeffrey saw a pool of black water. He knew the bottom was very close beneath the mini. Clayton sat on the hatch coaming, held his mask in place, and rolled forward, making hardly a ripple. Jeffrey sat, positioned his mouthpiece, held his mask, and rolled forward.

Jesus. His mask display said the water was 31° Fahrenheit—only salt content kept it from freezing solid. The water here was brackish, because of river runoff into the bay mixing with seawater from the Baltic.

Jeffrey moved around to warm up. His dry suit and long underwear did their job. He and Clayton clipped themselves together with a six-foot lanyard so they wouldn't be separated in the darkness and murk. Then they adjusted their flotation vests, admitting a little air; brackish water gave less buoyancy than seawater. They activated small flashlights fastened to their right forearms, and worked aft.

They saw the problem. A tangle of concertina snagged the main propeller's housing. Clayton reached for his compressed-air-powered wire cutters, and began to snip away.

The compressed air bottle ran low, and it got harder for Clayton to cut. He used brute force—Jeffrey knew Clayton, like all active-duty SEALs, had terrific upper-body strength. But eventually Clayton tired. He signaled for Jeffrey to take over, and handed him the cutters.

Jeffrey heard a buzzing in his ears. He checked his regulator, fearing an equipment problem. It was too shallow for nitrogen narcosis, or oxygen toxemia, or baro-trauma.

The noise got louder, seeming to come from everywhere at once. Underwater, at five times the normal speed of sound, it was hard for humans to judge direction to a sound source. But Jeffrey's dive computer had crude acoustic-intercept sonar.

The speedboat. It was coming this way. Jeffrey and Clayton turned off their pressure-proof flashlights. The buzzing got louder still.

Jeffrey saw a diffuse glow penetrating the water. The searchlight. The boat slowed. Jeffrey waited for the antiswimmer charges to come down. At this range, in the water, the blasts would rupture his organs. He and Clayton would die in slow agony, forced to the surface to be captured as blood oozed into their lungs.

The boat sped up again. It roared by almost directly overhead. Its prop wash jostled him and Clayton, and the mini bucked and the concertina jangled. No explosions.

But Jeffrey had dropped the wire cutters, and he'd forgotten to clip their lanyard—the cold was harming his judgment. He turned on his light, but didn't see the tool. He groped in the bottom muck, afraid he'd set off a mine. He found the cutters.

He had to use both hands, and forced himself not to grunt from exertion. Clayton held each ribbon of concertina steady, and Jeffrey held himself in place by treading water. Bottom mines or not, they took care to avoid leaving marks in the sand from their swim fins, though at this point Jeffrey thought it made little difference.

The last snagging piece of wire was cut. They checked that the mini wasn't damaged. Satisfied, they went back under the mini and emerged into the lock-out sphere. They closed and dogged the bottom hatch, signaled Meltzer, and he relieved the pressure in the sphere.

The operation had taken forty-five minutes. The Draegers still had plenty of endurance in their chemical oxygen regenerators, but the team was falling behind schedule yet again. Jeffrey and Clayton shook themselves off, then gave each other quick high-fives, still flush with adrenaline. Their faces were too numb from the cold to speak.

ON THE SHORE OF GREIFSWALD BAY

As the rest of the team got organized, Ilse, using her night-vision goggles, looked up at the fifty-foot chalk cliff. Through the swirling snow and enveloping darkness she could just make out the pines and firs along its upper edge. Somewhere above was the village of Lubmin, she knew, and a sea-surveillance radar site that swept the bay and the Baltic, plus German antiaircraft and anticruise-missile installations.

There was a hard knot in Ilse's gut that wouldn't go away. At least Durban, South Africa, had been home. Here was an alien landscape, giving no comfort at all. The snowfall was recent; there was barely an inch on the ground so far, and none in some spots scoured by the icy wind. The wind moaned hauntingly in Ilse's ears.

The cliff face ran east-west, above the narrow, sandy, ice-encrusted beach. To Ilse's left, east, the cliff and beach stretched for several miles, to Struck Island and then Peenemünde and the Baltic, all invisible with the snow squall. The SEAL team formed up in single file and began the route march in the other direction, to the landward, inner edge of Greifswald Bay.

Meltzer, in the mini with two SEALs held in reserve, was lurking somewhere in the bay. This was as close to their objective as he could drop them off—the inner bay was very shallow.

The razor wire along the water's edge had been easy to get through without leaving signs of intrusion. The SEALs used small grapnels to hold the coils apart, and everyone shimmied through. They knew from recon imagery that the beach probably wasn't mined—advanced synthetic aperture radar, though it couldn't see through water, gave resolution on dry land of under a foot.

The beach was, however, frequently patrolled. Clayton's team was following in the footsteps of the latest patrol, a good precaution in case the beach *was* mined. Everyone's footwear bore a tread like that of German Army boots, to blend in. At least there were no canine prints; there was a shortage of trained guard dogs Axis-wide.

There were wolves in the surrounding forests, but they usually avoided places humans went.

From now on the team would communicate and identify themselves by number, not name, for clarity and security. SEAL One, at the point, was one of the surviving enlisted men from *Texas*. So was SEAL Nine, who brought up the rear. SEALs Two and Seven and Eight had been with Ilse at Durban. Montgomery was Three, Jeffrey was Four, Ilse was Five, and Clayton was Six. To Ilse this made sense. Montgomery's people were well trained for winter operations; Clayton's men, pressed for this mission out of necessity as reinforcements, had drilled for the tropics. The SEALs most used to snow and ice were at the front and back of the column, serving as guides and security. Everyone else was mixed together, a well-integrated unit, with the vulnerable mission specialists, Jeffrey and Ilse, protected in the middle. Clayton carried one of the nuclear demolition charges; SEAL Seven had the second one.

Ilse concentrated on putting one foot in front of the other, following in Jeffrey's footsteps in the snow. The east wind, rushing along the base of the cliffs, howled and blustered relentlessly. Sometimes, in the distance, Ilse could hear the engine roar of German all-weather aircraft. Light, crisp snowflakes swirled everywhere. With the windchill, it was $-10°$ Fahrenheit. The white smocks everyone wore, for camouflage, helped break the wind; the silvered linings suppressed their signature on passive infrared. The effort of the forced march with a big backpack, and also lugging her Draeger, helped keep Ilse warm.

For a while things should be routine, she told herself, as long as the team keeps up the steady pace. The National Imagery and Mapping Agency satellites had shown that the German foot patrols came by at odd minutes after every hour, to be unpredictable. But the local army battalion's commander, it seems, craved order and precision: The exact time after each hour for each patrol followed a pseudo-random number sequence, so the schedule was actually set well in advance. The National Security Agency had detected the pattern, decoded the sequence, and predicted the schedule for tonight.

Step, step, step, step, inhale, exhale, inhale, exhale. One foot in front of the other, minute after minute, mile after mile. Still the driving wind howled, the snow swirled and got deeper. Still Ilse planted her feet wherever Jeffrey planted his feet. Partisans worked from the forests and marshes near the Polish border, the briefing notes said. They might have infiltrated, and planted mines of their own. At

Durban, Ilse remembered, the point man used a special radar mine detector, to spot sweep-resistant plastic mines. But Intel had warned that the Germans used a counterstrategy: mines with radar sensors, that detonated when you tried to detect them.

Ilse's breathing was heavy and her legs were sore and her back hurt. The approach march was very hard work. She had a sinus headache from the dry air, and her mouth was parched. Her earphones, under her ceramic battle helmet, hissed and crackled endlessly with static, but none of the team members spoke a word. She had to keep wiping the snow off her goggles and her lip mike. Her silenced electric ignition pistol in its holster was heavy against her thigh.

The SEALs all gripped their special machine pistols in their hands, scanning constantly for threats. They'd used white masking tape to break up the outlines of the weapons, and added white streaks to their face paint to blend in, given the weather. Their visors would be switching from image-intensification to infrared and back every half second, just like Ilse's. At latitude 55° north, in early evening in mid-December, it was pitch dark. Rush hour for the hectic night shift at the lab would be over by now, the personnel inside pressing ahead on the Mach 8 missiles. The road atop the cliff seemed deserted. The blackout of buildings and autos was complete.

Once more Ilse watched Jeffrey's back. She could see the hump of his heavy pack under his camo smock; the men's gear all weighed more than twice what hers did. The pack made Jeffrey look hunchbacked. He didn't seem to be limping, so she figured his old wounded leg must be okay.

Ilse started. The steady rhythm hypnotized her, and she'd lost focus on the time and where they were. Again she heard the voice in her earphones, frequency-agile low-probability-of-intercept microsecond radar impulses in the Ku band, deeply encrypted—much better for SpecWar commo than conventional radio. Also, or so they'd been told, the low-energy pulses were unlikely to set off a German antiradar mine.

"Contact!" SEAL One repeated.

"Report!" Clayton ordered. Everyone crouched low.

"Enemy patrol," SEAL One said. "Coming this way."

"Not on the schedule," Jeffrey said.

"They *changed* the bleeding schedule," Montgomery said.

"Into the water?" Jeffrey said.

"No time, with the razor wire. We'd leave spoor. Dead giveaway."

"Four, Six. Use proper procedure." Jeffrey shut up.

"One, Three. How many?" Montgomery snapped.

"Seven men, maybe eight."

"Team," Clayton said, "get behind these bushes. Drop your packs and Draegers, cover the bushes with your camo smocks, white side out. Take cover behind your packs and form a firing line."

Jeffrey did what he was told, draping his smock over skeletal scrub at the base of the cliff. He knelt behind his pack, using it as a shield. Around him lay rounded rocks the size of footballs, but there was no time to improve his cover.

"One, Six. Status?"

"Six, One. Any second now."

Jeffrey could see Ilse through his goggles. She was fifteen feet to his right. She had her pistol out.

Jeffrey drew his weapon.

"Team, Six. Weapons power up, weapons tight."

Jeffrey slid the switch on the butt grip. His pistol's safety diode glowed green. The bullet count read 18, a full clip: metal-jacketed hollow-point alternating with armor-piercing Teflon-coated. He checked the digital aiming reticle, superimposed on the view through his night-vision goggles.

"Team, Six. Steady," Clayton said.

Jeffrey's heart was pounding. He aimed his pistol out across the bay—this was its widest part, twelve miles to Rügen Island. The laser-interferometer-driven aiming reticle, superimposed on his field of view, bounced and jiggled wildly.

So much for my nerves of steel.

"Four and Five, Six," Clayton called in Jeffrey's earphones. "Status?"

"Ready," Ilse said. She sounded like she meant it.

"Ready," Jeffrey said, determined she wouldn't show him up. He heard the German footsteps now, and low murmuring voices. The voices stopped.

"They're still approaching," One whispered.

"Team, Six. Weapons off safe, selectors on semiauto only, but hold your fire. . . . Break break. Nine, Six. Report when their point man gets inside ten feet of you."

"Six, Nine. Understood."

"Team, Three. Aim low, so our bullets won't carry."

Jeffrey shrank behind his pack as the soldiers approached.

"Wass ist das?" he heard, and not over his headphones. What is this?

A weapon coughed.

"Weapons free!" Montgomery hissed.

Other weapons fired. The Germans' rifles, with sound suppressors, clattered on full auto as their receivers cycled and spent brass cartridge cases flew. Bullets smacked into the cliff face. The SEALs' caseless electric ignition subsonic rounds were completely silent, until their .50-caliber bullets thudded and crunched into organs and bone.

Ilse searched her front but had no targets.

"Five through Nine," Clayton shouted. "Flanking pivot left! Form an L-shaped ambush! Rapid fire!"

Ilse rolled across the snow and sand, saw Jeffrey do the same and block her line of fire. She rolled again, and Seven crawled up next to her. She began to fire at murky shapes when she saw muzzle flashes aimed her way.

"Eight and Nine, Six, go full auto!"

Ilse heard their weapons *puff-puff-puff* behind her. When her visor switched to infrared she could see the bullet traces, red-hot metal in friction with the air. Some of them hit home, and Germans grunted or writhed. Eight and Nine fired in short bursts. Enemy bullets snapped by overhead.

Ilse aimed her pistol at another German, who'd been driven against the barbed wire along the water. Before she could fire his muzzle flashed and something whacked the side of her helmet. The helmet flew off and she saw double. SEAL Eight riddled the German.

"Cease fire," Montgomery said. *"Cease fire."*

"Did they get off a warning?" Clayton said.

"Negative," SEAL Two said. "Nothing intercepted on my signals intel receiver. We didn't give them time."

"Anyone hit?" Montgomery said. "Team sound off."

The SEALs called in by number. When her turn came Ilse said, "Five." Then she heard, "Six. Seven. Eight. Nine," in different voices.

"Now what?" Ilse heard Jeffrey say.

"We have to make it look like partisans," Clayton said.

"Concur," Montgomery said. "Eight and Nine, secure our rear. One and Two, hold point. Everyone else, police up the bodies."

Jeffrey was glad the seven Germans were dead. The SEAL team couldn't take prisoners, and a wounded enemy soldier would be a major problem Jeffrey didn't want to think about. He surveyed the carnage. Blood soaked the snow and sand, looking black on his visors. On IR he could see the bodies were already starting to cool. None of Clayton's team were hurt, though Ilse had a gouge in the side of her ceramic bulletproof helmet, and two of the SEALs took enemy rounds in their flak vests. A quick check of the packs showed nothing vital was damaged.

"How do we make this look like partisans?" Jeffrey said.

"Disfigure the bodies," Montgomery said.

"What is it about you and cutting with knives?"

"It's my training," Montgomery snapped. "I don't *like* it, *sir*. I just have to *do* it."

"Sorry, Chief. What do you suggest?"

"Gouge out their eyes. Leave the corpses behind the bushes. Cover the blood with fresh sand and snow, but not too thoroughly."

"So it doesn't look like SEAL work?"

"Right," Clayton said. "Psychological warfare by the Resistance instead. . . . Then make it seem like we, *they*, came down the cliff in ambush and egressed back that way. Toss the German weapons and ammo out into the bay, since the partisans would collect them."

"Ilse," Jeffrey said, "how are you at climbing?"

"I like rock climbing."

"Think you can make it to the top and back real fast?"

"Yes. What about our footprints?"

"Trackers would read them as captured Army boots."

"Take these," Clayton said. He handed Jeffrey crampons and climbing rope. "Make it look good, plant them at the top. They're German brands."

"German?" Ilse said.

"Bought before the war."

"That's planning ahead," Jeffrey said.

"The CIA has whole warehouses full of useful stuff they buy from friends who might turn into enemies."

Jeffrey glanced at the bodies as Montgomery and Seven went to work with their K-Bar fighting knives. Jeffrey had to look away.

Jeffrey and Ilse climbed. The footing was uneven but firm, and the underbrush gave good handholds. The vertical set of the cliff precluded land mines—or so Jeffrey hoped. On the way down, he passed old bird nests in cracks in the rock. He knew the wetlands around Greifswald were an important breeding area in the spring.

In a few minutes he and Ilse were back on the beach.

"What do we do next?" Jeffrey said.

"Into the water," Clayton said. "We've covered about four miles along the shore so far. It's another mile to the Danische Wiek. We'd've gone back to Draegers there, anyway."

Montgomery came over. "To hell with this humping infantry-style. It's way too dangerous."

CHAPTER 20

"Team, Six," Jeffrey heard by skullbone induction, above the sound of his own breathing through his bulky Draeger mouthpiece. "Communications check," Clayton said. "Status check. Sound off."

When Jeffrey's turn came, through the built-in mouthpiece mike he said, "Four. Good to go."

He heard Ilse say, "Five. Good to go." Although she was Clayton's swim buddy, Jeffrey had unclipped from Montgomery and fastened his lanyard to hers to form a threesome.

Ilse was close enough for Jeffrey to see her cyalume hoop through the murk. The depth gauge on his dive mask read eighteen feet, salinity-adjusted. His dive computer told him the water temperature here was 37° Fahrenheit. The chronometer said that in barely sixty minutes, ARBOR's computer worm would expire. The team's unexpected extra swim had added more than an hour to their approach to the lab, burning up time they didn't have to spare. Once that worm went dormant and erased itself, any further intrusion by the SEALs would set off alarms.

Jeffrey floated horizontally, resting; to swim fast wearing a backpack, even one designed to be neutrally buoyant, was a bear. He listened as the team finished checking in.

The clandestine secure gertrude—the undersea counterpart to their frequency agile digitized-radar commo—worked well enough, even amidst the unstable haloclines formed by freshwater from the Ryck River's mouth, several thousand yards to the south. Jeffrey knew the Ryck skirted the north edge of Greifswald town itself. It emptied into the Danische Wiek, a small bay-within-the-bay, one mile wide at the point where the team swam across underwater.

The wind topside blustered again, stirring the shallow Wiek. Jeffrey was jostled by wave action. Now his dive display showed he had a sink rate of four feet per minute. He let more gas into his own and his backpack's buoyancy bladders.

"Six, Three." Montgomery spoke slowly and clearly. "First obstacle inspection complete. Confirmed the movement sensors are cased in titanium, and the land downlinks are fiber-optic lines we can't bypass."

"Three, Six. Very well," Jeffrey heard Clayton say. His voice was hollow and scratchy over the gertrude. Besides halocline effects, there was heavy flow noise, from the cooling water intake just ahead.

"Remove the bolts," Clayton ordered.

Jeffrey heard clinks, and grunting. He kept floating in the dark. Watching the amber inertial nav readout on his mask, as well as Ilse's greenish glow, he worked his legs to hold position. Otherwise, the readout told him, he kept drifting toward the intake pipe.

"Six, Three. The bolts are off."

"Three, Six. Open the access gate." Clayton's voice was tense and clipped.

Jeffrey forced himself to breathe evenly. If the security alarms *weren't* suppressed, they would know it soon. He heard a creaking sound.

"The flow rate is much faster than we expected," Montgomery said. "We're going to have to rappel in one by one, feet first, against the hydrodynamic drag."

"Copy," Clayton said.

"We are rigging the grapnels and lines."

"Copy."

Jeffrey waited.

"*Watch it,*" he heard on gertrude. Through the water he heard a whack, a scraping noise, then a *clunk.* The rushing of the inflow was louder than before.

"Report," Clayton ordered.

"We dropped a bolt cutter," Montgomery said. "The flow's so strong now it got sucked into the pipe. I think it fetched up against the first debris catcher. . . . One is inside. . . . Two is starting in."

Again, Jeffrey waited in the dark. This close to the surface, this close to shore, they dared not use their flashlights.

Montgomery swam up to Jeffrey, startling him. "Four, let's go." Jeffrey unclipped from Ilse, then attached his lanyard to the chief's equipment belt.

Soon they were at the intake gate. It was a giant fine-meshed titanium cage. Jeffrey was sucked against the outside of the cage.

"Hold on hard," Montgomery said. "Then stay still." Jeffrey gripped the bars. He felt Montgomery probing with his hands, checking Jeffrey's equipment by feel, cinching the straps and fasteners uncomfortably tight. Montgomery gave a final yank to the straps of Jeffrey's dive mask and mouthpiece/mike.

The chief unclipped his own end of their swim-buddy lanyard, and clipped the free end to the cage near the gate. This way Jeffrey was secured, but had some slack.

Montgomery tapped his shoulder. "Climb inside. Grip your regulator with your teeth *hard*. Face *up*stream, backward, *into* the flow, or your mask will get pulled off."

Jeffrey struggled through the access gate, into the cage. He had a surge of claustrophobia, for the first time in his life. He felt the water tearing at him, at his gear. The rapid flow began to chill him. It made a constant roaring noise.

Montgomery, himself clipped to the cage now with a spare lanyard, guided Jeffrey's hand to the guide rope. By feel, facing the flow and gritting his teeth, Jeffrey threaded the rope through the rappel fitting buckled to his weight belt. By feel, Montgomery checked him again.

Jeffrey heard thumps and clunks and almost pissed his pants. Were Germans setting up a crew-served weapon on the shore of the Wiek? The team was so shallow, machine gun or mortar fire would kill them easy.

"Relax, Commander," Montgomery said. "That's One and Two, cutting through the debris catcher."

Jeffrey looked at his vital signs on the mask display. His pulse was 132, his respiration 38. Too high. This was scary.

"Ready?" Montgomery said.

"Ready."

"Start down."

Jeffrey loosened the friction brake at his waist and slid into the pipe a little at a time. The pipe was less than five feet in diameter. His body partly blocked the flow, and made the suction stronger. The inlet was too constricted for someone else to work beside him—he was on his own.

Jeffrey tried to keep track of how far inside he'd gone, and which direction was up, underwater. In the dark, in the pipe, he relied completely on his heads-up display.

When he judged the distance was right, he turned on his flashlight. He started searching. Nothing. He went further in. Still nothing. Unless he found it, they'd have to scrub the mission. He slid along the pipe a little more.

There. He spotted the outer automatic blast-shield door, recessed into the top of the pipe. He traced the flange in the bottom of the pipe, into which the door dropped tightly shut.

He reached for the edge of the door. He lost control and spun wildly in the flow. Fighting panic and vertigo, he tried to brake himself by splaying arms and legs against the slippery pipe walls. His mask said his pulse was up to 170, his breath rate a ragged 52. He *had* to reach that door edge.

Almost losing his mouthpiece twice, he finally got a hand on it. The liquid jet stream tried to bend him double. He fought with all his strength. The noise of the cascade was deafening.

He pushed up. His orders said he had to make doubly certain. The blast shutter gave an inch or so, with increasing reluctance. He let go, and it came back down and stopped. It was spring-loaded, and held in place by an electromagnet or solenoid. So far, so good, for the mission ROEs.

Jeffrey switched off his light to save the battery. It was running very low, because of the cold.

Barely intelligible over the gertrude, Montgomery told Jeffrey to hurry up. Jeffrey went further into the pipe, in pitch darkness. Still the water roared in his ears. His own blood roared in his ears. His fingers grew numb, from effort and cold, the fast water flow the equivalent of an undersea windchill.

Jeffrey just kept sliding down the rope. He glanced at his inertial nav. *So far yet to go.*

He felt his determination flag—the cold was getting to him, and would only get worse and worse.

Jeffrey's jaw began to ache, but he dared not let up on his mouthpiece and trust the strap alone. If he should lose it, without first rotating closed the airway seal, salty water would get in the rebreather works. The caustic soda would turn to acid. Trapped deep in the pipe, with nothing to breathe and no swim buddy near, he'd drown for sure.

FORTY MINUTES LATER.

Ilse tried to rest, frozen solid. She'd begun to shiver, and had almost no feeling in her hands and feet and face. Her dark-adapted eyes could see well enough, by reflected glow from flashlights, as the SEALs worked above her.

Ilse glanced up. The whole team was bunched inside the accessway, several hundred yards into the cooling pipe. Below the maintenance ladder, beneath Ilse's feet, the water rushed. A fine mist filled the accessway, and droplets splashed her dry suit. Everyone still used the Draegers—the accessway was hermetically sealed, to avoid breaking the suction of the cooling flow. The Draegers protected the team from asphyxiation in the stagnant air, tainted by swamp gas from below, and maybe by chemical weapons to discourage intruders, from above.

Ilse clung hard to the ladder. Out of the water, her equipment regained its full weight. She glanced up again, impatient to get on with it. SEAL One was holding a stethoscope to the wall.

On Clayton's command, everyone helped each other out of their packs; they fastened the packs securely to the steel rungs of the ladder. They withdrew their weapons, removed the waterproof muzzle plugs, and inspected them carefully. They powered them up on safe with rounds in the chamber. They pulled out several kinds of grenades, and loaded the pockets of their combat vests. They donned their battle helmets and eye shields and night-vision goggles; they'd worn their flak vests, neutrally buoyant, all along. They put their dive knives in their packs, but retained their K-Bars and their survival knives. They also retained their Draegers, as gas masks.

Ilse realized Jeffrey had noticed she was shivering; he massaged her arms and legs. She tried to relax, and let him go to work. When his hands got too close to her backside, she shoved them away.

"Standard procedure," he said, enunciating inside his mouthpiece. "Against hypothermia. Works every time."

"Thanks," Ilse said, grateful for his help, and sorry she'd misinterpreted his explorations.

"It was good for me, too," Jeffrey said.

Ilse realized what he'd done. By flirting, he'd made her core body temperature rise fast, and her fatigue melt away. She made eye contact with him for a split second, then looked away before it went too far. *Inside a secret German lab, of all places. Just when I think I have Jeffrey figured out, he surprises me again.*

Ilse reminded herself why she was here. To help the SEAL team spy, and then escape, if espionage and escape were really possible. In any case, to help make *very* sure to thoroughly destroy the place. Beyond that, because of ARBOR's arrest, they didn't have much of a plan, and she had no idea what to expect from moment to moment.

Ilse glanced up. At the top of the ladder, SEALs One and Two worked to unfasten the manhole cover from underneath. Clayton kept eyeing his wristwatch.

"Ready," One said.

Clayton cleared his throat. "This is when we find out if they're waiting for us. . . . Weapons free."

The team poured out of the manhole as fast as they could and formed a perimeter. Jeffrey saw they were in a utility space. It was large and hot and humid, and deserted. Air whistled as it was drawn into the accessway. SEAL One used a handheld chemical sniffer.

"Air's clean."

Quickly the team retrieved their packs. SEALs One and Two resealed the manhole.

"We're here," Montgomery said. "ARBOR was supposed to have hidden a package."

"I don't see anything," Jeffrey said.

"Find it," Clayton said.

The team searched, systematically at first, then with increasing desperation. Inside storage cabinets, behind equipment, on top of pipes hung from the overhead. Jeffrey warmed up, then began to sweat. He opened his flak vest and unzipped the front of his dry suit.

"Trouble," SEAL One hissed. Jeffrey heard footsteps approaching steadily from around the corner of a drab, ill-lit corridor.

Everyone lifted their packs and hid them and knelt behind the pumps and transformers. Jeffrey pulled a dental mirror from his load-bearing vest, and peeked around the corner of an electrical switching cabinet. The cabinet bore the international symbol for DANGER—HIGH VOLTAGE: big red lightning bolts. Jeffrey wondered if he'd fry if a bullet hit the cabinet.

A guard entered the utility space. He approached the manhole, casually at first. He noticed the wet footprints. He reached for his walkie-talkie mike.

Jeffrey pulled his K-Bar and charged the man. The guard turned and raised his carbine. Montgomery charged from the other direction, also knife in hand. The guard turned toward Montgomery.

Jeffrey was on the man in a flash and Montgomery grabbed him from the other side. Simultaneously they plunged their fighting knives into the base of the German's neck, Jeffrey from the left and Montgomery from the right. Jeffrey flicked his K-Bar one way to sever the spine and the other way to cut the heart in two. He withdrew his knife the same time Montgomery pulled out his. Montgomery lowered the body to the floor, holding the head by the hair so blood wouldn't drip.

Montgomery flashed Jeffrey a grin. "Now who's who with knives, Skipper?"

"Any life-signs sensor?" Jeffrey snapped.

"We're clear."

Jeffrey and Montgomery wiped their knives on the guard's uniform blouse. From the uniform, Jeffrey could tell he was German naval infantry—not a marine, but a sailor who guarded a shore activity.

Clayton pulled a body bag from his pack; the team came prepared. "Help me get him in this. We need to lock in the body fluids and smells."

Jeffrey did as he was told. Around him, utility equipment whirred and hummed. He smelled steam and ozone and lubricant, hot metal and warm oil-based paint.

"Trouble," SEAL One said. More footsteps, more tentative than before. A security alert?

Everyone took cover. Again Jeffrey watched from his hiding place, using the dental mirror.

A man came around the corner. He wore a dirty orange coverall. Over his shoulder he carried a black plastic garbage bag. A point man in camouflage? A decoy?

The man saw the wet footprints. He knelt, and Jeffrey saw him notice drops of blood.

Montgomery charged with his K-Bar.

Jeffrey charged out, too. "No!" Jeffrey waved his arms at the chief. Montgomery pulled up short.

There was something odd about this man. He was old, and shuffled stoop-shouldered, more like a prisoner than a guard—he wore plastic sandals like beach clogs. He had a thick black mustache, so large and bushy Jeffrey wondered how he could eat or drink. In fact, the man looked malnourished. Strangely, he had a dark suntan.

No. His skin was brown. Jeffrey studied his face.

He's a Turk, Jeffrey realized. A *Gastarbeiter,* a so-called Guest Worker. . . . So the Germans are using forced labor after all.

The man said something in fluent German. Montgomery responded, barking questions. The man put down the garbage bag and stepped back. He gestured for the chief to open it. Montgomery covered him with his rifle, and told him to do it himself. Clayton ordered everyone else to stay behind cover. It might be a bomb.

The man knelt and untied the bundle. Out poured blank ID cards, a portable retinal scanner and a digital camera, a floor plan, two sausages, and a pretzel.

CHAPTER 21

SEALs One and Nine defended the bend in the corridor while the rest of the team parleyed. The Turk squatted on the floor; there was no place to sit except on bare concrete.

Montgomery spoke out of earshot of the man. "He says there's about a hundred of 'em in here. A lot of them lost their relatives in the big earthquake in Turkey in the nineties. They came to Germany to get away and find work."

"But *why*?" Clayton said. "The Axis keeps claiming they're not racist; they say even in Africa they're restoring law and order. Turkey's neutral, like in World War Two. Why would Germany *possibly* take the chance on antagonizing them like this?"

"Let me try," Ilse said. She walked over and sat down next to the Turk.

"*Wie heissen Sie?*" she said. In formal address: What's your name?

"Gamal Salih. *Und Du?*" And you?

He used *Du,* not *Sie,* a sign of affection in German. Ilse felt drawn to him at once, as to a kindly uncle, in spite of his tattered dress and smell. The Turk seemed remarkably poised, surrounded by commandos armed to the teeth. Up close, he didn't look as old as she'd first thought.

"Ilse," she said, touching her chest. "Ilse Reebeck."

"*Süd Afrikaner?*" South African?

He picked *that* up right away. "*Eine guter Süd Afrikaner.*" A good South African.

Jeffrey came over. Salih pointed to the rest of the team. "*Kampf-schwimmer?*"

"*Ja.*" Then Ilse said slowly in English, "U.S. Navy SEALs."

Salih nodded, as if they'd passed some kind of test.

"Why do they keep you here?" Ilse said in German.

Salih shrugged. "Labor shortage," he said in English. "The white Germans go to the Army. White Germans, they don't like cleaning garbage, washing toilets, sweeping floors. Instead, *we* wipe up their lubricant spills, pick up the shavings from their lathes." He made a gesture with his fingers, as if to say *Ouch.* Ilse realized the metal shavings must be razor sharp.

"So you're like janitors?" Jeffrey said.

"Slave janitors."

"They don't let you out?" Clayton said.

"Never." Salih grew angry. "My father was *born* in Germany. So was I. We were *citizens.* I was a building engineer, at an office tower in Frankfurt."

"Your English is good," Jeffrey said.

"What did you expect? Everybody studies it in school. Then I went to technical college. . . . You don't speak German?"

"No," Jeffrey said. "Just Arabic, and Russian."

"Prepared for the wrong wars, didn't you?"

"How'd you end up here?" Ilse said.

Salih sighed. "German antiaircraft winged one of your Tomahawks. It crashed near my house. . . . My family . . . They're all gone now."

"How'd you survive?"

"I was at the office."

Ilse hesitated. "I know how you feel, Mr. Salih. The survivor guilt, for being alive when they're not. I lost my family, too. Executed, or disappeared, for fighting the Johannesburg regime."

Salih nodded. "They said they were *hiring* us, for good money. Instead we're starved and beaten. *Betrayed,* by my own so-called countrymen." Ilse winced at his bitterness.

"Didn't you complain?" Jeffrey said.

"*Yes,* we complained. They hanged the spokesmen and made the rest of us watch. Now, we don't complain."

"But ARBOR—I mean the woman who is, was, helping us—she spoke with you?"

"She knew, how do you say it, *internal security* was getting close. She knew I was a sort of imam for the others."

"Like a priest?" Clayton said.

"More like a teacher. Turk Muslims, we're so-so observant. I'm forty-five, have my degree. Most of the others here, they're kids really, did menial work before the war. I'm the unofficial elder now, like it or not."

"Of the Gastarbeiter?"

"*Ja.* ARBOR, as you keep calling her, swore me to secrecy. She has a name, you know. Erika Rainer. She was six months pregnant. Did you know that?"

Ilse blanched. "What happened to her?"

"No one's been told. . . . She said you might still come, and I should try to help. I hope these ID things are helpful."

"They're not inventoried?" Jeffrey said.

"She wrote them off. She said she spilled coffee on them. She told me she altered their electronic serial numbers so they'll still read as valid when you use them."

Jeffrey gestured for Clayton and Ilse to follow him to a far corner, well away from Salih.

"We have a *big* problem, folks."

Clayton nodded, reluctantly. "We nuke this place, we'll kill a hundred innocent people."

"Wait a minute," Ilse said. "If this guy's telling the truth, then ARBOR knew all about the Turks. Why didn't she get word out?"

"Oh, boy." Jeffrey rolled his eyes. "Maybe she *did,* and Mossad decided not to tell us. They want this lab destroyed, real bad. Israel has no defense in depth, Ilse, the country's so small. A barrage of these new missiles could wipe out the whole population, Jews and anti-Axis Arabs both."

"So they withheld information?" Clayton said.

"I wouldn't put it past them. . . . Give me Salih's floor plan."

Clayton handed it over.

Ilse watched Jeffrey study it carefully. She translated some words for him.

"We have another problem," Jeffrey said. "According to this, the missile lab is subdivided into two hardened independent sections—one for the heavy test equipment and machine-tool manufacturing work, the other for the computer installation and offices and dormitory."

"Dormitory?" Clayton said.

"People must be working round the clock. This way they can grab some rest, then get right back at it. Besides, it's safer than living topside, right?"

Clayton studied the map. "So, we need to plant one bomb in each section." He glanced around the utility space, and eyeballed the overhead, the walls, the structural beams, the fire suppression system. "Based on what I'm seeing, this place is stronger inside than we thought. . . . With the aggregate volumes enclosed, the yields of our special items should just do the job, *but* . . . we can't put them just anywhere."

Jeffrey frowned. "That means we need to penetrate much further into the installation than we thought. . . . And we're still left with the problem of the Turks."

Ilse saw Jeffrey grimace, then start massaging his left leg. His old wound was acting up.

"Maybe we don't tell Salih what we're really up to," Clayton said. "Let him think it's a spy mission or something. When the bombs go off, it's not like they'll *feel* anything. The atmospheric overpressure alone . . ."

Jeffrey glanced at Salih, still squatting on the floor. He was eating an energy bar from one of the SEALs. Salih looked at Jeffrey and smiled.

"No," Jeffrey said. "This part's *my* decision. Leaving the Turks in the dark, and saving our own skins, that's cold-blooded murder. If it ever came out, which it will, it's terrible statecraft."

Ilse heard a muffled electronic tone.

"It's coming from that guard," Clayton said. Montgomery went to the concealed body bag and opened the zipper. He lifted the walkie-talkie; a light on it was blinking.

"LT," Montgomery called to Clayton, "it's some kind of general broadcast, like a message download. I think if I push this button we'll hear it."

"Do it," Clayton said.

Ilse listened. A computer-synthesized voice announced that a highest-level security alert was being sounded. An Army squad had been found killed several miles away. It might be a diversion, for some sabotage or espionage. Surface, naval, and airborne patrols were being strengthened. Lab work was to continue as normal. Perimeter security was being increased.

Ilse translated.

"I'm sure this manhole counts as part of the perimeter," Jeffrey said sourly. He glanced at his watch. "The computer worm expires any second. We're on our own."

"I think I'm supposed to press this button to acknowledge receipt," Montgomery called, holding up the radio.

"Do it," Jeffrey said.

"How long till they realize he's missing?" Ilse said, indicating the dead guard.

"Not long."

"Now what?" Clayton said. "The coolant discharge access hatch was supposed to be our way out, with *this* one, the inlet, as our backup. Do we just go ahead and blow the bombs, and kill us *and* the Turks?"

"If we have to," Jeffrey said, "that's exactly what we'll do."

Clayton's jaw set. He nodded.

Jeffrey waved for Montgomery. The chief walked over. "Chief, ask Salih exactly what ARBOR told him we're supposed to be doing here."

Montgomery talked to Salih. The chief came back.

"Spying."

That made sense, Ilse realized. ARBOR would've thought along the same lines the SEAL team took now.

"Okay," Jeffrey said, "let's keep him on a need-to-know basis. . . . Ilse."

Ilse turned to face Jeffrey.

"Get cleaned up and dressed and put on your makeup."

Ilse walked down the busy, carpeted corridor, one level below the utility space. Since the lab structure was dug into the ground, its basement, in effect, was at the top. The deeper Ilse went, the more helpless she felt. She was supposed to find her way around, see what was going on, try to gather intelligence, and report back to Jeffrey and Clayton. Because of ARBOR's arrest, Ilse had been drawn into this. Because of the Turks, things had gotten even more complicated. Ilse told herself wryly that a suicide mission, at least, had the advantage of simplicity. Now, with help from Salih in ARBOR's place, there might or might not be an upside: survival, and hard data on the Mach 8 missile project to bring back to Allied lines.

Ilse glanced up. The lab's massive armored roof, all of twelve meters—forty feet—thick, didn't make her feel safe. It made her feel trapped.

The overhead fluorescents had a bluish tinge. Ilse realized these were grow lights, to help the staff stay healthy and alert, to make up for the total lack of sunlight. Most of the people Ilse passed were men. Most of them, including the women, wore navy uniforms. They must have joined up—or been drafted—en masse when the war broke out. Their postures and gazes weren't very military. They acted more like engineers and scientists—without the lab coats and pocket protectors.

Ilse herself wore a white silk blouse, with navy blue jacket and knee-length skirt. Her shoes were plain black flats, with rubber soles. All had South African labels. Her clothes were wrinkled from being in her pack—but this was part of her cover story.

Around her neck she wore a chain from which dangled her smart ID card, loaded with a digital photo and retinal scan and other data. She lugged a briefcase, the big boxy kind that opened with flaps at the top. The briefcase was fine maroon leather. Inside were files and books concerning fluidics control, her alleged specialty.

She leaned to one side from the weight of the briefcase, and kept having to change hands to relieve the cramping in her fingers. She looked forward to being able to get rid of it—the case was *heavy;* someone should have thought to put it on wheels. Concealed in the middle, behind special plastic shielding to block gamma rays and neutrons, was a nine-pound hollow sphere of pure plutonium-239, surrounded by implosion lenses, a power supply, and arming circuitry.

A briefcase atom bomb.

On the upper level, amid the drab maintenance corridors, Jeffrey and Clayton and Montgomery followed Salih's lead. Actually, Salih shuffled behind them, and murmured directions in German to Montgomery as needed.

Jeffrey and the SEAL team leaders wore gray workmen's jumpsuits from their packs. Clayton also wore a full welder's mask, with a flameproof scarf, and welding gloves. Clayton carried arc-welding gear, including a portable transformer that ran off the standard German 220-volt three-prong outlet supply. Jeffrey lugged a heavy toolbox, of high-impact plastic with a matte beige finish. Montgomery's hands were free; he was the foreman of the work gang.

Clayton's welding equipment was real, all of German manufacture. The tools in Jeffrey's toolbox were real and German metric, too, except that under the top tray was the other one-kiloton nuclear device.

The threesome all wore their ID cards, except Clayton, whose photo was actually of SEAL Nine, who was hiding with the other enlisted SEALs; Nine was Caucasian. The intruders' military haircuts fit in well. As long as Clayton didn't have to remove his welding gear while a German watched, there was no way someone would know he was African-American.

Under his welding helmet Clayton wore night-vision goggles. Instead of being half blinded by the dark window of the mask, he could see very well.

Several times, Jeffrey's group passed lab personnel or guards, who hardly noticed them. After all, an *Untermensch* janitor and a handful of maintenance people weren't worth attention. They also passed more Turks, in their orange overalls, carrying pails from the employee cafeteria. Salih made a quick greeting and gestured to get back to work. Then he whispered to Jeffrey that, for the main body of Gastarbeiter on the night shift, those leftovers were breakfast. The lucky ones, Salih explained, worked as dishwashers.

The team came to an automated checkpoint, and everybody's ID cards worked perfectly—they'd uploaded themselves into the system using a modem socket in the utility space. Clayton faced away from the videocamera and lifted his welding mask and visor, and looked into the retina scanner. Salih had an ID card, too, though he said his access was very limited.

Ilse had to stop and put the briefcase down to rest. She still had a pounding headache, and massaged the side of her temple where the bullet grazed her helmet. Her heart sank when she spotted a heavy door blocking her progress. The sign on the door said TEST SECTION: UNAUTHORIZED ENTRY FORBIDDEN. Next to the door was a card reader and surveillance camera.

Near the reader was a water cooler alcove.

Ilse took two ibuprofen—made by a German company, in case she were searched.

She turned around and bumped into a man in uniform.

"Excuse me," the man said distractedly. He looked her up and down, and seemed puzzled. "I haven't seen you here before."

Ilse's heart pounded. Was there something wrong with her outfit, her bearing? Was her huge briefcase a giveaway? Had they found the dead guard?

She looked the man in the face, searching for words. He wore a naval officer's dress blues, with three stripes on his jacket cuffs: a full commander. He wore decorations: a *real* commander. He was handsome, blond, tall, and slim, in his mid-thirties.

"I'm, I'm new," she said in her best German.

"South African?" he said at once. He reached and examined her ID card—it didn't have her real name.

"What department?"

"Huh?"

"What department are you assigned to?"

"Um, fluidics control."

"The pepper subproject?" At least she thought that's what he said.

"The what?"

"Haven't you been briefed?"

"Um, no. I just got here tonight."

The officer chuckled. "Forgive me. You do look rather frazzled. What did you do to your head? Came in through Russia, did you?"

Ilse nodded. "By way of the Pakistan coast, then up through Iran on trains and buses. The food was terrible."

The commander chuckled again. "Everybody says that. We eat much better here, you'll see."

Ilse relaxed. He was good at putting her at ease. He had that command presence, like Captain Wilson. A certain charm and infectious upbeat mood, backed by a steely self-confidence that could turn ice cold in an instant.

"How did you get to Pakistan? By submarine?"

Ilse nodded dumbly. She knew that was the main way Germany and South Africa traded strategic personnel and resources—their war economies were each rather self-sufficient: Germany with all of Continental Europe's plunder, plus trade with Russia; South Africa from its long experience of trade embargoes under Old Apartheid.

"We have a Boer submariner here right now," the German commander said. "Arrived just a few days ago. I'm surprised, in fact, that they didn't send you through together."

Uh-oh. "Really?"

"Yes. He's a junior officer, visiting to master our new weapons system. I'd be glad to introduce you."

Now Ilse's heart was *really* in her throat. She'd been a senior Boer submariner's lover before the war, and met some of his crew, and others as his date at parties and receptions. If this junior officer should recognize her, a known resistance fighter . . .

"What department is *he*?"

"Fuel cryogenics."

"Maybe tomorrow, then," Ilse said. *Oh, shit, and I told Salih my real name. If they grab him . . . Now I don't have a gun, a knife, even a cyanide pill.*

"By the way," the commander said, "my name is Dieter Gaubatz. I'm in charge of missile payload integration. Atomic bomb, nerve gas, germs—take your pick. My department's motto is this: Any warhead, any target, mass destruction, unstoppable. Like it?"

"Succinct," Ilse said. "Hard to misinterpret."

"I made it up myself. But I neglect my manners."

Gaubatz shook Ilse's hand. His grip was bone-crushing.

Ilse squeezed back, hard as she could, and met him squarely in the eyes. *I may get turned into ionized plasma myself very soon,* she thought, *but boy, Commander Gaubatz, do I have a surprise for you.*

"You're assigned to the night shift?"

"Er, yes."

"Good. The best people are."

"Strictly speaking, I'm not on the payroll till tomorrow."

"Then why don't you rest? You look exhausted. No offense, I hope? Jet-lagged, *ja*?"

Ilse wiped some loose strands of hair from her forehead. She eyed the TEST SECTION door longingly.

"I'm so excited to be here, I can't sleep. I thought I'd take a look around, to get acclimatized."

"That's the spirit," Gaubatz said. "Germany and South Africa, marching side by side, a new world order. . . . Where's your luggage and overcoat?"

"Um, in the dormitory section. I just piled them on an empty cot."

Gaubatz hefted her briefcase.

"Groess Gott." Good God. "What do you have in this thing?"

"Er, some work papers and references. I like to keep them near me. For security, you know, and I do love my work."

Gaubatz smiled warmly. "Good. You'll fit in well."

Ilse stayed respectfully silent. Let *him* fill the silence. On mental pins and needles, she prayed.

"It's nice to meet you. I must be going." He moved to the door.

Once more, Ilse's heart sank. She tried to stall him. "Er, Commander, what's in there?"

"The wind tunnel, machine shops."

"Can I take a peek?"

"Ordinarily. . . . But we're set up for a major test."

"Room for another observer?"

"Sorry. I don't think so."

"But I've come so far."

"I understand. Space inside is very limited." Gaubatz swiped his card and eyeballed the scanner. The heavy door clicked open. He grasped the handle.

Ilse felt her goal slipping away. On the other hand . . . It amounted to double or nothing: If *he* were in there . . .

"Are there any South Africans at this test?"

"Er, not to my knowledge."

"Shouldn't *one* be, if it's so important? It would be a wonderful way to start my stay among you."

Gaubatz smiled and held the door for Ilse. "All right, then. I think you'll find this very interesting."

Jeffrey and Clayton held back while Montgomery peeked around the next corner.

"Bad news, LT," Montgomery whispered. "They've got four guards at the blast interlock to the other half of the lab. Three men, one woman. All with pistols, plus two submachine guns on shoulder slings. They look jumpy."

"They must have found the dead guard," Clayton said. "I'll never make it past them now."

Jeffrey nodded. The three of them had left all their weapons behind with the enlisted SEALs, because of the scanners and metal detectors. There was no way they could fight past these four naval infantry.

Salih watched Jeffrey from several yards away, pretending to wipe a spot on the floor with a rag.

"Shaj," Jeffrey said, "the chief and I can go through together, and leave you here."

"The problem's not me, it's the gadget. They may have *sensors*, you know, at that checkpoint. The box's shielding isn't good enough to sneak it by."

Salih tugged at Jeffrey's sleeve. "You need to sneak your box past the guards?"

Jeffrey nodded.

"You two go through here, say you're welders, *ja?* Me, I'll show the lieutenant the other way, through the air duct."

"Air duct?" Jeffrey said. Of course, there'd have to be one. But . . . "Won't they have intrusion detectors?"

"I can open the grills with my ID—yours won't work, so don't try it. I have access, to crawl through sometimes, to clean out the dust. It's a fire hazard if you let it build up."

"I know. But won't they have motion sensors inside? They'll know there's *two* of you going through."

"The guards disconnected them. Too many false alarms. Mice."

"Mice?"

"I used a toilet float on a string. Rolled it in, then pulled it back. Drove the guards nuts."

CHAPTER 22

"You'll need these," Gaubatz said. He handed Ilse a hearing-protection headset. "This whole area is sound-isolated, so we don't disturb our colleagues. It's a giant raft that floats on oil and rubber buffers, but the source level inside the chamber can exceed two hundred decibels. . . . And don't worry, this glass is armored and flameproof, just in case."

Ilse watched through the viewing port, fascinated, as technicians fueled the missile. The men wore rubberized protective suits. Frost formed on the hose they used. They stood on an antistatic mat. All their equipment was ceramic or plastic. Automatic fire-suppression nozzles ringed the test chamber ceiling.

"It's much smaller than I expected," Ilse said.

Gaubatz laughed. "This is a one-fourth-scale test article, made from the same materials as the full-size weapon."

Ilse blushed. "What's the capacity of the wind-tunnel?"

"Mach ten, though we won't go that high tonight. We do plan for the future."

"How do you get such a high speed in this confined space?"

"We've adapted magnetic rail-gun technology. It drives a system of rotary paddles in the high-pressure part of the loop."

"That must use a lot of power."

"It does. That's why we run these tests at night, when electric demand in the rest of the country is lower."

"What about the waste heat?"

"Tremendous heat, and also when the missile propulsion system runs. They just wrapped up a static test of the full-size engine. The cooling system was working hard."

"The missile's attached to that pylon?"

"Not exactly. You'll understand in a moment."

"The shape isn't at all what I expected."

Ilse studied the missile, trying to memorize every detail. It wasn't a flying telephone pole, or a shark with wings. It looked like a giant chisel, with stubby winglets near the back. Instead of a tail fin, control surfaces jutted from the edges of the winglets. Below the fuselage was a thin rectangular air intake. From this angle Ilse couldn't see the shape of the scramjet nozzles.

"Why isn't it painted?" The missile was mostly shiny silver or flat gray, but had patches in black or orange-gold.

"We didn't apply the ablative antiradar coating. It would make an awful mess, burning off in the test chamber. . . . The missile's defensive and targeting sensors are all conformal. They're liquid hydrogen-cooled, which at the same time preheats the fuel for optimum burning."

"Commander, where does the warhead go?"

"Weapons of mass destruction don't need to be at the *front*, do they? It's not like an artillery shell that actually *hits* the target. The payload bus is at the lifting body's center of mass, where the chisel widens."

The fueling technicians were finished. They withdrew. Others tidied up the test chamber. They left. On Ilse's side of the armored glass, engineers double-checked their instrumentation. The room in which she and Gaubatz stood was crammed with electronics cabinets and consoles, linked by fiber-optic lines and power cables.

"I have another question, Commander," Ilse said.

"Certainly."

"If this test is with a fourth-scale model, don't you have to adjust the results for the differences in air viscosity, and proportion the boundary layer turbulence, relative to the size of the full operational missile? That must be an extremely difficult calculation."

"*Ach.* Quite so." He smiled. "We've perfected the numerical methods involved. The work is done on our supercomputer. The results have already been validated, to a remarkable degree of accuracy."

"What's the purpose of this next test, then?"

"It relates to what *you'll* be working on. A key measure of weapon effectiveness is the probability of penetration to an Allied nuclear aircraft carrier through their entire layered defense, from long range. Live firing tests in the Baltic with full-size prototype missiles, and war-game simulations, also on our supercomputer, indicate that probability to be seventy percent."

"That sounds very good."

"It's remarkable, for expenditure of just one missile. But these missiles are very expensive, and even with mass production they'll be in short supply at first. We want to enhance the penetration probability to *ninety* percent."

Ilse nodded. "That way a salvo of a dozen would take out a whole carrier battle group, escorts and all. . . . Hmmm. And I suppose if you, I mean we, wanted to destroy some Allied cities with ten shots, it's better to kill nine of them than seven."

"The key is better artificial intelligence software for the autonomous counterthreat-evasion routines. Tonight we're checking out the latest software upgrade. It goes hand in hand with improvements to the fluidics elevon controls."

"Now I understand. Penetration probability enhancement research: PEPPER. . . . Does that team work here in the test center?"

"Oh, no. All that work's done in the computer-aided design-and-engineering lab."

"Where's that?"

"In the other half of the installation, near the mainframe."

There were *two* labs?

"They're almost ready now," Gaubatz said. "Put on your headphones."

Jeffrey glanced over his shoulder as the interlock's second blast door closed behind. They were in the other half of the installation now. No one was following them, and no one was in earshot.

"You're *good*," he said to Montgomery. "Remind me to never play poker with you, Chief. You bluff too well."

"Like I told them, not all loyal Germans were privileged to grow up in the Fatherland. It's not *my* fault I'm half-Irish, too—the English-hating kind. I know how to weld, and the Kaiserliche Marine needs skilled welders bad."

"What were you arguing about with that one guard?"

"First she asked me how we got inside, since there was no trace in her computer of me checking in."

"Oops. What'd you say?"

"We came in by truck, through the heavy shipping interlock. Didn't she have a record of any trucks? Then she wanted to see the work authorization. I told them we talked to Human Resources, and the place was a zoo. So, sorry about the lack of paperwork. Did they want the sewage system fixed or not?"

The floor began to shake, enough to tingle Ilse's toes.

"Wind tunnel start-up!" the engineer-in-charge announced on the loudspeakers. A big group of officers and civilians jostled closer to the viewing window, but they left her and Gaubatz room.

Through her headphone protection Ilse could hear a rushing sound, getting louder and higher pitched. She watched a big digital readout next to the window. It was up to Mach 0.80 already, rising steadily.

Gaubatz leaned closer and lifted one of Ilse's ear cups. "We're dispensing with a booster for the test. Any second now."

The number went to 0.90.

"All telemetry feeds nominal!" the engineer shouted. "Commencing the test!"

Suddenly there was another sound, a deep-toned tearing.

"*Scramjet ignition,*" the engineer said. The test staff, seated at the consoles, grew more intent on their displays.

The model missile rose from its pedestal. It wobbled slightly and steadied, facing into the wind tunnel slipstream. Ilse saw a subtle blue glow coming from the missile's rear—air molecules ionized by the searing hydrogen flame, itself invisible.

"Transition to supersonic!"

The meter read Mach 0.98, 0.99, 1.00, 1.01. . . . Ilse actually saw the air at the missile's tip seem to solidify for a moment, the bow shock as it broke the sound barrier—while also standing still. The fire suppression nozzles in the test chamber retracted into recesses. The pedestal retracted into the floor.

"Ramping up to hypersonic!"

The Mach number mounted quickly, 2, then 3, then 4, then 5. The missile's leading edge glowed dull red, from friction with the air. The noise was very loud now, a rumbling buzz and whining whistle. Ilse felt deep vibrations in the core of her gut. The missile continued to fly in place, untethered, maintaining position perfectly.

She leaned to Gaubatz and tapped his shoulder. "Is it radio-controlled?" she shouted.

"*Nein!* It's completely self-guiding, on smart autopilot!"

Ilse was impressed, and frightened. The precision of control was remarkable. Air rushed by the missile at thousands of miles an hour, yet it flew rock steady, varying hardly a centimeter against the orange-and-black position grid marked on the far test chamber wall.

"Going for full flight regime!" the engineer yelled.

Mach 6. Mach 7. Mach 7.9. Mach 8.

The missile body glowed hot orange, some spots even yellow—Ilse felt the radiant heat through the glass. Its exhaust was much brighter, too; a series of harsh blue rings streamed backward. These were standing shock waves, Ilse knew, perfectly stable and symmetric. They implied amazingly efficient fuel combustion and harnessing of thrust.

"Beginning active test of on-board artificial intelligence threat-evasion routines! . . . Threat simulations commencing! . . . *Infrared, on target vector!*" A make-believe interceptor's heat signature, as it approached the missile head-on.

Heat flares flashed. The missile jinked and dipped.

"*Tracking radar, forward sector!*"

A tiny phased-array antenna dropped from the test chamber overhead, outside the slipstream, and scanned the missile.

The missile zipped to one corner of the chamber, dashed back the other way.

"*Simulated overtaking antimissile missile lock-on!*"

Another antenna and heating element deployed from the floor, behind the missile this time.

The model did a corkscrew, a barrel roll, flew upside down.

"Ending test!"

The numbers wound down. The noise and vibrations diminished.

"Transition to subsonic!"

The Mach number held steady at 0.85 now. The pedestal rose up again.

"Scramjet shutdown!"

Robotic grapnels reached up from the pedestal, and locked onto the bottom of the missile. The missile engine stopped. The Mach number quickly fell to 0. The missile rested, heat ripples rising from its body.

Technicians reported to the engineer-in-charge.

"Test successful," he announced. "Software upgrades validated. Improved fluidics control on spec. All performance thresholds met."

People began to applaud. Several of the men pounded each other on the back.

Commander Gaubatz turned to Ilse and grinned. "We're on the way! An historic moment. This must have increased penetration probability by a solid ten percent."

"It's wonderful, sir," Ilse said weakly. *German science marches on.*

"Your job, for the next few weeks and months, my dear, is to help us get it up another ten percent."

CHAPTER 23

Jeffrey and Montgomery searched and searched for Clayton and Salih. They tried to not look as hunted and furtive as they felt. The pair were supposed to have come through an air duct somewhere, here on the far side of the interlock between the two halves of the lab, but *where were they?*

"Sir," Montgomery said, "maybe you and I should split up."

"That would make things worse."

Jeffrey heard an announcement over the public address system. Before Montgomery could translate, a guard came around a bend. He spoke to the two men sternly. Montgomery said something. The guard responded, then moved on.

"So?" Jeffrey whispered when it was safe.

"The staff's ordered to attend a security briefing. Right now, in the main auditorium."

"Where's that?"

"It's in this lab half. Follow me."

When someone broke out bottles of French champagne, Ilse yawned, then excused herself. She left Gaubatz in the test section, and tried to find a stairway to the next level down.

She knew she had to plant the bomb *under* the test section, nearer the structure's solid foundation. Clayton had warned her to avoid a vibration-isolated area. He wanted both bombs going off together, no matter what. If the one the SEALs would plant in the other hardened lab-half was triggered by its antitamper protection, the shock had to reach the bomb on Ilse's side as well, and still be strong enough to trip *its* antitamper.

For now, Ilse would just conceal the bomb. She wasn't allowed to arm it till she had met again with Jeffrey; he would give the rules-of-engagement go-ahead after she gave her report. Ilse felt a powerful craving for the team to *somehow* make it out of the lab, to get back to friendly lines, to carry a warning. From what she'd seen, this Mach 8 missile was a *much* greater threat than anyone realized.

There was an announcement over the loudspeakers, something about a security briefing. Attendance was mandatory for junior staff. Ilse ignored it. *Good, fewer people around.*

She reached the lower level and started scouting for a good hiding place for the nuclear device. She ran into a pair of naval infantry guards. They scolded her for trying to skip the briefing.

Ilse said she was new. They directed her to the auditorium. It was in the other half. She said she was lost, which was true. One guard said he'd show her to the interlock. Now she had no way to hide her bomb.

Still carrying the briefcase bomb, Ilse lingered toward the back of the crowd waiting to pass through the blast-door interlock. Employees were sent through in batches. Ilse noticed the guards were checking people's briefcases and bags. She heard one guard say something about a murder—a body had been found sprawled in a utility space, stabbed repeatedly. The SEALs must have taken him out of the body bag, to conceal their presence and widen the list of suspects, knowing the corpse was certain to be found eventually.

When it was Ilse's turn, she ran her card through the reader and looked into the retinal scanner.

A female guard reached for Ilse's ID, and studied it skeptically.

"How did you get in here?"

"I just arrived," Ilse said. "I'm new." She tried to smile.

"I *said,* how did you get in *here?* There's no trace in the computer of you ever coming from the other section."

Ilse blanched. The employee entrance to the facility, she realized, was in the other half, *and she'd never been checked in.*

She thought of running. She glanced through the nearer set of blast doors. The far set, inevitably, was closed—the interlocking made sure they'd never be ajar together.

"I, er, I, I can't understand the problem. It's certainly not *my* fault."

Ilse knew instantly that was the wrong thing to say, under the present circumstances. It was like pissing off a traffic cop at a roadblock—one who'd just lost a friend killed in the line of duty.

A male guard came over and fingered his pistol in its holster. Two other men quickly checked the rest of the crowd, then let them through. The blast door on this side swung closed, and stayed that way. Ilse was left alone with the guards.

"Your accent," the female said.

"I'm South African."

"Open your briefcase."

Ilse lifted it to the table, needing both hands. She unlocked the top, revealing the files and textbooks. She knew the guards might just be giving her a hard time out of nervousness or boredom. But . . .

The female guard hefted the case. "It's very heavy. What else do you have in this?"

"Um, my laptop."

"Put it through the scanner," the woman said to the man.

"No," Ilse said, thinking fast. "You can't. It's, um, it's a special machine. They told me the scanner fields would ruin it."

"Show it to me," the female said.

Ilse's heart beat so hard she was sure they could see her chest pulsating, or maybe the arteries in her neck. She tilted the case, at an angle away from the guards. She took out the dummy files and made as confused a pile of papers as she could. She showed the keyboard and screen underneath to the guards.

The woman guard's eyes narrowed. "Turn it on."

SIMULTANEOUSLY.

The auditorium held three hundred people. As far as Jeffrey could tell, every seat was taken. He and Montgomery stood at the back, trying to blend with the other standees.

A coarse fat man strutted onto the stage. He wore an expensive dark gray double-breasted suit. He stood at a lectern with a microphone. The man began to speak. Jeffrey didn't understand a word.

Ilse always imagined she'd sweat at a time like this, or feel cold and have the shakes. Instead, she felt nothing, like a robot.

I haven't heard from Jeffrey, but with that test chamber demonstration I've seen enough. I can't let them take me, or let them take the bomb.

"It needs a special password. For security." She began to enter the arming code. The device accepted it. Instead of starting the delay timer, she reached for the plastic shield that protected the instant-firing button. She lifted the shield; this also made the fissionable core preassemble.

Something beeped. "Increased radiation reading," the male guard said. He looked at Ilse and drew his gun.

Can I push the detonator button thrice before he shoots me dead? Ilse fixed her eyes on the guard. She was surprised how calm she felt. She pushed the button once. Then again. Once more and . . .

She had an idea.

"The magnetic storm." She kept her finger on the firing button.

"What?" the female guard said.

"It must be the magnetic storm. It's powerful now."

"You mean to tell me it broke your fancy laptop?"

"No, er, I mean, the security computer. Maybe that's why it doesn't show me coming in, and the radiation reading."

The male and female looked at each other.

Ilse took a breath. "Does your detector distinguish between alpha and gamma radiation? Does it show beta and neutrons separate or together? What's the integration interval? The alarm threshold? When was the last time you had it calibrated?"

The male guard shrugged.

"You're a technician?" the woman said. "Then who's your boss?"

"I was just at the wind tunnel test," Ilse stated. "With *Commander* Gaubatz. You can call him if you like." Ilse tried to act blasé.

The guards, all junior enlisted, hesitated. The point was, Ilse realized, they *weren't* traffic cops. They were naval infantry, and *she* knew a *commander*.

"You go ahead and call him," Ilse said. "*I* have work to do."

"Better hurry," the male guard said. "You'll miss the meeting."

Ilse left the weapon armed, just in case.

Ilse squeezed through a side door into the auditorium. It was crowded—she had to stand against the wall. She glanced across the crowd, and spotted Jeffrey and Montgomery. She looked away at once, in case they saw her and reacted and gave themselves away.

She noticed someone else looking at *her*.

Oh, God, it's that Boer submariner. He knows he knows me.

Ilse waved—what else could she do? He nodded, but seemed puzzled, like he was trying to remember how they'd met. *Now* she started to sweat—the room seemed unbearably hot, and not from the body heat of the audience.

A fat man stood at the lectern. There was a vicious set to his mouth, and he had hard, pitiless eyes.

"I think that we can rest easier now, with closure on this most unfortunate incident. Erika Rainer has paid the price for her treason, unrepentant till the end, hanged by the neck until dead, convicted by a tribunal which I chaired. I can assure you, the circumstantial evidence of her guilt was overwhelming. . . . The entire execution was recorded." He gave the URL on the lab's infranet, so people could download and watch. Ilse saw many in the crowd write the website name down.

"I need not remind you, this entire matter is top secret and is not to leave this installation."

He paused.

"And now I want to *reassure* you. Continue your work, with pride and confidence. Leave worries about internal security to me, and to my staff. They've proven their effectiveness. The last thing we need now is a self-destructive mole hunt."

He asked for questions from the audience, but there were none. Then someone brought him a note from backstage.

The fat man—the head of Internal Security, Ilse realized—turned to the audience and cleared his throat.

"Some of you may have heard that a guard was found brutally murdered this evening."

The audience stirred, alarmed.

The man raised his hands. "No, no. It's all right. A terrible tragedy for his wife and two young children, but the culprits have been found." The audience sat raptly. Ilse dreaded what she'd hear.

"You're aware of the stepped-up security because of the latest partisan attack, near the bay."

People nodded.

"It seems some of the Gastarbeiter became aware of the attack also. Two of them, in the most senseless copycat crime, decided to get in the act. They knifed a guard, repeatedly in the neck, using sharpened pipe-hanger brackets as makeshift daggers. Death was instantaneous. When we rounded up the Gastarbeiter, these two confessed at once."

What the hell is going on?

"They have already been punished," the fat man said. "Hanged while the others were made to watch. A search is being conducted for additional concealed weapons. . . . Now you see why we use them as forced labor. . . .

"I apologize for having to share with you these gory details. You deserve to know what's going on. Again, let me emphasize, things have been taken care of. Leave worries of security to Internal Security, and to the local Naval Infantry detachment."

The man paused again, drew a breath, and smiled.

A screen came down in front of the curtain.

"On a much more positive note, this imagery has just come in from our front lines. You're very privileged to see it before the general public. As you watch, bear in mind that these missiles, of foreign—Russian—manufacture, only do Mach two point five."

The lights began to dim, and martial music blared. Jeffrey realized it would be a wartime newsreel. *Some things never change.*

He glanced around. Diagonally across the auditorium, he made eye contact with Ilse, surprised to see her standing by one wall. He saw her briefcase. He realized she still had the other bomb—in the *wrong* half of the installation.

Now the lights were off. A picture came on the screen, a huge formation of merchant ships and escorts. It cut to one cargo vessel, flying an American flag. It cut to a frigate. It cut to a mushroom cloud blooming over the convoy.

Images from an unmanned aerial vehicle. No, more than one, judging by the angles and timing.

Fireballs burst from underwater. A makeshift troopship vaporized. Warships broke in half. More mushroom clouds rose skyward.

More undersea nuclear blasts. A liquid natural gas ship detonated.

The picture panned the horizon. *Three dozen* mushroom clouds? The convoy and escorts were decimated.

The picture cut to a container ship, no, a *troop*ship, sinking in a spreading inferno of flaming fuel. Black heads in the water, struggling amid the flames, without lips or fingers. A soldier, burned beyond recognition, being lifted into a helo. A woman soldier . . .

The picture cut to a nuclear submarine, pulling into a dock at an underground hardened base. A brass band played on the pier. On the sound track, the martial music continued.

Jeffrey studied every detail, desperate for clues on the sub's location. The camera zoomed to a man in dress blues on her bridge. A voice-over kept saying *Deutschland. Deutschland.* Germany. Germany.

The camera zoomed in more. No. Not "Germany."

Deutschland, the nuclear submarine. Jeffrey's heart raced. *Him.*

The naval officer waved, self-satisfied and smug. He puffed a cigarette. Jeffrey knew that face, that arrogant look. He seemed a little older, and even more sure of himself—as if that were possible.

It was three years now, but Jeffrey still felt the hate. The man who had tried to ruin Jeffrey's career at the Pentagon, through deceitful office politics, and trumped-up charges of sexual misconduct. The man who thought himself, even then, the best natural submariner in the world.

A man with an evil secret, even then. One of the main long-term conspirators behind the Double Putsch.

Now Freggatenkapitan, full commander, Kurt Eberhard.

•   •   •

Ilse had to wipe her eyes. She blinked as the lights came on. Good, let people think it's eyestrain, not grief and horror.

The fat man stepped to the lectern again.

"Naval Intelligence estimates the Allied losses at between fifteen and twenty thousand killed, and thousands seriously wounded or burned, along with the sinking of nine escort warships and over three hundred thousand tons of merchant shipping."

The audience grew even more excited. Several people cheered.

"As I mentioned, this was accomplished with Mach two point five missiles, against which Allied defenses are paltry enough. That, and of course *Deutschland*'s state-of-the-art nuclear torpedoes. In your mind, ladies and gentlemen, picture what we shall accomplish once our Mach eight weapon system becomes operational in the field."

He paused.

"I am very pleased to inform you that the latest wind tunnel test, just this evening, was a complete success."

More people cheered.

"Your senior director, now at a meeting in Berlin, has been informed. The High Command, I am proud to announce, has made the decision to go to full-scale mass production at once. . . . Work will begin immediately to ship the jigs and dies to our impenetrable factories dug into the Alps.

"With this big step, through all your efforts, we usher in a new age of warfare! Victory draws near! Long live the Fatherland! Long live our beloved Kaiser, Wilhelm the Fourth!"

A new picture came on the screen, the post-Putsch national flag: a two-headed black Germanic eagle, clutching the Hohenzollern crown, on a background of blood red.

The audience rose to attention as one, and sang the new national anthem.

Ilse forced herself to mouth the words.

As the crowd dispersed, Montgomery and Jeffrey approached Ilse.

"Follow me," she said, in German. She led them toward a ladies' room. Jeffrey carried the welding gear. Montgomery carried Ilse's briefcase, whose weight he seemed to hardly feel.

"Wait here," Ilse said. "I need to use the bathroom."

Ilse made sure no one else was in the restroom. Then she went into a stall, and bent over the toilet. To mental images of the burned woman soldier dangling on a stretcher in midair, her flesh all black and blistered, cracked and oozing blood, Ilse vomited. She thought of ARBOR—not a code word but a *person,* a pregnant woman with a name—also dangling in midair, and the pair of Turks.

Eventually there was nothing left to cough up. Ilse felt a little better.

Ilse opened the ladies' room door and waved Jeffrey and Montgomery in. Montgomery propped the door open with a spare welding rod, while Jeffrey searched nonchalantly for a security camera. Satisfied there wasn't one, Jeffrey plugged the welding transformer into a utility socket, where it could be seen through the restroom door. He had to make this look good—and also test the rig.

Jeffrey powered up the rig. He clipped the heavy ground cable to the stainless steel side of a toilet stall. He pulled a pair of dark goggles out of the rig's side compartment. He put them on and turned his face away. He applied the welding tip for a split second. There was a blinding flash, a sizzling noise, and an acrid smell. Droplets of hot metal spattered and burned his forearms through his coveralls. He held his breath and prayed, but the smoke alarm didn't go off. The smell lingered enough to give the scene authenticity: maintenance guys at work.

Jeffrey knelt by the side of the stall, ready to do it again if someone tried to enter the restroom. He waved for Ilse to stand in a corner, out of sight from the door. Now they had a place where the three of them could speak safely in English, to plot strategy.

For Jeffrey, Montgomery and Ilse summarized the head of security's speech.

"Someone in there knew me," Ilse added. "I don't think he remembered from where, not right away."

"Who?" Jeffrey said.

"A South African naval officer."

"Great. One more time bomb ticking on our heads."

"How'd you make out with Lieutenant Clayton and Salih?" Ilse said.

"We got separated. We don't know where they are."

"You think they were arrested?"

"If they were, we have a *major* problem. You heard what Shajo said: One bomb isn't enough to make an end to this whole place. . . . If they're okay, they'll head for the emergency rally point."

"How do we get back there? Going through the interlock again tempts fate too much."

"Salih said there was an air duct," Jeffrey said, "but we couldn't find it. It's not on the floor plan."

"Are you satisfied with the ROEs?" Ilse said.

"What did you find so far?"

Ilse told him and Montgomery about the missile test. They listened raptly. She also mentioned what Gaubatz said, that key people worked on this side of the interlock, in a separate computer-aided-design lab.

"Okay," Jeffrey said. "The ROEs are met. We're all expendable."

"But—"

"We just heard of three people martyred here, and saw tens of thousands slaughtered in combat. We can't let them down, nor everyone else who's counting on us."

Ilse hesitated only a moment. "I agree."

Jeffrey was surprised how determined she sounded. *We were just starting to really know each other, our moods and dislikes and desires, and now we're going to die.*

"Chief, you head upstairs. Find a guard. Ask them outright where's the air duct. Also, ask if they've seen a guy in a welding mask."

"That's risky, Skipper," Montgomery said.

"We'll have to chance it. Then come back here."

Montgomery left.

"Ilse," Jeffrey said, "I'll stay put, and keep pretending to weld. I want *you* to go back out there with your device. Find the computer center. Arm the bomb, then hide it somewhere good."

"It's already armed."

Jeffrey's eyebrows raised.

"I had some trouble with the checkpoint guards."

"Did you start the timer?"

"No. I almost had to use the instant-firing switch."

Jeffrey felt himself shiver. "Emplace it. Set the time delay for nine zero minutes, and start it running."

Ilse began to leave, then looked back. "Um, I, I want you to know, Jeffrey, it's been an honor working with you."

Jeffrey gave her a poignant smile. "It was good for me too, Ilse. I'm sorry if I seemed hard on you before, on the ship."

She came closer. "I, if only . . ."

"I know. In another life . . . I guess it just wasn't meant to be."

She turned to go, then turned back again.

"What if we can't find Lieutenant Clayton?"

"Then your bomb's all we've got. Half a lab's better than none."

CHAPTER 24

The first A-bomb was ticking. On the upper level, hiding behind a row of roaring fan blowers, Jeffrey and Ilse and Montgomery looked up at the entrance to the air duct. It was two meters off the floor, protected by a grating.

"Salih said he needed his ID to get inside," Jeffrey said.

"Want me to see if I can force it open?"

"We have nothing to lose, Chief."

"Yeah, that's for sure. Give me a boost, please, sir."

Jeffrey knelt and put his hands against the wall; Montgomery climbed onto his shoulders. The chief reached for the grating.

"It's open. Held with shims."

"It might be a trap," Ilse whispered.

"We have to take the chance," Jeffrey managed to grunt. He was still supporting Montgomery's full weight.

Montgomery jumped down. "Ilse, you go first."

Ilse climbed on Jeffrey's shoulders, and Montgomery helped her reach the air duct. With the grate swung open now, she chinned herself up and climbed inside.

Montgomery took the welding transformer and climbed on Jeffrey's shoulders again. Jeffrey almost collapsed from the weight.

The chief pushed the transformer into the opening. They might need the welder to emplace the other bomb, and abandoned somewhere here it might warn guards there were intruders.

Montgomery let Jeffrey stand, then linked his hands to make a stirrup. He boosted Jeffrey up.

Jeffrey clambered inside, and pushed the transformer forward—it was too tall to roll upright in the ductway. The metal case scraped loudly along the concrete. Jeffrey saw Ilse crawl further in, on hands and knees. When there was room, Montgomery leaped and chinned himself into the ductway.

"I can't reach the grate to close it," Montgomery said.

"Leave it," Jeffrey said. Soon enough, it wouldn't matter. Nothing would matter.

They crawled on. Eventually, past Ilse, Jeffrey could make out the other end of the duct, with another grate. Right in front of him, partly blocking his progress, was a constriction in the ductway: the visible edges of a titanium frame for an automatic blast door.

Jeffrey kicked himself; he wasn't thinking. Of course there'd be a blast shutter here. He tried to get the welder past the bottom edge of the frame. It was very awkward, in such confined space. Ilse couldn't possibly turn around, and Montgomery was behind him. Jeffrey had to do this by himself.

He levered the heavy transformer onto the lip of the frame, almost crushing a finger. He began to shove the rig forward. A little further . . . a little further . . .

The transformer slid through.

Crap!

Jeffrey pulled back just in time. The transformer dropped off the frame with a heavy thud, and the edge of the thick blast door snapped down like a guillotine. An alarm began to sound. *Trapped, on the same side of the lab as Ilse's bomb.*

Jeffrey heard guards running to the air duct. There was noise as someone positioned a ladder. He heard rifle charging-handles pulled back and released. Rounds slid into chambers, and selectors clicked off safe to fire—six or seven men.

A guard shouted something angry in German.

Montgomery shouted, too, then said something apologetic.

Jeffrey glanced back. Montgomery was holding his ID card over his shoulder so the guard on the ladder could see. Two other guards held assault rifles over their heads, aimed into the duct; Jeffrey just saw their forearms and their weapon muzzles—5.56mm caliber, the same as M16's. Jeffrey displayed his own ID, though he was too far in for the guard to read it. Montgomery pointed to the blast door, and shouted something more. He pointed again for emphasis.

The guard stepped down from the ladder. Another took his place, and covered them warily with his rifle. The alarm stopped. The blast door rose and reset. There on the other side was the welding gear. Ilse was gone. Montgomery pointed at the transformer, past Jeffrey's body, and spoke to the guard.

The second guard said something, nodded, and climbed down from the ladder. The rifles aimed into the duct disappeared.

Jeffrey heard a radio hiss and crackle. They must be talking to guards at the other end of the duct. *Ilse's end.*

Jeffrey climbed out headfirst at the other end of the air duct—that grate was swung wide open. Montgomery held his ankles till Jeffrey's hands could reach the floor. Awkwardly, Jeffrey stood. Montgomery handed down the transformer.

Jeffrey had an idea. He checked the coast was clear, so he could talk. "Chief, can you jam open the blast door with a welding rod?"

"Good thought, sir. Be right back." This way one bomb might be enough to kill both halves of the lab—or it might not.

Jeffrey saw a socket. *"Chief,"* he said in a whisper. Jeffrey plugged in the extension cord and lifted the rig to Montgomery. "Weld the rod in place. In fact, try to weld the door open."

Montgomery nodded. He backed in, dragging the rig. There were blue-white flashes, then more scraping of metal on concrete. The end of the rig reappeared.

Jeffrey grabbed it, then helped Montgomery down. He knelt so Montgomery could get back up to shut the grate, and remove any traces of the shims.

Ilse stepped out from behind a big steam manifold. It hissed and dripped. "Guards came by and did a sweep, but I evaded round these pipes till the ones on your side called them off."

Jeffrey smiled with relief. He gave her a hug, and she squeezed back.

"Let's get to the rally point." Jeffrey turned to Montgomery as they strode along, wheeling the welding rig, looking over their shoulders nervously, hoping they wouldn't be apprehended too soon, before they could turn the missile lab into a double nuclear Hell.

"You did it again, Chief," Jeffrey said to try to lighten the mood. "Faking out those guards."

"So I'll get an Oscar, posthumously. . . . This maintenance worker act is wearing thin, sir."

Jeffrey nodded. The guards might double-check and see there was never anything wrong with the duct that needed welding, and that Salih's ID, not a repair authorization, had opened the grates.

"Also, sir, the guard asked me if we'd seen a late-twenties woman with shoulder-length brown hair. *You*, Ilse."

"They're on to me."

"How did you get down from the duct headfirst so fast?" Jeffrey said.

"The grate didn't look like it could hold me, so I tried to do a parachute landing fall."

"You've had jump training?" Montgomery said.

"No. I told myself this was no time to clutch, and just *did* it. . . . I don't think I broke anything."

"The grates," Jeffrey said. "It's been nagging on my mind. I think Salih and Clayton are still on the loose. The way they left the ductway clear, those shims—it's like they were trying to plant a message for us. . . . I'm starting to have a new plan."

"There's another problem," Montgomery said. "That automated checkpoint we came through near the utility space, you remember, with Clayton and Salih. How do we get Ilse past it now? I'm sure they've invalidated her ID."

"We have to knock out the videocamera," Jeffrey said. "Then one of us can carry her on his shoulders through the floor-to-ceiling turnstile."

"Won't breaking the camera set off another alarm?" Ilse said.

"Sir, let me use the welding rig real quick, since they'll be watching on the fish-eye. I'll zap the camera cable."

"I like it. Then, if we can move fast enough, the alarm should work in our favor."

• • •

The alarm must have been silent. Past the turnstile, the threesome ran as fast as they could. They came to the spot where the rest of the SEALs were hiding. It was an especially hot, humid, and noisy cul-de-sac, where few lab workers or guards were likely to go, well concealed by big steel cooling pipes that also gave good cover from enemy fire.

SEALs One and Nine brought their weapons to bear, then waved Jeffrey through as soon as his group was recognized.

Clayton and Salih were there, huddled over a floor plan and recon photos. Clayton was suited up for battle. Salih held a pistol borrowed from a SEAL. Twenty other Gastarbeiter were there, also armed with borrowed pistols, or borrowed knives or grenades, or lengths of pipe. They weren't a rabble, but a disciplined formation in two squads.

"When we couldn't find you, sir," Clayton said, "Salih alerted his people. We were hoping you three would make it back on your own."

"I think there are guards right on our tail," Jeffrey said. It was better tactically for the first wave of guards to come to *them*. "Where's the toolbox?"

"Inside a T-joint access hatch, in a cooling bypass loop we closed the valves to isolate. . . . Where's Ilse's briefcase?"

"In a supply room in the other half," Ilse said, "down on the third level. Behind cartons of printer paper and water-cooler refill jugs."

"I know what's in your boxes," Salih said. "I'm a building engineer, remember? You'd never come this far just to spy. Do what you have to do."

"ROEs have been satisfied." Jeffrey checked his watch. "Lieutenant Clayton, arm and start your bomb, seven five minutes timer delay."

"Arm and start it, seven five minutes, aye." Clayton rushed off. SEALs One and Nine moved out to deepen the perimeter. One of Salih's squads followed each SEAL, crouching low.

Jeffrey and Ilse hurried into their black drysuits and flak vests. They pulled on urban warfare camo smocks—a pattern of broken shapes in white and black and gray, like shattered concrete and asphalt. SEALs Seven and Eight helped them don the rest of their battle gear. Jeffrey double-checked Ilse from head to foot, feeling very protective of her, especially now that they might have a chance to survive. She stood still for his close inspection, and made quick eye contact from very close, and there was something very intimate and special in her look.

Jeffrey turned to Salih. The Turk's stooped posture was long gone. His eyes sparkled in a way Jeffrey hadn't seen before.

"You held something back from us, didn't you?" Jeffrey said.

Salih grinned. "Need-to-know, Commander. In case you were captured yourself. After the first hangings, we reorganized from an ersatz labor union into infantry platoons in secret. A lot of the men did national service in the army, in Turkey or in Germany. I made corporal before I got out of the *Bundesarmee*." The German Army.

"Did your two men really confess about the guard?"

"I'm not good at making speeches. Those two volunteered, as soon as I explained things. They knew what would be done to them. I knew the rest of us would have to watch. *That* got my men fired up, far better than my words could."

Jeffrey gulped: *the self-sacrifice, the ruthlessness.* "I'm glad you're on our side, Mr. Salih."

"Call me Gamal."

"There are a hundred of you?"

"Some are massed at key points on the other side of the interlock, waiting to break cover when they hear the shooting reach them. The rest of us are here, or waiting near here. My men all know the only alternative to escape is death, from your bombs or from a German noose. We'll fight hard."

"How many more of you have firearms?"

"None so far," Salih said. "We'll get them the time-honored guerrilla way, from enemy dead. Some of you might reach the surface, with our help."

"*All right.*" It would be a slaughter, but with both A-bombs in place they had nothing to lose. The same idea had come to Jeffrey after crawling through the air duct—to join with the Turks and try to fight their way out together—but Clayton and Salih were way ahead of him.

Clayton returned. "The device is armed and set." Jeffrey looked at the SEAL team leader with new, heightened admiration.

"There's one change," Jeffrey said. "On the way out, we work past the test chamber, and grab the model missile."

"Concur," Clayton said.

"There's something else," Ilse said. "We should swing by the computer center. Before the A-bombs blow, we steal the drive disks outright."

Over Jeffrey's helmet earphones came, "Six, One, contact! Contact!"

Around a bend there was a crackling burst of assault rifle fire. Jeffrey heard soft sputtering, and whining ricochets, as SEALs One and Nine responded. A grenade went off with a flash and a sharp concussion, and there were screams.

CHAPTER 25

To sounds of more gunfire, Clayton finished his hasty briefing, telling everyone where to go and what to do and how to stay coordinated. "Keep them guessing! Keep up the pressure! *Don't stop for anything till we get out the front door!*" Each platoon had phase lines, and intermediate objectives, like any infantry assault. Clayton, Montgomery, and Jeffrey each commanded a platoon. Each of the SEALs, and Ilse and Salih, led a squad of Turks.

Jeffrey's group took off in one direction, Montgomery's in the other. Ilse and Salih stuck with Clayton, the headquarters platoon.

There was a deafening blast. The overpressure tried to burst Ilse's lungs. Her headphones crackled.

"Six, Nine. Turnstile down with C4!" That was SEAL Nine calling Clayton. Smoke and concrete dust began to fill the air.

Another burst of assault rifle fire, then more grenades.

"Six, Three! Three Platoon advancing toward trucking interlock!" That was Montgomery. Ilse knew his thrust was a feint, but one with a purpose. He *had* to secure their rear. With most of Clayton's scratch command half-starved Turks, they couldn't afford a fight on two fronts inside the lab.

Ilse followed Clayton round a bend. She leaped past dead Germans and Turks. Her own Gastarbeiter squad followed in her footsteps, lugging her pack. Some of her Turks stopped to strip dead guards of weapons and ammo, helmets and body armor.

"Their boots!" Ilse shouted in German—the Turks' sandals were pathetic and it was dead of winter outside. *"Take their boots!"* A spent round ricocheted past her head, then another. She bent lower and charged. She came to the wrecked turnstile; she vaulted over twisted titanium bars. It was raining. *What?* The sprinklers had gone off. She dashed through a waterfall, a ruptured overhead pipe.

She glanced back. Three of her Turks had weapons. She waved for them to fan out, to build a base of fire. For all their zeal, their combat skills were rusty; she didn't want one firing into her back.

"Six, Three," came over her headphones. "Truck interlock jammed as ordered. Mechanism fused with thermite grenades. We'll wreck the service elevator next." Ilse heard and felt a heavy blast. "Elevator destroyed."

"Three, Six. Casualties?" Ilse caught a glimpse of Clayton, firing on the run. He dropped a guard. Another fired at Ilse, hit one of her Turks. She dropped the other guard. A Gastarbeiter grabbed the fallen Turk's rifle.

"Achtung, achtung," came over the public address. "All staff proceed to safety areas. This is not an exercise."

"Five, Four," Jeffrey's voice called Ilse. "What was that?"

"The staff's taking cover!"

"Where?" Jeffrey shouted.

"Ten," Ilse yelled. *"Where?"*

"The dorm and the wind tunnel area," Salih said. "They're armored." Ilse relayed—Salih, now squad leader Ten, lacked a helmet radio; Ilse's number was Five.

"Three, Six," Clayton called. "Repeat: *casualties?*"

"Six, Three," Montgomery answered. "SEAL Seven is dead. We lost fifteen Turks. Rear secure. Beginning retrograde movement."

"Copy. What's your body count so far?"

"Ten enemy dead. All naval infantry. Eight's squad is sweeping the level beneath us now, blocking the stairways with cluster minelets to isolate the level under that."

"Three, Six. Copy."

"Six, Nine." Nine was also now on the level below, beneath the rest of Clayton's platoon. Nine led another squad of Turks—Ilse had seen them assaulting down a stairwell.

"Nine, Six. Go."

"They keep changing the encryption keys, to lock out captured radios. More naval infantry are mustering outside. I heard something about a freight train coming, with Army helo gunship escort."

"Nine, Six. Copy," Clayton said. "We're heading for the wind tunnel. Keep pace under us! Work with Eight's squad to cover your flank. Break break. Four, Six—status?"

"Taking heavy fire," Jeffrey said. "When's that freight train due?"

"Four, Nine. They said about four zero minutes."

"Six, Four. Reset your bomb, four zero minutes."

"*What?* You said seven five!"

"That's a direct order, Shaj."

"*I'm* in charge of the mission. We'll never get out of here in forty minutes!"

"Six, Four. With the ROEs, I rule."

Ilse heard Clayton hesitate. "Four, Six. Roger that, aye, aye. Break break. Nine, Six, you copy?"

"Six, Nine. Affirmative. I'll reset the bomb." Nine knew the anti-tamper disarm code.

"Four, Six. Status?"

"We're taking heavy fire near the air duct," Jeffrey said. "Unable to advance."

"Fall back," Clayton said. "When Three Platoon links up, assault the duct again."

"Copy."

"Six Platoon," Clayton said, "squads Five and Ten, to the second level now! *Follow me!*"

Jeffrey spun and fired and spun and ran. He tried to make every shot count, trying to slow down the German pursuit. He was the leader of Four Platoon, and Four Platoon was retreating. Something slammed Jeffrey's flak vest from behind but didn't penetrate, and he dropped to the floor and crawled. Jeffrey fired over his shoulder, then crawled more. A Turk, too slow, had his back stitched. He thumped hard to the concrete; his head bounced, then lay still.

Everywhere the sprinklers poured. *This is like house-to-house combat in a monsoon.* Rifle reports echoed harshly in the corridors and stairwells, making it hard to tell who was where. The Turks with German weapons made it worse.

At least the heavy sprinkler flow held down the smoke and cordite fumes, and suppressed the dust from shattered plaster and concrete. But it couldn't soften the broken glass from smashed fluorescent bulbs—Jeffrey's arms and legs bled. He had no choice: The enemy fire was too intense to duckwalk now.

Jeffrey's surviving men scrambled back around the cover of a structural load-bearing wall. They clambered over dead Germans, whom they'd killed just moments before. Among the lifeless navy blue, and the bright red blood, Jeffrey saw orange: dead Turks.

Desperate for cover as more enemy closed in, Jeffrey gestured for his men to pile the bodies as sandbags. He noticed these dead guards wore bandoliers of beanbag rounds, with taser stun-guns on their belts. The Turks had already grabbed the riot guns and twelve-gauge killing buckshot loads.

Bullets snapped overhead, or thudded into the bodies. One Turk raised his head too high—his skull exploded.

Jeffrey squeezed off three aimed shots with his pistol, using his helmet visor reticle, and hit one guard in the face. The German had pulled the pin on a offensive concussion grenade, but didn't live to throw it. It detonated under his belly. More gore pelted Jeffrey and his men, red and gray and purple. The deep puddles on the concrete floor were tainted with fresh blood.

Then Jeffrey saw something else among the dead guards' gear.

"Six, Four! Six, Four!" Nothing. More bullets snapped overhead. A Turk raised his shotgun blindly while he sheltered behind fallen friends, and answered with a deafening *boom*.

"Six, Four," Jeffrey repeated into his open mike. On his headphones he heard the others breathing, grunting, and cursing, and the sounds of battle in stereo. Up his nose he smelled spent high explosives, acrid bullet propellant, and pungent vomit and urine and shit.

"Four, Six. Go!" Clayton said at last.

"These dead guards have radiation detectors!"

"*What?*"

"Six, Five." Ilse's voice sounded, above more firing and more grenades and screams. "I had to show that lady guard my *laptop*."

"Team, Six," Jeffrey heard. "They're on to us. Pick up the pace."

Jeffrey's .50-caliber pistol was empty; the sound suppressor smoked. He loaded another clip. A grenade landed behind him. Its fuse train also smoked. A Turk grabbed the grenade and threw it back in time. Jeffrey ducked, and another searing shock wave overtook him—the engagement ranges were too short for fragmentation grenades. Burning debris pelted Jeffrey's legs, then was extinguished by the constant freezing downpour.

"Six and Four, Three," Montgomery said through the ringing in Jeffrey's ears. The chief was breathing very hard. "My flanks are linking up with yours."

The sounds of German firing increased. Every second that passed, the two A-bombs came closer to detonation. Every second that passed, German experts might find the bombs and disarm them—to prevent their going off too soon from blast shock from the firefight, Jeffrey had ordered their antitamper sensitivity set on low. The best way to protect the bombs, and the *only* way to escape, was to keep up the attack toward the front door of the lab.

Jeffrey heard a grunt and a gurgle on his radio. Then he heard a Turk shouting in German on the circuit. "Two's dead!" SEAL One translated. "A Gastarbeiter has his helmet."

Two Squad was leaderless now. "One, Four," Jeffrey ordered. "Have Two Squad merge with Eight! Then get Two's commo gear to Ten, to Salih!"

"Team, Six," Clayton snapped. "Next assault phase, *commence*."

All the remaining lights went out. Battery-powered blackout lanterns switched on from the overheads. The Germans shot them one by one. Jeffrey realized what the guards already knew: The Turks had no way to see in the dark.

Jeffrey popped an illumination flare. It ignited and he threw it toward his front. It skidded and hissed along the concrete, then burned brightly even in the endless indoor deluge. Weird shadows flickered on the pockmarked walls.

Jeffrey traded his electric pistol for the Turk's captured twelve-gauge shotgun. He showed the man how to use the backup iron sights on the SpecWar weapon, with their tritium dots for night work. They traded ammo.

Jeffrey jacked seven fresh shells into the big pump-action magazine under the shotgun's barrel. He looped a bandolier with twenty over his shoulder.

"*Forward!*" Jeffrey screamed.

•   •   •

Jeffrey fired at the ground, halfway between himself and a group of German guards. The deadly pellets bounced hard off the concrete, then tore on at kneecap height—they knocked the Germans down. Some of Jeffrey's men threw grenades. His squad hit the deck. Detonations flashed; the shock through the concrete punished Jeffrey's insides. SEAL One and his men dashed from around a corner. They poured fire at the guards from enfilade. Four Platoon had reached the air duct. They *had* to get through the air duct, or Montgomery's push through the interlock, to the other half of the lab, was doomed.

Another naval infantryman stuck an assault rifle out of the duct and sprayed Squad One. Two Turks fell, bellowing in pain, mortally wounded. SEAL One and his surviving squad returned the fire. The German's corpse dangled from the air duct.

"One, cover me!" Jeffrey shouted. Jeffrey grabbed an aluminum step stool, twisted and riddled from bullets and blast. Two of his Turks helped him toward the air duct. Jeffrey aimed his shotgun into the duct and fired and pumped and fired and pumped and fired and pumped. The bullets spewing at him from the other end of the duct subsided for a moment. He shoved the dead dangling German in front him as a shield, vaulted into the duct headfirst, and fired another blast. Two Turks came in right behind him with German assault rifles.

Jeffrey pushed the corpse-shield ahead. He crawled through slippery blood and gore. The Turks kept pace over both his shoulders, their bodies close, bonding in a way civilians could never know. The Turks kept firing toward the other end of the tunnel. Germans kept firing back. Bullets hit Jeffrey's helmet, his flak vest, with the force of baseball bats. One of the Turks was hit. Jeffrey fired another shell and crawled on; the dead guard he used as a mobile sandbag was being pulped. Another Turk took the place of the one left dead behind Jeffrey, and the threesome pressed on.

A German guard vaulted into the tunnel from the other end; he too used a dead man as a shield. Two other Germans climbed in behind him, and *that* threesome advanced. Halfway between them and Jeffrey lay the jammed-open blast door, the constriction giving a modicum of extra cover. Whoever reached it first would have a razor-thin advantage.

Jeffrey fired another shell, then another. The Turks on both sides emptied fresh 35-round clips, as the Germans fired back on full auto. Hot, angry hornets spat by in both directions; Jeffrey was struck by spent shell casings, and sand-blasted by concrete chips. His Turks died instantly; the Germans to his front also died.

The tunnel ahead was clogged. Jeffrey scrambled past the blast door. He tried to push the pile of bodies ahead of him, but they wouldn't budge—the Germans were barricading the air duct from the other side.

Jeffrey heard something on his headset. He was almost deaf; he turned up the volume.

"Four, Three! Four, Three!" Montgomery was calling him.

"Three, Four. Go!"

"You've *got* to take the far side of the interlock in enfilade! If my platoon goes through the blast doors unsupported, the interlock's a murder hole!"

"Three, Four. *We're trying!*"

Jeffrey reached to his load-bearing vest, grabbed a handful of C4 and a timer. "Back," he screamed to the new men crawling behind him. "*Back!*"

They understood. Jeffrey glanced over his shoulder, watched them pile out of the air duct entrance oh-so-far away, as their comrades beyond the duct mouth yanked them by the feet.

Jeffrey set the timer and shoved the charge into the jam-up of bodies. He crawled backward fast for all his life.

Men helped him down and they took cover and the C4 blew.

Flame and smoke belched from the air duct. More enemy fire belched from the air duct.

A Turk aimed his rifle into the air duct. Automatic fire killed him instantly. Another Gastarbeiter took his place. His forearms were shattered at once, and he fell back in paroxysms of pain.

"Four, Three," Chief Montgomery called. "We're pinned down, taking heavy losses. *We need support!*"

SIMULTANEOUSLY, ON THE LEVEL BELOW.

By the hot, smoky light of illumination flares, Clayton's platoon fought their way toward the entry to the test section. Ilse was their guide, keeping to the rear per orders, shouting directions to Clayton and SEAL Nine. On her headset she could follow the desperate see-saw battle raging on the level above. She heard the shouts and screams and weapon reports over the circuit, and felt the shock of grenades and C4 through the deck and through the air. The carpet here on level two was squishy from water and blood, and bodies slumped like tattered sacks of trash.

Resistance on the second level seemed weaker now. Were the Germans laying a trap somewhere ahead? Did they really know there was an A-bomb ticking, or more than one, or were they just not taking chances? Ilse was glad she'd thought to hide her case behind a pile of water jugs: The H_2O would help block gamma rays and neutrons.

Ilse heard Montgomery shouting for reinforcements. Salih offered to take some men and head upstairs, and Clayton said to go.

Ilse moved closer to Clayton. She passed a badly wounded German writhing on the floor. He was pimply-faced and looked barely seventeen. He kept calling, *"Mutti, Mutti."* Mommy. Tears streamed from his eyes.

Ilse shot him through the forehead, under the lip of his helmet.

Ilse reached the heavy door to the test section. It was locked. Of course. Salih had said the whole area was armored.

Clayton's men, the Turks, diminished in number but almost all of them armed now, crouched on both sides of the corridor. Two of them at the back, Ilse noticed, held big fire axes they'd broken from emergency-equipment cabinets.

SEAL Nine fixed lines of sticky detcord to the test section door. He started a timer and everyone pulled back around a corner.

The air itself seemed to solidify and heave. The door clanged to the deck. The men poured fire through the portal and charged inside.

Guards returned the fire and something knocked Ilse backward and knocked the wind out of her. She saw the stub of a bullet sticking from her flak vest, smoldering hot. Her breasts hurt. More automatic weapons spoke in both directions, but Ilse's throbbing eardrums barely heard. To one side of the control room a crowd of technicians took cover behind a barricade of desks and consoles, while a squad of naval infantry tried to hold off Clayton's platoon. Two of the guards, crouched behind overturned steel desks, had light machine guns mounted on bipods. They poured an endless stream of bullets at the

SEALs and Turks, pinning them down. Through the armored glass of the wind tunnel beckoned the model missile.

Clayton and SEAL Nine crawled for the inner door to the wind tunnel chamber, below the arc of fire of the bipod MGs. More guards tried to head them off. Ilse saw SEAL Nine clipped in the leg by a bullet. Clayton had one bootie heel shot off.

"Five," Clayton shouted, *"use grenades!"*

Ilse pulled two concussion grenades from her battle vest and pulled the pins and popped the spoons. She counted to three and threw them over the barricade. They exploded in midair. The MG fire ceased.

Turks charged the crowd of cowering technicians. For a split second the surviving guards were torn between who or what to protect, the staff or the missile.

The Turks opened fire on the German technicians mercilessly. The guards cut down some Turks, till Ilse and Clayton killed them, too. A pair of scientists with nothing to lose lunged for the fallen guards' weapons. The pair of Turks with fire axes blocked their path and cut them down. Ilse saw the ax heads rise and fall relentlessly, and red blood sprayed and bullets crackled.

The victims were in uniform. None had tried to surrender.

With a sharp *crack* SEAL Nine's detcord blew down the door to the test chamber. Ilse dashed inside. It was very warm in here.

She tried to lift the missile. It barely moved. She had to pull her gloved hands back—it was still scorching hot from the test.

"The fire nozzles!" she shouted, pointing at the overhead. She set the master selector knob to *"Wasser."* Water. Nothing happened.

SEAL Nine popped another illumination flare, and held it against a flame detector head. The water nozzles sprayed a freezing blast; the missile cooled. The Gastarbeiter dashed in and hefted the missile to their shoulders, then ran out like pallbearers with their prize. Seal Nine quickly bandaged his leg wound; it was minor.

Clayton and Ilse covered their rear as they withdrew. Ilse glanced into the corner of the control room. Blood dripped from the walls, and from the overhead. The Turks had left not one scientist alive. Ilse was revolted by the carnage. It was hard to tell where one corpse ended and the next began.

On second thought, Ilse ran and checked the light machine guns. "Light" was relative; these fired 7.62mm—.30-caliber—rounds.

One of the weapons was smashed, but the other worked. Ilse draped herself with belt after belt of ammo, till she could barely stand. She hefted the weapon and chased the rest of Six Platoon upstairs.

She passed some badly wounded Turks; it tore her guts to know they had to be left behind.

They pleaded for grenades, to try to take a German with them. She gave them what she had.

Jeffrey heard a strange whirring sound behind and wheeled in panic. He saw a huge pile of sandbags coming at him.

Salih shouted it was him, and Jeffrey realized he drove a heavy forklift. The bags held halite and rock salt.

"For the sidewalks and roads and parking lot," Salih said.

"I think they'll do."

Bullets poured steadily out of the air duct now, in short but vicious bursts. Jeffrey realized the Germans had set up a light machine gun on the other side.

"Six and Three, Five. Six and Three, Five."

"Five, go!"

"Shaj, Chief, there's no way we can make it through the air duct. The Germans have set up a static defense. We'll be cut to pieces."

"Five, Three, if we make a direct assault through the interlock *we'll* be cut to pieces."

"Maybe not," Jeffrey said while he rigged wads of C4 as booby traps around his side of the air duct. "Salih has something we can use as an armored car."

Ilse watched Jeffrey and Salih pull up with the forklift. Again she surveyed to the front.

Their side of the heavy blast doors gaped open. The doors into the other half of the lab formed a solid obstacle. Bodies of Turks and Germans littered the deck between the sets of blast doors. The walls were marked with bullet impacts and gore, and debris smoldered even with the sprinklers going.

"They've had too much chance to set up on the other side," Montgomery shouted. "Every time we move in and close this side so we can open the other doors a crack, they pour in overwhelming fire."

Behind them, one of Jeffrey's booby traps went off. SEAL One emptied a clip in the direction of the air duct, his weapon *puff-puff-puff*ing as it recoiled heavily. A German assault rifle chattered back, and ricochets zinged past. Another blob of C4 detonated by the air duct.

"Get that forklift in there!" Clayton shouted, pointing to the interlock. "Use the rock salt bags, the bodies, everything! Fortify a line, and then we've got to *go for it!*"

Everybody went to work, building a makeshift slit trench across the space inside the interlock. Everyone took positions, laying out spare ammo clips and grenades and flares. Salih still drove the forklift, with a good supply of sandbags left on the pallet as a shield. Jeffrey with his twelve-gauge shotgun, and Ilse with her light MG, climbed onto the back of the electric-powered forklift, protected by the sandbags in front. Now the team had armored, mobile, heavy firepower.

Montgomery worked the interlock controls, and the blast doors closed behind them. At the last second he tossed a thermite grenade at the workings on the other side, to isolate the Germans trying to outflank the SEALs through the air duct. One way or another, there'd be no retreating now.

Montgomery pushed the button on the wall to open the other set of blast doors, into the other half of the lab.

Nothing happened. "They've locked us out!"

"Try the manual override!" Clayton snapped. "They might not have fused the gears yet!"

Montgomery yanked open the utility hatch built into the wall. He heaved, and undid the linkage for the main hydraulic mechanism. He grabbed the giant hand wheel. SEAL One helped, and they cranked the outer blast doors slowly open.

They took fire at once.

Jeffrey let off five buckshot rounds. Clayton opened fire, and the surviving SEALs, One and Eight and Nine, did, too. Turks also started shooting as they gained good lines of sight. Ilse climbed atop the heavy metal cage that protected the driver's seat of the forklift from falling cargo. She waited . . . a little longer . . . a little longer . . .

She poked her MG over the top of the sandbags on the forklift and held the trigger down. A belt with a hundred rounds worked through her weapon rapidly. Hot spent shell casings flew everywhere, and her barrel smoked. From her vantage point well off the floor she pulverized the guards and furniture to her front. She changed belts.

"Go, go, go!" she screamed. She felt Salih floor the accelerator.

Salih charged. She pressed the trigger again, and swept her flaming muzzle back and forth. Beside her Jeffrey's shotgun boomed and boomed. The rest of Clayton's company maintained a base of fire from the sandbags in the interlock.

The Germans broke and ran. One guard glanced back—it was the woman who'd challenged Ilse before. Ilse cut her in half with MG fire.

"Achtung, achtung!" came over the public address. "All lab staff evacuate the installation. All lab staff evacuate the installation."

Ilse recognized the voice. It was the head of Internal Security.

Salih's improvised armored car sped down the main corridor on the upper level. Clayton, with SEAL Nine, followed on foot to one side, leading the rest of the team. Jeffrey stayed with the main force on the upper level. Ilse and Montgomery took Three Platoon to the deck below. More Turks emerged from hiding, and joined the fight.

Four—Jeffrey's—and Six—Clayton's—Platoons both kept advancing. The Germans kept falling back.

The forklift, with Jeffrey riding shotgun, sped round another corner. In front of them was a second line of German defense. Desks, refrigerators, massive piles of thick tech manuals, formed an impenetrable barrier. There were no stairwells beyond this barricade protecting the main entrance/exit interlock: There was no way to outflank. The Germans opened concentrated fire—their withdrawal had been a trap.

Salih and Jeffrey pulled back in the forklift. The sandbags at the front were riddled. Bullets punched through and nicked Salih in the arm and smashed the forklift's battery compartment. On momentum, one-handed, Salih steered around the corner in reverse. He and Jeffrey bailed out. Jeffrey stumbled over yet another dead German guard.

"Six, Five!" Jeffrey shouted. "I see different insignia! We're meeting reinforcements!" More naval infantry had come into the lab, to engage the SEALs as forward as possible.

Clayton, somewhere to Jeffrey's left, didn't answer.

"Six, Five. We can't advance!"

Still nothing. Jeffrey realized the guards were expendable, even if a nuclear demolition killed them all. It was far more important to keep Clayton's team from escaping with the missile and anything from the computer center, and let the remaining lab staff get away.

"Five, Nine," Jeffrey heard. "We're pinned down bad! Lieutenant Clayton's hit!"

SIMULTANEOUSLY, ONE LEVEL BELOW.

The computer center, a dead end in the floor plan, was heavily defended.

"We can't get in without damaging the disk drives!" Ilse said.

"We have to flush the Germans somehow," Montgomery said.

"The fire suppression system for the mainframe. I saw it. It's poison gas!" It worked by blocking oxidation—fires stopped burning, men stopped breathing.

Ilse and Montgomery and SEAL Eight pulled on their dive masks and put their Draeger regulators in their mouths. A handful of Turks grabbed breather packs from cabinets of fire-fighting gear. The others held back at a safe distance, based on Ilse's instructions.

"Move it!" Montgomery yelled to his assault team. Ilse and the men advanced, firing on the run, mowing down the guards who tried to protect the way into the computer center. SEAL Eight blew in the door with a deftly handled miniature satchel charge.

"Watch it!" Montgomery snapped. "Don't damage the disk drives."

"The emergency handle!" Ilse shouted. "There!"

SEAL Eight broke cover and reached for the big red handle for the gas. German fire hit him in the arms and legs. He grunted and clenched his teeth. He lunged again and grabbed the handle. As more bullets pounded into him he pulled the handle hard.

An alarm bell sounded and the invisible gas hissed. The guards tried to don their gas masks, but the masks did them no good: They asphyxiated. Other guards broke cover to reach the respirators stored in the computer center for just this reason. Ilse and Montgomery cut them down. The Turks in air packs moved in to mop up.

Montgomery checked SEAL Eight. He shook his head.

Ilse ran to the main memory storage units. These were big white cabinets with see-through doors, ranged in a circle so their fiber-optic interconnections would be as short as possible, and processor speed consequently high.

The superdensity disk drives themselves looked like stacks of platters, like old-fashioned records on a record-player changer; each drive wore a big number. Crude, but a way to prevent clandestine pilferage. Near the storage units were spare carrying cases, also numbered, locked inside another see-through cabinet. Montgomery broke open the doors of the floor-to-ceiling units. Alarms sounded immediately.

They had no idea which drives held what. Ilse and Montgomery took them all.

They loaded the magnetic drives into the carrying cases. They and the Turks with respirators lugged them out of the computer center and linked up with the rest of Three Platoon.

Ilse knew this was a desperate measure. The disks were fragile, and not saltwater proof, and unshielded on the surface the magnetic storm might spoil them all. She hoped National Security Agency data experts would be able to decode and reconstruct the key information.

Over her helmet radio she heard that Jeffrey's platoon was halted by another wave of guards, and Lieutenant Clayton was down.

CHAPTER 26

Jeffrey was in command now, and he'd run out of further options. He finished loading the back of the forklift with six small satchel charges. SEAL One jury-rigged connections in the battery box, to get enough current so the thing could move. The driver was a heavily bandaged Turk volunteer, already shot in a shoulder and one thigh, who knew he'd never make it far in any case.

Jeffrey yanked the igniter cords on the satchel charges together. He prayed the shock wouldn't trigger the A-bombs' antitamper. *They had no choice.* He fell back to where SEAL Nine was giving first aid to Clayton's pelvic wound.

The Turk driver screamed something and charged the German barricade. The German firing increased, and concussion grenades went off. There was a dreadful detonation, the loudest, hardest one so far.

Jeffrey charged immediately through the smoke. Now he held a German assault rifle in either hand, firing both at once. Ilse worked her light machine gun. Montgomery threw concussion grenades as far ahead as he could.

Surviving Turks charged after them. Others carried the SEALs' packs, much lighter from their heavy use of ammo and explosives.

Others brought the model missile, and the computer disks. Two men served as Ilse's ammo bearers now.

The combined satchel charges worked terrible havoc among the latest German position. Furniture and equipment were shattered beyond recognition. The blast broke so many overhead pipes, the sprinkler heads ran dry. Ammo cooked off as wreckage burned. The stench was sickening. Jeffrey's team paused to quickly salvage bullet clips and weapons—they were running dangerously low.

Jeffrey advanced again, firing and reloading constantly. He and Ilse and the rest of the team bled steadily from nicks and cuts: from bullets and broken glass, ricochet fragments, and flying shattered concrete and metal and wood. From the unending unbearable noise of battle they were almost deaf; Jeffrey's eardrums felt persistent pain and throbbing pressure. His rifle barrels were red-hot, and he knew they'd be drooping, making the weapons inaccurate—but at such short range it hardly mattered.

The team came to one last German position, barring the main interlock to the surface. Jeffrey spotted the fat man—the security chief—firing a pistol.

Jeffrey eyed his watch: four minutes till the A-bombs blew. If the interlock was jammed, the SEALs were trapped. If it wasn't jammed, more German reinforcements could come through any moment. Both Jeffrey's rifle clips ran empty. Next to him, SEAL Nine's ran empty.

"Use cold steel!" Jeffrey yelled. "The Germans *hate* cold steel." He caught Ilse's eye and shook his head, motioning her to save her remaining MG ammo—hitting the armored blast door walls, the heavy-caliber ricochets would go *everywhere*. Behind a structural column Jeffrey fixed a captured German bayonet to a captured German rifle. He loaded a fresh clip, his last, and chambered a round.

Jeffrey tossed Ilse his other rifle. He watched her fix a bayonet. He heard Montgomery shouting orders to the Gastarbeiter in German; they, too, fixed bayonets. Some Turks grinned.

Jeffrey tossed smoke grenades. Through the smoke he threw illumination flares.

Jeffrey cleared his throat. *"Charge!"*

•   •   •

Ilse lunged and parried and lunged and stabbed. Her rifle clip was empty; in close-quarters hand-to-hand fighting there was no time to reload. Everywhere around her, men screamed and grunted. She heard rips and thuds and clicks and crunches, as butts and bayonets clashed with each other or hit home. These barely registered on Ilse, as her combat mind focused in a tight tunnel-vision toward the front. Also in her mind she heard a constant scream of fear and panic, her own inner voice, but she had to keep on fighting. Any second she might die in agony. She cringed in naked vulnerability as she worked: The difference between life and death was random chance. She had no time for praying now—God helped those who helped themselves.

The Germans' backs were to the wall, the inner doors of the last interlock. The SEALs' and Turks' backs were to the wall, the A-bombs about to blow. Behind Ilse flames crackled, and harsh flares hissed. In front of Ilse macabre shadows danced.

Ilse found herself face-to-face with the head of internal security. He realized she was a woman, and aimed his pistol at her head with obvious delight. The hammer clicked on an empty chamber.

Ilse jammed her bayonet way down in his groin, just above the pelvic bone. She dug and lifted and dug and lifted, pinning the man against the inner blast door. His eyes widened and his mouth gaped. She twisted her rifle and worked the muzzle back and forth. Pink foam issued from his mouth, and his face turned white. He began to collapse against Ilse's weapon, shuddering and convulsing. Bright red blood spattered her cammo smock, and boiled against her overheated gun barrel.

She yanked free her rifle and plunged the bayonet into his chest, right at his heart. The weight of his body pulled her weapon down with him. She tried to remove the rifle but the bayonet was jammed, tight in his ribs.

She jumped—Jeffrey was tapping her on the shoulder.

"*Next phase!* We have to get through the blast doors *now.*"

Ilse looked around in shock. The Germans all were dead. SEALs and Turks worked over the latest bodies, reammunitioning.

A Turk ran up to the corpse of the security head, whom Ilse had left where he fell. The Turk gave back her light MG—she was still swathed in belts of ammo for it, though the belts were swathed in blood. Ilse stood under a broken water pipe to clean her gear. With a fire ax the Turk cut open the fat man's chest with a nauseating crunch, and freed the assault rifle. He grabbed it with a smile. A comrade tossed him a loaded clip.

ARBOR, and the martyred Gastarbeiter, were avenged.

Again the surviving company squeezed into the space between the inner and outer blast doors, missile and computer drives and all. This time there was no time to lay out sandbags, and they had no idea what forces they'd face on the surface.

Ilse lay flat behind her bipod-mounted machine gun. Montgomery opened the outer door a crack.

Cold air blew in. No snow. There was a blinding flash and a deafening *crack* as something impacted hard against the outside of the blast door.

"They've got an armored car!" Montgomery shouted—a real one.

SEAL One retrieved his pack and pulled out two small shoulder-mounted antitank weapons.

"Watch out!" Montgomery said. "These have a back-blast!"

Everyone scrambled aside. Ilse waited to be roasted alive by flame from the bazooka shells. Montgomery fired through the narrow space between the halves of the blast door. There was a roaring *woosh*, then a flaming blast outside.

The interlocking space was filled with plastic particles, not flaming gas—the recoilless antitank weapon was meant for use in confined space after all. The armored car was in flames—the shaped charge warhead burned through its thin armor. Its 75mm ammo began to cook off. The whole vehicle jumped and shivered, then the turret blew sky high.

SEAL Nine opened the blast door wider and Ilse and the others charged. The air was crisp but still. The ground was covered with four or five inches of snow. The sky was clear and bright. Ilse lifted her night-vision visors.

Above her, powered by the solar storm, a brilliant aurora flickered and pulsated, dancing sheets in evanescent red and green and blue, forming arcs and curtains and long converging lines. From her left, tracer rounds arced in the SEALs' direction. From her right she heard another heavy motor, another armored car. She saw the sparkle of its laser range-finder. SEAL One fired the other antitank rocket, but he missed.

The armored car fired, and a high-explosive shell tore up the dirt—its shock wave made the aurora seem to ripple. Turks rose and charged the armored car from opposite directions, while its gunner hurried to reload. The commander stuck his head out, and reached for the top-mounted machine gun. Ilse cut him down; his body draped the top hatch. The armored car's hull-mounted machine gun opened up. One Turk lived to reach its engine deck. His satchel charge exploded. The armored car exploded.

Jeffrey led his people instinctively to the right, away from the heavy machine guns and toward the bay, the water, a SEAL's best refuge. He knew his group was in the installation's parking lot. In the distance, by the auroral lights, Jeffrey saw people piling into buses. Some buses were already further off, on the road to Greifswald— surviving lab staff, rushing to safety. They were out of range of his weapons.

SEAL Nine had said there was supposed to be a freight train.

Jeffrey knew from intel that many westbound trains here were laden with explosive ordnance, manufactured in occupied Poland. Helo gunships escorted the trains to protect them from local partisans. This train wasn't on any known schedule, but the enemy must've seen the magnetic storm as a chance to sneak one through. Most trains used special radiophones that propagate along the rails. But now there'd be huge DC voltages coursing through, and the engineer was probably out of touch.

The German heavy machine guns on the left fired more bursts of tracer. In the parking lot, the SEALs and Turks tried to use the remaining vehicles for cover—their owners must have been killed, or told to get on a bus. Mercedeses and Porsches in the reserved section jumped and sagged as 12.7mm heavy MG rounds shredded their tires. Their windshields dissolved in greenish clouds of fragmented safety glass. Bullets clicked through sheet metal and clanged through engine blocks. Gas tanks blew, and liquid fire poured along the ground.

Jeffrey saw a neat row of BMW motorcycles, in gaudy colors. Tracers stitched them all, seeking out a running squad of Turks. Several men were hit. The 'cycles toppled like dominoes, then their gas tanks cooked off one by one, ignited by the heavy fire. The dead armored cars continued to burn merrily, throwing fireworks of their own into the air. Rubber, fuel, ammo, bodies, all gave off thick black smoke. Through the stinking fumes red tracers probed and pierced, sweeping back and forth, long killing bursts. Here on the Ryck River's floodplain, the land was flat; Jeffrey and the others were pinned down. They were all going to die, here in this parking lot.

Where the hell was that freight train? Had its helo gunship escorts spotted the action in the parking lot, and flagged the engineer down?

In the distance, from due north, Jeffrey saw a sharp flash. Instantly he heard a roaring sound, and a high explosive shell hit the far end of the lot. Four thousand yards away, atop the cliff that overlooked a cove, the Kooser See, a main battle tank was firing at them. Another flash, another tearing roar, another shell—this time it hit much closer. Jeffrey knew Leopard III's had 120mm cannon, almost as big as a modern cruiser's five-inch gun.

Where the *hell* was that train?

Another flash, due east this time, and another big shell blew the burning motorcycles to fragments. There was *another* tank, at the edge of the cliff across the Danische Wiek. Jeffrey's team was surrounded, cut off on low ground.

In the distance Jeffrey heard a train's air horn, and the growl of mighty diesel locomotives. *Finally.* Then he heard the beating of helo rotor blades. He looked at his watch—the A-bombs should have blown already! Had they been disarmed by German nuclear-munitions disposal experts? How good were Clayton's backup antisabotage devices?

The tank on the Kooser See cliff fired again. Wounded Turks writhed and screamed. The tank across the Danische fired again. It almost hit the model missile.

The diesel growl got deeper and louder. No! The train was going *faster.* They were rushing it on through, to escape this local threat. Once it passed the lab, the SEAL team's situation would be hopeless.

In a burst of anger and resentment, Jeffrey concluded the Joint Chiefs knew all along this raid would be a one-way mission. *We had to try, I guess.* He thought of the SEALs, the Gastarbeiter, him and Ilse, all sacrificed on the altar of military necessity. *Was it worth it?*

Suddenly the whole world *jumped,* and there was an ungodly sound like thunder from below: Clayton's nuclear booby-traps had beaten the German experts after all.

Atomic earthquake shocks repeated, and the ground began to move.

Ilse knew the soil at Greifswald was sandy, and the water table high. The lab structure actually floated in the soil, with pilings driven deep for added stability. The shock of the atomic detonations drove down beneath the lab, hit the underlying bedrock, then bounced back, over and over. The frequency hit a natural resonance of the massive structure. The soil around began to ripple in waves, literally liquefying. The shattered asphalt of the parking lot heaved up and down like sea swell.

Jeffrey yelled for everyone to use these temporary hillocks as opportunistic cover, and make their way northeast. Ilse ran and threw herself to the ground. She rose and ran again, past a burning Audi. Its vanity plate said GAUBATZ. As she watched, the plate's enamel burned off from the heat.

In the distance, the train whistle blew again. Then Ilse heard a harsh screeching that went on and on: The train was trying to stop. Still more tracer rounds followed the SEALs and Turks. Some of the men carrying the model missile were hit. Others took their places. Still others helped Clayton, who hobbled and bled.

Another heavy machine gun opened up from a different quarter. Ilse realized it sat on the speedboat pier that Jeffrey was trying to reach. Now they were caught in a terrible crossfire, between the MGs and the tanks.

Ilse rolled onto her back and reloaded in the snow. She watched and felt red tracers snap by right above her. She watched veils and rays and streamers in the ionosphere shimmer and play, beckoning to her in eerie silence from a hundred or a thousand kilometers up. She knew they were glowing atmospheric molecules, excited by the massive charges of the solar flare, a record-setting aurora that easily outshone the setting quarter moon. Ilse knew the energies involved in this otherworldly celestial display vastly exceeded all the nuclear weapons ever assembled on earth.

Ilse finished changing belts. She rolled again and fired.

Through a pair of binoculars held to his night-vision visors, Jeffrey could see helicopter gunships peel off from escorting the freight train. He watched the headlight of the train, at the front of a line of ten throbbing diesel locomotives. The boxcars trailed off into the distance, to the east, Poland—there were over a hundred of them. Jeffrey saw that the helos were heading right for him now. Their gunners fired bursts of 30mm cannon shells from their chin-mounted gatling guns, to test the weapons and test the range. Jeffrey had to duck as more machine gun tracers probed in his direction from the land, first from near the road to Greifswald and then from the speedboat pier. White-hot razor-sharp shrapnel whizzed by from different directions, as the tanks kept shelling the parking lot.

The earthquake shocks subsided. Jeffrey had a job to do, even if he'd never make it out alive. The lab structure, its massive roof jutting above the ground, seemed intact. He pulled out a handheld radiac. The radiation from the blast appeared to be contained—if there was a bad leak he'd know it, solar flare or not.

The helo gunships fired again, peppering the parking lot. Jeffrey really, *really* didn't want to die.

Ilse heard the screech of train brakes go on and on—the tracks must have been damaged by soil movement effects. Then there was a series of ten heavy, thudding rumbles, heard through the air and felt through the ground. Diesel fuel ignited as the locomotives' huge fuel tanks tore open. There was another staccato, thunderous noise as each freight car derailed in turn.

The freight cars began to pile up, then exploded one by one or in groups. There was a long series of blinding flashes, moving progressively away, back toward Greifswald. The ground trembled again. The airborne shock waves hit. It felt like sledgehammers were pounding Ilse's intestines and ovaries repeatedly, much worse than the twin atom bombs. She remembered to keep her mouth wide open, and put her hands to her ears—she was so deafened by now her radio was useless, even if it hadn't been overwhelmed by static from the sky.

Jeffrey watched, appalled, as the whole ammo train cooked off. He remembered now each freight car could hold one hundred tons. That meant a train a hundred cars long carried ten kilotons of high explosives—enough to take the whole neighborhood with it, including Jeffrey and all his team.

The effects were just like those of a nuclear weapon, without the fallout. Jeffrey saw helos knocked out of the sky by the endless explosions and shock waves. The aircraft fell to the ground or into the bay in pieces, as their fuel blazed in midair. Jeffrey saw the evacuating lab staff buses fall on their sides or go flying. They were swallowed by the spreading flames, pulverized by exploding crates of iron bombs and mortar shells.

Jeffrey heard a new kind of roar, from the north and from the east. Both chalky cliff faces gave way, under the burden of the tanks, because of the terrible seismic shocks. He saw the seventy-ton vehicles plummet into the water, making huge splashes.

He looked back toward the train. A narrow but mile-long mushroom cloud of glowing gas rose into the sky, tallest at the near end where the cars had blown up first. It seemed to reach for the aurora, and Jeffrey watched their colors embrace. Jeffrey drew grim satisfaction that his idea to move up the timing of the atom bombs had worked; by derailing the freight train, the ground around the lab—jutting into the bay between the Danische and Kooser—was mostly isolated from the mainland now, and from enemy reinforcements.

Then *things* began to come down—no radiation from this weird-shaped chemical mushroom cloud, but there *was* fallout after all.

A whole train wheel whizzed by and clanged into the parking lot and pulped a Turk. Another flew overhead, then skipped like a giant stone across the bay. Uncrated mortar shells whistled and tumbled through the air at random; some burst where they landed, some were duds. The burning, fulminating train gave off waves of radiant heat, so intense the snow was turned to slush. Shapeless pieces of steel and wood pelted the SEALs and Turks, some of it burning or red-hot. Jeffrey saw a blackened arm land nearby and steam. Then a German army helmet, human head still inside, plopped down next to Jeffrey and rolled across his legs. Pieces of sheet metal fell more gently, and clanged on top of asphalt or autos or Gastarbeiter. The rain of solid debris formed a nonstop counterpoint to the roaring and bursting of the ammo train, and the crackling of burning vehicles in the lot.

Jeffrey ordered his people forward. They *had* to reach the water, and a platoon or more of German soldiers was rushing down from the north, beyond the front end of the freight train. The machine gun on the pier opened up again—it had escaped the earthquakes and the conflagration, and its crew were angry men. Jeffrey hit the dirt.

Salih dropped next to Jeffrey. "I think I can make a diversion for you," Salih shouted. "If we all stay here we're dead men. I'll lead my people in the other direction, and we can try to join the partisans in the forest."

"No," Jeffrey yelled. "I want you to come back with us."

Salih shook his head. "I can't leave my followers." Nearby, Ilse's light machine gun fired at the heavy one on the pier. Rifles cracked on semiauto or crackled on full auto—the SEALs were long out of ammo for their sound-suppressed electric guns. Ilse's MG made a tearing sound, and the heavy MG bellowed. The approaching German soldiers' fire grew more effective, too.

A big wave hit the seawall. It broke, and drenched the parking lot with spray—a local tsunami, another effect of the massive explosions.

"Look, Gamal, we *need* you, to go in front of the U.N. It might get your mother country to come in on the Allied side, or at least give Third World neutrals second thoughts about joining the Axis."

SEAL Nine crawled up next to them. Ilse fired again, from a different position, at the German soldiers this time. Some of them spun and fell in lifeless heaps. The others continued advancing by squad, using fire and movement steadily. Jeffrey filled Nine in.

"Mr. Salih," Nine said, "I can stay and work with your men. An even trade, me for you." Nine's name was Andy Cooper, from northern Idaho.

Jeffrey didn't disagree with Cooper. A SEAL, training and leading a partisan group, would make a formidable force. There was a sick social Darwinism here—the surviving Turks were good but cautious fighters, and combat-blooded, too.

Salih turned to Jeffrey. "I can't swim."

"If we're lucky you won't need to. We'll try to capture a speedboat, or make a raft."

Salih looked at Jeffrey like he was crazy.

Montgomery crawled closer. "I think you should come with us, Mr. Salih. We SEALs are *good* at water egress." Once more Ilse's MG exchanged short bursts with the German soldiers. Their light MGs responded. The surviving heavy MG also tried to find and silence her. Salih shot at its emplacement on the pier. He didn't answer Jeffrey or the chief.

Jeffrey sent Cooper to fetch Ilse and have her give her weapon to a Turk.

Ilse crawled to the command group. Jeffrey filled her in.

"I agree, Mr. Salih," Ilse said. "I've had to go through this myself. We *need* you to speak out, to testify. . . . You can always return, reinsert through hostile lines. Look at *me*."

Salih hesitated, and Jeffrey could see his torment. The constant incoming fire and detonations in the distance wouldn't help him think.

"All right," Salih finally said. "I suspected this was coming . . . assuming *any* of us get out of here alive."

"I'll form up the men for a diversion," Cooper said.

"That German platoon is working closer," Jeffrey said. "I'm going after the machine gun on the pier."

A helicopter gunship tore in from over the water, its Gatling cannon blazing. Out of the corner of his eye Jeffrey saw Montgomery pull a Stinger from his huge equipment pack. He fired. The rocket roared at the helo. They connected. There was another bright flash, then a hard, sharp *bang,* and debris fell into the bay. The MG on the pier fired toward the source of the Stinger, and everyone blended into the now-wrinkled asphalt. Bits of pavement—secondary projectiles— pelted the group once more.

"I'm going into the water," Jeffrey shouted. He'd seen a boat tied to the pier. "Chief, keep that MG distracted!"

"We're out of missiles!"

Jeffrey swam under water in his Draeger. The surface roiled and chopped, from the earthquakes and landslides and tidal wave.

His dry suit was badly cut up, and he was quickly chilled. At least the cold reduced the pain of his minor cuts and wounds. He surfaced quietly under the pier, and spotted the fortified emplacement for the machine gun. From this close its report was very loud. Spent shells fell between the planks of the pier, and hissed on hitting the water.

From below, Jeffrey placed a satchel charge. He yanked the timer cord.

A guard saw something through the planks, and fired down with his assault rifle. Jeffrey dived away, and the bullets plunged past his right side—the guard had forgotten to account for the bending of light by the water, and his aim was off.

The satchel blew. The force of the air-burst was painful even underwater. Burning planks landed in the bay. Jeffrey stayed submerged for protection. When the rain of debris died down, he came to the surface. The emplacement was blasted to smithereens. Jeffrey cursed. So was half the pier, and the rowboat he'd seen tied up. His SpecWar skills were stale; he had used too much explosive.

He turned around and almost shit his dry suit. He saw a low-slung landing craft come right at him. Its top hatch popped open, and two heavily armed men aimed their weapons in his direction. They recognized him, then scanned the sky for threats. It was Meltzer's minisub, running in on the surface. He'd been watching through the periscope, and waiting for his chance.

Meltzer held the minisub against the remains of the pier with his side thrusters. The two SEALs who'd stayed in reserve with Meltzer dashed forward with a heavy mortar and mortar bombs, to help drive the approaching German soldiers back. There was another huge eruption from the ammo train, and everyone ducked.

"Chief," Jeffrey shouted above the noise, "give Nine and the Turks all we can spare of weapons and food and medical supplies!"

Montgomery nodded. "It looks to me like they've all got good footgear and overcoats by now!"

Turks and SEALs carried Clayton and eased him down the open top hatch. Jeffrey and Ilse handed down the disk drives. These too went into the transport compartment, including parts smashed during the battle. Jeffrey hoped they weren't impaired by the magnetic storm—at least the cases were nonconductive.

Last came the model missile, still largely intact. It barely fit through the wide top hatch, and had to be left awkwardly filling most of the lock-out sphere. Those who were staying behind bid farewell to those who were leaving. Cooper said he'd do everything possible to maintain a diversion, to draw forces from the bay.

Jeffrey threw some radiation sensors into the water, then closed the top hatch; the sensors would transmit in a few days, to show if the bay was contaminated. Meltzer got underway, following the narrow dredged channel leading from the pier.

Montgomery, watching the sonar, shouted that a speedboat was attacking. Jeffrey opened the top hatch—the water was much too shallow for the mini to submerge. Water splashed and sloshed as the minisub picked up speed. It had low freeboard; one shell through the hull and they were finished.

Jeffrey shouldered a Stinger that a reserve SEAL passed him from below. Jeffrey drew a bead on the speedboat. He was afraid the Stinger might not work, out here in the conductive seawater with the solar storm, but he got a tone as green tracers probed in his direction. He fired, and the missile tore away. It hit the boat, and fuel and ammo blew in wild secondary bursts. The aurora high above, reflecting off the choppy bay, plus the exploding ammo train, made a beautiful light show. Flying debris kept landing in the water all around.

Jeffrey dropped back inside and dogged the hatch. In the lock-out sphere, bending around and leaning under the missile, the two reserve SEALs were finished suiting up. Each held a compressed-air-powered underwater rifle, which fired depleted uranium bullets, deadly out to twenty or thirty feet.

"In case we meet enemy swimmers, sir, leaving the bay. They may try to block the hole in the concertina, or put limpet mines on our hull."

Jeffrey nodded. These men were *up*, clicked in, ready to fight. He knew he was in good hands.

Jeffrey went into the back to check on Clayton. The wound was through his lower left pelvis, from front to back. SEAL One said it must have been a 7.62mm round—.30-caliber. It hadn't tumbled, but cleanly pierced muscle and went right through the saddle of the pelvic bone, below vital organs and away from key blood vessels and nerves. Clayton was very, very lucky—he might even return to combat status. He was shocky, getting plasma from an IV, and groggy from a morphine shot, so Jeffrey didn't try to talk to him.

Jeffrey gave silent thanks that Clayton had survived; Jeffrey had grown very attached to the man, his forthright confidence and clear thinking under pressure. Jeffrey knew Clayton would be torn up inside over the deaths of three more of his men, plus so many fallen Gastarbeiter. It was just as well he was sedated for a while.

Jeffrey spoke gently to Salih, who sat with one arm in a bloody bandage and a sling. Salih seemed in mental shock himself, morose and distant. He began to murmur in Arabic, a Muslim prayer.

Jeffrey pulled himself away. He had much too much to deal with to get sentimental now, and didn't want to grow maudlin himself over their heavy losses. This was his own third SEAL raid, counting the one years ago in Iraq, and the loss of friends in combat never got easier.

Jeffrey chided himself. He'd sworn after the first time not to introspect; it just worsened the hurt. Plenty of chance after the war—if he lived and if the Allies won—to think back at reunions over beer or something stronger.

Jeffrey steadied himself as the mini started to roll in deeper water. Montgomery announced they were diving. Jeffrey heard the ballast tanks begin to vent. The continued detonations from the ammo train, transmitted through the water, boomed and reverbed like a distant thunderstorm.

Jeffrey went through into the control compartment, dogging the hatches after him. He squeezed behind Meltzer's seat. Ilse stood behind Montgomery; the chief was pilot again. In the rig for red, out of line of sight of the chief and Meltzer, Ilse reached and squeezed Jeffrey's hand.

Was she feeling it, too, the postaction emptiness? The elation of being alive fast turned to black depression over the wastefulness of it all? Jeffrey squeezed back, gratefully, and felt a bit less lonely. Ilse's touch lingered seconds longer than it should. Finally, she reluctantly broke his grip, and wiped a tear from her left eye. Jeffrey tried to make eye contact, but she stared stoically ahead, at the tactical plot. Speedboats and more helo gunships charged about, firing MGs and cannon at the water.

"Pilot," Jeffrey said, "ahead flank. Zigzag smartly. We need to get out of here before somebody with a depth charge or torpedo reaches the bay. Those sonar helos may come back, if their avionics aren't scrambled by the storm."

Montgomery acknowledged.

"Sir," Meltzer said, "if we make it through that hole in the concertina, what do you want to do? There's hardly any fuel left."

"Let me see the nav chart."

"We could try to bluff our way at one of the German bases on the Baltic," Montgomery said, "and get more fuel and have more options."

"I don't think so," Jeffrey said. "Even with comms disrupted by this magnetic storm, and power blackouts, they'll have fiber-optic land lines." Jeffrey was sure the alert would go out soon, if it hadn't already, even if German intercommand and army/navy connectivity were slow. Jeffrey knew his team's whole survival now came down to a race against German reaction time.

"Sir," Montgomery said, "we'll barely have enough range to reach the southern coast of Sweden at four knots. It's fifty nautical miles."

"It'll take forever," Meltzer said. "The Germans will cut us off."

Big cannon shells impacted close, probably from more Leopard III's, and Montgomery veered to starboard. Jeffrey held on tight.

"It's our only chance," Jeffrey said. "Make for neutral territory. Maybe we can escape-and-evade into the hinterland with our booty, and contact the American embassy or something."

There was another heavy explosion in the water.

"The mountains in the winter will be murder," Ilse said. "Stockholm's a long way from the southern coast."

"If the Swedes pick us up," Montgomery said, "and don't shoot us on sight, we'll be interned for the rest of the war. They'll keep our goodies themselves, sir, even give them back to Germany." Another big shell landed, somewhere ahead, and Montgomery veered to port.

"Ilse," Jeffrey said, "you have any other thoughts?"

"I wish I did."

Jeffrey stifled a heavy yawn. The adrenaline was wearing off, and he felt an overwhelming drowsiness. "Ilse, there's nothing more you and I can do right now. Let's go in back and try to get some sleep and let these guys do their jobs. Pilot, Copilot, your objective is the Swedish coast."

CHAPTER 27

THREE HOURS LATER,
IN THE GERMAN MINISUB.

Jeffrey jerked awake. He'd heard an explosion—it *wasn't* a dream. The transport compartment seemed half empty, because of the three SEALs killed in action, and Andy Cooper staying behind. Equipment packs littered the deck. The hard-drive cases were stacked near the chemical head.

Jeffrey glanced at Clayton and Salih. Clayton slept, but his color seemed good, and the SEAL attending him gave Jeffrey a thumbs-up. The reserve SEALs clutched their uranium-pellet air guns.

Salih looked very pale. "I'm seasick, and I'm feeling claustrophobic."

Jeffrey forced a knowing grin. "You just need something to do, Gamal. Remember your army first aid?"

"*Ja.*"

"Help us take care of the lieutenant."

Salih nodded, and stopped feeling sorry for himself.

"Let me see what's going on." Jeffrey went forward. In the lockout sphere he eyed the Mach 8 missile, and wondered if it would ever reach friendly lines.

Ilse was already up and in the control compartment. Jeffrey had noticed this at Durban—in combat she had boundless energy. She was getting to be quite a veteran. So was Meltzer.

Jeffrey read the display screens. The mini was making flank speed, all of twelve knots, on a course near due north. Their depth was one hundred thirty feet, in one hundred fifty feet of water. German frigates and patrol craft had them surrounded. The fuel gauge read five percent, and they were many miles from Sweden.

"That blast just now was an old design of torpedo," Montgomery said, "launched from a missile boat. Crappy software, made bottom capture, blew a hole in the mud."

More explosions sounded in the distance.

"Depth charges that time," Jeffrey said.

"We're stealthy," the chief said, "but they're closing in."

"Any mines nearby?"

"We're still in their submarine exercise area. . . . Of course, they could drop new mines."

"Where are all their training subs?"

"Warned away, we think, Captain," Meltzer said. "To give the combat-ready surface force an open field."

Jeffrey glanced at Ilse. She tried to smile back reassuringly— without success. "Can't we blend in?" Jeffrey said. "Pretend to be a training sub, like before?"

"What's that get us?" Montgomery said. "A POW cage, and a gibbet for Salih and Ilse."

"*Torpedo in the water!*" Meltzer said. "Bearing zero seven zero! . . . Constant bearing! Sounds like an SUT unit, Captain, wire-guided, launched from that Class one-thirty corvette east of us." A corvette was smaller than a frigate, but nimble and aggressive still.

"Range?" Jeffrey said.

"Seven thousand yards."

"Torpedo attack speed?"

"Er, thirty-four knots."

"Impact in six minutes," Montgomery said, "unless we keep running, and run down our peroxide."

"Pilot," Jeffrey said, "go shallow, thirty-three feet. Maintain flank speed. Steer two five zero." Away from that torpedo. "Copilot, stand by to equalize the lock-out sphere. Ilse, gimme a hand."

Jeffrey and Ilse went into the sphere. In a small locker was a case of three-inch chemical noisemakers. The mini took a steep up-bubble. The missile shifted, and Jeffrey almost broke an ankle. He and Ilse got the noisemakers out.

The mini leveled off. The air pressure in the sphere began to rise. Jeffrey and Ilse pinched their noses and blew. The pressure held at two atmospheres. The torpedo began to ping.

Jeffrey knelt and opened the bottom hatch. Water splashed from the mini's high speed. Jeffrey held out a hand. Ilse gave him a noisemaker. He threw it into the water, hard. She gave him another, another. Contact with saltwater would do the rest.

Jeffrey grabbed the intercom. "Pilot, make a knuckle, steer due north." He and Ilse held on as the mini banked into the turn.

Jeffrey dropped three more noisemakers, then closed the bottom hatch. Again he grabbed the mike.

"Equalize to one atmosphere, then go deep."

"How deep?" Montgomery asked on the intercom.

"Ten feet off the bottom."

Jeffrey and Ilse went into the control compartment as the mini nosed back down. The incoming torpedo pinged more rapidly.

"Torpedo still on constant bearing," Meltzer said. "Range decreasing fast."

There was a tremendous concussion, and the mini lurched and yawed. One of the wide screens went blank, and smoke came from the environmental control console. Meltzer cut the power there and sprayed with CO_2. An acrid stink lingered.

"We're still under control," Montgomery said. "That fish went for the noisemakers."

Jeffrey watched the tactical plot. The surface craft converged on the latest datum.

"New passive sonar contact!" Meltzer said. "*Bremen*-class frigate, bearing two eight zero, range twelve thousand yards. . . . *More* new passive sonar contacts, two helos, closing fast from two eight zero."

"We're never gonna make it," Jeffrey said. "We're almost out of fuel, and almost out of noisemakers. We lie doggo on the bottom, they'll just wait us out or hunt us down. Our environmental control is fried, and our battery's almost flat."

"Torpedo in the water!" Meltzer screamed. "From two eight zero, the *Bremen*. It's a prewar U.S. export, a Mark forty-six." A dangerous one.

Jeffrey eyed the nav chart. "Bottom the boat in this hollow just ahead on zero one five. Maybe we can hide in the terrain."

"*Air-dropped torpedo in the water! ASW helo overhead!*"

"Damn," Jeffrey said.

The Mark 46 dashed by with a scream and hit the lip of the hollow. The detonation shook the mini and warning lights came on. The air-dropped unit, another 46, spiraled down and also exploded nearby. The mini was shoved sideways against the bottom muck and boulders.

"Seawater leakage in the external battery cans," Montgomery said. Another console shorted out. Meltzer sprayed more CO_2, sparingly, but now they'd have to breathe it and the smoke—the mini lacked air breathers to go around, and the few undamaged Draegers wouldn't last long. The built-up CO_2 made Jeffrey sluggish and depressed. Ilse coughed. More depth charges blasted, much closer now, from the Class 130.

"*Another torpedo in the water!*" Meltzer said. "Bearing two nine five!"

"I'm sorry, people," Jeffrey said. "We tried. In the interest of saving as many lives as possible, I'm ordering the mini to surface and surrender."

Ilse looked at Jeffrey. He saw a sense of betrayal in her eyes. "I'm sorry."

Ilse wondered if she'd go to Hell for taking her own life. Was that better or worse than hanging, than dangling and kicking naked while she endlessly choked and her tongue tried to burst and her bladder let go? Was Hell better or worse than being gang-raped first and then strung up for the rapists to watch?

"Captain!" Meltzer shouted. "Latest torpedo now on diverging course! Screw-count and engine noise show it's an Improved ADCAP Mark forty-eight, targeting the *Bremen*!"

"Are you *sure*?"

"Confirmed! *Second* ADCAP in the water, targeting the Class one-thirty. . . . *New* passive sonar contact! Polyphems, torpedo-tube launched, aimed at the helos overhead!"

"What's going on?" Ilse said.

The message light blinked.

"Answer it," Jeffrey snapped.

"It's plain text gertrude," Montgomery said.

"On speakers."

"This is USS *Challenger*. Repeat, this is USS *Challenger*." The voice was scratchy and garbled, but Ilse knew it was the XO, Lieutenant Bell, the acting captain.

"They're on bearing two nine five," Meltzer said. "Range fifteen thousand yards."

Ilse saw Jeffrey grab the gertrude mike. Before he could answer, the roaring Polyphems hit the German helos in harsh eruptions. There were *pops* as debris impacted the surface. The wreckage made a rushing noise as it plunged to the bottom, then thumped into the silt. Something clunked onto the mini's top deck, then something else.

The high-explosive ADCAP hit the *Bremen*. The frigate's magazines went up. Reverb from the detonations drowned out the other sounds as the surface warship died. The other ADCAP hit the Class 130 corvette. The minisub rocked.

Jeffrey looked *furious*.

"*Challenger, Challenger,* this is Captain Fuller! What in God's name are you doing in the Baltic? I told you to get *out* if there was trouble!"

"Captain," Bell said, "we were ordered in by COMSUBLANT. Stand by for rendezvous and hangar pickup."

The minisub was docked, stowed snugly inside *Challenger*'s conformal hangar. The pressure-proof hangar doors were closed, the pressure relieved, the water in the hangar drained. Meltzer opened the mini's bottom hatch, mated to the top of the ship's forward escape trunk, aft of her sail.

Jeffrey went down the ladder first, and fast. He helped the enlisted SEALs pass a groggy Clayton through the trunk, then onto a waiting litter outside the trunk's bottom hatch, in *Challenger* proper. Clayton grimaced in pain from being manhandled, but with the missile in the lock-out sphere they couldn't bring a stretcher *up*. Clayton's wound—actually two, an entry and an exit hole—began to bleed again. The acting corpsman looked him over as Salih and crewmen carried the litter toward the wardroom, which doubled as *Challenger*'s operating theater. Salih's arm wound bled, too.

Ilse came down next, followed by Meltzer. Chief Montgomery stayed behind to deal with his men and their gear. Minisub maintenance specialists went up the ladder with tool bags.

Bell came to meet Jeffrey. "Sessions has the conn."

Jeffrey and Bell shook hands warmly. "Mission accomplished, so far," Jeffrey said. "Lab destroyed, intel gotten." Compared to Bell's crisp appearance Jeffrey realized how grungy he must look.

"Who's that guy with the big mustache?"

"A Turk guest worker turned resistance leader. He has quite a story."

Jeffrey heard more torpedo hits in the distance, then heavy secondary blasts. *Challenger* banked to port and then to starboard as she made a knuckle. From the feel, Jeffrey judged they were doing close to thirty knots, about as fast as they could go with their damaged pump-jet.

"Will you please tell me what's going *on*?" Jeffrey knew the ship was at general quarters—he saw the damage control and first-aid parties stationed.

He and Bell rushed along the corridor to the CACC. Ilse and Meltzer tagged behind.

"Mossad has a covert team in the mountains in southern Sweden, sir. They put up a Predator long-range recon drone with a laser downlink, to monitor Greifswald."

"Nosy bastards," Jeffrey said.

"They watched you come out of the lab with the missile. They must have contacted our embassy in Stockholm, and the attaché reached the Pentagon somehow, maybe land-line through Russia."

"How did SUBLANT reach *you*?"

"They activated a submarine commo satellite when it was over Denmark, then burned through a message before the satellite got fried by the solar storm. I'd raised the radio mast an inch when Milgrom heard your atom bombs go off, on the off chance . . ."

"How did you get through the Sound?"

"On the surface, Captain, the only possible way." The Sound was very shallow. "When German forces asked for the recognition code, we said in plain text we were *Deutschland*. We'd been on patrol too long, and our crypto books were stale. Surprise, poor visibility, no quick way to check . . . We fooled 'em."

Jeffrey looked Bell in the eyes, and saw Bell's confidence, his pride—he was shaping up as a worthy protégé. "That's damn fine work, XO." Jeffrey could picture it, too, that long run south: the endless minutes of vulnerability and nerve-racking suspense, moving further and further into enemy-held waters surfaced, waiting to be found out and destroyed at any time. "I don't think that's gonna work on the way out."

"I know, Captain," Bell said. "Still, it's good to have you back." Bell turned and gave Ilse and Meltzer congratulatory handshakes, too.

"It's good to *be* back," Jeffrey said. "Once they're cleaned up and rested, put Chief Montgomery and his men to work in the torpedo room, to help on damage control and the manual loading. . . . Messenger!"

"Sir!"

"When he can spare a moment have the acting corpsman issue depth-charge rations for everyone on the raid. I'll take mine in black coffee." Depth-charge rations were strong spirits.

"I'll have mine in coffee, too," Ilse said.

Jeffrey looked at Ilse: war paint, Band-Aids, torn-up body suit, hair going five ways at once.

"No, Ilse. Take yours straight. I order you to get some sleep."

Jeffrey looked around the familiar spaces, the fake wood wainscoting and flameproof linoleum floors. He smelled the smell of the ship, ozone and paint and warm electronics, lubricants and nontoxic cleansers. He saw all the faces he knew. *Home.*

"We're cut off and under attack, outnumbered ten to one, beyond any possible means of support, and I feel safer already."

They reached the CACC.

Jeffrey stood in the aisle, sizing up the situation. Their course was three one five, northwest, back toward the Sound.

"I have the conn."

"You have the conn," Lieutenant Sessions said. He went back to the nav console.

"This is the captain. I have the conn."

"Aye, aye," the watchstanders said.

Bell relieved one of his officers at Fire Control. Meltzer took the helm. COB was chief of the watch.

"Helm, slow to ahead two thirds, make turns for twenty-six knots. Right standard rudder, make your course zero nine zero." Due east.

"Captain?" Bell said. "That's back into the Baltic."

"XO, your timing to open fire was impeccable. Now we can't just run, we have to keep the enemy guessing."

"Sir?"

"I want to launch three brilliant decoys."

"Aye, aye."

"Program one to sound and act like *Seawolf*, and send it east toward St. Petersburg."

"*Seawolf*, St. Petersburg, aye."

"Preset one as the *Jimmy Carter* and aim it toward Gdansk. Let them think we have a major SpecWar op against the occupied Polish coast." The *Carter* was a *Seawolf* class, modified for SEAL mission support.

"Understood."

"Make the third one sound and act like *Connecticut*. Loop it northeast toward Stockholm and Finland, in international waters."

"*Connecticut*, loop it northeast, aye." *Connecticut* was *Seawolf*'s sister ship.

"That should confuse everybody for a while. Program all decoys for twenty-five knots, with ping-enhancers to emulate full-size hulls."

"Twenty-five knots, ping-enhancers, aye."

Jeffrey read his weapons status screen again. He needed the offensive power of the ADCAPs in tubes one and three, and the anti-aircraft power of the Polyphems in tube seven. The water to the northwest, the only route to possible safety, would just get shallower and shallower, magnetic storm or no.

"Launch all decoys through tube five. We'll let them run on their own, it's okay to cut the wires to reload."

"Understood."

"Then I want to fire three ISLMMs." Improved Submarine Launched Mobile Mines. "Target the mobile mines toward Rostock. That's the closest German naval base threatening our path to the Sound. Use tube five for the ISLMMs."

"Understood."

Jeffrey called up the chart for Rostock harbor, and used his light pen. "Preset the mobile mine warhead pattern to create a barrier due north and one mile past the breakwater, spaced one five zero yards apart, like *this*. When tube five's empty, reload one more decoy."

Bell began to enter commands on his console, and gave orders to the Combat Systems technicians on the starboard side of the CACC. Deploying all these units would take a while—*Challenger's* rate of fire was low from old battle damage. *Well,* Jeffrey told himself, *at least back on my nuclear-powered ship, I don't have to worry about running out of fuel like in that German minisub.*

"Helm," Jeffrey said, "when the last ISLMM is launched, my intention is to come left to course three one five." Northwest again.

Then comes the hard part. The Sound's so shallow we can only get through if we surface first.

NINETY MINUTES LATER, ON DEUTSCHLAND.

IN THE NORWEGIAN TROUGH

Ernst Beck knocked on the captain's stateroom door.

"Come!"

Beck entered.

"Einzvo," Kurt Eberhard said. He stubbed out a cigarette in irritation. "Still no contact on *Challenger?*"

"Nothing on our deployable hydrophone lines, sir. But we've received a high-priority message by secure undersea acoustic link. From Trondheim. The message is in captain's code."

"Give it to me."

Beck handed him the diskette. He watched Eberhard load it into his laptop.

"Look away." Beck heard Eberhard punch keys, the CO's personal passwords.

"Jawohl!" Eberhard exclaimed. *Yes!*

"Sir?"

"We're ordered to the Skagerrak at best possible speed. There's an American sub in the Baltic . . . that seismic activity we detected. The first shock *was* a low-yield atom bomb."

"Where, sir?"

"Greifswald."

"Greifswald? . . . We guessed the wrong target."

Eberhard shot him a contemptuous look, then rose from his desk. "None of that matters now."

Beck bottled down his anger. He followed as Eberhard took the short corridor to the Zentrale.

"We're ordered to find and destroy the enemy ship. Intel says it launched three decoys, acting like the *Seawolf* boats."

"Which is the real SSN, sir?"

They reached Control. Eberhard spoke distractedly as he studied his screens.

"It's believed to be USS *Challenger*. They somehow captured one of our minisubs. Our forces tracked it, certainly damaged it, but then it completely disappeared. Our listening nets heard no telltale flow noise of a dorsal load, so the mini must be in a conformal hangar now."

"*Challenger*'s, sir."

"There's no way they can escape!"

Beck nodded—there was *one* route out of the Baltic, and *Deutschland* would have plenty of time to cut them off. Coming so soon after the destruction of the two-part Allied convoy—by *Deutschland* and other Axis submarines—the loss of the U.S. Navy's *Challenger* would be an unbearable blow to enemy morale and fighting power.

"I have the conn," Eberhard said. "Action stations."

Beck took his position at the 1WO console. *Maybe this war will end soon after all.*

"Copilot," Eberhard said, "sever the hydrophone lines. Pilot, steer due south. Flank speed ahead."

"*Jawohl*," Jakob Coomans said. *Deutschland* banked and picked up speed.

Eberhard turned to Beck.

"I just hope we find them before some idiot frigate captain gets Fuller with a lucky shot."

CHAPTER 28

Jeffrey stood on the ladder in the sail trunk. On his orders, Meltzer held *Challenger* down with bow and stern planes, fighting COB's intentional positive buoyancy.

"*Battle surface,*" Jeffrey said to the local phone talker—the man was stationed with sound-powered phones in case the intercom system failed. Jeffrey heard compressed air roar as COB blew all main ballast tanks. Meltzer reversed the planes. *Challenger* breached.

Jeffrey undogged and hurled open the bridge hatch. A lookout—the messenger of the watch—came up right behind him. Then came Chief Montgomery, lugging a .50-caliber machine gun. Montgomery mounted the MG on a bracket he had deployed from the rear of the cockpit. Crewmen handed up heavy boxes of ammo.

It was pitch dark outside, and foggy again, and very cold. Behind Jeffrey, both photonic masts rotated, as the CACC prepared to take nav bearings visually, and scan for threats. *Challenger* was running the Køge Bugt, the shallows leading from the Baltic into the Sound. There were three men in the tiny bridge cockpit, all in bulky parkas over their flak vests, with life jackets over that; they could barely move. The air was clean—chemically, biologically, and radiologically—so at least they didn't need respirators.

Jeffrey switched his night-vision visors to full-time infrared, because of the fog. He still couldn't see much—fog blocked passive infrared. The CACC, and the electronic support measures room, fed him information through his intercom headphones, under his helmet. He also had a tactical display on a weatherproof laptop he'd brought up; the wires all led below. The lookout used image-intensified and electronically stabilized binoculars to probe toward the horizon and the sky. So did Montgomery—the fog could clear at any moment, leaving them totally exposed.

By inertial navigation they followed the route the German minesweeper and captured mini had taken on the way in. Jeffrey hoped there weren't new mines. The sail-mounted mine avoidance array was useless out of the water, and the one on the chin had been wrecked at Durban. Jeffrey had to save the LMRS. Kathy tried to use the bow sphere to search the water ahead, but it was difficult in these conditions.

"Maneuvering, Bridge," Jeffrey called on the intercom.

"Bridge, Maneuvering, aye. Willey here."

"Enj, I need flank speed."

"Sir, there's still the damage to the pump-jet from that two-twelve's weapon near the Azores. We get vibrations around thirty-two knots submerged."

"Will it get worse if we go faster, Enj, or is it a resonance that'll stop?"

"One way to find out, Captain."

"V'r'well. . . . Helm, Bridge."

"Bridge, Helm, aye," Meltzer answered on the intercom.

"Ahead flank."

"Ahead flank, aye."

Water began to cream over *Challenger*'s bow. Jeffrey felt it splash as some was deflected up by the streamlined fairing at the base of the sail. He felt the nasty vibrations begin just as Willey predicted, but they subsided as the ship accelerated more, as Jeffrey had hoped. *Challenger* reached flank speed and ran more smoothly, but flank speed on the surface was much slower than submerged—the unavoidable wave-making wasted power. Jeffrey heard a constant churning rushing as his command cut through the seas, and he felt a frigid wind on his face. The ship rolled badly, the sideways motion exaggerated here atop the sail.

Almost sixty miles to go before we can dive again. German command and control infrastructure would be in disarray with the solar storm, and *Challenger* had the element of surprise, but sooner or later she'd be found. Once localized, she'd be prosecuted to destruction.

Sixty nautical miles on the surface. An eternity. At least Jeffrey took comfort from his companions shoulder to shoulder.

"Fire Control, Bridge."

"Bridge, Fire Control, aye," Bell answered.

"We need all the firepower we've got. Spool up the gyros, all conventional Tactical Tomahawks in the vertical launch system."

"Bridge, ESM." The Electronic Support Measures room.

"Bridge, aye."

"Captain, we're picking up surface-search radars. WM-twenty-five track-while-scan fire control systems. Assess as *Bremen*-class frigates."

Jeffrey glanced at his laptop screen. One threat was to the north and one to the south, both about twenty thousand yards away—easy gun and missile range. They were converging on *Challenger,* and she'd entered the new dredged channel south of Saltholm Island. The narrow channel was for deep-draft shipping, and an SSN on the surface had deep draft—*Challenger* drew almost forty feet, and was really in a bind. If her stern dug in, due to bottom suction from the pump-jet intake, she'd take more damage there. If the stern was trimmed too light, to solve *that* problem, the pump-jet might suck air instead. *Challenger* also had no room to maneuver or evade to left or right; outside the channel the water was ten feet deep.

"ESM, Bridge. Is the return signal a threat?"

"Difficult to tell in these electromagnetic conditions, Captain."

It didn't matter—the frigates were faster than *Challenger* now, and the one to the north had her decisively cut off.

Jeffrey saw a flash to the north through his goggles: a strong infrared emitter, persisting, getting brighter fast.

"Bridge, ESM. J-band homing radar! *Inbound Harpoon.*"

The burning light in the fog got closer and Jeffrey could hear the Mach .85 antiship missile roar.

"ESM, go active. Try to spoof it!"

The light and noise approached Jeffrey steadily—a Harpoon warhead was deadly against any submarine. It came down to a contest between *Challenger's* low-observable sail and her electronic countermeasures, and the Harpoon's advanced target seekers and the frigate's counter-countermeasures. *Challenger* barely won, *this time*. The missile tore past the sail and Jeffrey felt its sizzling engine exhaust. It veered west, under external targeting control, to avoid the frigate to the south. It self-destructed with a hard *blam* and a stabbing glare. Jeffrey felt the shock and a wave of blast-furnace heat.

The fog bank cleared, leaving *Challenger* naked. The sky was overcast here. Jeffrey switched visor modes—the pixel gain control would keep the imagery from flaring, and help preserve his night vision. The blackout of the Swedish and Danish coasts was absolute.

Another missile was launched from the *Bremen* to the north.

This time the Harpoon came much closer before it missed and self-destructed.

"Bridge, ESM. They're defeating our countermeasures."

That was the problem with electronic warfare. Every time you radiated you gave something away, and the other guy responded. Jeffrey thought hard. He could fire ADCAPs at both frigates, but torpedo attack speed was barely a tenth of a Harpoon's. There was no time to switch the load in a torpedo tube.

"Weps, Bridge. Target an antishipping Tomahawk from the VLS at each of the *Bremen*s, smartly." The vertical launch system was twelve cruise-missile tubes built into *Challenger's* forward ballast tanks.

"Captain," Bell said, "we've no procedures for using the VLS on the surface."

"Improvise!"

"There's no way to flood the tubes after we fire. If we launch too many weapons we'll be too buoyant to dive!"

"There's plenty of water coming over the bow."

"Aye, aye."

Jeffrey saw two of the heavy pressure-proof VLS doors pop open. He saw another flash, another Harpoon launch. *Challenger* and the *Bremen* to the north were closing at almost sixty knots. The Harpoon came at his ship, more like six hundred.

There was a blinding flash and a terrible roar. Jeffrey and the others in the cockpit ducked instinctively. There was another flash and roar, and *Challenger* nosed and bucked even harder. Jeffrey was bathed in unbearable heat, and he choked on noxious fumes.

He peeked over the edge of the cockpit. Yellow-white flame receded fore and aft of the ship. The third Harpoon had missed, just barely. The Tomahawks sought their targets.

Before the frigates could zero in and jam the guidance frequencies, both weapons hit.

The frigate to the south was ripped by the Tomahawk, whose thousand-pound warhead was much larger than a Harpoon's. The frigate began to sink, blocking the channel, protecting *Challenger*'s rear. But the *Bremen* to the north, burning now, began to settle too. If it did, *Challenger* would be trapped.

Jeffrey had a clear view of the northern *Bremen*. The flames lit dense black smoke. The frigate was drifting sideways in the channel. Its bow was already level with the water.

Jeffrey ordered Willey to push the reactor hard. It was a race against time, and a fraction of a knot might make the difference. As if to mock Jeffrey, something on the northern *Bremen* exploded. An on-deck missile pod? Balls of fire spewed.

At last *Challenger* reached the sinking frigate.

"Helm, Bridge, all stop. Rotate the ship on auxiliary propulsors to true bearing zero four five. Then translate us due north. I want to shove that *Bremen* out of the way." Meltzer acknowledged.

Sharp concussions went off inside the *Bremen*. By now anyone still alive had abandoned the hulk. Jeffrey saw men in the water. Montgomery covered them with his machine gun, but they were in no shape to threaten *Challenger*. Jeffrey and Montgomery and the lookout were forced to go below and shut the hatch, because of the heat and smoke, and the secondary explosions and flying wreckage.

Jeffrey stepped on his intercom wire by mistake, and it yanked his lip mike askew. "Collision alarm!" he shouted down the ladder to the phone talker. The raucous siren blared.

In the CACC, Jeffrey knew, Bell watched the scene via photonics imagery. Still in the sail trunk, Jeffrey called it up on his laptop, to conn the ship. When they were very close he ordered COB to lower the masts.

Jeffrey was almost thrown from the ladder when *Challenger* nudged the starboard bow of the *Bremen* hard. He fixed his mike. He told Meltzer to use more forward auxiliary propulsor thrust, to lever the hulk aside, like a tugboat. Jeffrey heard more blasts through the hull. Shivers and jolts were transmitted from the steel side of the *Bremen* to the ceramic side of *Challenger*, right through her anechoic skin.

At last the pathway north was clear.

"Ahead flank! Make your course three four five!" Straight up the Sound.

Jeffrey climbed through the bridge hatch. There were bits of smoking debris in the cockpit and atop the sail. The Plexiglas windscreen was melted. He peered over the port side. By the glare of the burning frigate he could see *Challenger's* coatings were scorched. The sonar wide arrays were mounted low on her main hull's flanks, and Jeffrey hoped they weren't badly damaged. Montgomery climbed on top of the sail on his belly, and batted bits of frigate away. He fired a short burst as a test—the machine gun was okay. Jeffrey ordered COB to raise the masts.

Behind him, with one final shuddering detonation, the *Bremen* settled on the bottom; its superstructure protruded above the waves, still burning fiercely. The underwater blast caused several mines in the shallows to detonate sympathetically. Jeffrey doubted many German sailors in the water survived.

Challenger cleared another fog bank. She was free of the confining dredged channel, but the water was still so shallow she had to stay on the east side of the Sound, the Swedish side. The icy wind and freezing salt spray bit Jeffrey's face. Over his right shoulder Jeffrey saw another flash, quick and sharp: a naval defense gun on the Swedish coast. The shell landed a hundred yards off *Challenger's* bow, directly ahead of the ship. The bridge crew ducked as water fountained. Razor-sharp shell splinters pelted the sail.

"Helm, Bridge. Left standard rudder. We're violating Swedish neutrality."

"Bridge, Nav," Sessions broke in. "No can do, sir, unless we slow down. We need bottom clearance the way the pump-jet's digging in."

"ESM, Bridge. How are they tracking us? That gun's dead-on."

"Infrared laser, sir. There's no way we can jam."

"Yes, there is." The gun was off *Challenger's* starboard quarter, near Malmö, on a headland. "Chief of the Watch, raise the snorkel mast. Start the emergency diesel. Figure out how to put oil into the exhaust, to make a smoke screen." The diesel air intake had nuclear-biological-chemical filters, and detectors to warn of bad air, just in case.

Another Swedish shell landed, one hundred yards astern, again dead-on in azimuth. The ship was bracketed, an unmistakable message the next shell wouldn't miss.

Jeffrey heard and saw another gun open up, from near Copenhagen, on the occupied Danish side: incoming *German* fire this time. *Challenger* was caught in the middle. Her diesel coughed to life. Stinking exhaust poured from the vents in the sail, then dense smoke obscured the view aft.

"Helm, Bridge. Zigzag smartly!"

Meltzer turned hard right. A Swedish shell landed in *Challenger*'s wake. Another landed where she would've been if she had stayed on course. Another flash near Copenhagen, off *Challenger*'s port bow. Another German shell landed, almost as close. Dirty water drenched the cockpit. The stench of high explosives mixed with diesel fumes.

"Weps, Bridge. Target that naval gun by Copenhagen with a land-attack Tomahawk. Fire at will." Another VLS hatch popped open. This time the bridge crew knew to go below before the booster ignited.

They were past Copenhagen and Malmö now. They avoided the wreckage of the new bridge-and-tunnel that connected those two cities—started in the late nineties, finished in time to be destroyed by the Swedes as German forces flooded into Denmark. Jeffrey lost sight of the structure's stumps in his own smoke screen, streaming out behind the ship.

Despite ESM's efforts to spoof the gunnery radars, more German shells tried to follow from behind. Some came very close. Jeffrey ducked, and shrapnel whistled, and something behind him made a *whack*.

"Bridge, Control. Attack periscope photonics mast knocked out."

It was only a matter of time before a five- or eight-inch shell hit the hull. Ahead would lie more naval guns, and soon they'd be in visual range, and from that direction the smoke screen wouldn't work. Jeffrey ordered land-attack Tomahawks launched to take the guns

out. Again he and Montgomery and the lookout went below and felt
and heard the missiles launch. When the boosters were well clear,
they went topside.

"Fire Control, Bridge. I want to launch four more ISLMMs.
Preset them to loop up around Sjaelland Island. Lay a mine barrier
across the mouth of the Great Belt. Warships may be racing from
Kiel to head us off."

Bell acknowledged. He announced when each weapon was fired. It
was slow work loading tubes manually, especially against *Challenger*'s
constant pitch and roll. Jeffrey used lens paper to dry his goggles and
binocs, drenched again by flying spray; his weatherproof laptop was
holding up.

ESM announced more surface search radars, German corvettes
coming from the north. Jeffrey ordered ADCAPs fired to intercept.
Challenger passed an enemy fast-patrol craft, hiding in ambush in a
cove. He fired an antiship Tomahawk before it could launch its missiles. The Tomahawk burst viciously.

The ADCAPs hit their targets to the north, and Jeffrey saw bright
flashes. More loud booms rolled across the Sound. The water was
still very shallow, barely fifty feet, but at least the Sound was wide
enough now Jeffrey could evade the wrecks. *Challenger* entered a
snow squall, then came out the other side. Again Jeffrey cleaned his
goggles and binocs.

"It's awfully quiet in the air," Montgomery said. "We should've
stirred up one heck of a hornet's nest by now."

"I was thinking that," Jeffrey said. "Maybe our side sprang an info
warfare assault on Axis command and control. Saving something
really special, for a time like this."

"Then where are all *our* planes, sir?"

"Maybe the Axis did it to us, too."

In that case everything on and over the sea would come down to
map reading, guesswork, and the Mark 1 human eyeball.

Challenger was running low on ammo. The Germans held the
cards; soon they'd get their act together, and stop committing forces
piecemeal.

Ven Island lay ahead, in the middle of the navigable part of the
Sound. Ven was owned by Sweden, heavily fortified. *Challenger* had

to come left. This forced them closer to Denmark, where the channel was studded with shoals.

Soon *Challenger* would be in range of accurate fire from yet more naval guns, in line of sight above the horizon, where laser range-finding worked.

Then Jeffrey heard something worse than naval guns. He heard the clatter of helo blades to the northwest.

"Fire Control, Bridge. What airfield bears three one five?"

"A German army base on Sjaelland, Captain."

Jeffrey spotted the helos in his big binocs. The lookout said they were Tigers—brand-new attack aircraft. Their shaped-charge anti-tank rockets could easily blast through *Challenger*'s hull.

Montgomery leaped atop the sail and traversed his machine gun, for all the good it would do.

Jeffrey glanced at his search 'scope mast. It tracked the squadron of Tigers as they moved closer, strung out in line ahead.

"Fire Control, knock them down."

One by one a quadruplet of Polyphems broke the surface in their encapsulated launch tubes. Each lifted off, guided by fiber-optic wire and powered by a turbojet. The Tigers scattered, but the Polyphems' forty-pound fragmentation warheads shredded four helos. They burst into flames and crashed, but the other helos pressed on. Soon the eight survivors would be in rocket range, and it would take time to load more Polyphems.

"Bridge, ESM."

"ESM, Bridge, aye."

"Captain, static and propagation are fluctuating heavily. We're getting snatches of a big air battle shaping up due west."

"Range?"

"One hundred miles."

Hot-white light flared northwest, again and again. Balls of fire jetted toward *Challenger*—antitank rockets. Jeffrey screamed for the helm to zigzag. Once more he and the lookout ducked, and Montgomery dove headfirst into the cockpit. The chief landed on Jeffrey, knocking the wind from Jeffrey's chest.

The rocket motors roared. There was a red-white eruption. Waves of heat lashed the cockpit. A rocket had hit the after part of the sail, burning through the side of the structure, hardened for under-ice operations. Jeffrey glanced at the helos as they drew closer, just in time to see four more jink and then explode—another salvo of Polyphems hit home. He peered over the cockpit edge but couldn't see where the enemy rocket hit. He did see black smoke pour from the side of the sail. That part was free flooding, but it housed the floating-wire antenna winch. He ordered damage control parties to get in there from below with CO_2.

Four Tigers still lived. They ripple-fired their rockets, then turned away. The rockets tore the air and pelted the sea. Several hit *Challenger*'s forward hull, or rather the water cascading over it. They struck at a glancing angle to the surface, and the sea quenched their shaped-charge plasma jets. Others landed aft, and Jeffrey hoped they'd also failed to damage the ship—from the cockpit he couldn't see the after hull.

Another rocket hit the after part of the sail. Jeffrey ducked. One hit the outside of the cockpit. It burst, and hot gas and metal from its armor-piercing shaped-charge warhead jetted through and instantly burned a hole on the other side. Jeffrey and Montgomery, lying flat on the bridge hatch, looked at each other wide-eyed, amazed to be alive. Then they realized their life vests were on fire. They tore them off and threw them over the side.

Another four Polyphems pursued the remaining Tigers in the distance. They impacted one by one. The blasts and sheets of flame were much larger than the rocket hits on *Challenger*.

Jeffrey and Montgomery realized the lookout was gone, and the cockpit was spattered with smoldering gore.

Jeffrey saw Montgomery's machine gun was wrecked, and ordered him below—it was just too dangerous up here. The chief carried the ruined weapon down, and Jeffrey passed him boxes of ammo.

Now Jeffrey stood on the bridge alone, and they still had so far to go.

Jeffrey ordered the ship to slow momentarily. He wanted a man to mount the hull behind the sail, wearing a lifeline from the aft escape trunk, to do a close visual inspection for damage from the anti-tank rocket hits. If the hull had been burned through, even just partway, *Challenger* would never dive again.

They were past Ven Island now. The main hull was okay, but Willey reported the protruding top of the rudder looked like Swiss cheese. The fire inside the sail was out, but two firefighters had third-degree burns through their suits from shaped-charge blasts.

The choke point at the north end of the Sound was coming up fast. *Challenger* ran north at flank speed; wind whistled through the holes in the side of the cockpit. She wasn't meant for surface battle: She had no chaff dispensers, no magnesium decoy flares. Her ESM abilities were limited, just one mast with small antennas.

"Fire Control, Bridge."

"Bridge, Fire Control, aye."

"XO, I want to make some radar decoys. Take our radar reflectors and mount them on blocks of Styrofoam."

"Understood," Bell said. The radar reflectors were aluminum shapes with many right angles. Used on the surface in friendly waters, they helped the SSN show clearly on navigation radars, so she wouldn't be run down by a careless merchant ship.

"Confirm how many non-nuclear Tomahawks we have in the VLS." Jeffrey had lost count.

"Two land-attack, sir. That's all."

And they had two more in the torpedo room, which could be fired from there.

"Fire Control, target the suspected cable landing sites for the German hydrophone lines in our path."

"Which ones, Captain?"

Jeffrey reached for his computer, then realized it was wrecked— also from that antitank rocket blast. "Send me another laptop."

A new messenger handed one up, and Jeffrey plugged it in.

He called up the map with its classified data. "Fire Control, the ones on Anholt Island, Laesø Island, then Saeby, then Hirtshals." That would take *Challenger* through the Kattegat, and halfway through the Skaggerak if they were lucky. But there were more hydrophone nets between Hirtshals and the North Sea, and no more land-attack Tomahawks.

Before Bell could open fire, Jeffrey sensed—more in his gut than his ears—hard explosions in the distance to the west. Visibility was clear again, but he didn't see any flashes, just the amazing aurora still dancing overhead.

Face it, without this solar storm we'd never have even made it into the lab, let alone had the slightest prayer of making it home. . . . Weather has always been a critical factor in battle; now that includes weather on the sun.

"Bridge, ESM." Electronic Support Measures called again.

"ESM, Bridge, aye."

"Captain, that big air battle is heating up, and coming closer."

Two more VLS doors popped open. Jeffrey ducked below. Through the hatch he heard the roar of their boosters. He went back up and watched till the boosters separated, and the missiles rushed into the dark. Two more Tomahawks broached the water, from the torpedo tubes this time, and again their boosters roared. Then boosters fired on the land to the west and raced into the sky: antiaircraft missiles, pursuing the Tomahawks.

The choke point out of the Sound lay shortly ahead, barely three nautical miles wide between Helsingør in Denmark and Hälsingborg in Sweden. The Germans would be marshaling forces there for sure, or planting more mines, or both, to lay an impassable roadblock. Jeffrey knew that if he took the Swedish side of the channel now, with the Axis in hot pursuit, he'd draw both Swedish and German fire.

Jeffrey ducked as something roared at him out of the west. It was a pair of jet planes. They turned hard south, then waggled their wings as they receded. Jeffrey waved: Allied air cover at last.

The two aircraft came back. Their noses sparkled and red streamers darted out—they were German. Jeffrey ducked once more as 20mm cannon shells hit the water. The pilots corrected their aim, walking the tracers toward the ship. Jeffrey dashed below and dogged the hatch. He heard whacks and bangs as shells hit the side of the sail.

His ship was all out of Stingers, and Polyphems were useless against fast movers like these jets.

Jeffrey clambered down the sail trunk ladder, then dogged the second hatch. More cannon shells impacted.

"Bridge, Fire Control," Bell called in Jeffrey's headphones.

"I'm not on the bridge."

"Sir, we've lost the other periscope mast, and the ESM mast and the radio mast."

Challenger was blind and deaf, except for her sonars. And at flank speed on the surface, her sonars were almost blind.

"V'r'well," Jeffrey said. "I'm going up again."

"Bridge, Sonar," Kathy said. "Self-check indicates sail-mounted mine avoidance sonar, and under-ice sonar, are destroyed."

• • •

Jeffrey flung open the hatch. The sky was crystal clear now. The approaching air battle had definitely arrived. Aircraft tore in every direction, and dogfights raged at every altitude. Jeffrey saw tracers etching the sky. Missiles streaked like shooting stars. Airplanes exploded and wreckage pelted the sea. Above it all, the powerful aurora danced mockingly, from the zenith overhead to the horizon on every side, insensate and uncaring.

The combined roar of all the turbojets on full military power was so intense, Jeffrey was reduced to typing messages to Bell on his laptop. Bell answered the same way.

Bell gave him an updated tactical plot. Modern *Brandenburg* frigates and more Class 130 corvettes were charging through the choke point directly ahead. There were three of each detected so far. Another squadron of Tiger helos was closing in from the west.

Jeffrey tossed one radar decoy to port, and hoped the improvised counterweight would make it land in the water right side up. He counted to five and also threw the other decoy to port. The Class 130's each had eight Harpoons.

Each *Brandenburg* also had eight Harpoons, plus quadruple torpedo tubes with thirty-two Mark 46's aboard, and two state-of-the-art NH-90 antisubmarine helos. They also had active antitorpedo defenses—mortars and explosive nets—powerful against conventional fish, especially in such shallow water.

Jeffrey had few high-explosive ADCAPs left, and only four Polyphems. He had no ISLMMs, no antiship Tomahawks. The *Brandenburgs'* total load of torpedoes wildly outnumbered *Challenger's* antitorpedo rockets. The water was barely sixty feet deep—it was impossible to dive. The cleared channel was narrow again, its flanks studded with mines—it was impossible to turn away.

"Target the *Brandenburgs* with three ADCAPs," Jeffrey typed in despair. "Target the Tigers with Polyphems. Fire at will."

This was *Challenger's* last stand, and it was hopeless, and Jeffrey knew the Germans knew it. His brilliant decoys and noisemakers would be useless against enemy wire-guided Mark 46's, with the frigates holding visual contact on his ship like this. Jeffrey was forbidden to use nuclear munitions so close to neutral and occupied land, even in self-defense or self-destruction: The ROEs were inviolable.

Another aircraft exploded and fell from the sky. It crashed into the sea near *Challenger*. Friend or foe? Jeffrey couldn't tell. Flaming avgas marked its grave. Jeffrey saw no chutes. Still tracers and missiles ripped the air high above. Aircraft twisted and turned, and their cannon stuttered, and turbojets roared.

"Bridge, Sonar," Kathy Milgrom typed. "Eight torpedoes in the water. Mean bearing three five one, constant bearing, closing." Two of the *Brandenburg*s had fired a full salvo from their quadruple launchers, and would be racing to reload. The third *Brandenburg* was holding their first salvo in reserve.

"Helm, try to comb their tracks," Jeffrey typed. "Fire Control, arm the antitorpedo rockets." They were carried in nonreloadable launch tubes in the hull.

"XO," Jeffrey typed, "begin destroying crypto gear. Shred Top Secret documents. Jettison through the trash ejector."

Jeffrey saw hot-white flames to the west—incoming antitank rockets. Swelling glows to the north—inbound Harpoons. Quick, sharp flashes to the northwest—naval guns, more shells targeting *Challenger*.

Jeffrey felt the taste of defeat, more bitter than he imagined it could ever be. He saw more flames to the west, streaking through the sky, *more* incoming fire. He'd failed his crew and Ilse, and failed his country. Tears came to Jeffrey's eyes for everything he'd lost.

Above the cacophony all around he heard a different noise, a powerful whine. Were transport helos coming with Kampfschwimmer, to fight their way aboard? In despair Jeffrey turned with his binoculars. What he saw brought different tears to his eyes. Two dozen Royal Navy Sea Harriers came in fast from behind him, right above the waves. Their wings were heavy with antiship and antiaircraft missiles, and electronic warfare pods, and depth charges and smart bombs.

Their flight leader drew level with *Challenger*'s sail on the starboard side. He kept pace with the ship perfectly, so near that Jeffrey could touch his wing tip. Jeffrey waved. The pilot saluted. The Harriers attacked.

CHAPTER 29

Everything happened at once. Missiles streaked in all directions like a meteor swarm. Their smoky trails crisscrossed, lit by fires and flashes on every side. Decoy flares burned and silvery decoy chaff blossomed in the air. Antitank rockets streaked past *Challenger's* sail; one missed Jeffrey's head so close its engine exhaust burned his face. Another hit the sail port side, and more smoke spewed from the hole. Enemy helos, and Harriers, were hit by incoming missiles. They burst into flames and crashed into the sea. Enemy warships began taking hits.

Enemy Harpoons roared by, tearing momentary gaps in *Challenger's* trailing smoke screen, then disappeared. Tracer rounds stitched the sky. More helos were hit, and their rocket pods ignited and flew everywhere like angry bees; their torpedo loads went up in volcanoes of torpex and fuel. Vicious fountains of dirty water towered high, as antitorpedo rockets ripped through the sea and stopped incoming Mark 46's; enemy antiaircraft fire stopped another incoming Harrier. Conventional jets still tangled high above. Jeffrey knew an electronic warfare battle savaged the invisible ether, equaling in violence the battle he could see.

More antiship missiles leaped from beneath the surviving Harriers' wings, and homed on the German warships. More missiles left the surviving ships and tried to home on the Harriers and *Challenger.* More enemy five- and eight-inch shells landed in the water close to Jeffrey, and the whole hull shuddered and the grating he knelt on jumped. Enemy antitorpedo defenses flashed and raised more fountains. Jeffrey's ADCAPs reached the frigates and triple eruptions heaved; brutal concussions rolled across the Sound. Spent cannon brass rained from the sky, heavy and white hot. Shattered aircraft, friendly and enemy, also rained from the sky.

At last all six German warships were dead, settling in the water under merciless geysers of flame, or engulfed in searing fireballs as main magazines blew up. Jeffrey saw Harriers launching yet more missiles, and the naval guns on the Danish coast were pulverized.

Challenger came up on the hulks of the frigates and corvettes. Jeffrey gave quick conning orders to bypass the wreckage. He ducked as ammo cooked off and burning debris whizzed by. He choked on the acrid, stinking smoke, burning fuel oil and cordite and metal, burning rubber and plastic and flesh. The smoke coming from the fire inside the sail was thicker too, blending with the diesel exhaust from Jeffrey's smoke screen.

Harriers began to drop depth charges well in front of *Challenger.* They went off in yet more muddy fountains of watery rage, and sometimes there were secondary explosions: naval mines. The Harriers were clearing a path for Jeffrey's ship.

Challenger was through the choke point, out of the Sound, into the Kattegat at last. The bottom dropped off quickly here, not by much but enough. The Harriers' flight leader came back. He skillfully drew up right next to the sail. He pointed straight down, then to the north, then made a shoving gesture: "Go! Go!"

Jeffrey understood: Submerge, maintain flank speed. The Harriers would follow his wake hump, and take care of surface and airborne threats.

Jeffrey gave the pilot a thumbs-up. He ordered Meltzer to slow, so they wouldn't hit terrain as they dived. Jeffrey deployed the bridge cockpit's streamlining clamshells over his head—they were holed by enemy rockets, too. He went through the bridge hatch and dogged it shut.

He looked at the messenger standing at the base of the ladder, below the second hatch in the trunk. Jeffrey coughed on more acrid smoke, coming from inside the sail.

"Dive the ship! Dive! Dive!" Jeffrey felt the ship nose down. He

clambered below and dogged the lower watertight hatch, as water sprayed into the sail trunk through a leak. The trunk flooded, but the fire inside the sail was snuffed.

As Jeffrey reached the CACC, Kathy Milgrom announced, "Loud underwater explosions bearing two five zero! Range approximately one hundred thousand yards! Assess as ISLMM mine warhead detonation, and large secondary blasts!"

"Very well, Sonar." Something trying to cut *Challenger* off, a warship racing from Kiel, had just been sunk.

"Sir," Meltzer reported, "the ship is at periscope depth."

"Chief of the Watch, retract the foreplanes. Secure the diesel and lower the snorkel mast. Helm, ahead flank smartly. Follow the path through the Kattegat we took with that Delta four."

Meltzer acknowledged. *Challenger* was going much too fast to use the LMRS. Jeffrey took his seat. The ship vibrated heavily as the propulsion plant worked hard. The pump-jet cavitated heavily at such shallow depth.

"Fire Control, we'll have to rely on our remaining antitorpedo rockets if we trip a CAPTOR mine. Let's hope the Harriers can stay with us long enough." Bell agreed.

At flank speed—fifty knots on a good day—it would be two and a half hours to the Norwegian Deep. The Deep formed the gaping maw at the south end of the Norwegian Trough, well inside the Skagerrak, where the seafloor plunged to almost twenty-five hundred feet.

Another air-dropped depth bomb went off ahead of the ship— but how many could the Harriers possibly have?

Jeffrey called up the tactical plot. The air battle raged chaotically, almost impossible to follow by passive sonar. For now, there were no surface threats or enemy submarine contacts held, but sonar performance degraded badly at flank speed. There was extra-heavy flow noise from the holes in *Challenger*'s upper works; Kathy's people tried to filter it out.

Ilse came into the CACC, looking somewhat refreshed from her nap. She took her place at a sonar console. Kathy announced a Harrier was deploying a towed noisemaker sled, well ahead of the ship, to sweep for mines and to decoy Axis torpedoes. Jeffrey hadn't heard of this tactic before.

Another airplane crashed, somewhere to starboard. Another, somewhere to port. Above the sound of *Challenger*'s flow noise, another ISLMM went off at the mouth of the Great Belt. Kathy announced a huge twin secondary blast, same bearing and range: assessed as a German destroyer, its main magazines blowing up. But there'd be more such ships pursuing *Challenger*, far more than there were mine warheads in Jeffrey's improvised barrier.

TWO HOURS LATER.

In the CACC rigged for black, Jeffrey wore burn ointment on his face, but under it his cheeks blistered. His left leg ached, and his whole chest was sore, in spite of the mild painkiller and anti-inflammatory the first aid people had supplied.

Jeffrey hardly noticed his physical discomfort; a new surge of adrenaline coursed through his blood. The next choke point was coming, the constriction that marked where the Kattegat ended and the Skagerrak began. To port of *Challenger* lay Skagen, at the northeast tip of Denmark, surrounded by treacherous shoals. To starboard, still, loomed Sweden. At least her neutrality prevented the Germans from going nuclear here.

The water near *Challenger* was two hundred fifty feet deep. Kathy reported the last remaining Harrier pilot was jettisoning his noisemaker sled. He went for altitude. He veered east. Jeffrey knew that, rather than return to the U.K. when he reached bingo fuel, the pilot had stayed as antimine escort as long as he possibly could. Now, flying on the vapor in his tanks, he sought internment in Sweden, and Jeffrey silently wished him Godspeed. Dogfights raged again in the distance, but neither side had local air superiority now.

Jeffrey ordered Meltzer to slow to ahead one third. He ordered COB to deploy the LMRS. As *Challenger* slowed through thirty-two knots, her pump-jet vibrated—a mechanical transient datum that couldn't be helped.

Kathy announced several German warships rounding the headland at Skagen, charging toward *Challenger* from further out in the Skagerrak. Jeffrey ordered Bell to launch a brilliant decoy, set to run northeast at fifty knots, then parallel to the Swedish coast, to imitate *Challenger* trying to outflank the Germans.

The frigates and corvettes took off northeast, also at flank speed, which for them was thirty or thirty-three knots. The way past the choke point was clear. The LMRS showed no new mines on the track Jeffrey planned to take.

It was too easy. Those warships should've split up, with some prosecuting the fifty-knot contact and the rest of them guarding the gap.

Jeffrey realized he was being suckered. The Norwegian Deep was no place of refuge. He remembered the newsreel, *Deutschland* triumphant, the underground U-boat pen. It was hours now since the blast at Greifswald.

Eberhard. It had to be. Kurt Eberhard was waiting for him in the Norwegian Deep.

CHAPTER 30

Ilse held hard to her armrests as *Challenger's* bow nosed into a steep down-bubble. She tilted sideways uncomfortably in the rig for black.

"Helm," she heard Jeffrey's voice say in the dark, "make your depth twenty-three hundred feet. Chief of the Watch, engage nap-of-seafloor cruise mode. Maintain bottom clearance one hundred feet."

Ilse slaved one of her console screens to COB's forward-looking gravimeter view. She watched as the ship dove into the Norwegian Trough. The bottom dropped off rapidly. Ilse saw huge boulders go by, embedded in the muck. She knew they'd been transported here on glacial icebergs; when the icebergs melted, the boulders sank.

Ilse helped Kathy update their sound propagation models, as real-time data poured in on temperature and salinity outside the hull. *Challenger's* course was three one five, northwest, to the deepest part of the Norwegian Deep. But this was also taking the ship right at the coast of occupied Norway; freshwater river runoff, and the steep terrain rise at the far wall of the Trough along the shoreline, would affect target detection and counterdetection in tricky ways.

"Captain," Lieutenant Sessions said from the nav console. "Next course leg, recommend turn left on two three zero in three nautical miles."

"V'r'well, Nav."

Ilse glanced at her speed log window: still making fifteen knots. She called up the navigation chart. She overlaid the data COB had gathered through the LMRS on the way into the Skagerrak, two days ago that seemed like two years. The ship was following an Axis submarine safe-corridor—a *two-day-old* corridor; soon their data on the corridor would peter out. The LMRS worked in front of the ship again, ten thousand yards off, scouting for mines and enemy hydrophones, helping *Challenger* feel her way. Jeffrey said they were comparatively safe for now—the real threat would be *Deutschland* later. If this crapshoot through an Axis mine field was "safe," Ilse didn't want to think about later.

"My depth is twenty-three hundred feet, sir," Meltzer announced.

" 'Well the Helm." *Challenger* leveled off.

Ilse heard a pop and roar on her headphones.

"Surface impact datum," Kathy called. She gave the bearing and range—it wasn't close. "Assess as a fighter shot down. . . . No ejection seat hitting the water."

"Very well, Sonar. . . . Fire Control, your assessment?"

Bell cleared his throat. "Neither side has control of the air, sir. It matters less and less to us as we go deeper."

"Concur," Jeffrey said. "If you were *Deutschland*, where would you wait?"

"Where their ROEs let them go nuclear, Captain. Two hundred miles from Sweden. That's just before Stavanger, up the Norwegian coast, where the smooth shoreline first breaks up into hundreds of miles of islands and fjords."

"I concur, sir," Kathy said. "If I were Captain Eberhard, I'd wait near Stavanger. The seafloor there rises slowly to seven hundred feet and the coast to our right is a sheer cliff dropping into the Trough. Good conditions to capture our flow noise and tonals, while they lurk and listen."

"Then what do you think, XO? We go shallow? Sneak out of the Trough and try to outflank through the North Sea?"

"We can't afford more exposure in water a hundred feet deep, Captain. We'll be too exposed to enemy surface and airborne sea-denial forces, and we'd have to move very slowly. As the magnetic storm wears off, running shallow becomes too dangerous."

"Concur," Jeffrey said. "We need to stay as deep as possible, which is just what the Axis wants. We'll run into *Deutschland* head-on. With us on the move, she'll have the advantage of greater stealth. If we just sit in one place and try to hide, we put off the inevitable, and make everything worse. . . . Sonar, can you compensate for the collision damage to our port wide-aperture array?" That burning frigate, back at the south end of the Sound, had scraped and dented the hull-mounted hydrophones.

"Negative, sir. Substantial degradation in both gain and directivity."

"Then we need to stay on the *left* side of the Trough. Use it to shield our weaker side, and do our correlogram and instant-range-gate searches with the starboard array."

"Concur, sir." Kathy's throat sounded tight.

"There's no point in dawdling, people. We just give Eberhard more time to lay deployable hydrophone lines and perfect his sonar ray traces. Helm, make top quiet speed, twenty-six knots." Meltzer acknowledged.

Kathy turned to Ilse. "There's something you should know," Kathy said in an undertone. "My fiancé. I said his destroyer was vaporized."

"I remember. . . . You think it could happen to us?"

"Not that. . . . I didn't tell you . . . it was *Deutschland* that nuked his ship. *Eberhard did it to him.*"

Ilse ran more calculations as *Challenger* worked her way north. The ship nosed up, and Ilse eyed the gravimeter screen. *Challenger* followed the bottom as the seafloor rose off Kristiansand, Norway. Ilse switched to the large-scale navigation chart. The water depth would decrease gradually, then plateau for a while at fifteen hundred feet. They were one hundred miles from Sweden now; a while to go till Stavanger and the moment of truth with *Deutschland*. Jeffrey and Bell conferred, plotting strategy. Their tone, Ilse noticed, was much more collegial than during *Challenger*'s frustrating hunt for the 212 and 214 U-boats, before reaching *Texas*.

Ilse went back to listening on her headphones. A gale had blown in on the surface. Above the noise of wind and crashing waves, Axis frigates pinged. They dropped depth charges at random, and launched torpedoes at random, and *Challenger* struggled to hide. Here the freezing Nordic Current ran deep, under the last dregs of the warmer Gulf Stream from the Dover Strait. As a result the thermocline was drastic, the sonar layer almost impenetrable. *Challenger*'s out-of-phase emissions, from her active wide arrays and piezorubber tiles, helped suppress hull echoes. Enemy helo-borne dipping sonar probed deep, but too far away to be a threat—the helos lacked the electrical power, so their transducers lacked the punch, the effective range.

The LMRS was being recovered, to get another battery charge; the ship slowed to four knots. Kathy's people tried to use acoustic illumination from surface noise now, to detect mines ahead of *Challenger*. It might work, it might not. They might still be in an Axis safety corridor, they might not.

Ilse jolted. She heard an awful scream on her headphones.

"Torpedo in the water!" Kathy shouted. *"Incoming torpedo bearing two four zero!"*

"Fire Control," Jeffrey snapped, "stand by on the antitorpedo rockets. Sonar, what's the weapon?" Had they tripped a CAPTOR mine after all? Had they crossed a fiber-optic listening grid too close, and vectored in a 212 or a *Rubis*?

"Gas-turbine-powered, strong tonals, a heavyweight . . . A Russian export *wide-body Series sixty-five!*"

"*Deutschland*," Jeffrey stated, "*here*. She's the only thing the Germans have that fires a sixty-five." *Dammit*. Jeffrey's mind raced.

"Sixty-fives are nuclear-capable," Bell said—Jeffrey didn't need the reminder.

Ambushed. Out-psyched by that bastard already. Was Eberhard ruthless enough to go nuclear so close to neutral Sweden?

"Captain," Bell said. "Urge snap shot and turn away." Antitorpedo rockets were useless against a nuclear fish—their motors burned out well inside the atomic warhead's kill radius.

Jeffrey gave the snap shot orders; he had Bell launch a brilliant decoy, too. The 65 ignored the decoy.

"Helm, ahead flank smartly, make your course two four zero."

"Sir," COB said, "advise LMRS has not been recovered."

"Jettison the recovery gear."

The ship accelerated hard.

"Captain," Bell said, "we're aimed *right at* the inbound weapon."

Jeffrey smiled. "I know, XO." The ROEs forbade a nuclear countershot here, and running away toward Sweden was a losing proposition in more ways than one. Bell knew it, too—he gave Jeffrey a quick glance, but it showed a predatory eagerness for battle, not disapproval. Bell had clearly learned a lot in independent command of *Challenger;* his run into the Baltic on the surface was as "cowboy" as anything Jeffrey had ever pulled.

"Sonar, do you hold contact yet on *Deutschland?*" The ride began to get rough as *Challenger* built up speed.

"Negative, Captain. No tonals or flow noise."

Jeffrey had Bell fire another high-explosive ADCAP snap shot, straight ahead on two four zero; *Challenger* could launch weapons from any point in her speed envelope—but so could *Deutschland.* Jeffrey told Bell to have his first ADCAP go active.

"Unit is pinging. . . . No target return."

Jeffrey forced himself to count to ten. He glanced at Bell.

"Still no target return, sir. No Doppler whatsoever."

"Then *Deutschland's* hovering bows-on to us, canceling the echo." *Challenger* reached thirty-two knots, on her way to fifty fast. "He must have swum out his weapon at stealth speed on a random starting dogleg." The pump-jet shook, but held together; the worst of the shaking died down.

"Concur," Bell said. "Inbound torpedo range now ten thousand yards. Net closing speed one hundred twenty knots." The torpedo's speed plus *Challenger's.*

Jeffrey picked up the intercom mike for Maneuvering. "Push the reactor to one hundred twelve percent."

"Captain," Bell said, "unit from tube one still holds no target."

"Reload all empty tubes, conventional ADCAPs." This would take a while, and *Challenger* had very little time. Bell acknowledged.

"Oceanographer, match the gravimeter display with our most fine-detailed nautical chart. Find me something on the bottom that's not supposed to be there."

"Aye, aye," Ilse said.

"*Hurry.* Show me what you've got."

"Two mass concentrations, possible wrecks or SSNs, here and *here.*" Ilse's light-pen markings showed on Jeffrey's and Bell's screens.

"Fire Control, when ready aim an ADCAP at each point." The

ship's slow rate of fire was really hurting now. Still, *Challenger* charged at the incoming 65.

"One minute to incoming nuclear sixty-five lethal range if set on maximum yield," Bell said.

"Still no contact on *Deutschland*," Kathy said.

This is getting dicey.

"Sir!" Ilse said. "One mass-con fading! Conjecture it's in motion now!" The gravimeter couldn't track a moving object.

"Concur," Kathy said. "Broadband contact bearing two five zero, range fifteen thousand yards. Designate as Master One. . . . Mechanical transient, reactor check valves. Master One is *Deutschland,* going to flank speed."

But they'd need time to accelerate from a dead stop and then reverse course. That's what Jeffrey was counting on.

"Maneuvering, Captain, push the reactor to one hundred fifteen percent. . . . Helm, put us in *Deutschland*'s baffles if you can. Try to stay right on her ass." *Deutschland* knew the safe corridors, and at flank speed she'd act as minesweeper for *Challenger*—if *Challenger* survived long enough to get that close. If *Challenger* didn't survive, the closer Jeffrey could get to Eberhard, the more likely *Deutschland* might be damaged by her own atomic fish. . . .

Jeffrey watched his tactical plot. Both his ADCAPs converged on Master One, pinging, getting echoes off the back of *Deutschland*'s pump-jet. The kill radius of the incoming 65 would touch *Challenger* any second . . . but it also still touched *Deutschland*. The 65 kept closing.

"Fire Control, show me the kill zone at their minimum yield, one-tenth KT."

Bell typed; the circle shrank by half, to a diameter of less than five thousand yards. At that yield-setting, Eberhard was safe; *Challenger* wasn't. Jeffrey watched the screen. *Challenger* charged at fifty-three knots, the fastest she'd ever gone. The deck vibrated roughly. Console mountings jiggled; spring-loaded fluorescents bounced and squeaked.

"Incoming weapon is in one-tenth KT lethal range."

If I've guessed wrong . . .

"Master One is launching noisemakers," Kathy reported. "*Second torpedo in the water,* same bearing as Master One. Incoming, another sixty-five."

"Stand by on the AT rockets." There was nothing more Jeffrey could do. . . . The first 65 kept closing and closing. Jeffrey held his breath—*was it nuclear?* It got so close Bell destroyed it with two antitorpedo rockets; *Challenger* was pummeled by the blasts. It was conventional after all, but its high-explosive load was triple an ADCAP's.

More than enough to kill us all if just one 65 connects. How many does Deutschland *have?*

The sea was rent by gigantic detonations, both close and further away, as more AT rocket warheads burst and set off torpedoes sympathetically. *Challenger* shimmied and rocked.

Deutschland and *Challenger* kept exchanging salvos, even as *Deutschland* fled and *Challenger* chased; both ships defended themselves with antitorpedo rockets. Again and again the ocean heaved.

Both ships charged northwest as fast as they could, following the Trough around the southern coast of Norway. *Deutschland* would soon reach her own flank speed. Jeffrey knew from Intel her top quiet speed was faster than *Challenger*'s—was her flank speed faster, too? Jeffrey tried to herd *Deutschland* toward the left side of the Trough, the nearer side.

The ships were separated now by barely two thousand yards, too close for *Deutschland* to go nuclear even if Eberhard wanted to.

Deutschland launched four *more* 65's. *Challenger* fired another nonnuclear ADCAP—Jeffrey was down to only two remaining.

Two 65's veered left and hit the wall of the Trough intentionally. They blew and started an underwater landslide. Boulders disappeared from the gravimeter as they fell. They threatened to hit *Challenger*, and her AT rockets were no help.

That clever *bastard*.

Meltzer had to veer right to evade the avalanche; rubble pelted the hull. *Deutschland* gained a hundred yards of precious separation. Bell destroyed the last incoming 65's, but now was down to the last of *Challenger*'s rockets. *Deutschland* fired more AT rockets, and intercepted *Challenger*'s latest ADCAP.

There were no more torpedo engine sounds. The high-explosive skirmish was over, a draw. Meltzer held *Challenger* in *Deutschland*'s baffles; their utmost speeds were almost perfectly matched. Still both ships charged northwest.

ON *DEUTSCHLAND*

Ernst Beck watched his screens as data poured in from Weapons and Sonar. "Last conventional sixty-five destroyed by enemy AT rockets."

Beck glanced at Kurt Eberhard. Even in the rig for black, he knew his captain was livid.

"We're out of high-explosive torpedoes, and we're stuck in a high-speed stern chase. Fuller is too close for me to use atomic warheads, even if the *verdammt* Axis ROEs would let us now. We've no choice but to get well away from Sweden as fast as we can. . . . And *he* has no choice but to stay with us, or we'll get adequate separation to open fire first, before *he's* far enough away from Norway to shoot back."

"Concur, sir," Beck said. This whole situation was an accident of geography—but as always in war the geography, and the rules of engagement, were real. Axis ROEs did *not* protect occupied countries from fallout; Allied ROEs *did*.

Eberhard palmed the intercom mike with a feral grin. "Time for competitive speed trials, Einzvo. Let's see if we can outrun Fuller. Engine Room, Captain, push the reactor to one hundred fifteen percent."

Beck watched his speed log. Slowly the ship sped up, then held at 53.3 knots. The ride was surprisingly smooth, except for the usual fishtailing.

"Sir," Beck said. "Allied nuclear torpedo warhead yields are smaller than ours. *Challenger's* can be set as low as one-one-hundredth kiloton. If we draw apart too late, when we're far enough from Norway, they'll gain adequate separation for a shot at us before we can shoot back."

"Don't you think I know that?"

Beck studied the large-scale nautical chart. The Trough followed the Norwegian coast, north-northwest and then north, for two hundred fifty miles. Only then would *Deutschland* and *Challenger* reach open, truly deep water: the Norwegian Sea.

"Einzvo, I intend to follow the left-most safe corridor in the Trough. We need strong echoes from the escarpment wall, with short time delay, to keep an eye on *Challenger* astern."

"Concur, Captain." This was no time or place for a towed array. "Sir, enemy appears to have ceased firing."

"Out of conventional ammo, just like us. . . . Einzvo, what's enemy speed?"

"Fifty-three and one tenth knots."

"Separation?"

"Their bow dome to our pump-jet, eighteen hundred meters."

"With a speed difference of one-fifth knot, it'll be hours before either of us can open fire without a self-kill."

Beck nodded. "At least our close proximity discourages surface forces from interfering."

Eberhard pounded his console in undisguised anger. "It's an outrage our weaponry is so limited. Our Sea Lions are all nuclear, and the yields are much too large!"

"Captain, no one envisioned a scenario like *this*."

"The torpedo designers should be court-martialed and shot. When we return to base, I'll make sure that's what happens."

Beck shuddered. Eberhard would do it, too. Then Beck realized something. "Sir, *Challenger* may have more high-explosive torpedoes, saving them for some contingency."

"If so, Fuller's smarter than I thought. But he's not smart enough to get them past our antitorpedo rockets."

CHAPTER 31

Jeffrey sat at the command console, starting on another mug half full of coffee. The vibrations at 53.1 knots were so extreme, a full cup would've splashed. Jeffrey glanced around the CACC. His dark-adapted eyes showed some console seats were empty; the crew was having breakfast, or grabbing catnaps, or using the head, in shifts, of sheer necessity.

On the tactical plot, *Deutschland* raced through the Trough ahead of *Challenger*. Eberhard's ship was ever-so-slightly faster, and the separation grew to twenty-eight hundred yards. The enemy was in the sweet spot of *Challenger*'s bow sphere—advanced signal processors filtered out the own-ship flank speed flow noise. Jeffrey could see from the tonals and broadband how hard *Deutschland*'s power plant was working. He could see from his status screens the strain on *Challenger*'s systems, too.

"Captain," Sessions said. "Advise we are two hundred nautical miles from Sweden."

"Very well, Nav."

If we have a propulsion failure now, it's all over.

This was the moment Jeffrey feared. He turned to Bell, and tried to study the other man's face by the glow from the screens. "Here Eberhard can go atomic anytime he likes."

Bell shook his head. "We're too close behind him, sir. With a tenth-KT warhead, he'll want eight thousand yards between, at least, or he'd suffer serious damage."

"It's not that simple, XO. He could loop a weapon back behind us, outside our AT rocket range, then catch us from *astern*, more or less right *now*. We'd be in the lethal envelope; he wouldn't be." AT rockets only reached out to one thousand yards.

"Er, concur, sir. Sorry, I wasn't thinking. . . . But wait, it's not *that* simple either, Captain. A loop-around shot, set to come at us from behind, would have a long run to detonate, and a net overtaking speed of only twenty-some knots. He'd give us too much time to think, and we might fire a nuke right up his stern, and kill him for sure."

"You're right. Against *our* tenth-KT max-yield warhead, *he'd* be a goner. Even if he fired a nuclear torpedo to try to smash ours, with these geometries his own blast would take him with it. . . . And if *we* tried to loop a unit *ahead*, to catch *him* from off his bow, he'd have plenty of time to turn back at us and we'd just waste the weapon, we'd have to safe and abandon it."

Jeffrey took a deep breath. *ROEs, geometries, geography, and tactics. It was mind-bending, an unforgiving mental and physical marathon that could have at most one winner. This was undersea warfare at its best and worst.*

"Hmmm," Bell said. Jeffrey could see he was thinking hard. "Are you suggesting, sir, we take Eberhard with us if he does shoot now?"

"Consider the alternative, XO. We die, he lives. The U.S. is left with no ceramic-hulled nuclear submarine. With the new SSGN they're building, and *Deutschland*, Germany has two."

"Captain, *would* you take him with us now? I'd have to strongly object. We're barely thirty miles from Stavanger, and the gale is blowing *toward* the city. The population is fifty thousand Norwegians. The fallout—"

"I know, XO. I'd never ask you to concur and launch a weapon here." It would be in blatant violation of the ROEs.

"In another hour we draw abreast of Bergen, sir. The population there is a quarter-million-plus."

"I know, XO. I know."

There was no choice but to continue the desperate stern chase, and try to stay as close to *Deutschland* as possible, for as long as it took to get far away from Norway, and pray Eberhard couldn't open fire till Jeffrey could shoot back with nukes.

•   •   •

Ernst Beck returned from using the head. A messenger brought him a fresh mug of tea. He savored the drink, the sweetness of the sugar on his tongue, the way the hot liquid dispelled the stale, metallic taste in his mouth. *Deutschland* fishtailed again, and he almost burned himself. He put the mug in his cup holder.

Eberhard sat at the command console next to Beck, drawing arcs and measuring distances with his light pen.

"This is most unsatisfactory, Einzvo."

"Captain?"

"I need some way to lengthen the odds in our favor, or this action may become a double kill. *Deutschland* is far too valuable an offensive weapon to be expendable in exchange for *Challenger*."

"Concur, sir." What else could Beck say?

"At this rate it will still be hours before we're far enough away from Fuller to hit his ship down her throat from a safe distance. Before we can, he'll have separation for a lethal shot at *us* with his lower-yielding weapons. . . . It's unclear if we'll gain the separation *we* need to open fire before we both gain the Arctic Circle, at which point Fuller gets the ROE freedom *he* needs."

Beck knew the American captain and executive officer had to be thinking the same things. All either ship could do was pour on the speed. If and when the water got much deeper, slight differences in pump-jet efficiency might reveal themselves, due to greater sea pressure, and colder water going through the steam condensor cooling loops.

Secretly, Beck prayed their stern chase did reach the Norwegian Sea. He thought of what the fallout from an atomic blast could do this close to Norway, with the water less than three hundred meters deep. The tons and tons of radioactive steam. The effect of iodine 131 on children and expectant mothers. The effects of unfissioned uranium, and plutonium by-products and worse, on innocent people's lungs and bones and blood. . . . There were German citizens in Norway, too, and occupation forces, caught in this terrible conflict. Beck's country didn't need more casualties for military hospitals' overcrowded radiation wards.

But what was the alternative? If they reached the Norwegian Sea before achieving good separation, *Challenger* could sink them.

Eberhard told Beck to take the conn. The captain was going to his stateroom for a quick smoke and a piss.

Beck sat morosely at the command console, asking himself how this situation could ever have arisen. Not the fight between *Challenger* and *Deutschland,* but the whole war. What madness could ever tempt self-appointed national leaders to risk destroying the world, just to satisfy grandiose, self-referential dreams? All the people had to do was say No. Hadn't they learned that the hard way, in self-immolation under the Nazis?

Obviously not. Perhaps those who'd shared those awful memories firsthand couldn't pass on the warning strongly enough. Perhaps with the passing away of so many veterans, widows, orphans, and Holocaust victims, Germans forgot too much.

Beck shook his head to try to clear his mind of such troubling thoughts. He wished he could have another private talk with Jakob Coomans, to cheer himself and regain perspective, but he knew that wouldn't happen till the confrontation with *Challenger* was resolved. Beck almost wished he could share Eberhard's hate of this Jeffrey Fuller—it would make the needed mental savagery come to Beck much easier. Beck knew himself too well: He was a man who found it hard to hate.

Beck called up the navigation charts, to lose himself in shop talk in his mind. He watched the gravimeter, as the left wall of the Trough raced by. He eyeballed the different system status screens. He thought of old battles fought near here, Nelson at Copenhagen two centuries ago, Dogger Bank and Jutland in the Great War, the destroyer fights in the fjords at the outbreak of World War II, then the German attacks on the Russia-bound Allied convoys. *Deutschland* fishtailed again.

Beck had an idea. It was his duty to report it, though now he hated himself, and did so all too easily.

Eberhard came back.

TWO HOURS LATER, ON CHALLENGER.

After a quick snooze and a hearty breakfast of bacon and eggs, Ilse sat at her console. She was sifting through Cold War-era data from the Navy Meteorology and Oceanography Command. If the situation weren't so scary, it would have been fun—quite a switch from the tropics at Durban. For one thing, up here past 60° north latitude, there was little bioluminescence—the water was too cold. Ilse and Kathy had discussed using the ship's photonics sensors to trail the glow of *Deutschland*'s wake if *Challenger* lost contact. It wouldn't work.

The seafloor was getting much deeper—one thousand feet and dropping to twelve thousand over the next few hours—but the sound speed profile prevented strong convergence zones and deep sound channels from forming. Again, the water in the top few thousand feet was just too cold. Again, the search to recapture a contact once lost would be hard—and *Deutschland*, if lost, might well find *Challenger* first. Ilse knew they'd get no help from NATO's North Atlantic SOSUS hydrophone nets; the Axis had nuked the SOSUS at the very start of the war.

Ilse listened on her headphones for a moment. The gale raged topside. It would probably reach force ten—fifty-knot winds and fifty-foot waves—as they approached the winter Icelandic standing low-pressure weather system. This gale infused the sea with acoustic illumination, and encouraged both ceramic SSNs to hug the bottom for stealth; the seafloor here was smooth. The strengthening gale would also make it harder and harder for surface and airborne anti-submarine forces to function effectively. If *Deutschland* won the duel with *Challenger*, she'd escape Allied retribution—in the Norwegian Sea, Eberhard could vastly outdive any steel-hulled sub sent to attack him.

"The magnetic storm is getting worse," Kathy said.

"I know."

"NASA needs a new category," Kathy said. "G six."

"Beyond 'extreme.' Try 'cataclysmic.'"

Kathy hesitated. "I keep thinking about Roger."

"Your boyfriend?"

"He died up where we're headed. Last summer. The battle for Jan Mayen Island."

Ilse nodded grimly. The island was a nuclear wasteland now.

"Vaporized. His whole ship was vaporized. A cruise missile from *Deutschland*. I started having nightmares about it. I keep seeing him on the bridge, and then there's a flash, and his body boils away."

"Stop," Ilse said. She hesitated. "I know it hurts. I'm having night-mares, too." That was one main reason why she hated having to sleep.

Something appeared on the broadband waterfall display.

"Overflight," Kathy called out. "Low altitude, west to east. Mach point-eight-five turbojet, assess as an Allied ship-launched Harpoon."

"Very well, Sonar," Lieutenant Bell said. He had the conn while Jeffrey got some rest.

More Harpoons went by, also launched in the shallow North Sea off to port, aimed at something amid the Norwegian islands and fjords to starboard. "The shooting's started again," Ilse said.

More transients appeared on the waterfall, slanting sharply in the opposite direction.

"Overflights, supersonic, east to west," Kathy said. Ilse listened. Each transient sounded the same, a sonic boom followed by a roaring, tearing noise that surged, then faded.

"Rocket-assisted projectiles," Kathy called out. "Norwegian coast artillery. Assess as Bofors rapid fire one-twenty-millimeter guns." Manned by German crews.

"V'r'well," Bell said. "Surface forces skirmishing around our stern chase with *Deutschland* again."

Ilse knew no major warship afloat could keep up with their sustained fifty-three knots, especially in such rough seas. She knew none dared launch an undersea weapon for fear of hitting the wrong SSN. It was as if the ships and planes above Ilse were fighting a separate war.

The sonar tech next to her sat up straighter, and spoke to Kathy on a private circuit. Kathy sat up straighter, too.

"Aspect change on Master One. Master One is turning right!"

"Helm, *don't lose them.*" Bell grabbed an intercom mike. "Captain to Control."

Jeffrey showed in seconds.

"What is it?"

"*Deutschland*'s up to something, sir. They've turned toward the middle of the Trough. New course zero three zero."

"I have the conn."

"You have the conn."

"This is the captain. I have the conn."

"Aye, aye," Ilse said, along with the watchstanders.

"I don't like this, sir," Bell said.

"I know. They may have guessed we're favoring our left side for a reason." The damaged port wide-aperture array. "If we get in a turning dogfight we'll be at a sonar disadvantage. We're less maneuverable, too, with the top of our rudder shot up."

"Herd them back with another ADCAP?"

"With just two remaining, there's no point. He fires more AT rockets, and they're wasted. Worse, we'll telegraph we're low on conventional ammo, when we have to cease fire."

"So what do we do, sir? Keep following?"

"We have no choice. What's the separation now?"

"Almost four thousand yards."

"Two nautical miles . . . Far enough apart he may pull something nasty among the coastal islands."

"Think he'll try to lose us and make a getaway? Hide up a fjord, or put in at Bergen?"

"*Heck,* no. Not Eberhard. He'll try to lose us and get off a nuclear snap shot."

"*Challenger* has followed our turn," Beck reported. "Separation now thirty-six hundred meters, Captain." Two sea miles. Enough.

"Good," Eberhard said.

Beck studied his nav chart and gravimeter. Half an hour ahead on this course lay the rugged islands lining the coast of Norway. That's what Fuller was *supposed* to see, *supposed* to be thinking about.

"Brilliant decoy in tube eight is preset as ordered, Captain."

"Make tube eight ready in all respects, but do not open outer door."

Beck relayed commands. He watched the low terrain ridge on the bottom come at him rapidly. He activated the laser line-scan cameras on *Deutschland's* stern and sail and bow. He called up the imagery.

The seafloor rushed by below. Beck saw mud, and rocks, and caught a glimpse of a rusted oil drum, and a discarded liquor bottle. Then he saw a 150mm gun turret, lying on its side.

"Pilot," Eberhard said, "stand by for hard turn to port."

"*Jawohl,*" Jakob Coomans said.

"Einzvo, stand by to launch the decoy in tube eight. Set valve lineup for silent punch-out with an elastomer membrane water slug."

"*Jawohl.*" The membrane stored the force of ambient sea pressure; the weapon launch would be much quieter than with a water turbine or compressed air.

"Stand by to launch with same valve settings, torpedo tubes two and four."

Beck thought again of the people in Bergen, Norway. Tubes two and four each held a nuclear Sea Lion eel, armed and ready to fire.

"He's going to top that ridge in a minute, sir," Bell said.

Jeffrey nodded. "The time lag of echoes off the left wall of the Trough is less than twenty seconds here. Our bow sphere will cover to port. . . . We won't lose him."

Beck watched the gravimeter closely as *Deutschland* topped the ridge. He was so close to it now, the gradiometers clearly resolved the sunken mass to port. It was a hundred and fifty meters long, widest in the middle, narrowing at both ends, sitting flat on the bottom.

Now or never, Beck told himself. Would his idea work, or backfire?

"Tube eight," Eberhard ordered, "open outer door. . . . Decoy *los.*"

"Tube eight fired," Beck said. Now came the tricky part.

"Pilot," Eberhard said, "override flank speed rudder safeties."

Coomans acknowledged, his voice especially tough and confident now—no one knew better than Coomans how difficult this next maneuver would be.

"Port thirty rudder," Eberhard ordered.

Coomans acknowledged; the ship banked hard and hugged the terrain. Beck held tight to his armrests, and Coomans to his wheel—*Deutschland* weighed nine thousand metric tons submerged, a huge dead weight to try to turn so tightly at high speed. Coomans had to cut in the auxiliary thrusters to help. The copilot had to cut in on the stern-planes, to help Coomans maintain depth control.

"Decoy is operating properly," Haffner reported from Sonar.

"Stop the propulsion shaft," Eberhard ordered coldly as the g-force of the turn pressed Beck into his seat. "Full speed astern."

Deutschland shivered, strained, vibrated as she tried to slow. Beck tensed: Would *Challenger* hear? A red light flashed on Coomans's panel—the stresses on the rudder threatened serious, permanent damage.

Deutschland's way came off quickly. The red light ceased. Beck breathed again.

"All stop," Eberhard ordered. "Autohover." Coomans acknowledged once more. Beck detected the subtlest tone that Coomans was pleased with himself, at how well he'd handled the ship. *But had Jeffrey Fuller heard?*

"Shut down turbogenerators," Eberhard said. "Run essential systems off batteries."

The copilot relayed commands. The air circulation fans ceased.

"Decoy is on course zero three zero," Beck reported. "Speed fifty-three point three knots." He was sweating; the air already felt stale.

"*Challenger* tops the rise in ninety seconds," Eberhard stated. He gave Beck a piercing look. "Now we see if your idea works."

Beck swallowed and studied his screens—there was little time to fine-tune *Deutschland*'s position. "Sir, recommend rotate ship on auxiliary propulsors onto bearing zero four five, and translate fifty yards to starboard."

Eberhard gave the piloting orders.

Beck watched the photonics imagery screen. The mass on the bottom loomed out of the darkness. *Deutschland*'s bow was near its stern, her stern next to its bow. It was a sunken World War II German destroyer—Hitler's *Kriegsmarine* lost many in the opening battle for Norway. This one's bow was smashed—from a bomb or torpedo or mine, a collision at sea, or from impact with the bottom? Beck couldn't tell. The superstructure was mangled. The masts and funnels lay every which way.

"Open outer doors," Eberhard said, "tubes two and four."

"Doors open," Beck acknowledged.

Coomans had *Deutschland* nestled behind the destroyer beautifully now. Its gravitational and magnetic effects—and flow noise in the gentle bottom current—ought to hide *Deutschland* well. Beck listened to the sonar speakers for a moment. The wreck was old: no settling noises, no seeping fuel or air, no loose parts clanking. He checked the tactical plot.

"*Challenger* maintaining course zero three zero, Captain. Maintaining flank speed."

"Einzvo, stand by to fire tubes two and four, maximum yield, one kiloton."

Ilse watched her gravimeter and nav display as *Challenger* charged at the ridge. Slightly to left of the ship's projected track lay an old wreck, plotted on the chart.

"Fire Control, report," Jeffrey said.

"Master One maintaining course zero three zero, sir. Maintaining flank speed."

Challenger topped the rise. The bow sphere regained direct-path contact with *Deutschland*—she still made 53.3 knots.

"We'll reach the coastal islands in twenty minutes, sir," Sessions said.

"Very well, Nav."

Ilse watched her screens again as the wreck went by.

Wait a minute. . . .

"*Captain*. Wreck was anomalous on gravimeter."

"It looks normal to me," Jeffrey said.

"When we were closer, the sharper resolution . . ."

Jeffrey hesitated. "Helm, *hard left rudder!*"

Ilse was thrown against the back of her seat as the ship turned violently to port. *Challenger* banked into the turn so hard the centrifugal force kept her mug in its holder from spilling.

"The mass-con," Ilse said. "Look." It rippled and shrank.

"Mechanical transient," Kathy shouted. "Directly to port, near-field effects! *Reactor check valve transient.*"

"True contact Master One is accelerating," Bell said. "New course zero four five." Northeast. Eberhard's trick had been foiled, but *Deutschland* was getting away; her decoy sped into the distance.

"Chief of the Watch," Jeffrey ordered, "use auxiliary propulsors to put us in a sharper turn."

COB acknowledged. The g-force got even stronger.

"Master One is turning onto course zero three zero."

"Helm, as we come through the turn, make your course zero three zero."

Meltzer acknowledged. *Challenger* turned and turned. COB and Meltzer struggled to keep her from going into a snap roll, especially with the added weight of the flooded sail trunk high off the center of gravity.

Ilse saw something on the rear photonics imagery; she stiffened. A cylindrical object, sixty feet long, crossed *Challenger's* stern. A German minisub? Then Ilse saw the tentacles, and a humongous eye. A giant squid, the first sighting *ever* in its natural habitat here! Till now there'd been only dead ones found, washed up on the Norwegian shore. Ilse's heart ached to linger and study it. . . .

The ship leveled off. "My course is zero three zero," Meltzer said. *Challenger* chased *Deutschland* again.

"Fire Control," Jeffrey snapped. "Separation?"

"Thirty-four hundred yards." Less than before but not by much.

Ilse forced down her frustration: Eberhard had grabbed the initiative, *again*.

"That should keep him off balance nicely," Eberhard said. "Now for phase two of your plan, Einzvo. . . . It had better work *this* time. They've narrowed the separation by two hours' worth of pursuit."

"Understood." Beck knew it probably wouldn't be *that* easy. So far had just been the setup, to plant the seed of fatal doubt in Fuller's mind.

"Another ridge is coming up," Bell said. "There's another wreck behind it."

"I know," Jeffrey said.

"Think he'll play the same trick, sir?"

"He'll try *something*. This time the question'll be, which is his ship and which is the decoy?"

"We can use the gravimeter again," Ilse said. "Can't we?"

Beck watched the next rise coming up. It was higher than the first one, and the back side dropped more steeply.

"Pilot," Eberhard said, "starboard ten rudder, steer zero four five."

"Zero four five, *jawohl*," Coomans said.

•   •   •

"There's the other wreck on the chart," Jeffrey said. "This one's supposed to be a Royal Navy destroyer from World War One."

"Master One aspect change!" Kathy said. "Master One turning to starboard."

"New course is zero four five," Bell said.

"Helm, make your course zero four five."

"Sir," Ilse said. "That takes *Deutschland* further from the upcoming wreck."

"Concur," Bell said. "Our gravimeter resolution will not discriminate targets quickly enough this time."

"I know, XO. I'm sure that's what Eberhard plans."

"Captain, if he can gain adequate separation, he can hit us with a nuclear torpedo. The nearest Swedish border is over three hundred miles away, protected by tall mountains in Norway."

"I know, XO. We have a fifty-fifty chance of guessing right: Is it *Deutschland* at the wreck, or is it the decoy?"

Both ships were very close to Bergen now. The wind was blowing east. East of Bergen was Oslo, Norway's capital, twice as large.

"Brilliant decoys loaded in tubes six and eight," Beck said. "Flank speed, and courses, preset."

"Very well, Einzvo."

Beck watched his screens once more. The ridge approached quickly.

Deutschland topped the rise.

"Open outer doors, tubes six and eight. . . . Tube six, *los.* Tube eight, *los.*"

"Both tubes fired."

"Pilot, port thirty rudder."

Coomans acknowledged, even more confident than last time, almost cocky. *Deutschland* banked very hard.

"Both decoys operating properly," Haffner called. "Running steady at fifty-three point three knots, and emulating *Deutschland's* flank speed noises."

Deutschland herself lost way. Eberhard ordered the ship to stop and hide against the wreck.

•　　•　　•

"Captain," Kathy said. "Master One appears to have launched a decoy. Contact has split in two."

"Confirmed," Bell said. "One contact maintaining flank speed on course three five zero. The other also maintaining flank speed, on zero four five."

"So he didn't use the wreck at all this time." Again Jeffrey thought of Bergen and Oslo. He thought of *Challenger*'s crew and priceless intelligence payload, and the fact his ship was *not* expendable. *Which sonar contact should we follow?*

"Which one do we follow, sir?" Bell said.

Jeffrey hesitated, agonized.

"Captain?" Meltzer said.

Jeffrey decided to punt. "We'll split the difference, folks. Helm, head down the middle. Make your course zero two three."

Meltzer acknowledged; Bell nodded—he concurred.

"Fire Control, snap shot, ADCAP in tube one. Onto course three five zero, *shoot.*"

"Set. Stand by. Fire."

"Snap shot, tube three, zero four five, shoot!"

"Set. Stand by. Fire."

"Both units running normally," Kathy said.

"Sir," Bell said. "You said before this is pointless. He'll stop them with antitorpedo rockets."

"I know." Jeffrey smiled. "The ADCAPs are twenty knots faster than us. They'll run ahead and tell us what to do. . . . Decoys don't have AT rockets, XO. Eberhard has to shoot. Whichever contact shoots, that's Eberhard."

"Captain," Beck said. "*Challenger* has fired a Mark forty-eight Improved ADCAP at each of our decoys. Weapons are overtaking the decoys. *Challenger* maintaining flank speed on course zero two three."

"Perfect, Einzvo. Perfect."

"What's he waiting for?" Jeffrey said. "Our ADCAPs are getting too close."

•   •   •

"Both ADCAPs still chasing the decoys, sir," Beck said. "*Challenger* still making flank speed on zero two three. . . . Separation from *Deutschland* increasing rapidly."

"We're in Fuller's baffles now. He'll never hear our eels, till it's too late." Tubes two and four were reloaded with Sea Lions, with maximum yields preset. The sonar time delay off the left wall of the Trough and back was almost sixty seconds now.

"Open the outer doors, tubes two and four."

Beck relayed the commands. "Separation approaching six thousand meters, still increasing rapidly."

"Tube two, *los!* Tube four, *los!*"

"The ADCAPs are in easy range of his AT rockets now. *What is he waiting for?*"

"Captain," Bell said. "What if *neither one* is *Deutschland?*"

Jeffrey swallowed. "Helm, *hard left rudder!*"

Challenger swung to port. The blind spot in her baffles swung to starboard, away from the wreck.

"Torpedoes in the water!" Kathy shouted. "Two Sea Lions, one nine zero, closing speed seven five knots!"

"COB, use the side thrusters! Meltzer, get our bow left fast!"

The fates of a million civilians in Norway hinge on the rate of this turn.

"*Challenger* turning hard left," Beck shouted. "*Challenger* closing the range to *Deutschland* rapidly."

Eberhard cursed, then ordered Coomans to get underway to increase the separation.

Beck watched the plot as the Sea Lions both chased *Challenger,* and she led the eels round to the left, trying to catch up with *Deutschland*. The Sea Lions weren't in lethal range of the target yet, but the separation from *Deutschland* was still adequate. . . . It wasn't too late to end this all right here, just as Beck had intended: Kill *Challenger* and Jeffrey Fuller and God knows how many innocent people on land.

•   •   •

Ilse gripped her armrests as *Challenger* tore in a circle at flank speed—*Eberhard got in the first shot, after all.*

The bank of the turn was so steep, *Challenger*'s rudder began to act like stern-planes on full dive. Meltzer tried to pull up.

"We're in a snap roll!" Meltzer shouted; *Challenger* was out of control. The master ship control display showed the bow aim at the seafloor. The rear photonics sensor showed the pump-jet churn up the bottom muck. The two atomic Sea Lions gained on *Challenger*'s tail by the second. Both Sea Lions went active.

Beck watched the tactical plot in morbid fascination: *Challenger*'s in-extremis turning radius, versus *Deutschland*'s acceleration and the kill zone of the eels. Which outcome meant that Beck would win, and which that he would lose? What did he want endangered more, his body or his soul? "Separation now inadequate for nuclear weapons!"

"Einzvo, *safe the warheads*! Sever the wires! Pilot, maintain flank speed! Port thirty rudder, cut across *Challenger*'s wake as she turns! Make your course three three zero." Toward the left side of the Trough.

Beck safed the weapons. He felt relief, then felt doubled inner shame, both for what he'd tried to do and for his gladness that it failed—but throughout, he'd done his *duty*.

"We're inside *Deutschland*'s self-kill zone!" Bell shouted. "His weapons have to be safed!"

COB and Meltzer had barely recovered from the snap roll; the most immediate crisis had passed.

"Sorry, Captain," Meltzer said.

"Jesus," COB said, "that was close."

"Master One separation now forty-six hundred yards," Bell said.

"He regained his lead and then some," Jeffrey said. "He's also learned his turning radius is better than ours."

"We're all out of conventional torpedoes, too. Eberhard has to know that, sir—else you'd've launched a third one at the wreck along with the other two chasing those decoys."

Bell was smart, and fast—Jeffrey hadn't seen that last point quite as quickly; he drew some comfort from Bell's capable backstopping. *We've come a long way together since that argument we had.*

"Concur, XO, and we're much too close to Norway to use any nuclear fish. . . . Eberhard holds all the cards. Our options just keep getting narrower and narrower."

CHAPTER 32

SIX HOURS LATER.

At the command console, Jeffrey belched. He'd eaten lunch too fast, and gotten acid stomach. His bruised chest and his old leg wound still ached, and his face still hurt from the burns received in the Sound.

Good. The last thing he wanted to be was relaxed. The discomfort kept him on edge, kept him focused.

Ilse had grabbed another catnap, then eaten with Jeffrey, alone in the wardroom together. Now she was back at her console, too. The sexual tension between them during the meal—their first private time since they had both believed they'd die on the missile lab raid—had been electric, unspoken but unmistakable. Mutual desire and anticipation for the future, though intangible, seemed very real. For this, too, Jeffrey was glad. It helped him stay wide awake, and reminded him he had something to live for. Could Ilse become the soul mate he'd never before thought he might have, a fellow warrior of the opposite gender, the two of them a couple who braved the fires of battle side by side?

Now, in public, he and Ilse were strictly business—a lot had to happen before they could get back to such daydreams. Jeffrey pondered his screens; the relentless stern chase continued. As he watched, *Deutschland* and then *Challenger* dashed out of the north end of the Norwegian Trough. Both ships still hugged the bottom, in water thirty-three hundred feet deep. They were down in the Shetland Channel now, entering the Norwegian Sea, forced to head north-northeast at this point by a line of ancient volcanic ridges to port. Eberhard was undoubtedly using echoes off the closest ridge to keep tabs on Jeffrey behind him.

Over the last few hours, *Deutschland* had slowly widened her lead to six thousand yards. Jeffrey eyed the on-line nautical chart. This was the moment he'd waited for. The gale above now blew northwest, toward the ice cap and northernmost Greenland. The surface currents here formed a slow counterclockwise gyre. Airborne fallout would blow to a desolate wilderness. Seaborne fission waste would circulate with the gyre, as lighter elements floated and aged and heavy ones fell to the seafloor.

"Captain," Sessions called from the nav console. "Advise we are now two hundred nautical miles from Norway, the nearest friendly or occupied land."

"Captain," Bell recited formally, "advise rules of engagement now leave us weapons free with atomic warheads."

"Very well, Nav. Very well, Fire Control." Jeffrey and Bell went through the procedures to arm tactical nuclear Mark 88's and have them loaded in all four working torpedo tubes, the starboard-side tubes, odd numbers one through seven.

"Preset warhead yields, all weapons, to maximum yield."

Bell acknowledged and relayed commands.

"Make tubes one, three, five, and seven ready in all respects."

Jeffrey decided to wait. Much as he wanted to get in the first salvo, he also wanted just a bit more target separation. He was very far from home, and any further damage to his battered ship could well mean total ruin.

"Captain," Beck said, "advise separation now is fifty-five hundred meters."

Beck called the master weapons status page onto his main console screen. Nuclear Sea Lions were loaded in tubes one through eight, and armed—the port-side autoloader had gotten jury-rigged repairs at Trondheim; the starboard-side tubes still needed manual loading by chain fall.

"Very well, Einzvo. Set weapon yields, odd-numbered tubes, to minimum." Defensive, antitorpedo shots. "Set weapon yields, even-numbered tubes, to maximum." Offensive shots, against *Challenger,* who any moment would go weapons free by Allied ROEs.

Beck repeated the orders for confirmation, then relayed commands to the weapons officer. He confirmed to the captain when the orders were carried out. Beck shuddered to think of the cataclysm to come: Any detonation in deep water was fifty times as destructive as in air—water was very rigid, and had a much higher speed of sound. At close enough range, a one-kiloton Sea Lion could do to *Challenger* what the Americans had done to Hiroshima and Nagasaki combined. *Challenger's* warheads, one tenth the size of *Deutschland's,* were deadly enough.

"It's time to finish *Challenger* off," Eberhard said. "Make tubes one through eight ready in all respects."

"All tubes ready, Captain."

"Fuller won't hear it behind us. Open all outer tube doors."

"Outer doors are open." Beck was much happier now; they'd reached an isolated, unpopulated area, with ecologically favorable currents and winds. *A good choice for the final battleground.* The target separation for *Deutschland's* weapons was still narrow, but aggressive warshots followed by skillful tactical maneuvers might make up for that.

"Tube two," Eberhard ordered, "target *Challenger,* load sonar bearings, and *los!*"

Ilse listened on her sonar headphones, while she studied data on the Norwegian Sea, and tried to refine Kathy's ray traces.

Ilse heard it; Kathy said it. *"Torpedo in the water!* Inbound torpedo bearing zero one five, a Sea Lion!"

It's started, Ilse told herself. *The final confrontation, deep and with atomic weapons.* Everyone in the CACC felt the tension mount.

Jeffrey ordered a nuclear countershot, then a turn away, due east. Meltzer had to use the rudder gently, so they wouldn't break the wire at flank speed—which didn't help them any to evade the inbound torpedo. This countershot had better be telling. Jeffrey had to husband his ammo carefully; *Challenger's* rate of fire was dangerously slow. Bell launched noisemakers and jammers, which were also running low.

Ilse heard the two torpedoes, one Axis and one friendly, their nerve-jarring racket Dopplered up or down as they came at her or receded. She heard the gurgling hiss of the chemical noisemakers, too, and the undulating siren scream of acoustic jammer pods. *How can we possibly win? Deutschland has twice as many working tubes.*

Kathy reported that *Deutschland* had fired another Sea Lion. *Deutschland* changed course west, still making flank speed, and launched noisemakers and jammers.

Jeffrey fired another fish, this one aimed at *Deutschland*. Bell launched more noisemakers and jammers, then Jeffrey ordered another turn, south. *Deutschland* launched a Sea Lion to intercept Jeffrey's incoming fish, then launched another to intercept *Challenger*.

Deutschland launched *another* weapon at *Challenger*, then made a hard turn north.

Jeffrey watched the tactical plot. There were seven nuclear torpedoes in the water, tearing in all directions. Some chased *Challenger*, some chased *Deutschland*, some chased each other's torpedoes as nuclear countershots.

A sharp *crack* sounded through the hull. Jeffrey felt a big shove from astern, and the ocean all around was filled with terrible rumbles.

"Unit from tube one has detonated!" Bell said. "First incoming Sea Lion destroyed!"

Aftershocks hit over and over, as the fireball shot for the surface, throbbing as it blew outward against the sea pressure, then collapsed, then rebounded hard. The blast echoed off the surface, then hit hard. The ocean heaved as the fireball broke the surface and drove into the sky. The blast echoed off the ridge terrain to port and then hit hard.

Bell detonated another antitorpedo torpedo, and the punishment started again.

"Fire Control," Jeffrey yelled above the noise, "maximum yields, reload tubes one and three smartly!"

Kathy said they'd lost sonar contact with *Deutschland*.

The ocean shattered. Sledgehammers pounded *Deutschland*'s hull. Fireball aftershocks hit again and again, then blast echoes off the surface and the ridge.

Beck watched meaningful target data cease as the atomic sonar whiteouts blossomed. "Best guess for next snap shot at *Challenger* is due south, Captain."

"Too obvious. Let's bracket him." Eberhard ordered a two-eel spread; Beck complied.

Another of *Challenger*'s weapons went off. It snapped the wires to two of *Deutschland*'s Sea Lions.

Jeffrey tried to visualize the action in his mind. The computer data was meaningless and stale. Somewhere in that maelstrom Sea Lions sought him. Somewhere beyond the fireballs and tortured bubble clouds, *Deutschland* would launch more. Somewhere northeast a Sea Lion blew, set on maximum yield, lured perhaps by a noisemaker. *Challenger* rocked.

Jeffrey ordered a snap shot due north.

"Unit is running normally," Kathy said. Then she jolted. "*Inbound torpedo.* Sea Lion bearing zero six five! Range eight thousand yards and closing fast. *Torpedo has gone active!*"

Jeffrey heard the hard metallic *dinggg*. He ordered a defensive countershot; Bell acknowledged.

"If that inbound weapon's set at one KT," Bell said, "we won't intercept in time."

"Helm, hard left rudder. Make your course two seven zero." West.

"Lost the wire, tube seven! Inbound weapon tracking us due west."

"Helm, hard right rudder!"

"Unit from tube seven will fire on backup timer *now*."

The sea convulsed again. Fireball aftershocks, and terrain and surface blast echoes, were becoming almost continuous. Demons punched the ship from every side.

"Helm, hard left rudder!"

"Inbound torpedo still running," Kathy shouted.

"Confirmed," Bell said. "Interception *not* successful."

"Status of weapon reload?"

"All tubes empty. None will ready in time."

"Fire more noisemakers. Fire more jammers. Helm, make a knuckle smartly."

"Inbound weapon now in range-gate mode."

The *dingggs* came very fast.

"Helm, another knuckle." *Challenger* lost ground.

"No effect," Bell said. "Weapon separation now three thousand yards."

"More noisemakers and jammers!"

Bell complied, Jeffrey waited. Seconds ticked away.

"No effect. Separation now *two* thousand yards."

Close enough to smash our stern wide open, even set on lowest Axis yield.

Bell dutifully watched his screens, and uselessly reported, "Inbound weapon will blow any moment. No tubes ready to fire."

There was nothing more Jeffrey could do. He glanced at the back of Ilse's head, as she sat there in her earphones, bravely typing. *What wasted opportunities.*

Jeffrey waited to die. He'd failed the one hundred twenty people in his crew, and all their loved ones. There was a thud behind the ship.

"Weapon has fizzled!" Bell shouted. "Assess warhead was damaged by our countershot!"

In his mind, Jeffrey saw Eberhard's face. *We're not dead yet, you smug Prussian SOB.*

"Helm, hard right rudder. Make your course two seven zero." West again, and toward the volcanic ridges.

Jeffrey watched his weapons status screen. A Mark 88 was presented to the tube-one breach. Jeffrey and Bell did the arming procedures.

"Tube one is ready to fire!"

"Snap shot tube one due north *shoot*."

SIMULTANEOUSLY, ON DEUTSCHLAND.

There was a wall of noise and heat between *Deutschland* and *Challenger*. To Beck, the reverb coming through the hull was painful, deafening, and the sonars were virtually useless. Torpedoes, their wires broken by the blasts, ran out of control. Something exploded— a kiloton, one of Beck's own. Did it home on *Challenger*, on a bubble cloud, a noisemaker, or another torpedo? *Impossible to tell.*

The even-numbered tubes were reloaded. Beck and Eberhard

entered their passwords and turned their keys; the weapons were armed.

Suddenly Haffner at sonar shouted, "Inbound torpedo has come through the whiteout! Bearing one six two! Torpedo is one of our Sea Lions!"

It must have been damaged by blast, its safeties and guidance awry.

"Sea Lion has gone active! Sea Lion range-gating on *Deutschland*!"

"Snap shot, tube five, one six two, *los!*"

Beck launched the countershot. It would be barely in time, if that Sea Lion was preset at one KT—without the wire he couldn't tell its yield, let alone control it.

Deutschland still raced north, depth now fifteen hundred meters. Eberhard ordered more noisemakers fired. The errant weapon ignored the distractions. Noisemakers were almost useless this deep: the pressure.

It was time to detonate the defensive countershot from tube five. Beck punched the commands. "Unit from tube five has—"

The blast force struck.

"Another inbound weapon bearing two nine one!" Haffner shouted. "A Mark eighty-eight very close! *Near-field effects!*"

"Range too short for a countershot!" Beck yelled above the cacophony. "We'd be wrecked by our own eel! We're too deep for effective antitorpedo rocket fire!" The motor exhaust would be strangled: again, the pressure.

"*Verdammt,*" Eberhard cursed. "Make sure we take Fuller with us! Snap shot, tubes two, four, six, and eight, diverging spread northwest through southwest. *Los!*"

The Sea Lions leaped from the tubes. "All weapons fired!"

The inbound Mark 88 came closer and closer. Its *dingggs* came through the hull. Ernst Beck waited to die. He thought of his wife and sons—he felt sad and angry.

Something struck *Deutschland*'s sail a jarring blow.

"Mark eighty-eight propulsion noise has ceased," Haffner shouted.

"No apparent damage!" the copilot said.

"*Assess inbound torpedo as a dud.*" But this was no new lease on life, Beck knew; it simply meant more killing.

"Get the port-side tubes reloaded *now.*"

•　　•　　•

Challenger raced for the ridge. Meltzer pulled her nose up sharply to climb the face of the basalt formation. Jeffrey watched his screens. Tubes three and five were reloaded.

"Four inbound torpedoes in the water!" Kathy said. "Contacts held on wide aperture arrays. Two weapons off our starboard quarter, two off the port quarter, closing in passive search mode." Brilliant decoys wouldn't work: At five thousand feet deep, they'd implode.

Jeffrey and Bell armed the weapons in three and five as fast as they could, and launched them as countershots. Jeffrey ordered a turn due north, down in the valley behind the ridge. The four Sea Lions closed in hot pursuit.

More weapons went off in the distance—at what targets, real or false, Beck couldn't tell. *Deutschland* still fled north, to put distance between her and the tortured nuclear battlefield. Another weapon might come through the whiteout any moment.

One did, much too close. Eberhard ordered a countershot. The inbound weapon blew before the outbound one could intercept—the blast struck *Deutschland* at short range.

Unsecured objects in the Zentrale flew. Fluorescent lightbulbs burst. The command console died, and the backup analog speed log showed *Deutschland* losing way.

"Give me damage reports," Eberhard snapped.

Intercoms blinked and phone talkers shouted all at once. Beck reached for the call from Engineering.

"Excessive-shock reactor scram. Propulsion power lost. Control circuits may be damaged, safe restart will take ten minutes."

Deutschland coasted to a halt. Around her the ocean fulminated. Somewhere out there, Beck knew, more torpedoes plowed through the sea, searching for something to destroy.

"Autoloader bearing pin has sheared," the phone talker yelled. "Port-side torpedo autoloader out of action."

Jeffrey ordered Meltzer to slow, to try to make less noise, to hide. *Challenger* was shielded from the worst of the whiteout to the east by the intervening ridge crest. Maybe the inbound torpedoes would run right past him in the chaos.

Challenger's latest two antitorpedo shots went off beyond the ridge. The shock waves bent over the crest, and rattled the ship. It was impossible to tell if there were still incoming weapons.

Jeffrey ordered Kathy to have her people listen hard, for signs of *Deutschland* or her torpedoes.

Something detonated against the opposite side of the ridge— again, the warhead's force bent up and over the crest. The gravimeter showed gaps in the ridge: an avalanche. The local seismic seawave struck, knocking *Challenger* askew. The ship rolled and bucked until Meltzer and COB got her righted again.

A torpedo came over the top of the ridge off *Challenger's* stern. It pinged, then pinged again—Kathy heard the echoes above the landslide; it was close.

Jeffrey ordered flank speed.

Bell fired the 88 in tube seven as a countershot.

The Sea Lion warhead went off first, off the port quarter, then the blast reflected off the ridge and back again from starboard. Jeffrey's skeleton tried to fly apart inside his body. He tasted copper—his gums bled, gouged by a capped tooth.

Challenger coasted to a stop.

Propulsion power was lost. Jeffrey grabbed the red handset for Damage Control back aft. Willey said there was a fire in Engineering, then the line went dead. Jeffrey ordered everyone to don their emergency air breather masks. He waited for the phone talker to report— the sound-powered phones were backup for the intercom. Jeffrey knew the news would not be good. Damage that halted the ship always had to be serious. Here, it could be their undoing.

CHAPTER 33

Ernst Beck made his way aft, past damage control parties at work. He passed the wardroom and mess, where first-aid men treated the injured. He had no time to stop and give encouragement or comfort. He noticed the ship's lay preacher, himself a first-aid tech, making his rounds.

Beck went through the heavy watertight door, into the spotless stainless steel corridor leading beyond the reactor. With all the shielding and massive machinery surrounding him now, the noise outside the hull seemed less.

Beck glanced to his right. In there, beyond the shielding, the core lay dormant, boron carbide control rods thrust between the zirconium-clad uranium-235 plates. Pressurized water still circulated, carrying off thermal energy as short-half-life by-products decayed. But there was nowhere near enough heat to generate steam to drive main turbines, or even auxiliary equipment. Without the turbines spinning, there was no current from the turbogenerators. Without that current, the permanent-magnet propulsion motors were still. The ship could hardly surface and run on emergency diesel here. All power had to come from the batteries.

The batteries were needed to restart the reactor, once the safeties triggered by the battle shock were reset, and the fast-unscram procedures were complete. But the batteries were also needed to run the combat systems, which used very high electrical demand. Time was of the essence.

Beck went through the watertight door at the far end of the corridor. He was in the engine room now—it was hot and humid here, and much too quiet. The engineer stood and supervised, as senior enlisted technicians and junior officers checked the status of control circuits and equipment. Others studied readings from the reactor core, of temperatures and neutron flux.

Everyone worked confidently and efficiently. Beck was hardly needed. He watched as the first group of control rods was lifted, by just enough to enter the restart power range. The operators went through their automated checklists. One Leutnant zur See flipped through thick hard-copy reference manuals, independently verifying key parts of on-line procedure.

The engineer nodded, satisfied. "Very well, Reactor Operator. Lift the next control rod group to restart-level power." This step also went well.

Beck palmed an intercom mike and reported to Eberhard. Eberhard ordered Beck to the Zentrale. Eberhard told him Coomans had gotten the port-side torpedo autoloader working again.

SIMULTANEOUSLY, ON __CHALLENGER__.

Jeffrey fidgeted as he watched his automated damage control displays. He drew a breath and exhaled. Around him twenty other air masks hissed and whooshed. Jeffrey was still so used to being at the scene in drills or combat—with Commander Wilson in charge in the CACC—it was emotionally trying to just sit and wait.

But Jeffrey *trusted* Bell, his XO now back aft; Jeffrey *made* himself relax. He told himself he still had a ways to go to learn the captainly ways Commander Wilson had long since mastered.

"Captain," the phone talker said. His voice was muffled through his mask. Jeffrey looked up. "Damage Control reports fire extinguished, sir."

"How long to propulsion restart?"

The phone talker relayed the question.

"Five minutes till the ship can answer Maneuvering bells."

"Very well." Jeffrey knew there was no point in asking Willey to hurry—he already was. *When would another torpedo come over the ridge?*

"Call the XO forward," Jeffrey said.

"Aye, aye."

Bell was there in moments, slightly breathless from his dash in a heavy air pack. Jeffrey made a point of thanking Bell for his help.

"Navigator," Jeffrey said, "take the conn."

Sessions unplugged his mask, came to the command console, and plugged in again. "This is the navigator. I have the conn."

The watchstanders acknowledged through their masks.

Jeffrey cleared his throat, and pointed around the CACC. "XO, Sonar, Oceanographer, Assistant Navigator. Strategy session at the plotting table."

Everyone took deep breaths, pulled on intercom headphones, put their masks back on, and used duct tape to get good seals; the local CACC intercom circuits were working. They joined Jeffrey at the horizontal nav console, and plugged back in.

The assistant navigator, a senior chief, brought up a large-scale nautical chart.

"We've broken contact with *Deutschland*," Jeffrey said. "Now, fight or flight?"

"*Deutschland* has more options than we do, sir," Bell said. He pointed to the digital chart. "They can try to come after us, or evade. If they want to evade, they can head northeast, into the Barents Sea, and take refuge in Russian waters."

Jeffrey nodded. The Joint Chiefs' global ROEs forbade American warships from entering the Barents Sea, to avoid a confrontation with Russia that might escalate.

"They could go southeast," Kathy said, "back the way we came, to Norway or the Baltic. . . . They could even run the Greenland-Iceland-U.K. Gap, sir, into the North Atlantic, and head for a base in France, or threaten our convoys again."

"Concur," Jeffrey said. "And if they head north under the ice cap, they can sneak up over the top of the world and try to run the Bering Straits, on the Russian side, and break into the Pacific past Alaska. From there they could go anywhere."

"*We* have only one real choice," Bell said. "Under the ice cap we might blunder into Russian SSNs, guarding their boomers, and anything could happen. The friendly waters right off Northern Greenland and Arctic Canada are much too shallow anyway. That leaves the GIUK Gap for us. Into the North Atlantic and home, or temporary refuge in Great Britain."

"Not the latter," Jeffrey said. "We're too tempting a target. I don't want to bring danger following *us* to the British Isles, with atomic weapons so recently fired."

"I have to agree," Kathy said. "Although there's the same problem with going to the U.S. East Coast. I mean, triggering a nuclear exchange at a base or near the shore . . . At least we'd have the whole Atlantic for defensive measures first. Losing an Axis tail, linking up with Allied surface and airborne and undersea forces . . ."

"I concur with Sonar," Ilse said. "If we transit the Atlantic, we give time for heads to cool. We can try to avoid something awful in direct retaliation for the Greifswald raid."

Jeffrey nodded. Ilse and Kathy had an important point. The U.K. was smaller in size and population than the U.S., and the Brits were hurting bad in this third Battle of the Atlantic. The U.S. could take more damage and keep up the fight. Cold-blooded, but there it was.

"All right," Jeffrey said. "But let's get back to the main question. We know we want to destroy *Deutschland*. Do we try to do it now and here?"

"Captain," Bell said, "you started this by asking if we wanted to escape."

"I don't think we have an alternative, XO. *Deutschland* and the Axis high command can't afford to let us get away, because of the model missile and the hard drives. Eberhard's most likely decision is to continue pursuit."

"Assuming he isn't badly damaged," Ilse said.

"Yes, assuming that. Even if he doesn't regain contact soon, he'll be somewhere in our rear, hunting us. As we approach the GIUK Gap, we may encounter one or more Axis *Amethyste II*'s on barrier patrol. They'll know the Gap's our only practical escape route, too."

"A pair of those in front," Bell said, "and *Deutschland* behind . . . I don't like those odds one bit."

"Nor do I," Kathy said. "Any datum we made, fighting other German SSNs, would draw *Deutschland* immediately. There's partial deep sound channel coupling through both passages in the Gap."

Jeffrey'd already made up his mind, but it was good to hear the others check his thinking and agree.

"Now, how do we find *Deutschland* before she finds us?"

"Captain," the phone talker called, "Engineer reports, Ready to answer all bells."

"Very well," Jeffrey said. "End of briefing. I have the conn. . . . Helm, ahead one third. Make your course zero two five."

Meltzer acknowledged.

"XO, I intend to proceed five nautical miles up this canyon, turn to starboard, and take a peek back over the ridge."

Beck was leaning over Werner Haffner's sonar console when the Zentrale phone talker spoke.

"First Watch Officer, sir, the engineer's compliments, and reactor is in full-power range. Ship is ready to answer all bells."

Beck went back to his own console, now rebooted, and repeated the message to the captain, who'd surely heard the talker himself— but this was procedure.

"Very well," Eberhard said.

Beck saw Eberhard was examining the large-scale nautical chart. Eberhard typed, and the same image came on Beck's screen.

"So, Einzvo? What would you do now?"

"If I were *Challenger,* sir, I'd head southwest, toward one of the passages between Greenland and Iceland and Scotland."

"Yes, that's his obvious egress path. Your sonar search plan?"

"Sir, *Challenger* will surely continue to hug the terrain, for acoustic masking."

"Tell me something I don't know."

Beck swallowed. "I suggest we first proceed to the top of the nearest ridge, then listen with the advantage of height and conceal-ment." The series of parallel ridges ran north-south; the nearest lay just west of where *Deutschland* and *Challenger* had had their incon-clusive nuclear skirmish.

"What makes you think *that* will work?"

"*Challenger* is in a bind, sir. If she goes fast she'll make more noise, and we'll detect her from a distance." The noisy damage to her rudder, from the surface battle in the Sound, had been impossible to miss. "If she goes slow, she'll be closer, and that much easier to lo-calize."

"Pilot," Eberhard said, "steer two zero five." To the south-southwest. "One-third speed ahead."

"Steer two zero five, *jawohl*. One-third speed ahead, *jawohl*." Coomans glanced at Beck for a moment, as if to give him a mental shrug.

Beck *was* miffed. Eberhard hadn't even replied to Beck's suggested plan.

"Sir, may I ask your intentions?"

"Work our way further south at the near side of the nearest ridge line. Then proceed to the crest at four knots."

Ilse and the others sat in their air breather masks, with intercom mikes underneath. She heard Sessions report they'd made the progress north that Jeffrey wanted.

"Very well, Nav," Jeffrey said through his mask. "Helm, make your course zero six zero." To the east-northeast. "Make turns for five knots."

Ilse watched her gravimeter screen, set to the forward-looking view. *Challenger* drew closer to the talus slope at the western base of the volcanic ridge line. The ship put on a steep up-bubble as Meltzer took the slope. On the display Ilse saw the ridge flank passing under her, very close.

She looked down at the deck, and reminded herself that all this imagery was *real*. The ridge *was* there outside the hull. The jagged basalt *was* right there under her feet. She glanced at own-ship's depth; the two-tons-per-square-inch sea pressure was also real.

She switched to the bird's-eye view gravimeter mode. It showed the ridge from above, with *Challenger*'s position marked. The own-ship icon slowly scaled the ridge, at an angle.

The gravimeter could see through solid rock—and through the boiling ocean of a sonar whiteout. The display showed the other side of the ridge, and the floor of the Shetland Channel just beyond. Ilse wondered what waited out there. To the gravimeter, a moving SSN would be invisible.

Beck watched his screens as *Deutschland* slowly climbed the east face of the ridge.

Beck saw something on the sonar readouts.

"Hole-in-ocean contact on starboard wide-aperture array!" Haffner shouted. "Ambient sonar contact as well! *Near-field effects.*"

"It's *Challenger*," Beck said. *The two ships had met head-on at point-blank range.*

"Pilot," Eberhard snapped. "Flank speed ahead!"

"Reactor check valve transients directly to starboard!" Haffner shouted. "Tonals imply *Challenger* accelerating. . . . Aspect change! Signal drawing toward our baffles."

"She's turning to try to follow us," Beck said.

"Not she. *He*. Fuller. *Pilot, starboard thirty rudder.*"

They'd found *Deutschland*, and *Deutschland* had found them. Ilse held on as *Challenger* banked steeply into a very hard turn to starboard, building up momentum as she went. The deck began to vibrate as the ship fought for flank speed.

"Contact still held on Master One," Kathy said. "Relative bearing is constant."

"We're in a turning dogfight," Jeffrey said.

The two ships tried to follow each other into a tightening circle; turning radius in a sub depended on rudder angle, not speed. *Challenger* hit thirty-two knots; the pump-jet's heavy shaking began.

"Bearing rate on Master One!" Bell said. "Master One is drawing into our baffles!" *Deutschland* was winning the contest for position.

Challenger topped forty knots, on the way to fifty. The ride was *very* rough.

"Sir," Bell said. "At close enough range *Deutschland* may try to cripple our pump-jet by ramming it with a safed Sea Lion, or even fire at us with her antitorpedo rockets." The only fish that worked this deep that either side had were nuclear.

"Concur, XO," Jeffrey said. "We have unknown damage back there already, and Eberhard knows it. He heard that shaking, too."

A sudden rumbling roar got louder, then another and another. There was a *bang-bang-bang*, then a staccato plinking against the hull.

"That was a salvo of rockets," Bell said. "A broadside, depleted-uranium buckshot. . . . No apparent damage, sir."

"A ranging shot, to scare us."

Deutschland and *Challenger* danced their ballet. On the gravimeter Ilse watched the ridge crest turn in a dizzying circle beneath her. *Challenger* hit fifty knots.

Jeffrey ordered COB to blow high-pressure air into the sail trunk. Ilse heard compressed air roar, then a rushing whistle as water was forced out through the leaks in the flooded trunk. The noise changed to a gurgle.

Jeffrey ordered Meltzer to reverse his rudder, hard, and follow the ridge slope down, back the way they'd come.

It took a moment for *Deutschland* to react. She tried to follow.

Jeffrey ordered COB to flood ten tons of variable ballast. Ilse knew that trick would help them build speed down the slope. Sonar tracked Master One behind by echoes off the ridge flank.

Challenger leveled off, racing northward in the canyon.

Jeffrey told COB to secure the high-pressure air—Ilse realized they'd blown the trunk dry to prevent another snap roll; the sail trunk flooded again. Jeffrey told COB to restore neutral buoyancy.

The close-in flank-speed stern chase resumed, the roles now reversed: *Challenger* in the lead, with *Deutschland* hard on her tail. The canyon floor got gradually deeper.

"Target separation eighteen hundred yards," Bell said. Too close for a Mark 88 on lowest yield without self-damage. *Deutschland* gained on them slowly.

Jeffrey grabbed a spare sound-powered phone, and yelled through his mask. "Maneuvering, Captain, push the reactor to one hundred twenty percent. . . . Yes, I *know* Admiral Rickover would turn over in his grave. Do it, Enj, or we'll join him."

CHAPTER 34

FOUR HOURS LATER.

Kathy came back from another catnap and sat down next to Ilse; Jeffrey and Bell had also taken turns with snatches of sleep. All around Ilse, things in the CACC bounced and jiggled. Her backside was numb from the constant vibrations, and from sitting in concentration. At least the crew was out of their respirators now. Ilse glanced at the speed log: 53.3 knots.

She busily sifted through her METOC data files, and typed. She worked hard to help refine the models and numbers for Kathy's people. This constant drill under pressure was giving Ilse a whole new appreciation of her work and the ocean around her. She felt a facility and skill level she never imagined possible.

What she was doing was critical. The slightest change in Master One's noise echoes would give clues to Eberhard's intentions and equipment status, if detected quickly enough. It was difficult, but vital, to sift out *Challenger*'s flank speed flow noise perfectly. The water depth was now almost nine thousand feet; the water temperature was a steady 34° Fahrenheit.

"We're matched to the tenth of a knot down here," Bell said. The greater pressure and lower temperature helped the propulsion plant slightly. "But time's on Eberhard's side."

Ilse knew Bell was right. After all their discussion before, Jeffrey was heading for the polar ice cap anyway. . . . *Oh.* South toward the GIUK Gap the water got much shallower—there, *Deutschland* could use her high-explosive Series 65's, and *Challenger* had nothing non-nuclear to answer with, and precious few AT rockets and noisemakers left as well.

Ilse thought about the enemy right behind them. There were over a hundred men inside *Deutschland,* living and speaking and moving around, intent on killing Ilse and Jeffrey and everyone else on *Challenger.* Ilse pictured Kurt Eberhard, at a command console like Jeffrey's—she knew Eberhard's face, from that newsreel. Jeffrey and Bell seemed to like and trust each other more and more; Ilse tried to picture *Deutschland*'s XO. What sort of man was *he?* How did *he* feel, reporting to Eberhard?

At once, a machine-scream filled the air: the sonar speakers.

"Inbound torpedo in our baffles!" Kathy shouted. "A Sea Lion, screw count and Doppler indicate closing rate twenty-two knots!"

"He's doing it," Jeffrey said. "Trying to break our pump-jet by collision with a safed Sea Lion. . . . Once he cripples us he can bash away at our sonar arrays with more Sea Lions and AT rockets, then draw off when we're blinded and finish us with a weapon that *isn't* safed."

Bell cleared his throat. "Impact in three minutes."

Beck controlled the Sea Lion himself. Sonar, and the weapons techs, fed his console data on the eel and *Challenger*'s pump-jet. With his joystick he tried to keep the eel icon on his screen centered on the pump-jet bull's-eye. The weapon pinged continually. The range dropped by ten meters per second, as the Sea Lion overtook *Challenger* from behind with a speed advantage of twenty-two knots: the weapon's seventy-five compared to the target's fifty-three. There was no way to vary the weapon's speed; its only other setting, for stealth attack, was much too slow.

"Intermittent blue-green laser illumination," the weapons officer said. "*Challenger* has activated stern photonics sensors."

The Sea Lion closed steadily, but it began to buffet in the enemy's wake, the flank-speed turbulence. *Challenger* whipped her stern away, and the Sea Lion ran up her starboard side: Beck had missed.

"Bring it around for a reattack," Eberhard said.

Beck tried again to ram. He was better at handling the turbulence this time. He waited for *Challenger* to turn. Her stern began to swing right. He followed. Fuller's rudder turned hard the other way, and her stern-planes tilted as she banked. The Sea Lion missed again, glanced off the target's starboard quarter, and ran on beyond. *Challenger* resumed course.

"Pass control to me," Eberhard said. "We need to get this over with."

"Sir, I'm starting to get the hang of it."

"You've had two tries already."

"Sir, recommend we launch another weapon. Let's *both* try, together. We can catch him in a pincers, and he's ours."

Eberhard and Beck rushed their safed torpedoes at *Challenger* in sync, to box her in, to smash her propulsor.

At the last moment *Challenger*'s bow reared up sharply, and her pump-jet dipped. Beck and Eberhard tried to follow with their joysticks. *Challenger*'s bow nosed down, her pump-jet lifted. Both Sea Lions passed under her, scraping along her hull, then veered away.

"Lost the wire, tube two," a weapons tech called. Eberhard's eel was wasted; he cursed. There was no change in *Challenger*'s speed or trim.

Eberhard ordered another weapon launched. Again Beck looped his back for a coordinated try. Beck had to admit he was enjoying this strange little contest: bludgeon *Challenger* till she was paralyzed and blind, then sneak off to a safe distance and deliver a good one-kiloton coup de grâce.

"Two inbound torpedoes overtaking again," Bell called. "One from port and one from starboard. . . . They're closing in more smoothly than before!"

"Practice makes perfect," Jeffrey said. "I want to try something else, hit their torpedoes with AT rockets."

"Sir, this deep their motor exhausts barely function."

"They won't need to. Once they're launched they'll fall back toward our wake. Set their warheads to blow at the right moment, and the depleted uranium buckshot ought to hurt the Sea Lions or their wires. . . . Besides, what choice have we got? We can't let them take us alive."

The Sea Lions bore in steadily. Beck and Eberhard watched for *Challenger*'s next evasive move. Beck's heart pounded, but it exhilarated him. Up or down? Right or left? He tried to anticipate.

"Rocket motors!" Haffner shouted. "Antitorpedo rockets."

The noise was muffled, choked. There was a double *boomf*.

Eberhard's Sea Lion engine noise grew ragged; it lost speed. He moved it out of *Deutschland*'s way just in time. Beck's weapon lost its wire but not velocity. It crashed into the seafloor with a drawn-out crunch.

"This is *useless*," Eberhard said.

"Concur, Captain. We're just wasting ammo."

"*Damn him* for his clever tricks."

Beck hesitated. "Sir, we need *some* way to break contact with this Fuller, get separation, and find him again."

Ilse watched the latest frightening game of thrust and parry. Again it was a draw. Earlier, *Challenger* had to stay on *Deutschland*'s tail to keep Eberhard from going nuclear near land. Now, *Deutschland* needed to stay on *Challenger*'s tail, or Jeffrey could get off the first effective A-bomb shot. Ilse looked at the charts again. This stern chase could go on for thousands of miles, up past the North Pole and beyond.

But it couldn't go on forever. There on the chart, on the far side of the winter Arctic ice cap, stretching from horizon to horizon, was the solid land mass of Russia. Much nearer lay Spitsbergen, owned by Norway, now Axis-controlled. Every minute, *Deutschland* forced *Challenger* closer toward unfriendly waters backed by hostile shores.

"They're still holding position in our one-eighty, sir," Bell said. Jeffrey nodded.

"Sonar. Oceanographer. I want you to give me *some* way to break contact with *Deutschland*, get separation, and find her again."

CHAPTER 35

On the gravimeter, Ilse saw the canyon *Challenger* followed grow narrower. Ahead lay a different formation of ridges, barring the Shetland Channel from the huge Norwegian Basin to the northeast. These new ridge lines, their crests sawtooth-jagged, ran northwest. If *Challenger* continued straight, she'd have to climb the wall into the Basin—the Basin was open and flat.

Despite the stress, Ilse smiled: Above the constant flow noise on her headphones, she heard whales playing. There were many here, between Norway and the ice cap. Then she pressed her headphones closer. "Oh, *bizarre*."

Kathy heard it, too. "Captain, *Deutschland* is calling us on underwater telephone."

Jeffrey hesitated. "Put in on the speakers."

". . . Not your fault . . . Your own uncaring commanders . . . sent you in over your head." Eberhard's voice echoed and reverbed on the gertrude, like the announcer in a sports stadium. He was almost drowned out by the steady hissing at flank speed—*Challenger's* hull and sail and control planes tearing through the water—but it was definitely Eberhard.

"Jesus," Jeffrey muttered. Ilse helped Kathy's people clean up the signal.

"Accept my truce. . . . Let us be chivalrous. . . . I promise you safe passage . . . to internment in Russia or Sweden." The voice was crisp, blasé, superior. The English was perfect, the accent aristo-cratic.

"He can't be serious," Bell said.

"He wants to get under my skin."

Ilse turned to look at Jeffrey. He stood, and steadied himself against the ship's vibrations by grabbing a stanchion on the overhead. Ilse saw him frown, then smile and grab the mike for the underwater telephone.

"Hiya, Kurt. Whazzup, buddy?" Jeffrey unkeyed the mike, and laughed. "That should piss him off nicely." Eberhard didn't answer. Jeffrey keyed the mike again. "Why should I trust you?"

"I make my offer sincerely . . . as one naval officer to another . . . as warrior to warrior . . . across the gulf between us. . . ."

"Melodramatic, don't you think?" Bell said under his breath. "Typical Eberhard."

"I make this offer . . . for old times' sake. . . . We once worked to-gether. . . . Let us do so again, for peace."

"*Old times' sake?*" Jeffrey said to Bell. "*Wrong* thing to say."

"You have one minute . . . or I withdraw my offer . . . and you die."

"Ooh," Bell said. "Think he means it? Has some new secret weapon up his sleeve?"

"It's bull. If he had something, he'd've used it already." Jeffrey keyed the mike. "You're a mass murderer, Eberhard. . . . I'd love to see you hang for war crimes."

"You *fool.* I'll crush your ship like a cheap cigar."

"No. I'm gonna blow *your* Teutonic ass to Hell."

Prolonged silence. Jeffrey hung up the mike.

Both ships kept charging north along the bottom. Ilse eyed her gravimeter once more.

"Captain," Sessions said, "we're at the way-point."

"V'r'well, Nav. Helm, left standard rudder. Make your course three one five." Northwest.

Meltzer acknowledged. *Challenger* settled on course, still mak-ing flank speed, down in a new canyon—a different valley squeezed between parallel ridge lines that ran on for another hundred miles.

The water got deeper and deeper. *Deutschland* followed close behind. Over the speakers, Ilse could hear a steady rumbling now, not from flow noise, nor from *Deutschland*, not from crunching icebergs on the distant ice cap edge, nor from some far-off nuclear battle.

"Live volcanoes on the seafloor, Captain," Kathy reported. "Bearing three one five. Range one hundred nautical miles, matches the latest charts."

These volcanoes, Ilse knew, lay at the northern extremity of the tectonic-plate spreading seam that formed the Mid-Atlantic Ridge. They were a recent offshoot of the same magma hot spot that caused lava flows on Iceland. Ilse knew, because it was her job to know, and it was her recommendation to head there.

"Perfect," Jeffrey said.

Eberhard hung up the gertrude mike, and smirked.

"Aspect change on *Challenger*," Haffner said.

"Confirmed," Beck said. "*Challenger* steadying on new course three one five."

"Exactly as I predicted. Pilot, steer three one five."

Coomans acknowledged.

Beck could just make out a rumbling and burbling over the speakers. "Live volcano field now one hundred sea miles ahead."

"Perfect, Einzvo. How are you and Haffner coming on the new acoustic holography module?"

"We'll be ready, Captain."

"Perfect."

TWO HOURS LATER.

Jeffrey sat at his console. *Challenger* at this point had run at flank speed, with her reactor pushed as hard as he dared, for longer than ever in her short but exciting life as a warship.

The ride was still very rough. Jeffrey knew from Bell that crewmen who took their coffee with milk and sugar had taken to not bothering to stir; the constant tossing and bouncing did it for them.

The men thought this was funny; morale was high. Everyone aboard had heard by now of Jeffrey's strange conversation with Kurt

Eberhard. Whatever the German had sought to achieve, his ploy backfired. The crew was more determined than ever—their fatigue, and any self-doubts, melted away.

Was this because the crew saw Jeffrey, and their banged-up boat, as the underdogs? What *had* Eberhard been trying to achieve? The enemy Fregattenkapitan was a coldly rational man.

Jeffrey stared at the gravimeter and listened to the sonar speakers. There ahead of him, close enough now to be sharply resolved on the screen, was a group of active volcanoes. The noise was like a mix of rolling thunder and ten thousand boiling witches' cauldrons. Jeffrey felt a tightness and a tingling in his chest: This was the most risky, if not downright insane, maneuver he'd ever even *thought* to pull in a submarine. Now here they were, actually *doing* it, and not even on their own but with a determined opponent on their tail fixated on sinking them before some natural phenomenon could.

Challenger began to rattle and buck in a different way than before; the ride was choppy, the ship rolled back and forth. She rose and dipped, forcing Jeffrey into his seat, then forcing his stomach toward his Adam's apple.

"Captain," Meltzer said as he fought his controls, "advise encountering volcano-related turbulence."

"Maintain course and speed." Jeffrey *knew* this would be very dangerous.

"Sea temperature and chemical content fluctuating rapidly," Ilse said. "Average water temperature rising almost one degree per second."

"Constant variable ballast adjustments needed," COB reported. He worked his panel actively.

"Very well, Oceanographer, Chief of the Watch."

"Captain," Kathy said, "advise acoustic sea state has risen to thirteen."

"V'r'well, Sonar."

Jeffrey's plan was simple: If you're blind and going into a knife fight, you lure your sighted opponent into a dark room. If you're deaf in one ear, and your opponent has good hearing, you take him somewhere deafening.

Jeffrey heard a crunch on the speakers.

"Hull popping," Kathy said. "Self-noise transient."

Jeffrey wasn't surprised—*Challenger* had just gone through her test depth: ten thousand feet. The ship would have to endure every conceivable peril Mother Nature could throw at a deep-running SSN before this one-on-one battle with Eberhard was over with.

"*Deutschland* still pursuing," Bell reported. "Separation twenty-two hundred yards. No sign of change in *Deutschland*'s course or speed."

"Very well, Fire Control."

"Mark eighty-eights loaded and armed in tubes one, three, five, and seven, sir."

"V'r'well."

"Captain, advise those are our last four Mark eighty-eights."

Jeffrey sighed. This was it. The finality was somehow comforting.

"Sea Lions loaded in tubes one through eight, Captain. All weapons armed."

"Very well, Einzvo."

"Sir, advise those are our last deep-capable nuclear torpedoes."

"We know from our two skirmishes that Fuller's rate of fire is very low, and he has only four tubes working. Eight eels will be more than enough."

Jeffrey watched as the volcano field got closer and closer. There were five main erupting cones, formed roughly in a cross twenty miles wide: one in the center, one at each of four corners. These were young seamounts, disgorging molten rock from deep within the earth. Though it didn't show yet on the gravimeter, Jeffrey knew they were growing steadily, as the earth's core leaked and fresh-born rock piled up. More magma—called lava once it emerged from the ocean floor—welled out of side vents on the volcanoes' slopes. The seafloor here was 11,500 feet deep; the craters at the seamounts' peaks rose two or three thousand feet above that.

Jeffrey ordered Meltzer to steer just to the right of the volcano at the southern tip of the cross. He ordered the sonar speaker volume lowered; the rumbling and sizzling and crunching from directly ahead were extreme. Bell reported *Deutschland* still on their tail. Jeffrey wondered if Eberhard was frightened, too, taking his ship into a live volcano field, and so close to his crush depth. Eberhard was not a man to know fear easily, but this place, of all possible places, might well remind him of his ultimate mortality.

Jeffrey called up the basic sonar data, a summary of what Kathy and Ilse and the sonarmen were working with. He windowed the surrounding water's temperature and density and dissolved mineral content. Chemical sniffers mounted on *Challenger*'s hull showed him just what Ilse had told him to expect: The local ocean was a corrosive soup of sulfuric and hydrochloric acid. It was very warm, with chaotic hot spots that were impairing *Challenger*'s cooling systems. As they approached the flank of the cone that Jeffrey called South, the acoustic sea state and hydrographic measurements shot higher.

Way above their heads, Jeffrey knew from the magnetometers, the solar storm still raged. Up there, too, the gale continued; any survivor of this confrontation who somehow made it to the surface in a life vest would die of exposure rapidly. Intermittently, Kathy reported crashing and tumbling from big icebergs, broken from glaciers on the Icelandic coast, driven here by winds and surface currents. Truly this was a submariner's Hell.

"Helm," Jeffrey said, "stand by for a hard turn to port on my mark."

"Understood."

"Sir," Bell said, "we'll unmask our weaker side to *Deutschland*, our damaged port wide-aperture array. We'll lose him."

"He knows we've been favoring our left side, XO. He'll expect us to turn to starboard. We've a better chance of *him* losing *us* by going to port."

Bell nodded. He and Jeffrey grabbed their armrests as *Challenger* dipped suddenly; water heated by lava was less dense, reducing buoyancy. They held on again as *Challenger* plunged upward—caught in an updraft now, as that less-dense water, itself positively buoyant, raced for the surface.

"Helm, hard left rudder, *mark*."

"Hard left rudder, aye. No course specified."

Jeffrey watched the gravimeter, and the ring-laser gyrocompass. "Slow to ahead one third, turns for ten knots."

"Sir," Beck said, "we've lost sonar and wake turbulence contact with *Challenger*."

"Good," Eberhard said. "Then they've surely lost contact with *us*. Pilot, slow to one-third speed ahead, RPMs for ten knots. Starboard twenty rudder, steer zero four five."

Coomans acknowledged.

"Status of the acoustic holography routines, Einzvo?"

"Engaged and working, sir."

"He thinks he's evened the odds, coming here. He's no idea how well we can see in his supposed darkened room."

Beck nodded. These brand-new signal processing routines used *Deutschland*'s wide-aperture arrays to map out the entire three-dimensional noise field structure, on both the near and far sides of a sound source, no matter how chaotic and intense that field might be. Originally invented to analyze jet and missile engine performance in wind-tunnel testing, and ideal for use with both *Deutschland* and her quarry in a slow-speed stalking game, they should spot *Challenger* even here amid the live volcanoes.

All around *Challenger*, five live volcanoes roared and burbled. There was constant seismic activity, too, adding to the noise. A volcanic eruption, or a massive avalanche, or an earthquake and resulting seawave surge—any one of them could do in *Deutschland* and *Challenger* both. As Jeffrey had reasoned earlier, an even exchange here—both vessels sunk—was a big strategic gain for the Axis, with Germany's new SSGN almost ready for sea.

Jeffrey scratched his head. His scalp itched; he needed a shower badly. He made himself stop; it didn't look good.

"He'll probably patrol in a circle," Jeffrey said. "Eberhard needs to keep moving, or we might spot his reactor shielding and core on our gravimeter. . . . If one of us goes outside the outer ring of cones, the other might spot him there while still concealed. So neither of us is gonna leave the inner maelstrom till this issue is resolved."

"May I ask your intentions, Captain?"

"You may *ask*, XO. If I were sure of the best next steps, I'd've told you already. . . . So, what do we know?"

Bell opened his mouth, but was interrupted by a big blast from outside. Ilse shouted that it was a magma eruption on the left flank of the central cone, the one they were calling Middle. The noise lessened, and the buffeting died down. Kathy reported she detected no torpedoes in the water—that blast hadn't given *Deutschland* a hole-in-ocean or ambient-echo sonar contact on *Challenger,* but the threat was always there. Jeffrey ordered Meltzer to move the ship, just in case.

There was a sound like rolling thunder, and once more *Challenger* rocked.

"Seismic event on West," Ilse reported. "Probable magma subsidence, resulting lava dome collapse."

Jeffrey waited while Kathy's people listened again for an inbound weapon.

"XO, Sonar, Oceanographer," Jeffrey said, "we need to do a recon. Get more water measurements, and better gravimeter resolution, too. We'll patrol clockwise for now, take the chance Eberhard's gone the other way, off on the other side of Middle. Helm, take us closer to volcano West."

Soon Lieutenant Willey called; at least the intercom was repaired. He warned Jeffrey that the temperature of seawater intake to the main condensor cooling loops was rising rapidly, and the efficiency of the propulsion thermodynamic cycle was being degraded. They might suffer boiler-feedwater vapor lock, and stall the turbines.

If Jeffrey's ship did stall, *Deutschland* could spot the stationary mass concentration on her gravimeter; gravimeters were immune to the local acoustic conditions and turbulence.

And with propulsion degraded, we couldn't evade an inbound weapon either.

Jeffrey saw Bell hesitate.

"Captain, I must advise, with only four remaining Mark eighty-eights, both self-defense and sure destruction of our target will be difficult."

"I know it, XO."

Another terrible rumble came through the hull.

"Magma outburst!" Ilse said. "South flank of volcano North."

Challenger shook, then dipped and rolled.

"Seismic seawave," Ilse shouted. "Assess an avalanche on North."

Jeffrey had the glimmer of an idea. If they could somehow predict one of these outbursts, and get into proper position, they might use the noise to get a sonar contact off *Deutschland.* Of course, this could backfire and give *Challenger* away, and Eberhard might get in the first and fatal shots. Or, the outburst might not behave as expected and itself deal *Challenger* the lethal blow. But with his own port-side wide-aperture array in bad shape, and some of his other sonars wrecked completely, Jeffrey knew he had no choice; time was on Eberhard's side.

Jeffrey told COB to activate all ship's passive photonics sensors, and window the pictures onto one of the vertical wide-screen displays. So far there was just darkness.

"Oceanographer."

"Captain?"

"Let's check out the west flank of Middle from closer range."

"Sir? There was just a magma outburst there."

"Let's go take a look."

"Magma outburst!" Haffner shouted. "South flank of volcano North!"

Deutschland shook, then dipped and rolled.

"Seismic seawave," Beck shouted. "Assess an avalanche on North!"

"Any contact on *Challenger?*"

"Working, Captain. Holography needs time to exploit the acoustic illumination. . . . No object identified as *Challenger.*"

"He may be hugging terrain, trying to use shadow masking."

"Recommend we gain some altitude for a better look-down aspect angle." In a strange way Beck was enjoying himself now. This was a pure contest of will and technology between *Challenger* and *Deutschland,* and he could focus solely on survival and success with a clear conscience. Let them sink Fuller's ship, here in this ecological wasteland, and help speed the larger war toward victory.

"Concur, Einzvo," Eberhard said. "Pilot, decrease depth. Keep us three hundred meters off the bottom. Maintain search pattern within volcano field. We'll find him. We have sonar superiority, and he's outgunned."

CHAPTER 36

Challenger cruised the west side of the central volcano. The ship moved at three knots, taking careful measurements. Jeffrey ordered the sonar speakers turned off altogether, because of the noise; Ilse used her headphones, with the volume set well down. Even at dead slow, the ship shook and jostled as it had when she'd made flank speed before. The volcano field was never still, and the shocks transmitted through the water never ceased. Ilse wondered when something on *Challenger* would break.

Jeffrey ordered Meltzer closer to the bottom, despite the risk of a crash into terrain. They needed better data, if Ilse was to have a hope of forecasting how these magma outbursts behaved.

On passive photonics, with the gain at a factor of one hundred thousand, she began to see something. The scientist in her was fascinated. The common sense in her said this was madness—volcanologists on *dry land* had been killed getting too close to their subject of study. . . .

Ilse stared at the screens. Lava poured from a side vent in Middle's cone. It glowed bright orange, before quickly quenching to red, then turning dark as it cooled more. There was no steam as the molten rock emerged and hit the seawater; the pressure at eleven thousand feet was much too great.

The lava was *alive*. As Ilse watched, it cascaded and spattered. The lava's surface hardened quickly in the cold, often forming a glassy, brittle shell, only to shatter as more glowing rock, at 3,000° Fahrenheit, forced its way from inside. The lava formed strange shapes, some resembling huge cow patties, others extruded toothpaste.

The glowing lava gave its own illumination. The imagery rippled from the heat. Ilse saw large pillow lavas. One resembled a cracked egg: the hardened surface broke, and the liquid rock inside poured out and hardened like a yolk.

Challenger neared another active vent, and the picture grew brighter. Here lava emerged with greater force. Ilse watched red chunks and cinders erupt and cascade like fireworks in slow motion. *Challenger* trembled constantly, from immense geological forces transmitted through the water.

On her headphones, Ilse listened to the accompanying sounds. The lava rumbled as it upwelled through faults and dikes, then gurgled as it flowed through tubes and fumaroles. As new hot lava forced the cool young rock ahead of it downhill, the advancing front made a crunching, scraping, clinking noise.

"Oceanographer. Recommendations?" Jeffrey's voice pulled Ilse from her reverie.

"Er, to predict large-scale behavior we need to examine more of this face. Build a recent history of the cone flank."

"What do you think, XO?"

"If we want to regain contact with *Deutschland*, sir, it *is* better to linger in one area. If both of us keep moving, the chances are great we'll *both* just go in circles and keep missing each other."

"Captain," Kathy said. "Ilse and I discussed something earlier. In this acoustic sea state, low-frequency look-down pings are unlikely to be detected by an adversary. Properly tuned sound energy will penetrate the seafloor, and give us valuable geologic information."

Jeffrey turned to Ilse. "This isn't a scientific research expedition, you know."

"Sir, we *need* that kind of data to time the seismic events. If you want to use that tactically against *Deutschland* . . ."

"Very well. Go active at your discretion with ground-penetrating sonar."

•   •   •

"Captain," Ilse said, looking up from her console a few minutes later, "recommend switching photonics to active laser line scan."

"That's risky," Jeffrey said.

"Understood. But we're too far from hot lava to gain illumination now. Line scan will provide the fine-resolution data I've got to have."

"Chief of the Watch, activate all look-down laser line-scan cameras." COB acknowledged.

As *Challenger* moved along, Ilse studied her screens. The terrain here was a jumble of layers made at different times. Ilse built a picture of how and when each lava flow had formed, their origins and sequencing. She saw large and squared-off blocks, with light and darker swirls and marbling, where molten basalt had thickened in alternating bands as its mineral content varied; this gave further clues about the Middle cone's behavior. These blocks were blown out from the central crater in some giant explosion, or they'd fallen from the rim in a violent avalanche. Either way, their sparkling, crinkled surfaces suggested they were very recent. Ilse realized the next outburst would probably produce more such huge projectiles, and one might come smashing through *Challenger*'s hull.

Kathy's people continued gathering ground-penetrating data, and passed it to Ilse. From density variations below the floor, Ilse was constructing a map of the active magma chambers, their sources in the earth's mantle, and their vents into the sea. Using Doppler she could actually follow how the magma moved, when it did move.

"What do you want to examine next, Oceanographer?" Jeffrey asked.

"The large subsidence that's just west of Middle, at the bottom of the slope." Jeffrey gave the helm orders.

Jeffrey watched the photonics intently. *Challenger* moved over a wide bowl in the seafloor, a lava lake whose surface had hardened before the underlying lava drained away, back into some crack or chasm. The lake roof then collapsed, except for isolated pillars jutting from the floor. As *Challenger* passed the far wall of the bowl, Jeffrey saw where lava had emerged and cooled in stages, forming distinct layers, their broken edges now exposed. At Ilse's request, Jeffrey ordered Meltzer to make another pass over the bowl, from a different direction, so she could grab more data.

When *Challenger* reached the center of the lake, the ship trembled strangely.

"Subsurface noise increasing rapidly!" Kathy said. "Assess as new outflow onto the lake floor. *Advise clear datum smartly!*"

Jeffrey snapped helm orders.

It was too late. While Jeffrey watched, lava burst from several fissures in the lake bed. The bowl began to fill. The lava glowed bright red. The ship was struck by thermal updrafts. Lava hardened, then cracked and flowed again. *Challenger* bucked and buffeted; heated water gave less buoyancy.

"Make turns for fifteen knots!"

Meltzer acknowledged as he fought the turbulence. Jeffrey watched his screens, horrified, as more and more lava poured up into the lake. It sloshed and rippled now, like water splashing in a bathtub. *Challenger* began to sink.

"Chief of the Watch, pump all variable ballast!" At this depth it would take forever. "Deploy the bow-planes!"

"Bow-planes are jammed! Bow-planes will not deploy."

"Sir," the phone talker said, "Engineer reports main steam-loop vapor lock."

Challenger began to slow. The ship and everyone on it were about to be broiled alive, or worse, entombed and baked within the pool of glowing lava.

"Switch all battery power to propulsion." The fans stopped, and nonessential consoles darkened. "Helm, put stern-planes on full rise."

It was close, but they just made it, past the bowl and into somewhat cooler water. The ship's depth stabilized.

"Oceanographer, I thought we were going to *predict* these things!"

"Sir, we have outstanding data *now*. The next event won't take us by surprise."

Main propulsion came back. Jeffrey felt almost giddy with relief. He admired Ilse's outward calm—but had he done the right thing relying on her expertise like this?

"Oceanographer, I need your prognosis."

"Something big should happen soon. This lake refilling so fast is a positive sign of it. . . . Based on the pattern of seismic activity, and underground magma movements beneath the central cone, I predict another powerful outburst from Middle's western flank, in an hour."

"And after that?"

"They'll probably recur, at more or less regular intervals, at least for a while."

"Okay," Jeffrey said. "I think we're as ready as we'll ever be. Let's hope this gives the datum on *Deutschland* we need, without boiling us like lobsters. Helm, bring us close to Middle's western flank, and position us with the starboard wide-aperture array facing *out*."

SIMULTANEOUSLY.

"Still nothing, Captain," Beck said.

"Time is on our side, Einzvo. Fuller's coming here is like him playing Russian roulette. Every time a lava vent acts up, he pulls the trigger again, and makes another acoustic holography datum along some sector of the volcano field. Sooner or later he'll chamber the loaded round—with us in the right position to detect his transient—and then we have him cold."

Beck studied the nav charts. *Deutschland* continued her search.

"Now that we're sitting against a time bomb, Captain," Bell said, "may I ask your plan?"

"I've revised my thinking, XO, given our paltry ammo supply. I intend to find *Deutschland* by letting him find *us*. Next time this lava vent blows, we'll be acoustically backlit nicely on a broad arc off our starboard side. Eberhard'll think we blundered. I'm betting he'll let loose some snap shots. Then we strike."

"What if he's somewhere else when the magma outburst hits?"

"We'll try again. What's the rush?"

"Sorry, Captain, I just want to get this over with."

"So does Eberhard, believe me. That's what I'm counting on. That's why I tried to piss him off before, on the phone, and I'm betting he called for the same reason, to goad me."

"I'm worried, sir," Bell said, "that this magma explosion may finish us before Eberhard does."

"I'm not disagreeing, XO, but with hardly any useable weapons left, what choice have we got?"

Kathy requested permission to go active again on the ground-penetrating sonar—Ilse wanted to update her information on the pressure buildup in the underlying magma chamber. She'd obviously heard Jeffrey and Bell talking; everyone in the control room had.

"Permission to go active," Jeffrey said. "Update at your discretion. . . . Fire Control, we need to put our weapons out there *now*, so we catch Eberhard by surprise, inside the defensive ring of his own atomic countershots. That's the only way we'll have a prayer of scoring a hit."

"Sir?"

"I want to launch all four working tubes, and loiter our weapons at stealth speed, like a smart mine field, halfway between us and the volcano to the west."

"Er . . . concur," Bell said. "He has to come through there eventually. Whether he's heading north or south at the time won't matter from our perspective."

"Exactly. The mobile mine field's our tactical trip wire."

"Captain, four torpedoes doesn't make a very big mine field."

"I know."

Outside *Challenger*'s hull, the sounds of rumbling and gurgling grew louder and louder.

ONE HOUR LATER.

Deutschland rounded the north face of Middle, heading southwest.

"Contact on acoustic holography!" Haffner shouted. "Definite SSN hull, beam on to us, silhouetted against west face of Middle!"

Beck sat up straighter. "Confirmed! Clear picture of noise field near Middle is forming on port wide-aperture array. *Challenger* backlit against seismic rumbling from west face of central cone."

"*Achtung,* Einzvo," Eberhard said in triumph. "Snap shots, tubes one through four. On bearing to *Challenger, los!*"

"Torpedoes in the water!" Kathy shouted. "Two, three—*four* inbound torpedoes in the water!"

"It's too soon," Bell said. "The magma hasn't blown yet. Our weapons are out of position."

"Inbound torpedoes bearing three one seven," Kathy said. Northwest. "Range nine thousand yards, closing fast!"

"Pull our units back and use them as countershots?" Bell said.

"Inbound torpedoes are diverging," Kathy said.

"Assess he's trying to get us in a pincers. *Captain.*"

"There's no point in using our eighty-eights defensively. Let his Sea Lions get closer. Oceanographer, how soon till that magma blows?"

"Any minute," Ilse said. "I think."

"Sir," Bell said, "advise we move away from the cone flank smartly."

"Not yet. *Deutschland* is probably beam on to us, using her wide-aperture arrays. Don't ask me how she found us, the point is that she *did.* . . . Sonar, go active on the bow sphere. *Ping.* Give Fire Control the target range and bearing. Tell me which way *Deutschland*'s stern is facing."

There was a high-pitched *eeeee.* It fluctuated wildly in strength and frequency, to make it hard for the target to actively suppress.

Kathy waited for the echo. "*Deutschland*'s course is one eight five." Eberhard's baffles pointed north.

"Okay. Okay. Fire Control, send our weapons at *Deutschland* in two pairs. The eighty-eights furthest from her, go right at her bow at maximum attack speed *now.* Sneak the closer units in behind her stern in a stealth approach."

"What if Eberhard goes to flank speed?"

"He'll think he doesn't need to; we might track his noise on passive without giving him pings to track *us,* and he has his own wires to protect."

"Understood." Bell went to work. "But what about the incoming torpedoes?"

"Hold your fire."

"We *have* nothing to fire."

"Eberhard doesn't know that."

"Two Mark eighty-eights inbound from directly ahead," Beck called out.

Eberhard launched the Sea Lion in tube five as a defensive countershot. Beck reported the inbound weapons were diverging, closing in on *Deutschland* from her port and starboard bows.

"They're still under wire control?" Eberhard said.

"Apparently, Captain."

"Then he hasn't reloaded either tube."

"Concur."

Eberhard launched another countershot, the Sea Lion in tube six. "Send one at each Mark eighty-eight."

"Understood."

"Status of our salvo from tubes one through four?"

"Good wires. All units approaching *Challenger* in a fan spread. Bypassing the lava lake now."

"*Challenger's* response?"

"None yet, Captain. Not since that ping."

"Well, he certainly knows where we are. Either he's waiting for our units to get closer, or he's had a bad equipment casualty. Either way he's doomed. Keep tubes seven and eight in reserve, just in case."

"Understood."

"I want to check our baffles. Pilot, starboard twenty rudder."

In *Challenger's* CACC, the noise of torpedo engines was drowned out by a double blast. *Deutschland's* two antitorpedo torpedoes went off simultaneously, so that neither one would suffer warhead fratricide. Because of the geometries involved, the concussions arrived at *Challenger* one half-second apart.

"Lost the wires," Bell shouted, "units from tubes one and three. Assess both units destroyed. Good wires, tubes five and seven, stealth approach in *Deutschland's* baffles."

"Update our firing solution. Sonar, go active."

There was another ping, with a different random pattern of strength and pitch.

"Aspect change on *Deutschland. Deutschland* turning to starboard."

"Send units from tubes five and seven at maximum attack speed."

"*Captain,*" Bell said. "Four Sea Lions are inbound at *us* at maximum attack speed."

"Sit tight, XO. We can't move till we break all Eberhard's weapon wires."

"What's Fuller doing *now*?"

"Nothing, sir," Beck said. It didn't make sense.

"He's panicked, or they're arguing what to do. Crew discipline's collapsed on *Challenger*. It's beautiful, mental torture before they die."

"*Torpedoes in the water in our baffles!*" Haffner screamed. "They're close! Near-field effects!"

"Flank speed ahead," Eberhard bellowed. "Snap shot, tube seven, minimum yield, into our baffles. *Los!*"

Deutschland picked up speed.

"*Damn* him," Eberhard said.

Beck stared at his tactical screen. "It's impossible, sir. *Challenger's* just sitting there."

"Has Fuller lost his mind? He used all four tubes at *us*. Our Sea Lions are so close he'll never intercept them now, even if he launched more units."

Deutschland hit twenty knots.

"Inbound torpedoes diverging," Beck said.

"Snap snot, tube eight, minimum yield, into our baffles, *los!*"

Deutschland fishtailed, hitting thirty knots.

"Inbound torpedoes still closing, sir." They were much too deep for noisemakers or decoys.

"That *madman*. He's committed suicide, just to get at *me*."

"Captain," Beck said. "*Challenger's* weapons are too close. With their maximum yield, or our minimum yield, we'll take heavy damage either way." *He's clever, this Fuller. The two weapons off our bow were ones he meant for us to see. They were a ploy, to lull us, while he snuck two more behind our stern. It worked: We were blindsided.*

"Pilot, stern-planes on full rise! Emergency blow on hydrazine!"

The bow nosed for the surface. The hydrazine roared as it forced seawater from the main ballast tanks.

"*Lost the wires, tubes one through four!*" Beck watched *Deutschland's* depth decreasing rapidly—but the American 88's still overtook. If Eberhard ordered the last two Sea Lions detonated now, *Deutschland* would destroy herself. The ship hit forty knots.

"Cavitating!" Haffner shouted. The pump-jet was making noise, even this deep, because of dissolved volcanic gases in the water.

Fuller's weapons began to ping in range-gate mode. Sonar conditions were disturbed, but sound rays took the same path coming and going. The inbound torpedoes would follow the twisting path of each ping's echo, right up *Deutschland*'s stern. *Yes, this Fuller is a clever one.*

By rote Beck called out the ever-closing distance to the two weapons. The ship hit fifty knots. Coomans kept reporting *Deutschland*'s depth. The climb from three kilometers down was taking an eternity. The 88's would be in lethal radius long before *Deutschland* reached the surface.

Jeffrey watched the data feeds. "I think we have him, XO."

"Sir, unless you *do* something, *Deutschland* has us, too."

"Helm, ahead two thirds. Left standard rudder, make your course due east."

Meltzer acknowledged.

"Captain," Bell said, "that takes us right at the live volcano. Inbound torpedoes' range is four thousand yards, overtaking us by fifty knots!"

"Helm, thirty degrees up-bubble. Take us through Middle's central crater plume."

"Sir," Bell said, "do you know what you're saying?"

"The lava lake was a dress rehearsal."

Ilse heard more distant blasts.

"Units from tubes five and seven have detonated!" Bell said. "Solid hits on *Deutschland*!"

The blast force of the 88's reached *Challenger*. The inbound Sea Lions pinged.

"Helm, ahead flank!"

"Sea Lions in lethal range at one KT any moment!"

Challenger entered the volcano plume.

In a flash, Ilse realized what Jeffrey was doing. The rising, dispersing heat and chemicals of the plume created a giant acoustic diffuser. The vertical sound-speed profile would refract all sound rays *up,* far more sharply even than normal in the bottom isothermal zone. The plume would also cause the sound rays to diverge— to spread and weaken—in the horizontal direction, because sound speed was highest at the central axis of the plume. When *Challenger* was well into the plume, the Sea Lion pings would weaken drastically, and the weak echoes would diffuse even more while bouncing back.

The Sea Lions, their wires snapped, would seem to lose the contact. Their blue-green laser target discriminators wouldn't sense a noisemaker or decoy. They'd assume the target had put on a burst of amazing speed and escaped, or turned hard out of their search cone, or that the weapons themselves had suffered a hardware or logic flaw. They'd either rush off in a different direction, to try to regain contact, or detonate, in a last-ditch try to kill their receding target.

When they detonated—outside the immediate zones of the fireballs—the shock wave would act like sound: It *was* sound. It, too, would be bent up and diffused, as it passed through the plume, and with luck would deflect harmlessly above *Challenger;* the extent of ray refraction was independent of sound intensity.

Sometimes, Ilse had to admit, Jeffrey amazed her. The one big question was, would it work?

Then there was the wild card: the magma outburst, now overdue.

ON DEUTSCHLAND

Deutschland was dying even as she drove for the surface. All the hours of chase and searching, all the plans and strategy, had given way to these last few savage seconds of guessing and outguessing— and *Deutschland* had lost. Beck manned his station grimly. Along both sides of the Zentrale men sat broken-necked or stunned; only Beck's headrest, as *he* faced forward, prevented whiplash from the Mark 88 A-bomb blasts astern.

Damage reports came in from all over the ship. There was bad flooding in Engineering and in the torpedo room. There was a bad electrical fire in equipment near the enlisted mess. Eberhard ordered Coomans aft, to take charge at the fire. The Leutnant zur See copilot took over the helm; the relief pilot was dead.

"Sir," Beck said. "We're losing positive buoyancy. We're losing the ship."

Eberhard ran to the copilot's station. He worked the controls for the conformal hangar.

"Einzvo, use the minisub. Save as many men as you can."

"Captain?"

"*Verdammt,* you have a family. *Go,* there isn't time."

Beck eyed a pressure gauge as smoke filled the Zentrale. *Deutschland* peaked out at four hundred meters, then started to go back down.

There was an explosion somewhere aft—the pressure of the blast burst Beck's eardrums.

"Captain!" Beck shouted. He saw Eberhard juggling the ballast controls. The captain picked up a sound-powered phone and yelled into the mike, but Beck couldn't hear.

Eberhard turned to Beck. "For God's sake, go!" Beck read his lips.

Werner Haffner moved in his seat. Beck unbuckled Haffner and slapped him and he rallied. "Sonar, *come.*"

Beck and Haffner ran aft, choking on the smoke, gathering crewmen as they could. They had to use a ladder to bypass the fire. Beck saw Jakob Coomans lying on the deck, unconscious. Beck lifted him in a fireman's carry, and struggled toward the conformal hangar lock-out trunk.

"Abandon ship!" he shouted to the damage control parties, and to anyone else he saw. "Follow me!" More crewmen followed.

Beck's hearing began to come back. Coomans revived and moaned. He coughed, then vomited blood. Beck could feel Coomans's abdomen growing rigid and distended. *Severe internal injuries.*

Beck slipped on blood and vomit and fire-fighting foam. He slid downhill, aft. *Deutschland* was sinking by the stern.

He reached the lock-out trunk. Men helped him carry Coomans up the ladder, into the minisub. Beck ran into the control compartment and powered up the systems. Men kept climbing the ladder into the central sphere, then clambered in back. Smoke came up through the bottom hatch. More men came and filled the hyperbaric sphere around the hatch.

Beck eyed the mini's instruments. Eberhard had flooded and equalized the hangar, and the doors were fully open. *Deutschland's* depth was seven hundred meters. That meant the mini's was seven hundred, too. At eight hundred the mini would implode with the hangar equalized, and *Deutschland* was dragging her down.

There was a deep thud from below, from aft. The ship's rate of descent increased sharply. Something must have given way, increasing the rate of flooding. The minisub's hull creaked.

"That's it," Beck shouted. *"Close the bottom hatch."*

The moment the mini's board went straight and green Beck released the hold-down clamps. The mini was free. He drove for shallower depth. He dared not surface with the mushroom clouds above. The minisub was sluggish with the weight of all the men.

He activated the sonar speakers. Above the other noise he heard a terrible whistling: *Deutschland*, flooded, plunging for the ocean floor at over one hundred knots. There was a thunderous *crack*, the ship impacting the basalt bottom. Beck knew *Deutschland* would have smashed into a million pieces.

Beck let a surviving crewman, qualified in the mini, take control. Beck went aft and did a head count. Including himself, there were eighteen men aboard. *Eighteen saved out of ten dozen.*

But Jakob Coomans lay flat on the deck. Haffner looked at Beck and shook his head. "I'm sorry, sir."

Beck knelt and cradled Coomans in his lap. He tried to smooth Coomans's hair, and wipe the blood from his lips and nose. Coomans, cynical but shrewd, always knowing just what to say, to lighten Beck's mood or restore his perspective. Coomans, a good man by any measure, and the closest thing to a friend Beck had had on *Deutschland*. Jakob Coomans was dead. Beck's captain, Kurt Eberhard, was dead—to the very end, Beck had never understood the man. *Deutschland*, Beck's *ship*, his home at sea, was dead. Beck sat there, tears streaming. Such a horrible, horrible waste.

"Sir," Haffner interrupted. "What do we do now?"

"What?"

"What should we *do*, sir? Head to Iceland and internment?"

"No." Beck pulled himself together. "Let me look at the charts." He went into the control compartment. He studied the data: fuel supply, drinking water, battery levels, air. He measured distances, and eyed the prevailing currents. He thought of the ceramic-hulled SSGN, almost ready to put to sea. She'd need battle-hardened men, and a good XO and sonar officer. Beck had a *duty*, to try to continue

the fight. He thought of his wife and young twin sons. He had a duty to *them,* to get back, and to protect them.

Beck turned to the pilot. "Make four knots, steer zero three zero."

"*Jawohl.* Our destination, sir?"

"Spitsbergen. We'll drift as much as we can, ration our emergency supplies. . . . Seven hundred sea miles. . . . It should take about a week. We'll make contact with our forces there." *Challenger* may or may not have survived—Beck didn't know, but Intel would find out eventually.

Haffner stuck his head in the control compartment. "Sir, what should . . . What should we do with Chief Coomans?"

"When it's safe, we'll go shallow, and equalize the sphere. We'll bury him at sea."

SIMULTANEOUSLY, ON CHALLENGER.

Ilse yanked her seat belt tighter as *Challenger* fought the worst turbulence she'd ever experienced. On the bird's-eye view gravimeter mode, Ilse saw they were right above the volcano's central crater cauldron.

"Contact with inbound torpedoes fading," Kathy said.

"Engineer reports we're going into vapor lock!" the phone talker said.

"Helm, maintain flank speed."

Ilse watched her speed log. Flank speed could only give thirty knots. Behind *Challenger,* a Sea Lion exploded, inside what should've been lethal range. The blast was muffled, but still it jarred the ship. Another Sea Lion blew. The shock lifted *Challenger's* stern. Meltzer fought his controls.

"Switch all batteries to propulsion," Jeffrey ordered.

Another Sea Lion blew. *Challenger* was making barely twenty knots, going more on momentum than on her pump-jet. She drifted deeper in the crater. The CACC air grew warm. Jeffrey ordered the fans turned on again. Still the air grew warm.

"Hull popping!" Kathy said. "It's *expansion* noise."

"We're being cooked!" Bell shouted.

"At least it'll help us float." A bigger hull should mean more buoyancy, but it wasn't enough. The ship kept sinking.

The final Sea Lion blew. Once more *Challenger* plunged and bucked. Ilse stared at the gravimeter. The ship was down inside the crater now, lower than the lip of the wall. They were trapped, and churning lava beckoned.

There was another gigantic eruption astern—the magma outburst, at last. It was more powerful than all four Sea Lions combined. *Challenger*'s stern reared up even more, and everything in the CACC shook violently; the ship was heading down, closer and closer to the lava.

"The gravimeter!" Ilse said. "Look!" Before her eyes the rim of the crater gave way. "An avalanche!"

"Captain," Bell shouted, pointing, "head through *there!*"

"Helm," Jeffrey ordered, "steer for that gap in the wall!"

On her photonics screen, Ilse watched as *Challenger* barely fit through. The ship continued sinking, plunging for the rock-hard seafloor three thousand feet below, carried by a seismic seawave, pacing the gigantic boulders tumbling down the seamount's slope. *It's turning into a double-kill after all, us and* Deutschland *both.*

"Chief of the Watch, give us buoyancy! Blow the sail trunk. Blow the safety tank. *Blow everything you can!*" Jeffrey grabbed the mike for Maneuvering. "Enj, get our power back or we've had it!"

The roar of the avalanche made it hard for Ilse to hear. Two thousand feet to unforgiving impact with the bottom. One thousand. Five hundred. *Two* hundred.

And then, as *Challenger* entered colder, denser water, she regained positive buoyancy and propulsion power came back. Almost miraculously, *Challenger* hurried away.

"Captain," Kathy said. "Large object heading toward the bottom fast! Heavy flooding and breaking-up sounds!"

"Object is *Deutschland,* sir," Bell said.

"*Put it on speakers.*" There was a horrendous crash, followed by endless banging and clunking, as pulverized wreckage scattered and hit the bottom. There was a continuing *whoosh,* as all the air and fumes in *Deutschland*'s shattered hull and ballast tanks rose to the surface to mark the ship's grave.

"Helm," Jeffrey said, "make your depth eight thousand feet. Left standard rudder, make your course two one five."

Ilse looked at a nav chart. Course two one five: the GIUK Gap.

Ilse turned to Jeffrey and smiled. Jeffrey grinned back. *They'd done it.* They'd done it.

Bell pointed at a chronometer. It was 0005, Zulu time.

Zulu time was also Greenwich Mean Time. *Challenger,* up near the Arctic Circle—not all that far from the North Pole—happened to be due north of Greenwich. It was 24 December 2011.

"Hey, everybody," Jeffrey said. "Tonight's Christmas Eve!"

EPILOGUE

NEW YEAR'S EVE.

NAVAL SUBMARINE BASE, NEW LONDON

The Navy tugs moved USS *Challenger* toward her berth in the new hardened underground pens, blasted into the high bluffs up the Thames River opposite Groton, Connecticut. Jeffrey stood in the cockpit atop the sail. He eyed the nontoxic smoke screen that blocked the sky but gave his ship concealment. He heard the roar of F-18's and F-22's flying top cover. He couldn't hear the racket in the ether, as aggressive electronic countermeasures helped ward off Axis attack.

Inside *Challenger*, Jeffrey knew, things were very crowded. Here on the bridge, things were crowded, too. Besides the regular lookouts, standing in safety harness up on the sail roof itself, Captain Taylor, from USS *Texas*, and Ilse Reebeck stood next to Jeffrey in the cockpit. Ilse pressed against Jeffrey every time *Challenger* rolled, and she seemed to enjoy the body contact. Jeffrey desperately wanted to hold her hand, but it was out of the question with Captain Taylor there. . . .

After leaving the erupting volcano, Jeffrey had examined the site of *Deutschland*'s impact with the bottom: The wreckage *was* real, the German SSN truly destroyed. Then a message through the deep sound channel ordered *Challenger* to rendezvous with HMS *Dreadnought* in the North Atlantic. *Texas* had won her duel with the

German *Amethyste II* after all. The ceramic-hulled *Dreadnought* evacuated the survivors from *Texas,* then transferred them to *Challenger,* using her Royal Navy minisub. *Challenger,* out of ammo, the German mini with the missile back inside her internal hangar, was the field ambulance. *Dreadnought,* freshly provisioned, all eight tubes and her autoloaders working, provided armed escort, until Jeffrey could link up with U.S. Navy forces near the East Coast. Jeffrey and Kathy Milgrom even got to visit with their Dutch uncle and mentor Commodore Morse for a little while—*Dreadnought* was his flagship for an undersea battle group. They shared a drink in Morse's cabin, in honor of the holidays and *Challenger's* success. Morse told Jeffrey an attempt would be made to salvage *Texas,* using gas bladders robotically placed in the flooded engine room. Till then, two Royal Navy SSNs stood guard.

Now, *Challenger* was inside the pen. The blast door interlock was closed behind her. Lining the underground pier were hundreds of people. These were the welcoming committee, wives and children and parents and friends—and girlfriends—of the two hundred plus souls *Challenger* was bringing safely home. Jeffrey also saw a group of people wearing black, comforted by chaplains of several faiths; not everyone had made it.

As *Challenger* nudged the deep draft separators against the concrete pier, Jeffrey noticed several figures in dress blue. He counted seven captains and four admirals. With them was Commander Wilson, *Challenger's* CO, looking refreshed and well.

The moment the aluminum brow was in place, Captain Wilson strode onto *Challenger's* hull. Jeffrey climbed down through the sail trunk to meet him; the trunk was damp, from the flooding, and it stank. Ilse went below. Chief Montgomery and his SEALs tenderly carried Shajo Clayton's litter up through the weapons loading hatch. Wilson spoke to Clayton and shook his hand; both men smiled warmly. Shajo, Jeffrey knew, had a Special Warfare commando's million-dollar wound: a Purple Heart, a Silver Star *at least,* a paid vacation to convalesce, then an almost certain return to combat status.

Wilson surveyed his command. He looked very hard at Jeffrey. *"What did you do to my beautiful boat?"*

Jeffrey felt self-conscious standing next to Wilson. The captain's uniform was spotless, beautifully starched. His shoes had a mirror-hard shine, and the three gold rings on each jacket cuff gleamed.

Under Jeffrey's salt-stained parka, his khakis were wrinkled and dirty—at least he'd had time to shower and shave, in spite of the water rationing.

Jeffrey glanced around, following Wilson's gaze. For the first time in weeks, he could see *Challenger* from outside. The periscope and antenna masts were ragged stumps. Aircraft cannon shell hits, and shore defense gun shrapnel, pockmarked the sail. Shaped-charge antitank missile hits holed the sail and the top of the rudder. The anechoic coatings and piezorubber tiles were shredded in some spots, and missing altogether in places. The sail-mounted under-ice and mine avoidance sonar complexes were smashed. The whole ship's upper works were scorched along her port side. From this angle, *Challenger* looked like she'd been through the wars indeed.

"I've left my patrol report on your desk in your stateroom, Captain."

"I read it already. A copy of the copy you gave to Commodore Morse. The German mini, the model missile, the hard drives, Mr. Salih—they'll be offloaded when all these civilians are gone. . . . This is for *you*." Wilson handed Jeffrey an envelope.

"What is it, sir?"

"Orders. You're being detached. To the Prospective Commanding Officers Course. Your class started last week. You have a lot of catching up to do, and you've got some blind spots you better fix real quick."

"Er, I don't know what to say, sir." PCO school was a necessary step to Jeffrey's own, official, independent command.

"Then don't say it. . . . This is for my weapons officer."

Another envelope.

"Orders, Captain?"

Wilson nodded curtly. "Prospective Executive Officers School. He earned it."

Jeffrey saw Wilson held a third envelope. "Where's Miss Reebeck?" Wilson said.

"Her stateroom, sir."

"We're sending her through the Basic Submarine Officers Course. . . . This isn't charity. Her government-in-exile paid a fee."

"Lieutenant Milgrom?"

"She stays with the ship."

Jeffrey just stood there, numb. He was being discharged from the vessel that was his only real home, home for three months that felt like a lifetime. The ship's company was being broken up, as she was readied for dry dock and badly needed repairs.

Wilson shooed Jeffrey off the quarterdeck, toward the brow. "I'll have your luggage sent. You're missing class." Then Wilson's manner softened, and he actually gave Jeffrey a smile. "You did well, Mr. Fuller. Enjoy your New Year's Eve."

Jeffrey walked onto the pier. The families and friends were growing impatient. *Challenger*'s A-gang, the deck hands, part of Bell's department, were already waving and shouting to their loved ones. Jeffrey spotted Lieutenant Bell's wife, beaming and great with child. Jeffrey knew not to bother to look to the crowd; there'd be no one waiting for *him*.

Jeffrey shook hands with the senior officers standing near the brow. His squadron commodore, and group rear admiral, pounded him on the back.

Finally, it all sank in. The *schools*, at the *New London base*. For six weeks, Jeffrey and Ilse would be together on dry land.

Jeffrey decided, then and there, to ask her out for tonight—they'd usher in the new year, 2012, *together*.

ACKNOWLEDGMENTS

The research and professional assistance that form the non-fiction technical underpinnings of *Thunder in the Deep* are a direct outgrowth and continuation of those for *Deep Sound Channel*. First I must thank my formal manuscript readers: Commander Jonathan Powis, Royal Navy, who was Navigator on the nuclear submarine HMS *Conqueror* during the Falklands Crisis; Lieutenant Commander Jules Steinhauer, USNR (Ret.), World War II diesel boat veteran, and carrier battlegroup Submarine Liaison in the early Cold War; retired senior chief Bill Begin, veteran of many SSBN "boomer" strategic missile deterrent patrols; and Peter Petersen, who served in the German Navy's *U-518* in World War II. I also want to thank Navy SEAL reservists, Warrant Officer Bill Pozzi and Commander Jim Ostach, for their feedback, support, and friendship.

A number of other navy people gave valuable guidance: George Graveson, Jim Hay, and Ray Woolrich, all retired U.S. Navy captains, former submarine skippers, and active in the Naval Submarine League; Ralph Slane, Vice President of the New York Council of the Navy League of the United States, and docent of the *Intrepid* Museum; Melville Lyman, former CO of several SSBNs, and now Director for Special Weapons Safety and Surety at the Johns Hopkins Applied Physics Laboratory; Ann Hassinger, research librarian at the U.S. Naval Institute; Richard Rosenblatt, M.D., formerly a medical consultant to the U.S. Navy; and Commander Rick Dau, USN (Ret.), Public Affairs Director of the Naval Submarine League.

Additional submariners and military contractors deserve acknowledgment. They are too many to name here, but standing out in my mind are pivotal conversations with Commander Mike Connor, at the time CO of USS *Seawolf*, and with Captain Ned Beach, USN (Ret.), brilliant author and one of the greatest submariners of all time. I also want to thank, for the guided tours of their fine submarines, the officers and men of USS *Alexandria*, USS *Connecticut*, USS *Dallas*, USS *Hartford*, USS *Memphis*, USS *Salt Lake City*, USS *Seawolf*, USS *Springfield*, USS *Topeka*, and the modern German diesel submarine *U-15*. I owe "deep" appreciation to everyone aboard the USS *Miami*, SSN 755, for four wonderful days on and under the sea.

Similar thanks go to the instructors and students of the New London Submarine School, and the Coronado BUD/SEAL training facilities, and to all the people who demonstrated their weapons, equipment, attack vessels, and aircraft, at the Amphibious Warfare bases in Coronado and Norfolk. Appreciation also goes to the officers and enlisted personnel of the aircraft carrier USS *Constellation*, the Aegis guided missile cruiser USS *Vella Gulf*, the fleet-replenishment oiler USNS *Pecos*, the deep submergence rescue vehicle *Avalon*, and its chartered tender the *Kellie Chouest*.

Foremost among the publishing professionals who influenced my work is my wife Sheila Buff, a non-fiction author with more than two dozen titles in birdwatching and nature, wellness and nutrition. Then comes my literary agent John Talbot, who lets me know exactly what he likes or doesn't like in no uncertain terms. My editor at Bantam Dell, Katie Hall, so accessible and responsive, who always insists on the highest standards and shows me how to meet them. My publicist at Bantam Dell, Chris Artis, for his constant enthusiasm and keen attention to detail. Thanks also to the late Grace Darling, formerly of the Council on Foreign Relations, one of the most wonderful people I have ever known. And finally, to personal friends Larry Carr, Roy and Linda DeMeo, Susan Farenci, Marty and Carol Goldstein, Betty and Larry Steel, Gil Nachmani, Rochael Soper, Carole Taub, and Linda Karr and Bernie Scutaro.

GLOSSARY

Acoustic holography   A technique for studying in detail a complex three-dimensional sound field using sophisticated signal processing mathematics applied to data from a rigid planar array of hydrophones. The sound field from a target source or sources may vary over time as to both spatial arrangement and signal strength. A submarine's *wide-aperture arrays* (see below) may serve as the planar array of hydrophones.

Acoustic intercept   A passive (listening only) sonar specifically designed to give warning when the submarine is pinged by an enemy active sonar. The latest version is the WLY-1.

Active out-of-phase emissions   A way to weaken the echo that an enemy sonar receives from a submarine's hull, by actively emitting sound waves of the same frequency as the ping but exactly out of phase. The out-of-phase sound waves mix with and cancel those of the echoing ping.

ADCAP   Mark 48 Advanced Capability torpedo. A heavyweight, wire-guided, long-range torpedo used by American nuclear submarines. The Improved ADCAP has even longer range, and an enhanced (and extremely capable) target-homing sonar and software logic package.

AIP   Air-independent propulsion. Refers to modern diesel submarines that have an additional power source besides the standard diesel engines and electric storage batteries. The AIP system allows quiet and long-endurance submerged cruising, without the need to snorkel for air, because oxygen and fuel are carried aboard the vessel in special tanks. For example, the German Class 212 design uses *fuel cells* (see below) for air-independent propulsion.

Alumina casing   An extremely strong hull material which is less dense than steel, declassified by the U.S. Navy after the Cold War. A multilayered composite foam matrix made from ceramic and metallic ingredients.

Ambient sonar   A form of active sonar that uses, instead of a submarine's pinging, the ambient noise of the surrounding ocean to catch reflections off a target. Noise sources can include surface wave-action sounds, the propulsion plants of other vessels (such as passing neutral merchant shipping), or biologics (sea life). Ambient sonar gives the advantages of actively pinging but without betraying a submarine's own presence. Advanced signal processing algorithms and powerful onboard computers are needed to exploit ambient sonar effectively.

ARCI   Acoustic Rapid COTS Insertion. The latest software system designed for *Virginia*-class (see below) fast-attack submarines. (COTS stands for "commercial off-the-shelf.") The ARCI system manages sonar, target tracking, weapons, and other data, through an onboard fiber-optic local area network (LAN). The ARCI replaces the older AN/BSY-1 systems of *Los Angeles*-class submarines, and the AN/BSY-2 of the newer *Seawolf*-class fast-attack subs.

ASDS   Advanced SEAL Delivery System. A new battery-powered minisubmarine for the transport of SEALs (see below) from a parent nuclear submarine to the forward operational area and back, within a warm and dry shirtsleeves environment. This permits the SEALs to go into action well rested and free from hypothermia, real problems when the SEALs must swim great distances or ride on older free-flooding SDVs (see below).

ASW   Antisubmarine warfare. The complex task of detecting, localizing, identifying, and tracking enemy submarines, to observe and protect against them in peacetime, and to avoid or destroy them in wartime.

Auxiliary maneuvering units   Small propulsors at the bow and stern of a nuclear submarine, used to greatly enhance the vessel's maneuverability. First ordered for the USS *Jimmy Carter*, the third and last of the *Seawolf*-class SSNs (nuclear fast-attack submarines) to be constructed.

Bipolar sonar   A form of active sonar in which one vessel emits the ping while one or more other vessels listen for target echoes. This helps disguise the total number and location of friendly vessels present.

CACC   Command and Control Center. The modern name for a submarine's control room.

CAPTOR   A type of naval mine, placed on or moored to the seabed. Contains an encapsulated torpedo, which is released to home on the target.

CCD   Charge-coupled device. The electronic "eye" used by low-light-level television, night-vision goggles, etc.

CERTSUB   A certain hostile submarine contact.

COB   Chief of the boat. (Pronounced like "cob.") The most senior enlisted man on a submarine, usually a master chief. Responsible for crew discipline and for proper control of ship buoyancy and trim, among many other duties.

Deep scattering layer   A diffuse layer of biologics (marine life) present in many parts of the world's oceans, which causes scattering and absorption of sound. This can have tactical significance to undersea warfare forces, by obscuring passive sonar contacts and causing false active sonar target returns. The layer's local depth, thickness, and scattering strength are known to vary by one's location, the sound frequency being observed, the season of the year, and the hour of the day. The deep scattering layer is typically several hundred feet thick, and lies somewhere between 1000 feet and 2000 feet of depth during daylight, migrating shallower at night.

Deep sound channel   A thick layer within the deep ocean in which sound travels great distances with little signal loss. The core (axis) of this layer is formed where seawater stops getting colder with increasing depth (the bottom of the *thermocline*; see below) and water temperature then remains at a constant just above freezing (the bottom *isothermal* zone; see below). Because of how sound waves diffract (bend) due to the effects of temperature and pressure, noises in the deep sound channel are concentrated there and propagate for many miles without loss to surface scattering or seafloor absorption. Typically the deep sound channel is strongest between depths of about 3,000 and 7,000 feet.

Elastomer membrane water slug   A method, for quietly shooting a torpedo from a torpedo tube, which is powered by using a large, very strong, and stretchable plastic disk inside a tank within the submarine to store the potential energy of ambient sea pressure itself. This technique can be less noisy than current alternatives using electric or hydraulic turbines, or compressed air, to drive the slug of water which gives the torpedo a starting shove on its way. (The torpedo's own engine then propels it to the target.)

ELF   Extremely low frequency. A form of radio that is capable of penetrating several hundred feet of seawater, used to communicate (one-way only) from a huge shore transmitter installation to submerged submarines.

EMBT blow   Emergency main ballast tank blow. A procedure to quickly introduce large amounts of compressed air (or fumes from burning hydrazine) into the ballast tanks, in order to bring a submerged submarine to the surface as rapidly as possible. If the submarine still has propulsion power, it will also try to drive up to the surface using its control planes (called "planing up").

EMCON   Emissions control. Radio silence, except also applies to radar, sonar, laser, or other emissions that could give away a vessel's presence.

EMP   Electromagnetic pulse. A sudden, strong electrical current induced by a nuclear explosion. This will destroy unshielded electrical and electronic equipment and ruin radio reception. There are two forms of EMP, one caused by very-high-altitude nuclear explosions, the other by ones close to the ground. (Midaltitude bursts do not create an EMP.) Nonnuclear EMP devices, a form of modern nonlethal weapon, produce a similar effect locally by vaporizing clusters of tungsten filaments using a high-voltage firing charge. This generates a burst of hard X rays, which are focused by a depleted-uranium reflector to strip electrons from atoms in the targeted area, creating the destructive EMP current.

ESGN   Electrostatically suspended gyroscopic navigation. The latest submarine inertial navigation system (see *INS* below). Replaces the older SINS (ship's inertial navigation system).

Fathom   A measure of water depth equal to six feet. For instance, 100 fathoms equals 600 feet.

Frequency-agile   A means of avoiding enemy interception and jamming, by very rapidly varying the frequency used by a transmitter and receiver. May apply to radio, or to underwater acoustic communications (see *gertrude* below).

Frigate   A type of oceangoing warship smaller than a destroyer.

Fuel cell   A system for quietly producing electricity, for example to drive a submarine's main propulsion motors while submerged. Hydrogen and oxygen are combined in a reaction chamber as the "fuels." The by-products, besides electricity, are water and heat.

Gertrude   Underwater telephone. Original systems simply transmitted voice directly with the aid of transducers, and were notorious for their short range and poor intelligibility. Modern undersea acoustic communications systems translate the message into digital high-frequency active sonar pulses, which can be frequency-agile for security. Data rates well over 1,000 bits per second, over ranges up to thirty nautical miles, can be achieved routinely.

Halocline   An area of the ocean where salt concentration changes, either horizontally or vertically. Has important effects on sonar propagation and on a submarine's buoyancy.

Hertz (or Hz)   Cycles per second. Applies to sound frequency, radio frequency, or alternating electrical current (AC).

Hole-in-ocean sonar   A form of passive (listening only) sonar that detects a target by how it blocks ambient ocean sounds from farther off. In effect, hole-in-ocean sonar uses an enemy submarine's own quieting against it.

HUD   Heads-up display. Laser holography is used to project tactical information onto a transparent plate within the user's field of view.

IFF   Identification-Friend-or-Foe. A radar or sonar system for identifying one's own aircraft or vessel to friendly units, for tactical coordination and to help avoid friendly fire. Encrypted pulses are transmitted when the IFF system is "interrogated" by properly coded pulses from another friendly IFF. Of course, the IFF can be switched off when at *EMCON* (see above).

INS   Inertial navigation system. A system for accurately estimating one's position, based on accelerometers that determine from moment to moment in what direction one has traveled and at what speed.

Instant range-gating   A capability of the new *wide-aperture array* sonar systems (see below). Because each wide-aperture array is mounted rigidly along one side of the submarine's hull, sophisticated signal processing can be performed to "focus" the hydrophones at different ranges from the ship. By focusing at four ranges at once and comparing target signal strengths, it is possible to instantly derive a good estimate of target range. The target needs to lie somewhere on the beam of the ship (i.e., to either side) for this to work well.

IR   Infrared. Refers to systems to see in the dark or detect enemy targets by the heat that objects give off or reflect.

ISLMM   Improved submarine-launched mobile mine. A new type of mine weapon for American submarines, based on modified Mark 48 torpedoes and launched through a torpedo tube. Each ISLMM carries two mine warheads which can be dropped separately. The ISLMM's course can be programmed with way-points (course changes) so that complex coastal terrain can be navigated by the weapon and/or a minefield can be created by several ISLMMs with optimum layout of the warheads.

Isothermal   A layer of ocean in which the temperature is very constant with depth. One example is the bottom isothermal zone, where water temperature is just above freezing, usually beginning a few thousand feet down. Other examples are (1) a surface layer in the tropics after a storm, when wave action has mixed the water to a constant warm temperature, and (2) a surface layer near the Arctic or

Antarctic in the winter, when cold air and floating ice have chilled the sea to near the freezing point.

Kampfschwimmer German Navy "frogman" combat swimmers. The equivalent of U.S. Navy SEALs and the Royal Navy's Special Boat Squadron commandos. (In the German language, the word Kampfschwimmer is both singular and plural.)

Krytrons Extremely fast-acting electrical switches used to detonate all of the implosion lens components in a nuclear warhead at exactly the same time.

KT Kiloton. A measure of power for tactical nuclear weapons. One kiloton equals the explosive force of 1,000 tons of TNT.

LIDAR Light direction and ranging. Like radar, but uses laser beams instead of radio waves. Undersea LIDAR uses blue-green lasers, because that color penetrates seawater to the greatest distance.

Littoral A shallow or near-shore area of the ocean. Littoral areas present complex sonar conditions because of bottom and side terrain reflections and the high level of noise from coastal shipping, oil drilling platforms, land-based heavy industry, etc.

LMRS Long-term mine reconnaissance system. A remote-controlled self-propelled probe vehicle, launched from a torpedo tube and operated by the parent submarine. The LMRS is designed to detect and map enemy mine fields or other undersea obstructions. The LMRS is equipped with forward- and side-scanning sonars and other sensors. Each LMRS is retrievable and reusable.

Mach stem A phenomenon resulting from a nuclear explosion at an optimum height in the air. The Mach stem produces an extremely destructive shock wave moving along the ground. It results when the blast's initial shock wave bounces off the ground and then moves quickly through the now-heated air to catch up with and merge with the original shock front still moving outward from the airburst itself. This merging multiplies the overpressure greatly and is an important factor in the effectiveness of tactical nuclear weapons.

MAD Magnetic-anomaly detector. A means for detecting an enemy submarine by observing its effect on the always-present magnetic field of the earth. Iron anywhere within the submarine (even if its hull is nonferrous or degaussed) will distort local magnetic field lines, and this can be picked up by sensitive magnetometers in the MAD equipment. Effective only at fairly short ranges, often used by low-flying ASW patrol aircraft. Some naval mine detonators also use a form of MAD, by waiting to sense the magnetic field of a passing ship or submarine.

MEDEA A study group comprised of civilian scientists and U.S. Navy oceanographers, formed at the request of *METOC* (see below), to study classified Navy oceanographic databases, and then report on the value of possibly making public some of that data so as to support advances in oceanography, understanding of the ocean environment, and related public policy.

METOC Meteorology and Oceanography Command. The part of the U.S. Navy which is responsible for providing weather and oceanographic data, and accompanying tactical assessments and recommendations, to the Navy's operating fleets. METOC maintains a network of Centers around the world to gather, analyze, interpret, and distribute this information.

Naval Submarine League (NSL) A professional association for submariners and submarine supporters. See www.navalsubleague.com or call (703) 256-0891.

NOAA National Oceanic and Atmospheric Administration. Part of the Department of Commerce, responsible for studying oceanography and weather phenomena.

OBA Oxygen breathing apparatus. A self-contained respirator pack used on submarines to move around freely during emergencies such as fires. (Crew members are also supplied with breather masks that plug into nozzles in special air lines, for use while manning their stations or lying in their racks.)

Ocean Interface Hull Module Part of a submarine's hull that includes large internal "hangar space" for weapons and off-board vehicles, to avoid size limits forced by torpedo tube diameter. (To carry large objects such as an ASDS minisub externally creates serious hydrodynamic drag, reducing a submarine's speed and increasing its flow noise.) The first Ocean Interface has been ordered as part of the design of the USS *Jimmy Carter,* the last of the three *Seawolf*-class SSNs (nuclear fast-attack submarines) to be constructed.

PAL Permissive action link. Procedures and devices used to prevent the unauthorized use of nuclear weapons.

Photonics mast The modern replacement for the traditional optical periscope. The first will be installed in the USS *Virginia* (see *Virginia class* below). The photonics mast uses electronic imaging sensors, sends the data via thin electrical or fiber-optic cables, and displays the output on large high-definition TV screens in the control room. The photonics mast is "non-hull-penetrating," an important advantage over older 'scopes with their long, straight, thick tubes which must be able to move up and down and rotate.

Piezo rubber   A hull coating that uses rubber embedded with materials that expand and contract in response to varying electrical currents. This permits piezo-rubber tiles to be used to help suppress both a submarine's self-noise and echoes from enemy active sonar (see *active out-of-phase emissions* above).

PROBSUB   A probable (but not certain) enemy submarine contact.

Pump-jet   A main propulsor for nuclear submarines which replaces the traditional screw propeller. A pump-jet is a system of stator and rotor turbine blades within a cowling. (The rotors are turned by the main propulsion shaft, the same way the screw propeller's shaft would be turned.) Good pump-jet designs are quieter and more efficient than screw propellers, producing less cavitation noise and less wake turbulence.

Q-ship   An antisubmarine vessel disguised as an unarmed merchant ship to lure an enemy submarine into a trap. First used by the Royal Navy in World War I, in actions against German U-boats.

Radiac   Radiation indications and control. A device for measuring radioactivity, such as a Geiger counter. There are several kinds of radiac, depending on whether alpha, beta, or gamma radiation, or a combination, is being measured.

ROE   Rules of engagement. Formal procedures and conditions for determining exactly when weapons may be fired at an enemy.

SDV   Swimmer delivery vehicle. A battery-powered underwater "scooter" used by SEALs, wearing scuba gear, to approach and depart from their objective.

SEAL   Sea Air Land. U.S. Navy Special Warfare commandos. (The equivalent in the Royal Navy is the SBS, Special Boat Squadron.)

7MC   A dedicated intercom line to the Maneuvering Department, where a nuclear submarine's speed is controlled by a combination of reactor control rod and main steam throttle settings.

SOSUS   Sound surveillance system. The network of undersea hydrophone complexes installed by the U.S. Navy and used during the Cold War to monitor Soviet submarine movements (among other things). Now SOSUS refers generically to fixed-installation hydrophone lines used to monitor activities on and under the sea. The advanced deployable system (ADS) is one example: disposable modularized listening gear designed for rapid emplacement in a forward operating area.

Synchrolift   A kind of gigantic forklift or elevator used to move an entire submarine at a shore base or a shipyard.

Thermocline   The region of the sea in which temperature gradually declines with depth. Typically the thermocline begins at a few hundred feet and extends down to a few thousand feet, where the bottom *isothermal* zone (see above) is reached.

TMA   Target-motion analysis. The use of data on an enemy vessel's position over time relative to one's own ship, in order to derive a complete firing solution (i.e., the enemy's range, course, and speed, and depth or altitude if applicable). The TMA mathematics depends on what data about the enemy are actually available. TMA by passive sonar, using only relative bearings to the target over time, is very important in undersea warfare.

***Virginia* class**   The latest class of nuclear-propelled fast-attack submarines (SSNs) being constructed for the U.S. Navy, to follow the *Seawolf* class. The first of four currently on order, the USS *Virginia*, is due to be commissioned in 2004. (Post–Cold War, some SSNs have been named for states, since construction of *Ohio*-class Trident missile "boomers" has been halted.)

Wide-aperture array   A sonar system introduced with the USS *Seawolf* in the mid-1990s, distinct from and in addition to the bow sphere, towed arrays, and forward hull array of the Cold War's *Los Angeles*-class SSNs. Each submarine so equipped actually has two wide-aperture arrays, one along each side of the hull. Each array consists of three separate rectangular hydrophone complexes. Powerful signal processing algorithms allow sophisticated analysis of incoming passive sonar data. This includes *instant range-gating* (see above).

BIBLIOGRAPHY

ALEXANDER, COLONEL JOHN B. *Future War: Non-Lethal Weapons in Twenty-First-Century Warfare* (St. Martin's Press, New York, 1999).

BAKER, A. D., III. *Combat Fleets of the World 1998–1999* (Naval Institute Press, Annapolis, 1998).

BALLARD, ROBERT D., with WILL HIVELY. *The Eternal Darkness: a Personal History of Deep-Sea Exploration* (Princeton University Press, Princeton, 2000).

BEACH, CAPTAIN EDWARD L. *Salt and Steel: Reflections of a Submariner* (Naval Institute Press, Annapolis, 1999).

BLANK, LIEUTENANT COMMANDER DAVID A., Professor Emeritus Arthur E. Bock, and Lieutenant David J. Richardson. *Introduction to Naval Engineering* (Naval Institute Press, Annapolis, 1985).

BODANSKY, DAVID. *Nuclear Energy: Principles, Practices, and Prospects* (AIP Press, Woodbury, NY, 1996).

BROAD, WILLIAM J. *The Universe Below* (Simon & Schuster, New York, 1997).

BURCHER, ROY, and LOUIS RYDILL. *Concepts in Submarine Design* (Cambridge University Press, New York, 1995).

BURN, ALAN. *The Fighting Commodores: Convoy Commanders in the Second World War* (Naval Institute Press, Annapolis, 1999).

CLANCY, TOM. *Submarine: A Guided Tour Inside a Nuclear Submarine* (Berkley Books, New York, 1993).

Committee for the Compilation of Materials on Damage Caused by the Atomic Bombs in Hiroshima and Nagasaki, translated by Eisei Ishikawa and David L. Swain. *Hiroshima and Nagasaki: the Physical, Medical, and Social Effects of the Atomic Bombings* (Basic Books, New York, 1981).

CONSTANCE, HARRY, and RANDALL FUERST. *Good to Go: The Life and Times of a Decorated Member of the U.S. Navy's Elite SEAL Team Two* (Avon Books, New York, 1997).

CREMER, PETER, translated by Lawrence Wilson. *U-Boat Commander: A*

Periscope View of the Battle of the Atlantic (Naval Institute Press, Annapolis, 1984).

CRENSHAW, CAPTAIN R. S., JR. *Naval Shiphandling* (Naval Institute Press, Annapolis, 1975).

DANIEL, DONALD C. *Anti-Submarine Warfare and Superpower Strategic Stability* (University of Illinois Press, Urbana, 1986).

DOENITZ, GRAND ADMIRAL KARL, translated by R. H. Stevens. *Memoirs: Ten Years and Twenty Days* (Da Capo Press, New York, 1997).

DUNCAN, FRANCIS. *Rickover and the Nuclear Navy: The Discipline of Technology* (Naval Institute Press, Annapolis, 1990).

EARLEY, PETE. *Family of Spies: Inside the John Walker Spy Ring* (Bantam Books, New York, 1988).

ENOCH, CHIEF GUNNERS MATE BARRY, with GREGORY A. WALKER. *Teammates: SEALs at War* (Pocket Books, New York, 1996).

ERICKSON, JON. *Marine Geology: Undersea Landforms and Life Forms* (Facts on File, New York, 1996).

FLUCKEY, REAR ADMIRAL EUGENE B. *Thunder Below!* (University of Illinois Press, Urbana, 1997).

FRIEDEN, LIEUTENANT COMMANDER DAVID R., ED. *Principles of Naval Weapons Systems* (Naval Institute Press, Annapolis, 1985).

FRIEDMAN, NORMAN. *U.S. Submarines Since 1945: An Illustrated Design History* (Naval Institute Press, Annapolis, 1994).

FUERBRINGER, WERNER, translated and edited by Geoffrey Brooks. *Fips: Legendary U-Boat Commander 1915–1918* (Naval Institute Press, Annapolis, 1999).

GATCHEL, THEODORE L. *At the Water's Edge: Defending Against the Modern Amphibious Assault* (Naval Institute Press, Annapolis, 1996).

GORMLY, CAPTAIN ROBERT A. *Combat Swimmer: Memoirs of a Navy SEAL* (Onyx, New York, 1999).

GORSHKOV, ADMIRAL OF THE FLEET OF THE SOVIET UNION S. G. *The Sea Power of the State* (Pergamon Press, Oxford, England, 1979).

HAFFNER, SEBASTIAN, translated by Jean Steinberg. *The Ailing Empire: Germany from Bismarck to Hitler* (Fromm International, New York, 1989).

HASKELL, W. A. *Shadows on the Horizon: The Battle of Convoy HX-233* (Naval Institute Press, Annapolis, 1998).

HEINE, JOHN N. *Advanced Diving: Technology and Techniques* (Mosby Lifeline, St. Louis, 1995).

HERVEY, REAR ADMIRAL JOHN B. *Submarines* (Brassey's, London, 1994).

HUGHES, CAPTAIN WAYNE P., JR. *Fleet Tactics: Theory and Practice* (Naval Institute Press, Annapolis, 1986).

KANFER, STEFAN. *The Last Empire: De Beers, Diamonds, and the World* (Noonday Press, New York, 1993).

KEEGAN, JOHN. *The Price of Admiralty: The Evolution of Naval Warfare* (Penguin Books, New York, 1988).

KEMP, PAUL. *Underwater Warriors* (Naval Institute Press, Annapolis, 1996).

KIELY, DR. D. G. *Naval Electronic Warfare* (Brassey's, London, 1988).

KOTSCH, REAR ADMIRAL WILLIAM J. *Weather for the Mariner* (Naval Institute Press, Annapolis, 1983).

MACK, VICE ADMIRAL WILLIAM P., and COMMANDER ALBERT H. KONETZNI, JR. *Command at Sea* (Naval Institute Press, Annapolis, 1982).

MCINTOSH, ELIZABETH P. *Sisterhood of Spies: The Women of the OSS* (Naval Institute Press, Annapolis, 1998).

MEDVEDEV, ZHORES A. *The Legacy of Chernobyl* (W. W. Norton & Company, New York, 1992).

MEYER-LARSEN, WERNER, translated by THOMAS THORNTON. *Germany, Inc.: The New German Juggernaut and Its Challenge to World Business* (John Wiley & Sons, New York, 2000).

MULLIGAN, TIMOTHY P. *Neither Sharks Nor Wolves: The Men of Nazi Germany's U-Boat Arm 1939–1945* (Naval Institute Press, Annapolis, 1999).

O'KANE, REAR ADMIRAL RICHARD H. *Clear the Bridge!* (Presidio Press, Novato, CA, 1997).

PAKENHAM, THOMAS. *The Boer War* (Random House, New York, 1979).

PAKENHAM, CAPTAIN W. T. T. *Naval Command and Control* (Brassey's, London, 1989).

RHODES, RICHARD. *The Making of the Atomic Bomb* (Simon & Schuster, New York, 1988).

RHODES, RICHARD. *Dark Sun: The Making of the Hydrogen Bomb* (Simon & Schuster, New York, 1996).

Scientific Utility of Naval Environmental Data: A MEDEA Special Task Force Report. Edited by Dr. Kenneth E. Hawker, Jr. (MEDEA Office, McLean, VA, 1995).

SONTAG, SHERRY, and CHRISTOPHER DREW, with ANNETTE LAWRENCE DREW. *Blind Man's Bluff: The Untold Story of American Submarine Espionage* (Public Affairs, New York, 1998).

STEFANICK, TOM. *Strategic Antisubmarine Warfare and Naval Strategy* (Lexington Books, Lexington, MA, 1987).

STUBBLEFIELD, GARY, with HANS HALBERSTADT. *Inside the U.S. Navy SEALs* (Motorbooks International, Osceola, WI, 1995).

STUERMER, MICHAEL. *The German Century* (Barnes and Noble Books, New York, 1999).

UHLIG, FRANK JR. *How Navies Fight: The U.S. Navy and Its Allies* (Naval Institute Press, Annapolis, 1994).

URICK, ROBERT J. *Principles of Underwater Sound* (Peninsula Publishing, Los Altos, CA, 1983).

Watch Officer's Guide: A Handbook for All Deck Watch Officers. Revised by Commander James Stavridis (Naval Institute Press, Annapolis, 1992).

WOODWARD, ADMIRAL SANDY, with PATRICK ROBINSON. *One Hundred Days: The Memoirs of the Falklands Battle Group Commander* (Naval Institute Press, Annapolis, 1997).

The following periodicals were also consulted extensively:
Aviation Week and Space Technology: McGraw-Hill, New York, NY.
The Day, Military Matters: The Day Publishing Company, New London, CT.
Naval War College Review: Naval War College, Newport, RI.
Sea Power: Navy League of the United States, Arlington, VA.
Sky and Telescope: Sky Publishing Corp., Cambridge, MA.
The Submarine Review: Naval Submarine League, Annandale, VA.
Undersea Warfare: Superintendent of Documents, Pittsburgh, PA.
U.S. Naval Institute Proceedings: U.S. Naval Institute, Annapolis, MD.

ABOUT THE AUTHOR

JOE BUFF lives in Dutchess County, New York, with his wife. *Thunder in the Deep* is his second novel.